ONE AND ONLY SUNDAY

A Women of Greece Novel

ALEX A. KING

For my mother, who survived Greece

And for B & C, always

KIKI—AGE 12

The old woman was in a coma, again—a long one, this time. Twelve-year-old Kiki Andreou shoved the spoon into her grandmother's mouth. It was heavy with pink roe paste that smelled like the day-before-yesterday's catch.

"My Virgin Mary! Your mother is trying to kill me," her grandmother said, rocketing out of the bed she'd been in for weeks.

"She's not trying to kill you," Kiki told her. Except, she kind of was, wasn't she? Attempted murder was her mother and grandmother's *thing*.

"Why else would she feed me *taramasalata*? It is not fit for Albanian dogs!" Then she bolted back to the bed, jerked the sheets up around her neck. "Shh." She stared sightlessly up at the white ceiling. "Your mother is coming."

Sure enough, a moment later, Margarita Andreou stuck her cosmetics-painted face around the corner. Her dark matte lipstick did the talking.

In the 90s, matte lipstick did a lot of talking.

"Yes, yes, I am trying to kill your grandmother. We could use the spare room." Not a word from the woman in the bed. "Kyriaki," her mother continued, "we are having coffee with the Boutos family

ALEX A. KING

tomorrow—all of us. Except *Yiayia*. Her we will leave behind. Wear something nice, and be good for once, eh?"

Then she was gone.

"I told you so—yes?" *Yiayia* said, sounding far more satisfied than a walking dead woman should sound. "When they took her from me in the hospital after she was born, I believe they swapped her for a Turk."

THE TWO FAMILIES MET THE NEXT AFTERNOON. LOUSY WEATHER, but that didn't stop them sitting outside, under the *taverna*'s blue and white umbrellas on Agria's promenade. The gulf was a waving, choppy grey, not its usual blue-green glass. Stubborn people, the Greeks. It was summer, and summer meant sitting outside, whether they liked it or not.

Kiki was already tired of hearing her parents and their best friends complain. When they started talking politics, she got tired of that, too. She ignored them right up to the part where they began talking about weddings.

Specifically, her sister Soula's to the Boutos's son, Stavros. He was Soula's age, a year older than Kiki.

"Hey, Soula," she called out to her sister, who was three tables down, chatting to a group of German tourists. Very sociable girl. Dark-haired and dark-eyed like Kiki, but cut from a slightly more vivid bolt of fabric. "Mama and *Baba* are marrying you off."

"To who?"

"Stavros."

"Boutos?"

"Yes."

Stavros Boutos. A skinny kid who somehow managed to wrangle his way out of this social gathering.

(Like many Greek sons, Stavros was a Mama's boy. He didn't want to come? Okay, no problem.)

Soula's laugh fizzed all over the *taverna*. "They cannot do that, I'm a lesbian."

Helena Bouto's face went blank. "Margarita, your family is from Lesbos? All this time, I did not know. How long have we been friends?"

Forever, more or less. The two women bounced on the same knees as babies, made the same mischief after they transitioned from walking to running. They were *koumbaras* (maid/matron of honor) at each others weddings. As adults, they knelt and swore the same allegiance to the gods of too-much-makeup.

"No." Mama's mouth puckered. Her disapproval, Kiki thought, looked a lot like a goat's butt. "My family is not from Lesbos."

"But ... Oh."

Everybody looked at Kiki. Even at twelve, she knew this wasn't going anyplace good.

"Lucky we have two daughters," Mama said.

"Is she a lesbian, too?"

Mama looked at Kiki with steel in her eyes—knives, mostly. "I do not know. Kiki, are you a lesbian, too?"

The girl named after the day of rest blinked. "Yes."

Mama smacked her around the head. Not hard. Just enough to toggle her switch. "How about now? Are you still a lesbian?"

Kiki said, "No."

"Good. Then you can marry Stavros."

Kiki Bouto—no S. Greek men often scored an S on the end of their last names, probably to make up for losing that second X chromosome.

Overcompensating, Soula would say.

Whatever. She didn't want to be a Bouto. Andreou was a good last name. Nobody had an S.

Very fair.

———

SUNDAY. THE DAY OF REST. THE DAY GOD FLOPPED FACEDOWN ON His new grass and muttered something about how being the parent of everything was exhausting.

See also: Popular Greek names.

Kyriaki was the second daughter, so they hung her mother's mother's name around her neck. Soula was the lucky one. Her name, in its full form, meant immortality, and—in a slightly ironic twist—came from her father's mother, a woman who died before she and her name-sake had a chance to meet.

For the record, Soula was not a lesbian. She only played one when her mother tried to marry her off to unappealing family friends.

Not that there's anything wrong with being a lesbian; Agria had its own, except people there tended to call them *wives*.

BY THE TIME KIKI WAS THIRTEEN SHE THOUGHT SHE WAS PRETTY smart and very grown up.

"If I have to marry Stavros, I'm going to date lots of other boys first."

When she declared this solemnly to her mother, Mama said, "I do not think so! If you are a smart girl, do not talk to boys. They will pretend to like you, but they are only after one thing."

She went to her father. "What are boys after?"

"Your dowry and my sanity," he told her.

Insanity didn't seem so bad. Mental instability ran in the family.

Exhibit one: *Yiayia* and her frequent (and frequently convenient) comas.

Exhibit two: The great-uncle dangling from her father's branch of the family tree, the one who tied a brick around his neck and jumped into an overflowing bath tub. He cracked his skull on the faucet and spent the rest of his life working in Amsterdam as Candy Box. Crazy made Candy Box rich.

Kiki went to her sister for the real scoop about marriage and boys and what they wanted.

"What's a dowry?" she asked Soula.

"It's when your parents pay some guy to have sex with you."

"But that's prostitution," Kiki said, wide-eyed.

"Grown-ups call it marriage," the older Andreou girl said confidently.

"But what if you have sex before you're married?"

"Your parents have to pay more money."

That sounded to Kiki like sex before marriage really paid off for a guy.

Soula knew everything—even more than Kiki—including the best place to play *Spin the Bottle*. One steaming afternoon, they carried an empty *retsina* bottle Soula scored from the Great Market (Great, in this instance, meant dingy, dusty, and run by a man who knew how to squeeze blood out of rocks, and allegedly demanded ten drachma from a couple of kids who wanted an empty box for their kitten) to an alcove behind the high school, large enough to hide several teenagers and a bottle.

Stavros trotted to the school alongside the Andreou girls. He was a zero to Soula, built like a pencil, with pants that refused to stay on his hips. He was a zero to Kiki, too, which bothered her. Shouldn't her future husband be a number greater than nothing?

Soula muttered something about how Stavros was like a brother, which made this whole thing feel too much like a Virginia Andrews novel, in her estimation.

"Did that woman ever meet a story she couldn't shove incest into? No," Soula said, with all the authority of her fourteen years.

Their fourth was Leonidas Karas. The Karas boy was fifteen, and rumor had it he'd been shaving since thirteen. One of those triple threats (tall, dark, handsome in a cut-from-stone kind of way), girls all over town (and way, way out of town) liked him. They liked him ever harder when he showed promise on the school's basketball courts. He gave Kiki a tingly feeling that made her want to do bad things like kissing and holding hands.

"They say he's got hair around it," Soula whispered to Kiki behind her hand.

"Around what?"

"You know—*it*." She pointed at her crotch.

Kiki nodded like she was worldly, then parroted what their mother had told her once. "That's so you don't put your mouth on it."

Soula giggled in her cloud of *Love's Baby Soft* perfume. "They want you to put your mouth on it! And they will say *anything* to get it. *Yiayia* told me so, and it's true."

"How do you know?"

Her sister shrugged. "I just do."

Kiki's hands shook as she spun the bottle. She didn't want to put her mouth on *it*. Like the dowry thing, it didn't seem very fair to girls. What did girls get?

As luck would have it, the bottle spun out of control, rolling into the bushes.

"Your turn," she told Soula, partly relieved and mostly disappointed.

"I'm only here to supervise," she said, waving her hand. "I've got a boyfriend. Maybe two."

Kiki spun again. The bottle slowed. And then stopped. Right between Leonidas and Stavros.

Tie.

"Choose," Soula told her. "It's ladies' choice."

Kiki's gaze shifted from one to the other and back again. Stavros, her future husband, or Leo, the boy who made her think a road trip to hell might be fun. Because good Greek girls don't take fun road trips to hell with their husbands.

"I can't," she stammered.

Soula's arms curled around her shoulder, and she leaned in close. "You do not have to choose Stavros just because you are to be married. Now is for living."

Smart girl, her sister.

Kiki went into the bushes with Stavros anyway, because Mama had a way of sitting her non-corporeal self on one shoulder, flicking Kiki's ear whenever she strayed off her Mama-designated path.

"Come on," he said. "Let me show you my disappearing finger trick. Girls love it."

What girls? They were supposed to get married. "Do you want to hold my hand?" she asked.

"Later," he said, pulling up her denim skirt.

It was a good trick, one she wanted to share with Leo.

"Let me show you my disappearing finger trick," she said when it was Leo's turn.

Big bad Leo looked worried, but he unzipped his jeans anyway. "There's nowhere for your finger to go."

"Trust me, you'll love it. Turn around."

Good guy Leo, he turned around. What was he talking about? Of course there was someplace for her finger to go.

Kiki showed him her new trick.

"You're crazy," he screamed. Jeans still unzipped, he bolted.

2

KIKI—AGE 28

There is a special place in hell for people who enforce childhood promises on adults, and Margarita Andreou is on her way there in a pale blue dress with a modest neckline.

It's Kiki's wedding day, but does Kiki want to get married?

That's a big fat Greek NO.

"Today I hate you," Kiki tells her mother's reflection in the tall, oval mirror.

"Of course you do," Margarita says casually. "And I hate my mother, too. Why do you think I am always trying to kill her? When I am old and feeble, you will try to kill me. That is how it is in our family."

Kiki glances over at Soula, who is shimmying into her bridesmaid's dress. Mama's choice—of course. Kiki isn't the kind of woman to inflict that shade of green on anyone she loves. Still, Soula being Soula, she forces the dress to suit her. She's old school glamorous is Soula, with that black-blue hair (salon-bought) and red lipstick. The kind of woman who—when she lights up a rare cigarette—makes a person forget lung cancer isn't cool.

"What about Soula? She's not trying to kill you."

"She took her turn when she was born, that ungrateful girl. There I was, giving her life, and what does she do? She almost kills us both."

"I don't want to do this," Kiki says. "My hair ... I'm Medusa."

Soula jumps in. "Mama, look into Kiki's eyes. Let's see if she can turn you to stone."

"You are almost thirty, what else can you do? Work?" Very convenient, the way her mother sidesteps Soula's offer.

Lipstick skates over Kiki's lips. A daring shade of her-lips-but-dimmer. Not her choice, but on this day, what is? Despite her objections, she's a good little Mama-bot, isn't she? "I work now. And marriage isn't a job."

"Of course marriage is a job—a thankless job. You are a teacher." Usually it's Margarita's hands that punctuate her sentences. Today, it's a hairbrush, in between smoothing invisible stragglers from her own neat French twist. Wave, wave, goes the brush. "That is not work, that is torture. Why you want to raise other people's children?"

Kiki wants to shake the stupidity out of her head. Only on Mama's planet is a teacher not a real job. Kiki teaches junior high and high school English (the two schools are mixed in together, in the same building), and when she's not physically present, work is swallowing her free time. If teaching is not work, then why is it so much, well, work?

Mama doesn't understand. She chose family over a career, and now that her daughters are grown, her marbles are rolling all over the floor. Nothing to do except keep trying to off *Yiayia* and sell her daughters to family friends.

Now it's time for Kiki to stuff herself into that awful dress. Stand her next to the wedding cake, nobody will be able to discern which is cake and which is woman, unless they get a good look at her sad, sad eyes.

Jesus, this stinks. Everything from the dress to the groom. Inside her head she screams for help.

"I really don't want to do this."

"So don't do it," Soula tells her, voice husky from a long night of wine and laughter. Last night—Kiki's last unmarried night—they partied like her world was ending.

Which—in her estimation—it kind of is.

The older Andreou sister wins a slap around the ears from their mother.

"She has to do it," Mama's fuchsia-colored mouth says. "Otherwise the family will be shamed. Do you want the family to be shamed? I do not think so!"

The argument rides to the church with them in a white limousine. Bicker, bicker, all the way up to the front doors.

St George's isn't the church Kiki wanted, but the Holy Mother is too small to hold all the family, the friends, the friends of family, the friends of friends, and the tourists who want to gawk at a Greek wedding. So it's here, or cast the guests out into the late April sun. If she was marrying a man of her choosing, she would have fought for the Holy Mother. It's tiny but it's personal, and not just because the priest is her cousin.

It's where she goes to beg for freedom.

Everyone is packed into the bigger church. It's strange, she knows most of these people, but right now they're one long smear. Only a few faces stand out: cousin Max and his American fiancée, Vivi, her daughter Melissa (also one of her students), Kostas and Max's mother —her aunt—and her about-to-be in-laws. *Yiayia* is there, too in her wheelchair, head slumped on her chest.

She's in a coma—a different one this time.

Kiki glances from mother to sister, shrugs. Something's missing. That would be the groom. "So where's Stavros?"

Stavros should be out here. That's how Greek weddings go. The couple meets at the door, and then they walk in together. A Greek woman doesn't stroll into marriage on her father's arm. Fathers palm their daughters off on the groom as quickly as possible.

"Not here yet." The voice comes from the church's open doorway. Stavros's *koumbaros* (best man) and best friend, Akili. He's holding the *stefana* (flowery halos, tethered together with a single ribbon to symbolize the union), in one hand, punching letters into his phone with the other. The thing about Akili is that he's an ass. And like any ass, he doesn't miss an opportunity to kick her in the teeth. So the lack of kick means he doesn't have clue one where Stavros is.

"He will be here," Mama says. "Or I will cut off his—" she wiggles her little finger.

Is Kiki mad?

Nope. Every second that passes without Stavros showing up is a better one. Obviously he doesn't want to be here any more than she does. He just got smarter, that's all, and skipped church.

Too bad he didn't let her know so she could skip church, too.

Time ticks onward. The spring sun is transforming this wretched dress into a torture device. High afternoon now, and all she wants is a *frappe*. She needs the caffeine punch. This is how lamb feels on the rotisserie, Kiki thinks. Every last hair on her head is scraped into a high, tight ponytail, before exploding into manmade curls. Beads of sweat creep between the captive strands. She wants to shake the whole mess loose, rip off the dress, roll her bare skin over the concrete until she quits itching.

Almost worth doing it to watch Mama explode. She deserves it for this ... this ... *wedding*.

Inside the church, the natives are restless. No air conditioning, all that incense. There's the eager hum of gossip behind hand-covered mouths. Usually the entertainment starts after the wedding, but she's okay with them getting started early. If the town is going to gossip about her, well, it could be worse, couldn't it? Stavros standing her up outside the church is pretty benign.

People start flooding up the steps, dressed in celebratory threads. Another wedding is on its way. Hopefully one with a groom. The bride shows up in a limo identical to Kiki's. She's wearing the dress Kiki wanted, a simple slim column. Kiki remembers her from school, back in the days when she was a fledgling bitch.

"What's the matter, Andreou. Did you get stood up?"

"I think so. Isn't it wonderful?" Kiki says sweetly. No way can she be mean when she's feeling this great.

Best day ever.

Gathering up her skirts, she stomps into the church, as much as anyone can stomp in pencil-thin heels. "Everybody out," she announces. "The groom is a no-show, and there's another wedding about to happen."

Hooray!

NICE DAY FOR A WEDDING. NOT KIKI'S WEDDING, BUT *A* WEDDING.

Everyone congregates outside the church. Nobody wants to leave—what if something dramatic happens and they miss it?

"Hold up your hand if you've heard from Stavros since last night," Soula hollers.

Nobody has heard from Stavros since last night—not his mother, not his father, not his friends.

"Well," Soula says, bunching up that ugly green dress, "he's not coming." She looks at Kiki. "Beach or dancing?"

"Beach first. Dancing later."

Mama's hand snaps out, grabs Kiki by the curls. "She cannot just leave her own wedding!"

"What wedding?" Soula says, repressing a grin. "There is no wedding. No Stavros means no wedding."

It's the best news ever. Kiki can't help herself—she laughs.

And laughs.

And laughs.

Beside her, Soula starts to cackle. Two women laughing this hard, it sounds like a chicken coop outside the church. It's infectious. The priest is the next to fold. Kostas Andreou is her cousin, which means he knows this whole wedding thing wasn't Kiki's idea. About a thousand times since he joined the priesthood, she has wandered into the Holy Mother, begging God to shut this particular door and shove her out a window.

And look, it worked. Here is her window.

Everything is good. Everything is fine. If the bride is laughing instead of crying, then the guests feel okay about laughing in front of her, as opposed to behind her back.

"This is not funny!" Mama barks. "How do you think it looks, eh? My daughter stood up by that—"

Thea Helena moves into range with a granite face. She's in a silvery silk dress that's wilting like warmed lettuce. "By that what, Margarita?"

It was a rare childhood photo that didn't capture the two women together, but now Mama is standing under the spotlight's hot glare while her best friend tries to snap a new picture that speaks of an alternate ending to their lifelong friendship.

The answer dies in Mama's mouth.

Things are bad when Margarita Andreou's mouth dries up. It's one of the signs of a very small, very Greek apocalypse.

Kiki slides into her mother's orbit, changes the subject to something that won't cause a friendship derailment. "I hope he's okay."

"Why wouldn't he be okay?" Same question, two mouths.

Both mothers dive to touch the nearest red thing—in this case, a clutch held by somebody's aunt's third cousin. Kiki doesn't know her name, but from the way she slaps at the women with her bag, it's obvious that somebody's aunt's third cousin has mistaken them for purse-snatchers.

(It's a Greek thing, the touching red when two people speak the same words simultaneously. If they don't, it's a sign they're going to fight.)

"I'm sure he's fine," Kiki says.

And she *is* sure. This is Agria, a small town on the Pagasetic Gulf, near the foot of Mount Pelion, where death is mostly natural causes, and crime is something that happens to a cousin's uncle's best friend's chicken. It's big news if someone steals an armload of firewood.

Okay, so years ago there was a flasher, and that same summer one of the local cops died when a pair of clowns robbed one of the village's two pharmacies. But those are outliers.

Accidents are few and generally limited to tourists accidentally wandering into the merciless Greek traffic, or someone falling out of a tree they shouldn't have been climbing to begin with. And they're easily fixed with liberal applications of rubbing alcohol or vinegar. Need the big guns? Use both.

So the odds that Stavros Boutos is anything other than okay are extremely low. He's probably holed up somewhere with a bottle of ouzo and a couple of his favorite naked friends, doing her the favor of a lifetime.

Tonight, she'll crack open the champagne and toast her thanks. To life, to Stavros, to freedom.

"Kiki ..." Soula nods toward the road.

Snugging up to the curb is one of the town's police cars. She knows the young constable from school, and she knows Detective Lemonis by sight and reputation, mostly. There's no mistaking him for anything but the law; even in plainclothes he looks like he knows how to sniff out trouble and slap it with cuffs.

They tramp up the stairs, gazes combing the crowd. A hand shoves Kiki forward. Mama. Somebody has to be the mouthpiece, so—tag —she's it.

"Is there a problem, Detective?"

"Helena and Kristos Boutos, are they here?"

Her hot Greek blood turns cold

❧ 3 ❧

KIKI

The door to this subtle cage swings open, and the detective walks in; Lemonis, the man who cracked the Boutos-Andreou wedding party like a nut. Three fragments sit on plastic chairs around a metal table that's seen more scratches than a cat's litter box. The other shards, who knows what became of them?

Like she doesn't know.

They hurried back to their houses to change, and now they're moving from yard to yard, swapping gossip and speculation.

Detective Lemonis dumps a pile of platitudes on all three of them, apologizes, as though he's the one who pulled Stavros's plug. They drive with him to the morgue. To identify the body, he says.

In the back of the police car, Kiki whispers, "Maybe it's not Stavros."

A small light appears in his mother's eyes. "That must be it. They have the wrong person."

She takes *Thea* Helena's hand, pulls it onto her lap, two pallid rocks dumped in a nest of statin and tulle. "That's it, I'm sure of it. It happens all the time."

Yeah, on TV. Which means she isn't sure at all, is she?

Down a long pale hall they walk, into the room where death dwells.

The morgue attendant jumps into action when the detective nods. It's just business as usual to the attendant; she can tell by the way he moves on well-lubricated joints. He could do this in his sleep, show the dead to their families.

But it's not Stavros, remember? Mistaken identity. They're here to see a stranger.

She clutches hope with her manicured nails, all the way up to the unveiling, when *Thea* Helena's hand falls away from hers.

Stavros. Dead. Wearing the Scorpions T-shirt he scored when the band played Athens.

Kiki can't look at him, so she looks to his parents. These two people are stone. And why wouldn't they be? Their son is the coldest thing they've ever seen.

Lemonis clears his throat. Waiting on confirmation or denial.

Now she looks at the man who slid the bauble his mother chose onto her finger. A beautiful, meaningless ring.

Cold pebbles pour into her stomach. "That's him. That's Stavros."

Thea Helena turns on her, face contorted with fury. "How can you say that?"

"Margarita," *Theo* Kristos says.

The older woman glares at her husband. "It is not Stavros. Just someone who looks like him."

"It's him," Kiki tells Detective Lemonis.

Thea Helena shoves her. "*Skasmos*!

Kiki wants to shut up, but she can't. "It's him." Quieter this time.

A slap arrives and it's a good one. *Thea* Helena serves it up, hot and fresh, on Kiki's face.

It's a hard wallop, but her up-do doesn't budge. She touches her cheek with one hand. It comes away grey and damp. Tears. Funny, she didn't realize she was crying.

"I'm sorry, *Thea* Helena, it's still Stavros."

She should go. She's not family; doesn't matter that she's been calling them her aunt and uncle since she first learned to speak.

But it's Helena who stalks away.

"That is not my son," she yells, finger stabbing the air as though it is her enemy's heart. "That is *not* my son."

DETECTIVE LEMONIS DISHES WHAT HE KNOWS, MORE OR LESS. KIKI can tell he's keeping secrets.

Somebody found Stavros this morning, face down on the old rail tracks that run through town but go nowhere, and haven't for years. One bullet through the heart—but one is all it takes if it's an accurate one.

"Right now I am inclined to call it a suicide. The gun was in his hand."

He looks at Kiki—looks at Kiki like he's imagining her in stripes instead of this stupid dress.

"My son would not kill himself," *Theo* Kristos says.

Kiki's head bobs up and down like a parrot's. "Stavros is—was—a man who loved his life."

The stories she's heard, Stavros loved life a lot, and as often as he could.

"Well," Lemonis says, "we are still investigating. As soon as we know something you will be hearing from me. I am sorry."

KIKI HIDES IN THE WORST HIDING PLACE SHE KNOWS: HOME. IT'S the second layer on a three-layer cake. She and Soula live a literal stone's throw away from their parents. It's the Greek way. Build a house, then build a house on top of that. Keep going until all your children are doomed to live under your roof for their share of eternity. Greek parents like the idea of making the rules forever. And by the time the parents are dead, those children have spent years looking forward to ruling their own children.

Lucky Soula, she scored the top bunk. Eldest's choice. Kiki is sandwiched between the two.

Agria is a place where no-one locks doors unless they're tourists, so Mama comes and goes as she pleases—and she usually pleases when her girls aren't home.

Tonight, Kiki locks the door.

There is no hiding if people can walk in and find you.

This warm home she made puts its arms around her, walks her to the bedroom where all her pillows wait.

Stavros was supposed to be here after today, sharing this house, this bed, these plump pillows Kiki collected over the years.

Instead, he broke off their engagement in the most permanent way.

Nice of him to consult her. An "I don't" would have sufficed. It's so Ancient Greek of him, killing himself instead of telling their families "No."

Bitchy, irrational, cruel, and she knows it.

Stavros is dead.

Forever.

Nobody recovers from that, except zombies and vampires. And that's not really living, is it?

She takes a brief trip to the kitchen.

No glass; Kiki doesn't feel civilized enough for a long-stemmed flute. She wants the champagne naked, straight out of the bottle.

A long, cold swallow of bubbles.

Stavros had sixteen years to say goodbye.

Suicide. It's unthinkable. Was the idea of marriage to her that awful? She's no angel, but she's a good woman. Attractive, or so they say. *They* being the few guys she covertly dated along the way. She wasn't the only one; Stavros had more than his fair share of girls and women, too. But his flings weren't kept in a jar, with a tightly-screwed lid.

And why not? He is—was—a good-looking man. Not her type, but that wasn't his fault. No more than not being his type was her fault.

Poor *Thea* Helena and *Theo* Kristos. Everything that mattered to them is gone. And poor Stavros. If only she'd known things were that bad. Then they could have worked together and done ... *something*.

A hand knocks on her front door.

"Go away."

Back to bed, just her and the bottle's green curves.

Here is her closed door, her open window. Here is her freedom.

Isn't it supposed to taste sweeter than this mouthful of ashes?

❧ 4 ❧

HELENA

Helena Bouto wraps herself in black. Two years is the appropriate mourning period for the loss of a child, but she knows she'll wear black forever. People here will judge her—people she has known all her life. Forever black is the color of widows, they will say, but never to her face.

Let them talk, they who have the luxury of still-living children, and they who have never been mothers.

A massive pot boils on the stovetop, its water black. One at a time, she dunks her clothes in sadness. What wasn't already black becomes black, or a close-enough cousin. Then it's onto the clothesline, where the dye stains the earth. Soon this patch of grass will be as dead as her happiness.

It's not just one child she has lost, but the others to follow. The grandchildren, the great-grandchildren. Now she is a loose end, cut and fraying. Her family's line ends here with her. She had an older brother, but he was lost during the *Regime of the Colonels*. Lost! He was not lost. The soldiers executed him for supporting King Constantine and his family.

Kristos, her husband, has nothing for her. And so they are even. He goes to work, he comes home, and they sit in front of the television without speaking.

Three dead people in this family, but two are still breathing. Some would call that a miracle, but Margarita knows better. There are no miracles for a woman with a dead child, unless that child climbs out of his grave to join the living.

The police are worse than useless.

Suicide. Bah! Her boy did not live a coward's life. Stavros was strong—a man. Her family does not make cowards. It was murder. Helena knows it in her bones.

What else could it be? Her son would never, *never* kill himself.

The Boutos family do not own a car, so she walks to see Detective Lemonis. Everything in town is within walking distance. For everywhere else there's a reliable bus service and taxis.

Detective Lemonis is accommodating, respectful. Of course he is. No expression on his face, but his eyes are watchful, weighing her words, her actions and reactions, for signs.

He does not believe it either, that Stavros killed himself. That is what she hopes today, two days after her son's death.

He walks her to an airless room—not his office, but a place designed for asking questions. Overhead, a fan stirs the heat, but all it is doing is batting the same balls into the corners.

She spits her accusations across the table, into the detective's face.

Click goes his pen. Then another click. *Click, click*, in time with the spinning blades directly above them.

If she wasn't already half mad, the repetition would make her crazy.

"*Kyria* Bouto, believe me when I say that we are considering all the possibilities, at this time."

Is he blind? Stupid? Always she has heard that the Lemonis boy is a good policeman, smart. But here he is showing her he is the biggest *vlakas* in town.

"Possibilities? There are no possibilities." She shivs the air with her pointed finger. "There is only one probability. Stavros would never kill himself. Why would he? His life is happy. He is surrounded by love."

She will not correct herself, will not swap the present tense for past. Stavros will never be past tense for her.

The detective pockets his pen.

"Go home, *Kyria* Bouto. This time is difficult, and you have much to do. Let me do my job, and as soon as I know something, you will know, too."

Two days ago the handkerchief in her hands was white with pink flowers. Today it's black; the flowers boiled away in the steaming dye. She twists it this way and that, wringing its cotton neck. "Do you promise?"

"I promise."

That is a mouth, she thinks, *used to delivering empty promises to desperate ears.*

❦ 5 ❦

LEO

The plane is still breathing heavy. Doesn't stop the cops shoving their way down the tight aisle. Not regular cops—the military kind. And they're coming right for him, as fast as they can. Which means not very. They're big, fit guys, but today's planes were built for yesterday's slighter people.

"You Leonidas Karas?"

Leo thinks about lying, but they know his face or they wouldn't be asking the question. He's lucky they're asking at all.

"Last time I looked," he tells them. Last time he looked was a couple of hours ago, while he was filling out the customs and immigration paperwork. Leo's a good Greek boy (light on the good, fifty-fifty on the Greek), but his passport is US issued. It's been a long time since he was home. About fifteen years.

Long enough that he figured he'd dodged Greece's mandatory national service.

Apparently not. They don't care that he's got fifteen years in each country, which makes him as much American as Greek.

They hoist him up by the arms. "Bags?"

Leo points at the overhead lockers. "In there. The black one."

Joke is on them: all the bags are black. So they give him one arm, but snap it back into place after he's done pointing.

The two MPs escort him off the plane. Leo knows everyone's watching. A sea of whispers swells behind him.

"Whatever it is, I probably did it," he tells the flight attendant. She's pretty, in that faded English way.

She smiles, gives him the approving up-down look. "I bet you did."

He thinks about getting her number, but there's no time. Anyway, there are a lot more fish in that sea and he's a good fisherman.

Though it's looking like fish are going to be out of season for a while.

That's okay. Leo has fresh divorce papers in his pocket. Things didn't work out between him and Tracy, so they said their goodbyes in a courtroom. He gave her the house as a parting gift. Now he's home-less. Greece is the last stop on his travel agenda. Between here and California he's seen a few airports and a lot of beautiful women. He threw his half of the community property into a storage unit and turned in his notice—effective immediately. Good thing he's his own boss.

He's glad to be off the plane. Airlines don't sell seats for shoulders like his. Part of him is always spilling into the aisle. He came by the body honestly. Good genes and a lot of lifting—animals, mostly. Comes with the territory when you're a veterinarian and your speciality is livestock.

Off the plane, into the airport. Different airport to the one he left on his way to the US all those years ago. The old one is rotting on a piece of priceless land. Lots of security with guns litter the terminal. They look even more paranoid than the guys at LAX, which is really saying something.

You guys expecting a Turkish invasion?" he asks, nodding at the rent-a-cops and their guns.

He gets nothing from the two amigos—nothing all the way to Immigration. A military cop either side of him, the Immigration officer doesn't say much, either. Not even the customary "Welcome home." She stays sour until his passport's stamped red. Probably she thinks it's bad form to welcome a guy home when he's got the law clinging to his ass like this is the Savannah and he's the lion's dinner.

Through customs; nothing to declare but this pair of goons he picked up.

"You guys want to carry my bags, or is the muscle for show?"

"Very funny."

Out into the full frontal assault of the sun. He'd forgotten its sting —different to the one back—

Home.

His parents are in Florida, his wife's gone. He's a man without an anchor, which means he should feel free. But he doesn't. Mostly it feels like he's free-falling with a noose around his neck. This place is the closest thing he's got to a hometown—a home he hasn't seen in years. They've both changed, so how's that going to work out? Leo knows there's no going backward, only forward

So why is he here?

Why not?

There's family here. Family he hasn't seen since he left. They don't know he's coming, so he'll be a surprise. But he told his Facebook friends, didn't he?

He turns to the guys in green. "*Malakas*, both of you," he says, big grin on his face.

Now their brick faces crack, spread wide until all three men are cracking up.

"Welcome home, asshole," they say.

A lot of back-slapping follows. There was a time Yianni and Yiorgos were like brothers. The past few years they've been Facebook friends, liking pictures and family updates he's posted. Both guys are married with families; Agria's a town they visit on special occasions, when their mothers' nagging drags them home.

"You had me fooled," he says. "I didn't recognize you guys at first."

Coming back after fifteen years is like waking up from a longterm coma: the names are the same but the faces have moved on.

Yianni shoves his hands into his pockets. "We knew you soon as we saw you. Ugliest guy on the plane—easy to spot."

They swap small talk on the sidewalk. The sun beats him with its fists. It's not as cruel as the sun in the US's southern states, but there's some weight behind its punches.

"So you guys going to give me a ride to Agria, or do I have to catch the train?"

They look at each other. Then back at him. Yeah, these guys are a ride, but not a ride home.

"So it's like that," Leo says.

His old friends nod. It's like that.

"We have to take your passport. Sorry, man."

Leo slaps it into Yiorgos's hand. Now he's stuck here until they say, "Go."

THE DAY'S JUST GETTING STARTED. HOT, BUT NOT TOO HOT. Smoggy, but not too smoggy. It's no Beijing (circa today) or Los Angeles (circa 1984), but the air is thicker than it used to be. Athens is a big city, and all those people, a city gets messed up fast. Greece is a country with problems, these days. Not just money and corruption, but pollution.

As soon as they get out of Athens, the car cuts southwest, headed for Kalamata—birthplace of the Kalamata olive, home to the base where Greece trains its soldiers.

The road ahead is shimmering. Heat rises in dense sheets. The windows are open, the air conditioning off. Spring comes in, snuggles right up to him. Feels good at first, until the sweating starts.

"So what happens next?" he asks his old buddies.

"Five weeks of basic training. Then you'll get five days to visit the family. After that, who knows? They could send you anywhere."

Nice decorations in this car—they look like seat belts. Yianni and Yiorgos aren't wearing them, so he doesn't either. Which means he can lean forward to talk. "Any way out of that?

"They make exceptions, sometimes."

"For what?"

Yiorgos glances over at him. "Bigger problems than you've got, my friend."

"How long do they keep you, these days?"

"Nine months."

Nine months. Damn.

Leo bangs his forehead against the seat. He's heard the stories about guys who came to Greece on a family vacation and got hooked. The family went home while the guys stayed to complete their service —no choice. But he figured it was one of those urban legends. Something that happened to a friend of a friend of an uncle. Unreliable tales from unreliable witnesses.

Now here he is, the friend of a friend of somebody's uncle.

He could run but he won't. Duty matters.

And he's a man with nothing much else to do. May as well be useful.

"Do I get a phone call?"

"Calling your zoo keeper?"

He laughs. "Parole officer. Just kidding. My folks. Have to check in if I'm going to be out of range for a while."

"Mama's boy."

They all laugh at that, because it's standard operating procedure for Greek sons, but Leo's mother is a hundred-percent American.

"You know it," he says as his phone gets busy reaching out to make a connection.

"Leo?" Dad asks. "Where are you?"

"About that," Leo says, and tells him the good news. He's in Greece. For the next nine months. Well, ten if you count basic training. "Why, you guys missing me that much?"

Not exactly. They need him—Mom needs him, Dad says. But what he's really saying is that he needs Leo. Because Mom has cancer of the fast-moving kind. Pancreatic. No surviving that unless it's caught early, and Mom's wasn't caught early.

Curse words spray the inside of his head. *Think, Leo, you dumbass.*

"Okay. Okay. I'm coming home."

He doesn't say when—he can't. The army took his passport, which means he's going nowhere without a new one.

"I need my passport and I need you guys to turn this car around."

They exchange glances. "Orders, man."

"Can't you pretend I wasn't on the plane or something?"

No can do.

"Just wait until I tell your mothers," he mutters.

What's he going to do? Who you gonna call?

(Hint: Not the Ghostbusters.)

The USA's home on greek soil—who else?

He makes his dad a promise he's not sure he can keep, then calls the US Embassy in Athens. He wastes the next hour of his mother's life bouncing from line to line.

No.

No.

No.

A lot of "No," and not nearly enough "Yes, we'll get you home."

As far as they're concerned he is home. And he's Greece's problem until he's served his time. Mom doesn't have an endless supply of time.

Now his old friends feel like new enemies.

✿ 6 ✿

KIKI

Times have changed, and the bishop is a compassionate man. He grants the Boutos family permission to give Stavros a Greek Orthodox funeral. Suicide is not the anathema it used to be.

It's the afternoon before his funeral, and mourners shuffle up to the coffin one-by-one to leave their final kisses on Stavros's cheek. St George's priest has come to the Boutos home to conduct the *Trisagion* —the Greek prayer service for the dead.

Kiki looks at Stavros in his wooden box set up in the dim living room, Mama on one side of her, Soula on the other. *Yiayia* is somewhere in the house, taking a hiatus from her latest coma. No way was she going to miss all this excitement.

"Kiss him," Mama says.

That's what they're supposed to do, take turns dropping goodbye kisses on his cheek, but Kiki's not big on kissing the dead.

"If you are not going to kiss him, at least pretend! Otherwise how will it look, eh?" Mama doesn't wait for an answer. "Bad. Very bad, Kiki."

"Where was he shot?" Soula asks.

"Soula!" their mother hisses.

"Through the heart," Kiki tells her sister.

"Poor Stavros. Interesting suit. Is that—"

"Yes."

His wedding tuxedo. Very ugly. *Thea* Helena's choice. Looks like something the 70s coughed up. The best place for it is six-feet underground with her wedding dress and the green thing their mother had Soula wearing. But not like this.

Yiayia rolls up in her wheelchair, cranes her neck to take a good gander. "He looks like wax."

Poor guy, *Yiayia* is right: he looks like one of Madame Tussaud's rejects.

"Mama!" Margarita hisses.

"What? All I said is that he looks like wax. Your father looked like wax when he died, too. But old wax left in the sun too long. And he was yellow because of his liver. Wrap some flowers around him, and he would have looked like a *lambada*."

NOT THAT *LAMBADA,* THE SILLY (OKAY, AND CATCHY) SONG FROM 1989 that had us all humping legs, South America style, and in 1990 spawned a movie—

No, you can't really call it a movie. More like ... cruelty to captive audiences who paid for entertainment and wound up sitting through the visual equivalent of waterboarding.

Anyway, before the song and the movie and the dance, there was the Greek *lambada*, a long, thin candle wrapped in ribbons, flowers, and various other decorations, made for Easter's midnight Service of the Resurrection.

MARGARITA ANDREOU CLOSES HER EYES, PLEADS WITH SOME HIGHER power. "A *lambada*. What is wrong with you, Mama?"

"Nothing. I came here to see if Stavros was really dead or just pretending."

"Who pretends to be dead, Mama? Who?"

"Elvis."

"Elvis is dead," Kiki tells her grandmother, but *Yiayia*'s grabbing the coffin's rim, hoisting herself into a standing position.

"How can he be dead when *Kyria* Marika saw him at the beach ten years ago? Dead men do not sunbathe, because—*po-po*—the smell. His death was theater for the media so they would leave him alone to eat his sandwiches on the toilet. Maybe Stavros wants to be left alone, too. Did he like sandwiches?" She reaches into the coffin, pinches his nose. Gets up close. "It is okay, Stavros. If you are alive I will not tell anybody. It will be our secret, eh?"

"My Virgin Mary," Margarita mutters. "Get her down from there before Helena calls the police to come and take us all away."

Yiayia glances over her shoulder. "I think he might be dead. So far he has not opened his mouth to breathe. Does anyone have a mirror?"

"No mirrors, *Yiayia*," Kiki tells her. With a one-two-three she and Soula wrestle the old woman back into her chair.

"Stavros is dead," *Yiayia* announces in her outside voice. "I made sure."

The room stops.

"Why are they looking at me like that?" she asks her granddaughters. "I was trying to be helpful.

St. George's bells won't quit crying. They weep all morning, a slow, plodding sound that escorts them first to the church, then to the graveyard. Everyone walks, following the crawling hearse. They, too, are slow and plodding.

Spring. Too much sun and too much green for a funeral. Fall and winter are better suited for burying the dead, but Stavros had other plans.

It is a black sea of people that pours into the graveyard.

There are levels of mourning, and defying them is a metaphorical spitting on the deceased. A widow wears black for the rest of her life. One year for a sister or daughter. Forty days for a friend.

(Men wear black armbands, because the people who make the rules naturally favor themselves.)

But what is Kiki? She's not any of those things. She's the abandoned bride. Not quite a widow, and not a sister or a friend. Yet Mama dished up the bad news the day after Stavros's death: "Two years, Kiki, or everyone in town will hate you."

Everyone meaning *Thea* Helena. The rest of the town won't hate her, but they'll talk. Oh, how they love to talk. Gossip is Greece's unofficial national sport.

Everyone—not just *Thea* Helena—is watching her. This is the part where she's supposed to hurl herself at the coffin, wailing. It's practically law.

Except she's not, is she?

One day she might wail over a descending coffin, but not today. Like any number of depraved sexual acts, she's saving that for someone special.

Mama nudges her. "Go."

"No," Kiki says.

"You have no choice! What will people say?"

Mama is a mallet; it's nothing for her to hammer Kiki until she's flat and compliant. But Stavros's death is the beginning of something new.

A door has closed, a window opened, and there's no hand waiting to shove her out. If she wants to jump, it's her choice.

Arms folded. "No, Mama."

She's not alone in her stone shoes. *Thea* Helena stands close by, her feet clinging to the patch of grass she's chosen. The woman Kiki has known all her life doesn't blink, doesn't move. Her head is turned away from the grave, looking out toward the road. Kiki wonders if she sees the pickup truck parked there, with Romani piled in the bed. They're watching this Greek tragedy intently, as if they're trying to figure out who is Electra, who is Antigone, who is Oedipus.

———

ANCIENT GREEKS LOVED THEIR TRAGEDIES. MODERN GREEKS STILL

do. Now they prefer it closer to home, preferably in a neighbor's yard. That way the seats are free and front row.

But in the old days, they were happy to pay to watch the misfortunes of others. For a country that once embraced homosexuality as commonplace, they sure didn't take to happy endings—not for a long time, at least.

Not many of those tragedies have survived the time travel. Only three Ancient Greek tragedians made the leap. Sophocles, the rich kid, who may or may not have died choking on a grape. Euripides, who died after a dog attack. And Aeschylus, who was known as the father of tragedy, and also as the man who died after an eagle dropped a tortoise on his head.

And now here is Stavros Boutos, writing his tragedy from the afterlife.

"GO," MARGARITA HISSES.

"Mama, stop," Soula says. But their mother isn't in a listening mood. She lets out a huge melodramatic sigh, then flings herself at the coffin, hand curled around Kiki's wrist, wailing and weeping. Her fingernails bite.

"Poor Stavros," she cries. "Oh, the poor boy! Why did God steal him from us? Whhhhhhy?" She nudges Kiki. Whispers, "Just do as I do." Then her howling continues.

Very dramatic. A fantastic performance. Kiki hopes she has a Margarita Andreou at her funeral someday. But she can't join in. Like Helena, she's watching the road. It's not a big road, but it leads to a bigger road, and that road leads to another road that goes someplace that isn't here.

She longs for that mythical someplace, where she can wear colors that aren't black.

7

HELENA

The funeral happens. She refuses to participate. Participation is confirmation, and Margarita prefers not to believe. St George's bells cry for someone else's son, not hers.

The wailing women fall on top of another man's casket.

Home again, where—for some reason unknown to her—people have gathered to eat.

The condolences that roll out of their mouths afterward are a mistake—they have the wrong woman.

She refuses the *koliva*. Let the others choke down the honey-sweetened wheat grains. "May God forgive him," they say as they spoon the traditional funeral food into their mouths. "May God forgive him."

Why does God need to forgive a saint?

People kiss her marble cheeks. Those smooth slopes of skin are wet from so many lips. Is it hot in here? Is it cold? Her brain can't decide. She shivers inside her black dress with its wilted lace collar.

"Excuse me." She pushes her way out of the room, collecting condolences as she goes. They stick to her back, follow her into the bathroom. Even after the door is locked, and she's sitting in the tub with a towel over her head, she hears apologies hailing against the door.

Why are they all so sorry? Their solemn faces will evaporate the moment they step out her front door. By the time they've eaten their fill, and returned to their homes, Stavros Boutos will be forgotten.

If they think of him it at all, it will be to give thanks to God that He did not take their sons.

At first she doesn't hear the knock. It's small, timid. The second and third are bolder, made by a persistent hand.

"Come in," she says from under the towel. Someone steps in, slides the small bolt closed behind them. Then suddenly she's not alone in the tub. Her husband curls himself around her, becomes her protective shell.

Between them they shed so many tears it is a wonder they do not drown.

❧ 8 ❧

KIKI

Soula is a woman with a lot of good ideas. This one arrives late afternoon, while the sisters sit on Kiki's small balcony. Agria is arching its back, stretching after its siesta. But the evening's cooler air hasn't arrived yet, so it's a long, luxurious waking.

"We should go on your honeymoon. You will feel better after a trip to Paris."

Okay, so not one of Soula's best ideas.

"I don't think so," Kiki says.

"Okay." She dims, then brightens. "We could go together."

"I don't feel like going to Paris. Besides, I'm in mourning. And so are you."

"The only mourning I'm doing is on your behalf. Can I go on your honeymoon?"

"Alone?"

Soula shrugs one slim shoulder. It's pale—for her—but then summer hasn't turned on all its tanning lamps yet. "No. I will take someone."

"Who?"

"I don't know. Who would you take?"

"Stavros."

Soula gives her a meaningful look. Sisters know things other people don't. "I mean who would you really take to Paris, the city of love? I know you are not a nun."

"There hasn't been anyone in ages."

"Really?"

"Really."

THEIR PARENTS WEREN'T THE ONLY ONES WITH AN AGREEMENT. BUT the one between Kiki and Stavros was flexible, invisible to everyone but them.

Over ouzo, they hammered out the terms. Took five minutes.

"Whoever you want, as long as no one knows," Stavros said.

"Whoever you want, as long as no one knows," she agreed.

"And after, what do you want, Kiki?"

"After we're married?"

"Yeah."

She shrugged. "I'll be the best wife I can be. You?"

Time stretched. It took an eternity for him to pour another glass. "Whoever I want, as long as nobody knows."

KIKI DATED, BUT SHE DATED SMART. ONLY MEN WITH ONE LEG IN Agria and their other leg in another town, another country. That way they weren't going to stick around and cause problems.

Problems, meaning a hunger for something long-term.

Some would say that made Kiki as wild as Stavros.

And others would say, if they held degrees in armchair psychology, that Kiki was looking for a way out of town, out of her engagement.

People say lots of things. Sometimes they're true.

SOULA ASKS, "WHAT ABOUT STAVROS, DID HE HAVE SOMEONE?"

Kiki gives her the *are-you-kidding-me?* look.

"I meant one woman, not all the women. Someone special."

"Who knows? We never talked about it. We never talked about anything."

"Do you think that would have changed after you married?"

"Probably not."

They sit in silence for a while, watching their piece of the village come back to life. Slowly, the neighbors begin their evening scuttle.

"This is a blessing."

"Soula ..."

Her sister shakes her head, long, sleek strands whipping her shoulders. "Trust me, it is a blessing. Stavros was shit, and now you don't have to be *Kyria* Shit."

Wow, now there's a revelation. She never saw that coming. All these years, it seemed like Soula was okay with Stavros, the way you're okay with one boob being slightly bigger than the other.

"Why do you hate him so much?"

Soula gets up, leans her elbows on the balcony's metal balustrade. Evading the truth. Not her sister's way at all. Usually Soula delivers truth like a hammer. *Smack*! in the face of the person who needs the reality check.

"All these years, he could have stopped the wedding. Our mother, she doesn't listen. Complaining to her is like throwing words into the wind. But *Thea* Helena would have listened to Stavros if he'd said, 'No.' But he did not say no, did he?"

"I don't know."

"Yes, you do. He never told her, 'No.' And you know why?"

"Why?"

"Because Stavros was a *mounaki*. He wanted women *and* a wife from a good family to make his business look good. He was greedy."

(*Mouni*: slang for the female anatomy; it's that word, you know, the one that begins with C and rhymes with *hunt*. A *mounaki* is a teeny tiny ... uh ... *mouni*.)

It's true and Kiki knows it—has known it for years. But did she want to believe it? No. Who wants to believe they're marrying a jerk?

Nobody. When a marriage is arranged, you get who you get, and hope for the best.

"I knew what he was, Soula."

"Did you? Then why go through with it?"

Kiki joins her sister at the balustrade. "Because I'm monumentally stupid?"

Soula grins. "You really are."

"I know."

It's a flimsy piece of fiction, because they both know she's anything but stupid. Still, it's less lame than the truth: Kiki never met a man she liked better. There's never been a man worth the inevitable fight with her mother or the punch in her reputation's throat.

And people here look for any excuse to deliver that punch.

Things would be different, Kiki knows, if there was a man worth the fight.

✿ 9 ✿

HELENA

She refuses to see that woman.

Why should Margarita have a child—two children!—while she has none?

Margarita comes to her with apologies spilling from her mouth, from her eyes. Helena does not want her apologies. They are worthless and hollow. A woman with all her children still living cannot know true sorrow—only its shadow. A shadow is not tangible; you cannot hold it in your heart the way you hold naked grief.

"What do you want from me?" she says, tongue numb and thick against her teeth.

Eyes wide, surprised. "I do not want anything from you. I am here to give whatever you need."

Helena scoffs at her foolishness. "Are you a necromancer? Can you snatch Stavros away from death?"

"Helena ..."

She cannot abide the pity in the other woman's eyes. It is if she is seeing her lifelong friend for the first time. Black is not her color, she thinks. But then whose color is black if its purpose is for mourning the dead? Black suits the young, the passionate, those who know nothing of loss. On middle-aged and elderly women it is a sign their season has long passed.

"How are your daughters, Margarita," she says bitterly. "Are they well?"

"Soula is fine. Kiki is—"

Helena leaps on what. "What is Kiki? Is she grieving? You cannot tell me she is sad Stavros is dead. We both know she did not want to marry him."

"Of course she did." Margarita's tears spill into a black handkerchief. "Our whole family loved Stavros like he was one of ours."

"One of yours? One of yours? He was never one of yours! He was mine!"

"Helena, please."

"Go." Quiet. The calm before the storm.

The other woman doesn't go. She stands her ground, that fool. "No. You need me."

Helena leans in close enough to smell her perfume. Something with too many flowers. What is it Margarita wears? She can't recall. She smells powdery, flowery, funereal. "I need *nothing* from you. Go."

"I am staying."

"Go."

Silence.

"Go!"

Nothing. Mother of Christ, she cannot stand all the sympathy in Margarita's eyes. It disgusts her. Who is she that she needs sympathy?

"Go," she screams. "I do not want to see you!"

Margarita fades away.

Good, good.

STAVROS HAD MANY FRIENDS. NOW THEY COME, DISPENSE apologies, and then they go. But one sticks.

Akili comes all the time to visit. Like her, he cannot let Stavros go. And why should they? What harm is there in holding the dead close so they can never fully leave?

Like her Stavros, Akili is a beautiful boy. As children, Stavros was spaghetti and his friend was a *loukoumada* (a honey-drenched donut), but the army rolled them together and baked two fit men.

When he comes it is to sit with her in the afternoons before Kristos returns from work. He watches as she makes careful stitches on a circle of white fabric. Today it is a leaf she makes—one of the last, then this tablecloth will be complete.

It was for Kiki and Stavros, but now it is for nobody but herself.

She will never use it. Instead, it is destined to join all the other things in Stavros's room that she cannot bear to touch.

"The police spoke with me the other day," Akili says gently.

"When?"

"The day after ... after they found him."

"Oh? What did they say?"

"Nothing. Only questions."

"Questions! They ask the wrong people."

"They asked about Kiki."

Helena lifts her eyes away from the silk leaf. "What about Kiki?"

"They asked if maybe she had a reason to be angry at Stavros."

It is a careful woman who speaks her next words. "What do you think—does she?"

"A reason, maybe. A good reason? No."

"What reason is that, that not so good reason?"

Her son's best friend scans the other neighborhood yards for signs of eavesdroppers. Then his gaze settle back on the needlepoint in her hands.

"Maybe she heard stories about Stavros. Lies, but maybe she mistook them for truth."

"What stories?"

"Stories. Every good-looking man has stories."

"About women?"

"Some of them."

"But they are not true."

He glances up at a pair of Romani women shuffling along the street, wandering from yard to yard. "No, not true."

"Stavros was a good boy. And you are a good boy, too. I am glad you come."

He lifts her hand away from the white cotton circle, holds it in his "Stavros will never be dead to me."

She squeezes her hand. "Or to me.

❧ 10 ❧

KIKI

Greeks never forget the dead. Ever.
How can they when they're almost drowning in memorial services?

Three days. Nine days. Forty days. Three months. Six months. One year. And every year after, if the family wishes. A Greek Orthodox priest is a busy man, constantly reminding the living that the dead are still dead.

Three days after Stavros's funeral, everyone's back at his grave, listening to the priest repeat himself.

Good times. Lots of blame and resentment whizzing through the air.

Stavros is dead, Kiki is alive.

Doesn't seem fair to Team Stavros. Why does she get to stand there in her knee-length black dress and those reasonable heels, when Stavros is stuck in his wedding suit forever?

TEAM KIKI HAS ITS OWN COMPLAINTS.

"Why is Helena looking at you like that?" *Yiayia* prods Kiki with her elbow. "What did you do?"

"Nothing."

"Nothing," Margarita repeats, though her face is busy ignoring her family.

"Nothing." *Baba* pats Kiki's hand. "My Kiki is a good girl. What could she possibly have done?"

He's the perfect counterweight to her mother. She's cut from a tiny piece of cloth, and he almost needs to stoop his way under lintels. She's dark-haired, dark-eyed, he's fair-haired with hazel eyes. He takes life as he finds it, but when she finds life she assumes it's lying.

"Nothing," Kiki repeats.

"Something," *Yiayia* continues. "Because they are shooting things at you with their eyes."

It's true. Stavros was shot only the once, but it's a wonder Kiki's still breathing with all the holes they're punching in her.

Not *Theo* Kristos, though. He just looks sorry, eyes cast at the ground, shoulders slumped. One hand rests on his wife's waist, but it brings comfort to neither of them.

"You did pinch Stavros's nose," Soula tells their grandmother.

"I was doing everyone a favor," *Yiayia* says. "If he was alive, we could have avoided all this."

Her family is three-ring circus: Soula, Mama, *Yiayia*. *Baba*'s the quiet one, the man who knows when and how to leave a room. Which leaves Kiki to the monkeys, the clowns, the lions.

Stavros's family isn't a circus. They always came to the Andreou home for their serving of entertainment. The adults would form a pack and toss their combined three kids into the streets to play.

Mostly this meant Soula would pelt Stavros with uncomfortable questions about his burgeoning manhood.

"IS IT BIG?" SHE ASKED ONE SUMMER EVENING, WHILE THEY HUNG out on the big stone steps by the high school's basketball courts.

Stavros dribbled the ball. "Is what big?"

"You know," Soula said slyly.

"Oh. That. It's huge."

"Prove it."

"Prove it how?"

"Show us." She elbowed Kiki. And when Kiki muttered, "Oh, Jesus," Soula said, "Don't you want to know what you're getting before you buy it? What if it's defective?"

"It's not defective." He unzipped and showed Soula the goods she wanted to inspect.

Kiki didn't look, did she? She didn't want to marry Stavros and she didn't want to see his dick. Although seeing it was inevitable, at some point, she supposed.

"Well," Soula declared with all the authority of someone who'd seen a few, "you are not done growing yet, anyway."

KIKI SANK INTO THE DIRT (WELL, CONCRETE) THEN AND SHE'S sinking into the dirt now. Doesn't matter that she's standing on grass, the soil below wants her. All she can think about are all the times she tried throwing her life into reverse, going back to the day when the Boutos-Andreou deal was struck, and rolling another outcome. But Margarita refused to hear a word of it.

"I DON'T WANT TO MARRY STAVROS," SHE HAD SAID ONE AFTERNOON, while her mother was stringing clothes across the yard. Election day. Which meant only their green clothes saw soap and water that morning, because their family was a PASOK (the Panhellenic Socialist Movement; PASOK is an acronym that only works in its native Greek) family, and the color of Greece's left wing was green. Soula waltzed past in a red dress and won a slap behind the head from their mother and orders to march back into the house and find something green, lest the rest of town think they supported KKE, Greece's communist party.

(Greeks wear their political affiliations proudly, and condemn those who vote the other way with sullen looks and snide remarks about how their mothers lie down with donkeys.)

"Of course you want to marry Stavros. You just don't know it yet."

"I am sure she knows it, Mama," Soula said.

"You. In the house. Now."

(Yeah, Soula went back inside, but she kept the red dress and shimmied out the back door to see a boy about some cigarettes.)

"I really don't want to marry Stavros. I'm sure of it."

"You are fourteen. What do you know about anything?"

"I know I don't want to marry Stavros."

Mama tacked a green shirt onto the line. "Okay, you do not have to marry Stavros," she said, voice frolicking through a meadow with ponies and cotton candy.

"Really?"

Snap went the steel trap. "No."

Kiki stormed towards the steps, flipping her mother off inside her head.

"I saw that," Mama called out.

Sometimes, Kiki thought at the time, Mama was like one of those spiders whose whole head is made of eyes.

(Okay, so only eight eyes, but that's a lot of eyes.)

Kiki took a stab at the REWIND button regularly after that, always with the same outcome.

"You have to marry him, Kiki. Otherwise how will it look? What will it do to my friendship with Helena, eh? You only think of yourself."

Or, "Ha-ha-ha. You are a very funny girl, Kiki. No."

Or, "Did anyone hear that? I thought I heard someone whispering, but look, there is no-one here. It must be the ghost of a very silly girl who has no idea about life and what she wants."

Very compassionate mother, that Margarita Andreou.

During her eighteenth year, Kiki pulled a Soula.

"Guess what?" she said over Mama's chickpea soup. "I had sex with twelve sailors this afternoon."

A shocked silence, then lunch went on as usual.

"Oh well," Margarita said passively. "Good thing it was not thirteen. That is a very unlucky number."

Yiayia reached across the table for the bread. "Thirteen! That must be some kind of family record. One after the other, or did you take a break?"

"Mama, Kiki was joking," Margarita said.

"*Panayia mou*, why am I not in a coma? Nobody does anything exciting in this family."

"I do," Soula said.

Mama fixed a steel eye on her. "Go on, Soula. Tell us what you do that is so exciting."

"Roma men," the fifteen-year-old told her mother proudly. "As many as I can find."

A sharp intake of breath. "Tell me you did not just say *tsiganes*."

"And if I did?"

"There will be no kissy-kissy with *tsiganes* in this family while I am alive or while I am dead. Keep it up, both of you, and you will lose my blessing."

Worst thing ever to a Greek child, losing their mother's blessing. That means their mama is teaming up with God to turn their collective back on you.

Fend for yourself in this world, because God and Mama don't care.

Once that happens, every bad thing that follows, from chipped nails to death, is your own stupid fault.

Should have listened to your mama, ungrateful child.

Kiki quit poking her mother with sticks after that. She quietly accepted Stavros's ring and all its consequences.

Mostly quietly.

Okay, sometimes she complained, but never too loudly. And now here they are, listening to a priest remind them that this is day nine of a world without Stavros. She would cry, but her tear ducts know what her mind hasn't fully processed yet: she's free.

🦂 II 🦂

HELENA

The walls in the detective's office huddle together. They stand too close to one another for her to breathe comfortably.

She paints a portrait of Stavros as an angel, a man without sins or the kind of stains that might entice someone to do wish him harm. Kiki she paints in dense shadows, a fallen angel who acted upon lies.

Akili is her backup. The dear boy, he underscores her words with nods and sounds that confirm she speaks the truth.

When she's done talking, the detective leans back in his chair and tap-tap-taps his pen on his desk.

They have come uninvited and he is unhappy to see them, she thinks. Or maybe he is unhappy that she and Akili are doing his job for him. Who enjoys being usurped in their own kingdom?

"So you think Kyriaki Andreou killed Stavros?"

"Who else?" Palms up. "There is no one else, only Kiki."

"And she did this because she has heard stories that are not true?"

"People have killed for much less," Akili adds.

They have delivered a gift into his hands, so why doesn't he move? He should be running for the door, gun in hand, to toss Kiki into one of their cages.

Helena sighs. Useless, ineffectual man. This is who people rely on to keep them safe? Ridiculous.

"Come, Akili, we are wasting our time." She leaves the chair, the office, the worthless man behind the desk.

"Kyria Bouto?"

She glances back at the worthless man. "Yes?"

"Think carefully before you speak your suspicions to other people. You know what it is like here."

"What is it like here, Detective?"

"Take care that you do not destroy an innocent woman's life—if she is innocent—with gossip and rumors."

12

KIKI

Everyone tiptoes around Kiki. They have mistaken her for glass. Except *Yiayia*. Her grandmother, at least, speaks to her in her same old bold when she shows up for lunch.

"I wonder who will die next? Agria has not had a funeral since Stavros."

Cutlery screeches across a plate. "Mama!"

"It's only been a couple of weeks." Kiki slides into her chair. "Not in a coma today, *Yiayia*?"

"Eh, maybe tomorrow. Today the gossip is too good. Maybe I want to spread a little myself."

In a small village like Agria, gossip is a renewable resource. People here will still be talking behind each others backs, long after the Middle East's wells have gone dry and its people are begging the world to buy barrels of sand.

The whole family is at the kitchen table. It's lunchtime, which means (if you're Greek) it's dinnertime. Margarita dumps a bowl of pasta on the table, a bottle of ketchup, chunks of roughly-cut bread.

"For this I work so hard," Kiki's father says. "Spaghetti and ketchup. Who eats spaghetti and ketchup?"

His wife snatches away the plate. "There was a time children in this country went hungry. They would have been grateful for spaghetti *without* ketchup. But are you grateful? No!"

Hand outstretched. "Just give me the plate, Margarita."

"No. You do not like my cooking." A camper could pitch a tent on Mama's bottom lip.

"I like your cooking just fine—when it *is* cooking."

She gives him the plate, but she makes sure she knows it's a hardship. Kiki doesn't make eye contact with her sister. If she does she'll crack.

"So what are you going to do now, Kiki?" *Yiayia* says. "You need to get out there, find a new boyfriend."

Margarita throws her hands skyward. "This is why I keep trying to kill you, Mama. Kiki cannot go out and find a new boyfriend. We are still in mourning. How will it look?"

"Like she wants sex," *Yiayia* says. "Later we will get dressed up, eh? We can cruise the promenade together, maybe find some nice penis."

Prayers mumbled from Margarita's mouth: *Please God strike her down. Let the devil take her.*

"When's the last time you got laid, *Yiayia*?" Soula winks at Kiki, who hides her smile behind a chunk of bread.

"Twelve comas ago. He came to collect the garbage, but I told him your mother was not home."

Mama picks up her own plate, walks it to the garbage can. Dumps everything, including the plate. The screen door slaps the frame when she leaves.

Everybody starts eating except Kiki. She toys with the spaghetti a moment before setting aside the fork and the bread. Nobody looks at her when she stands. They don't want to see, don't want to know. The funeral is over and it's all so sad, yes, but to them this is the season of healing.

How can she heal when, on some level, she's believes she's the reason for Stavros's death? All her wishing and hoping, God or the gods heard her prayers and conspired to teach her a lesson: Here's what happens to good Greek girls when they want to defy their parents wishes. It's not logical; his death, suicide or not, was not about

Kiki. The universe didn't just hand Stavros a gun because Kiki might have hitched her wish for freedom to a falling star or fifty.

But the mind goes where it goes, and hers is trotting down a guilty road.

Kiki finds her mother pulling weeds from the potted plants. Not a one of her plants are in the ground; they all live and die in red-painted captivity. When an oil or olive container spills its last drops, it wins a coat of bright red paint and time in the sun to dry. Soon the gardenias will sprout their buds, and by July she'll be drunk on the scent of them, day and night. To Kiki, they are summer.

She kneels beside her mother. "Can I help?"

"Eat. Otherwise why do I cook?"

"I'm not hungry."

"Then do not complain to me later when you are hungry and there is no food."

"I'll eat it later."

Her mother sets aside the small trowel like it's killing her. Since Stavros died, Mama isn't Mama. She has abandoned makeup, styling her long hair, painting her nails. "What do you want, Kiki?"

"To see if you're okay."

Margarita sighs, picks up the trowel again. She digs at the dirt as if it's the problem. "You have lost the man you were meant to marry, a man you did not love. But I am losing a friend because of this, and her I do love."

"I did love him. Just not like that."

"Not all people who get married are in love."

"You and *Baba* were."

"Yes, and look at us now. We cannot draw two breaths of the same air without fighting. What is love, Kiki?"

"I don't know. But I think it's supposed to be everything."

Mama reaches over, taps her on the forehead with a dirty finger. "Then you are a fool."

***

GREECE HAS ONE OF THE SHORTEST SCHOOL YEARS IN THE WORLD,

but this semester still has more days on its calendar. Those tickets to Paris Soula mentioned lie in wait inside Kiki's handbag. Something has to be done with them, and soon.

She goes to school in a fog.

"Take some more time," the principal urged her. But she can't. To be at work is to be busy, and busy is good. It tricks the mind into believing all is well. At the front of the room with chalk in her hand, Stavros is still alive and juggling funny money for his clients.

That small act of forgetting makes her smile.

How strange: grief has given her a kind of amnesia. Now sometimes she has to remind herself that she didn't love him.

The chalk is damp in her hand. She sets it on the blackboard's lip and returns to the desk at the front of the room. She feels like a paper cutout. The kids haven't noticed. It's business as usual in here. They're passing rumors around the room, exchanging notes and glances. Not a one of them is about her. If they know, they don't care. Teenagers blow their own bubbles and live inside them until the world stabs them with a reality-shaped needle.

She smiles, but hides it in the stack of test papers her desk, when she overhears Melissa Tyler doing English with a Greek accent. They all do the same thing, her native English speakers. There's a handful of them in the school, raised in other countries and brought here by their Greek parents when the homesickness overwhelmed them.

"Ooooh, look," one of the boys says, "it's the police. Somebody is in trouble."

The meerkats pop their heads up, rush to the windows that run the length of the room. Kiki goes, too, but she's the last one to peer out and down to where a police car has parked itself outside the tall iron gates that surround the school.

A couple of constables get out. She knows them both. She taught them when they were younger and she was fresher. Good students, but when it comes to English, most of them are. Television and movies make her job easier.

And harder. It's not easy shaking the slang out of their sentences.

A cold arm curls itself around her shoulders, gives her a squeeze.

You like jail? it says. *Because jail would love a woman like you. They're here for you.*

But that's ridiculous. What business do they have with her?

She already sat on the sad side of their table, answered their gentle questions as honestly as she knew how. What other business is there?

She taps the chalk on the board. "Back to your seats."

"But—"

"Please."

They like her so they go, with a couple of stragglers casting curious glances out the window. She does her best not to look. And her best is pretty good. She barely flinches when a hand raps on the classroom door. She tells them to come in, but the door's already halfway open.

"*Despinida* Andreou?" Respectful. Trepidatious, too. A few years ago the two cops were backsides in this room or one like it.

Suddenly someone is showering inside her, and they've set the water to COLD.

"Who's dead this time?"

"Detective Lemonis sent us. He wants to ask you some questions."

"Okay," she says. "Okay." Her kids' faces are blurring together. "Stay right there," she tells them. "And be good."

When she shuts the door behind her, the room explodes. A chatter bomb. Kids are ostriches: if a grownup can't see them, then a grownup can't hear them.

THEY PUT HER IN THE WAITING ROOM, SO SHE WAITS. No magazines, no books, so she reads the inside of her eyelids. A door opens, closes. Kiki's eyes stay shut.

THEY THINK YOU KILLED STAVROS. WHY ELSE WOULD YOU BE HERE?

She opens her eyes because her reading material sucks, and because someone is breathing in her face.

"At first I thought you were dead, but no you are just lazy." The voice is old, scratchy, like it's coming at her from a phonograph cylinder.

Now there's an old man in the seat across from her. He's on the downhill slope toward ninety. Suitcases under both eyes. Pants hitched up to his armpits. A toupee that isn't fooling anyone. In one hand is a figurine—a crouching man with big thighs and a chin-grazing anaconda.

"What's that?" she says, nodding at the statue.

"A fertility statue. I think he likes you."

"By the looks of him he likes everyone."

"*Ha-ha*." He points at her with the wood's wood. "Why are you here? Solicitation?" His eyes light up.

"My fiancé died. I think they think I killed him."

"Bah!" He waves a disgusted hand at the thin air. "You did not kill anyone. I saw you in a vision. But your bottom was smaller and your melons were bigger. It was a sign, so we came here to find you—me and Laki!" He holds up the statue.

In a Greece everything is a sign, except street signs. Street signs are there mostly to give drunk drivers a place to nap until the cops show up. Sneezing is a sign someone is gossiping about you. If someone throws salt at you, you can be sure you are an unwelcome guest. Crows bring death. Sometimes they steal your jewelry. (They're like very small relatives—with wings.)

Kiki goes to the counter. "If I say I did it, will you get me away from this guy?"

The constable looks up from his newspaper. "Is that a confession?"

Never mind. Back to the chair.

"You are very pretty," the old man says. "Twenty years ago, I would have pounced on you."

"Twenty? Try fifty."

"Forget it," he scoffs. "You are pretty, but you are not that pretty."

A door sings its song, and Detective Lemonis appears.

"Come in," he says.

THE DETECTIVE'S OFFICE IS A SMALL ROOM AT THE BACK OF THE building.

Smart, hiding the windows from the street. No throwing a brick or a Molotov cocktail through a window you can't see.

At least he takes her to his office, not an interrogation room. Still, she feels tiny and insignificant on the far side of his desk.

"At first the evidence seemed to be pointing toward suicide, but now it's pointing to something else," he says.

"You think I killed Stavros," she says flatly. Of course they do. And she understands why. She's suspect *numero uno*, the reluctant fiancée, the wronged woman. They went out there with a muck rake, flipped over the piles of gossip, and heard for themselves the stories about Stavros's dick and the places it went without her.

"Kyriaki Andreou. Twenty-eight. You teach at the high school. You and the deceased have been engaged for how long?"

"We've been here. You already know."

"Humor me."

"Since I was twelve. Sixteen years."

"Arranged marriage?"

Spring is inching toward summer. Light sweat glues her dress to her chest. She tugs at the black fabric, but her skin won't let it go.

"Yes."

"And it took you this long to set a date?"

"We were busy."

"Doing what?"

Putting off the wedding, mostly. "Establishing our careers."

"How did your families feel about that?"

"I can't speak for the Boutos family, but my mother was sure I was trying to kill her."

"Kill her?"

She lets out a long pained sigh, an exact replica of Margarita's. "The normal Greek mother's litany. '*Oh, Kiki, why are you doing this to me? I need grandchildren, and Soula is so busy selling houses that she will never marry. Look at her last boyfriend—poor man, she dumped him for being boring. What does she expect? All men become boring, sooner or later. If you want excitement in your life, you must have lots of children to torture.*' "

Lemonis jots something down in his notebook.

"Did Stavros have any enemies?"

She gives him the old are-you-kidding look, because ... is he kidding? "He was an accountant. Everyone is an enemy if they don't like the way you add the numbers."

Stavros was a lot of things (mostly sexual things of a nefarious nature), but he was a good accountant. Nobody ever talked about how Stavros Boutos counted their numbers wrong—*wink wink*.

"Any *real* enemies?"

"Arranged marriage. We weren't exactly close, Detective. But town gossip says no. If anything, Stavros was one of those people who never met a stranger. He would drink with anyone, socialize with anyone. He made fun for himself and those around him." Which is why Akili clung to his leg like a horny dog.

In this small office is where she realizes how little she knew Stavros. They played together as children, shared a few colorless kisses in their teens, but that's it. His friends weren't her friends. They ran with different crowds. There were stories about him, yes, but Agria is filled with stories—more than the *Naked City*'s eight million.

Detective Lemonis goes on. "He was an angel, according to his mother."

A short blunt laugh. "An angel? No. He's a Greek son, which means his mother—like yours, no doubt—thought he was Jesus Christ."

"His best friend—"

"Akili? You're talking about Akili, right?" Nothing. "Akili is a snake. Big mouth, small brain. You can't go anyplace but wrong if you listen to Akili."

"You sound bitter, *Despinida* Andreou."

(*Despinida* = Miss)

"Bitter? No. Honest."

Back to his notes. "Do you own a gun?"

Is he high? This is Greece. Who has guns in Greece? Almost nobody, that's who. "No."

"Do you have access to a gun?"

"Detective, I don't know anyone who owns any kind of gun. And I didn't kill Stavros."

The detective doesn't look convinced. Kiki's sure he sees a look of guilty faces whose mouths talk innocent talk. And now that he's looking at the real deal, he can't tell the difference.

Do anything long enough and you wind up blind to the alternatives.

"It was not suicide," Lemonis says, shoving away from the desk. "Impossible. No residue on his hands. And all those houses around the train tracks, yet nobody heard the gunshot? Here nobody dies without making noise. There are no secrets."

"Except," Kiki says slowly, "the ones we pretend we have."

"That's right." He nods over his notes. "I don't think you did it, *Despinida* Andreou. But his mother thinks you are guilty, and she is not the only one."

"Akili. Like I said: snake."

The detective shrugs.

It's a cold blade through her heart. But she can't be angry at Helena. Disappointed, yes, but not angry. The woman has known her since birth, watched her live and grow. At times she's been a confidante, a soothing hand on her mother's ruffled feathers. Kiki loves her like a second mother.

"She just lost her son," she says carefully. "She'd say anything to point the finger in a direction that makes sense."

"You are not angry that she is accusing you of murder?"

"She lost her *only* child, Detective. Can you imagine? Wouldn't that make you crazy and desperate?"

"How saintly of you."

Not saintly at all. *Thea* Helena's loss is, on some level, Kiki's gain. What Kiki feels is a slow, steeping guilt that won't ever let her dry out.

"I'm not a saint. I just want to be left alone."

Whether he likes it or not, she's done here. The chair scrapes across the floor as she stands.

"I read the paper," she continues. "I hear the talk. Vivi Tyler is a friend of mine and my cousin's fiancée, and I know you've got it wrong before, Detective. And in exactly the same way."

"No one heard the shot," he reminds her.

"You've forgotten one important thing about this place. Even the most ... *attentive* people hear only want they want to hear, see only what they want to see. What is it you want to see and hear, Detective? A murder or the truth?"

No more old man in the waiting room.

Now he's doing his waiting outside—for her, apparently.

"Do you want a ride?" he asks.

She looks at the moped leaning on its prosthetic leg. "On that? Does it even run?"

"I offer you a free ride and you complain? Women, all you do is complain. And Greek women are the worst." He shakes his finger in her face. "You complain sixty percent more then other women."

Kiki walks. Perfect weather, but there's a cloud overhead that won't let her leave. It's been stalking her since the wedding that never happened, and it's moving closer.

Agria is slowly gaining its summer kilos. Tourists are trickling in now, but in another month they'll be a full pour. That's fine; the people who come here are good. They like Greeks and they like a good time. And Greeks know how to show visitors a good time.

"*Kalimera*," she says, waving. Once, twice, three times she says *good morning* to faces she knows. Even in her black mood she doesn't throw away her reputation as a polite woman. Once is all it takes. Forget to say hello and they throw you into the social dungeon with the chicken thieves and adulterers.

Behind her, the moped gargles.

He's following her, isn't he?

That's a big, neon YES, he's following her.

"Socrates," he calls out. "I am Socrates Karas."

Karas.

Ha-ha.

Now there's a name from not nearly enough years ago. Which branch of the family is this monkey swinging from? She stops, takes a good look. Now she remembers: he's the patriarch. Leonidas's grandfather.

"What do you want, *Kyrios* Karas?"

"You think this is my idea? No! Laki. He is the one who tells me to speak to you."

Ha-ha. Very funny man, this lunatic. "Why?"

He shrugs. "Do I look like I know? If I knew, I would be speaking instead of following you like a dog. Can I pinch your *kolos*?"

"My Virgin Mary," she mutters.

"I would pinch her *kolos*, too."

FORGET ITALIANS—GREEK MEN ARE CONSUMMATE ASS PINCHERS. They start young. It's nothing for a ten-year-old boy to pinch an ass he likes when it walks by.

Greek men do everything early. Except make their own beds.

For that they have mothers, then wives.

"*YIA SOU, KYRIOS KARAS.*"

Yia sou. It's one of those allen wrench phrases that means more than one thing. It's hello, it's goodbye.

Kiki means goodbye.

But the old man takes it for hello. When she speeds up, he follows.

And now Kiki feels like a jerk, because the day is getting hot and he's getting older. Annoying or not, the last thing she wants is another death on her hands.

She stops in the nearest patch of shade, a wide, dark rectangle, cast by the backside of a taverna.

"Why are you stopping? Are you weak? You look strong, like the ox."

This guy ... "I'm stopping for you, so you don't drop dead."

"Bah! I am immortal. Nothing can kill Socrates Karas. And they have tried."

"Who tried to kill you?"

"Eh." He shrugs his way into the shade, alongside her. "The Turks, the Greeks, the snakes, the ocean, the gods. And one time, my wife, because I pinched her mother's *kolos*."

"Just say what you've got to say. Please. I have to get back to work."

Socrates's grin is a mixture of gums and gold. "Okay. Listen carefully. Laki tells me that you will meet a man soon."

"Do you want me to cross your palm with silver?"

"Silver? You are cheap. But no—no silver. What I tell you is for free. You will meet a tall, dark, handsome man. And also you will go to jail. What?" He holds up the statue, looks it in the eyes. Zones out for several moments. "Apparently Greece's current economic crisis is a Turkish plot to seize Greece for itself."

"Sounds rational." On Mars, maybe.

"You will see." Socrates shakes a finger at her. "Laki is never wrong, except for those few times when he is. He makes many, many predictions for the future and thinks we should write a book."

"You should do that," she tells him.

"I will. But we will be seeing each other again very soon."

God, no. "How is your grandson, Kyrios Karas?"

"Which one? I have many."

"Leonidas. The one who went to America." Before she had a chance to apologize for showing him the disappearing finger trick.

He shrugs. "Why ask me? You will find out soon."

13

HELENA

S tavros is not dead.

Dead men do not laugh at their mothers and say, "Mama, you're overreacting—again. You get these ideas in your head and make yourself miserable, and for what? Nothing."

"I saw you with my own eyes," she tells him.

"Theater. I had to make everyone believe I was dead."

"Why?"

"Why?" He shakes his head. "Because you and *Thea* Margarita were forcing Kiki and me to get married. Wasn't any other choice."

"You could have said."

"We tried. But you two, you wouldn't listen."

"That is not true."

He slams his fists on the table so hard its feet skip across the marble tile. "Don't lie, Mama. You stole my choices when I was too young to stop you. And now look at me."

This trick her mind plays is a cruel one. She is both sadist and masochist.

"You are not dead," she says.

"Mama ..."

"You are not dead!"

He pulls up his Scorpions T-shirt, the one he died in. "Then what is this, Mama? What is it?" His fingers touch the bullet-made hole. "Nobody escapes this."

"You will. I will go to Hades and drag you back myself!"

HELENA DOESN'T TELL KRISTOS ABOUT THEIR SON. HE'LL MISTAKE her for *trela* if she does. She isn't crazy, just desperate. But he will not see desperation, only insanity.

She packs a small bag and waits for the taxi to ferry her away. The cabdriver does not require gold coins—euros will suffice. At her command, he takes her to the bus station in Volos, where the air is stale and the exhaust fumes form clouds of despair.

One after the other, tin cans rattle up to the boarding bays. They dump old passengers for new, then they're gone with a burp and a drawn-out groan.

Which bus does she take? Which bus goes to the mouth of Hades?

The names blur together.

A bus going west is the one she needs, bound for the place where three of Hades' rivers meet. That is where she will find the bones of the old *Necromanteion* and bargain for her son's life.

But with what? What does she, Helena Bouto, possess that Hades could possibly want?

What is the price of a life?

Another life, of course.

The only life she has to swap is her own, half-used, its soul sick with grief. In no way a fair trade. Hades will not want her stale leftovers.

She picks up the bag that's never been anywhere but home, walks back to the where the taxicabs wait. Begs one to ferry her home.

Until she has something worth trading, she will not believe Stavros has gone.

It cannot be borne.

14

LEO

Five weeks in basic training. A few months ago he'd have said five weeks was nothing.

Now it's too much.

He filed his complaints, gave his reason, and now the army's deciding whether to give him a green light or red.

If you had volunteered like you were supposed to, it would be different, they told him.

If they say he has to do it, he has to do it. No choice.

The training itself isn't a problem. It's more fun than his marriage was, near the end. Not that it was all bad. There were great times, then good times, and okay times. Near the end, there were times.

Both of them tried to make things work. Too bad it wasn't a simultaneous effort.

Now here he is in green splotches, taking orders from some barking kid he doesn't respect. Leo is the oldest of the bunch, and the brat won't let him forget it. Calls him '*Papou*.'

Yeah, right. If he was the brat's grandfather, he'd put that kid over his knee and paint his butt red.

Five weeks. Followed by nine months. Too much time when his mother's got a couple of months or so—max.

NOT LONG NOW UNTIL HE GETS A FEW DAYS RESPITE. FOR THAT HE'S going back to Athens on a camping trip. Destination: the US Embassy's front door step. That way he's not just a voice on the phone, he's a person. An American.

If the army doesn't release him first.

"Hey, *Papou*. Pick up the pace!"

Little bastard.

When he gets back to the barracks, there's a messenger waiting with a big, fat "No" in his hands.

15

KIKI

The body snatchers have been hard at work. These women look like Kiki's friends, but they've been hollowed out by strangers.

Star Trek had it wrong. The only fuel they ever needed was a half-dozen or so Greek families. They could have zipped all over the universe at the speed of gossip.

Marianna is not the first to snatch away her friendship, just the most recent. "Kiki? What are you doing here?"

"Oh, I don't know. Looking for a friend?"

"Kiki ..." Tired, wary. No offers of hospitality. "Is it true? Do the police think you killed Stavros?"

She coughs up a laugh. Because—really? Don't her friends know her better than that?

Good thing for her she and Soula aren't cut from the same blue and white cloth, because Soula wouldn't waste a second reminding Marianna that it wasn't long ago the same police accused her husband of sexually assaulting a Swiss tourist.

They had the wrong guy, but Kiki came everyday to give Marianna a place to cry.

What does Marianna give her?

Nothing but a handful of salt, flicked in her direction.

No sleep for the falsely accused.

Kiki spends her nights imagining herself in stripes. It's not a good look. Never wear clothes that don't flatter even a tall, slender woman.

The warmer nights pull her onto the small balcony overlooking the yard. Most nights, she hears the soft hum of Soula chatting into her phone. Her words are indistinct, but her tone is gentle, happy. Sometimes she laughs; a throaty, intimate sound.

On this mid-May night, Soula's voice wears armor. Her words are tough, sharp. Someone's taking a beating. The woman knows how to win fights and stand on the bodies afterward, banner held high.

It's not long before her front door slams. Espadrilles dance down the stairs to the yard and all its obstacles.

"Where are you going so late?" *Yiayia* says.

"Nowhere," Kiki hears her sister say.

"Does this nowhere have a big penis?"

"Not every destination has a penis, *Yiayia*."

Their grandmother grunts. "Then why else go out so late?"

Light floods the yard. Mama sticks her head out the door. "What is wrong with you? People are trying to sleep!"

"What people?" *Yiayia* says. "There is only you complaining."

Mama disappears. The door slams.

Soula tosses her final words over one shoulder. "Good night, *Yiayia*."

The Mini buzzes away.

❧ 16 ❧

HELENA

She follows Stavros into the kitchen.

"I'm starving," he says. "What's for breakfast?"

"Anything you want."

"Toast with olive oil."

Toast with olive oil. Stavros has always loved that.

She makes toast, drizzles olive oil over the top. Slides it in front of him.

But he doesn't touch it.

"Eat," she says.

"I'm not hungry, Mama."

"Okay. You don't have to eat."

He sits there not eating, her beautiful boy. And she sits there watching him, wondering if he is happy.

"We should not have insisted you marry that girl. It was a mistake."

Silence.

"She is too much like her sister. Too independent. She would never have stopped working when your children came."

Silence.

At least Stavros doesn't leap to Kiki's defense the way he used to.

That is something. That is ... Something.

❧ 17 ❧

KIKI

May twenty-first, Kiki walks to the Boutos home, gift in hand. At dawn, the bells chimed for Saint Helena and the women and men who share her name, in all its variations.

Greeks don't do birthdays unless you're a child. It's the name day that matters.

"*Kronia polla, Thea* Helena," she says, wishing the woman many more years.

"Kiki!" Helena waves. She rushes to the gate, arms open wide, pulls Kiki into her arms. "Let me look at you," she says. "What a beautiful girl you are. Come, see Stavros. He is inside. I will fix you something to eat—you look too thin. Are you well?"

Ten seconds ago she was a woman, now Kiki is a goldfish, mouth opening and closing and opening.

"I'm fine." The words squeak out. It's clear Helena is anything but fine. But how deep do the cracks go?

Answer: All the way.

Stavros is in the kitchen, all right. Not in the flesh, but in latex. Someone (Helena) has glued a headshot of Stavros to the face of a blowup man-doll.

"*Thea* Helena ..."

"Stavros, look who has come to see you," Helena crows. "I will fix something for you both to eat, then I will leave you two lovers to talk."

What's she supposed to do? Sit and talk to the doll? Kiss it on both paper cheeks? What's the proper etiquette for greeting an imaginary son? She looks at the beaming mother. "And you, how are you, *Thea* Helena?"

Thea Helena wags a finger in her face. "Soon you will be calling me *Mama*, yes?"

Kiki sits slowly. Any second now, she expects the older woman to shatter.

"Where is *Theo* Kristos?" she asks cautiously.

"Mind your own business, *putana*!"

The words fly out of the crimped edge of Helena's mouth, but the words are meant to be her son's.

Now is when anyone else would run, but she's on a goodwill mission.

Helena switches personalities, puts on her own. "Stavros! You will not speak like that in my home! Poor Kiki, he didn't mean it, my doll."

Maybe Stavros didn't mean it (dead men don't mean much, do they?) but *Thea* Helena's stake was expertly kicked into her chest.

"I know," she says slowly. "It's been a difficult time for the family."

Helena's face is innocent. "Oh? How so?"

"With Stavros's death." She sets the words out there gently, waits for the crash of breaking glass.

"Stavros is not dead, he is here!"

Switch.

"I'm dead because you killed me, *putana*!"

Okay ... "I have to go," Kiki says.

"Stay! You haven't eaten yet. Don't mind Stavros, he's having a bad day. He woke up on the wrong side of the bed—the wall side."

Kiki hovers in that uncomfortable position between air and chair. Her ass says, sit, her head tells her to scream "Fire" and run.

Her mouth is a lousy mediator. It says, on her behalf, "Just coffee, please."

Yeah, thanks for that, mouth. Now she's stuck here in the Craziest

Place on Earth, making polite conversation with *Thea* Helena and Stavros's eternal grin.

She slides her feet into the older woman's metaphorical shoes. How else does a parent cope with losing a child? It's the act of a desperate woman. Someone has to get her some help—someone being Kiki, because who else is there? *Thea* Helena won't talk to Mama, and *Theo* Kristos is grieving in his own invisible way.

In the meantime, she plays along.

"How's work, Stavros? Are all the numbers adding up right?"

"Very good accountant, my Stavros." *Thea* Helena glows. "The best in Greece."

"In the world," Kiki says. When the coffee comes, it's cold and missing its sugar. Kiki drinks. It tastes like her life.

❧ 18 ❧

HELENA

After Kiki is gone, Helena drops into the chair beside Stavros.
"Don't say anything. Please."
The good son says nothing.
"I'm losing my mind. Maybe it's already gone."

✣ 19 ✣

LEO

A stranger comes to town.

No, not really. But he may as well be. It's been about that long.

The bus passes out at the curb. The way its engine dies, it might never get up again.

He steps off the bus and into *deja vu*. He's been here before, but in a smaller, younger body, getting on the bus with his Greek father and American mother, who hated the place. As the lights of Volos faded behind them, she said, "So long, God forsaken shit-hole." His father choked on his cigarette, jabbed his thumb at Leo. Leo, the kid, didn't care. Hearing his mother swear was like watching porn. It was exciting, dangerous, and eventually someone would need tissues.

"Leonidas!"

There's only one person standing there, calling his name. A man older than dirt—and Greek dirt is older than most.

"*Papou?*"

"Socrates. *Grandfather* makes me sound old, and I am in my prime." He opens his arms. "Come here!"

Leo accepts the hug and gives one back. "How did you know I was coming?"

"A vision told me you would be on this bus."

"A vision?"

"Yes, that is what I say." He looks Leo up, down. "What is with the uniform?"

Five weeks and it's like he was born in the thing. "I'm in the army."

"What for? Are you stupid? Because when you left here you were not a stupid boy. But who knows what happens in America? They do many stupid things."

"No choice, *Papou*. They snatched me off the plane."

And took his passport. And threw him into basic training. And denied him clemency. He spent this morning appealing to the US Embassy, but they showed him their best shrugs. Now here he is, searching for alternatives.

"Socrates."

"Socrates."

"Okay," his grandfather says. "We can fix that. I do not have a basement, but you can dig one under my house and hide there."

Leo slaps him on the back. "Great idea. Let's do that."

"The older I get, the better my ideas are. When I am dead I will be Greece's biggest genius. Can you drive?"

"I can drive."

"Can you drive a motorcycle?"

"Sure."

"Good. You drive. I will sit on the back and watch the girls."

It's a moped built for one. Two is risky, at best, and its heartbeat doesn't have much enthusiasm. His grandfather helps by throwing out a bunch of encouraging curse words. Nobody violates religious figures like the Greeks.

The moped does what it can. Soon they're putt-putting through the streets of Volos, down to the road that hugs the gulf.

It's like he remembered, but more vivid. His childhood memory is of a watercolor, but this is an oil painting. The Pagasetic Gulf is a bowlful of blue-green marbles, constantly shifting. Saints Constantine and Helena's church is still on its urban corner, flanked by a park and the sea. It watches over the promenade and the long string of *tavernas*.

Today a man is scraping its backside with a bucket and brush, brushing away the FACK spray-painted on its rock.

Leo laughs. Things never change.

"Stop," Socrates hollers in his ear. "I lost my hair."

There's traffic both ways, but not too much, so Leo does a quick u-turn. Sure enough, there's his grandfather's toupee sitting in the opposite lane. From here it looks like roadkill. One car zips over it. Two. The synthetic hair flaps in the breeze.

"Can't you get a new one?"

"It is my lucky hair. I won it in a donkey race."

"Donkeys race?"

"It was a very slow race." He nods to the hair. "In my vision, you pick up my hair."

It's the least he can do. Leo parks the moped, snatches up the hair, leaps back in time to avoid being hit by a truck filled with watermelons and Roma.

"We curse your sons with four nipples!" one of the men yells.

Leo laughs. What else can he do—they're already gone.

Sons. He wonders if he'll ever have them. Or daughters. Daughters would be nice. Healthy, happy, that's what matters.

Too bad he and Tracy could never agree. Before they married she was determined to have kid and so was he. Right up until his sister-in-law had a child with Down's Syndrome. Then Tracy started singing a different song, where the chorus was "No kids. Not ever."

The no-kids thing was one of many nails in the coffin.

Socrates slaps his hair into place, then they're rolling again toward Agria.

Agria. It's a suburb of Volos now, but from what Socrates has been telling him, you don't say that too loud. Agria, to the people who live there, is still Agria. They refuse to be a subset.

St George's fills its same old slot at the southwest end of the promenade. Butted up against its right flank is the playground where he used to hang. It's wild with children today. Parents everywhere; there never used to be any.

"That's new," he says. "Almost no parents when I played there."

"Very new," Socrates tells him. "There was a murder, and now everybody is crazy. Bah! They act like we have not seen murder before. We have seen plenty of murders, but we called them accidents. It is this detective. He sees murder everywhere, even when it is a hangnail."

"Who was it?"

"Kristos and Helena Boutos's boy. He was hungry, so he ate a gun. Or someone fed it to him."

"Vaguely familiar."

"A wild boy. But a very good accountant. And now everybody thinks his fiancée did the murder."

"Did she?"

Socrates scoffs in his ear. "If anyone can kill a man it is a woman. Especially an angry woman. But I know that woman and she is not angry, except at me."

"What did you do, Socrates?"

"Maybe I pinched her bottom."

"Maybe?"

"Eh, maybe. Her bottom is a very nice bottom."

The moped chugs along the waterfront. After all this time and his body still remembers the way home. It knows when to take a left at the grimy old waterfront supermarket, and left again at the Agria's first apartment building on Drakia Road.

His grandfather's house sits on the same old corner, across from a tiny bakery and a shack that pretends to be a grocery store. Chickens everywhere. Turkeys, too. The old cat lounging in the bakery window watches the birds with one open eye. The other eye other doesn't give a damn.

Same old dump, his grandfather's place. Hasn't seen whitewash in what looks like forever.

They used to live here, with Socrates, when he was a kid. His mother hated that, too. It's one of a million reasons why they left.

Yeah, it's definitely the same-old, right down to the outhouse sitting next to the chicken coop. No chickens, but there's a stack of newspapers sitting outside the outhouse door.

"No toilet paper?"

Socrates slaps him on the back. "What do I want toilet paper for?

Better to wipe on the Greek news. That is what I think of the politics now. Come, you can have your old room. The bed is still there."

"Hey, *Papou*, do you have a phone?"

"Socrates. It is in the kitchen. Who you need to call, eh?"

"My folks."

"Give your mother and brother my love, but give your father a little fart, eh?"

IT'S ONE OF THOSE OLD ROTARY PHONES. WITH A CORD. BEEN A while since he saw one of those.

When he lived here there was no phone. If you wanted to talk to someone, you did it the Greek way: stand in their front yard and yell. So this is progress.

He'd use his cell phone, but it's dead. No Internet meant there was no paying the bill. Yeah, yeah, there's auto-pay for everything now, but sometimes companies have a way of randomly snatching out more than their designated share. It's not that he doesn't trust them, it's that he doesn't trust them.

He laughs at himself, because for this one thing he should have trusted them. Then he wouldn't be relying on his grandfather's antique.

He dials his mother's cell number, but nothing. Just her prompting him to leave a message. Leo's not big on leaving messages, so he calls Dad next.

Dad's not busy. He picks up on the second ring.

"Dad, it's me."

"Leo? Where are you?"

"Still in Greece. I'm on leave."

Mumble mumble, then: "Still in Greece? How soon will you be back?"

"I don't know. How is Mom?"

"Not better, but not worse."

His father almost sounds convinced of his own lie.

20

KIKI

The kitchen is hot, steamy. There's a breeze floating through the window and door, but it's only passing through.

"Have you spoken with *Thea* Helena recently?"

Mama looks away from the pot she's stirring. It's thick with *rizogalo*.

YOU WANT DIABETES? COME, EAT SOME OF GREECE'S RICE PUDDING. It's made of sugar, rice, and a half dozen cans of *NOYNOY* (pronounced *noo-noo*) evaporated milk. One bite and you'd better start shopping for a larger wardrobe. Or take the whole bowl and call a doctor the morning.

"NO. SHE WILL NOT SPEAK TO ME." THE SPOON STIRS FASTER, acting out Mama's frustrations.

"I went to see her today."

"So?"

"She needs help."

Now Margarita Andreou abandons her spoon, looks at her daughter with twenty-eight years of exasperation. "Kiki, you cannot help somebody who does not want to be helped."

Sure she can. It happens all the time.

———

WITH HER HANDS ON THE WHEEL OF SOULA'S MINI COOPER, KIKI runs away.

("Why must you buy a red car, Soula?" Mama had said when her sister bought the Mini home. "Red! People will think you are a communist! Only the communists buy red cars.")

"Take it," Soula insisted when Kiki asked to borrow her car. "I can catch the bus—no problem."

"Are you sure?"

"Always I am sure of everything."

Now here she is zipping up Mount Pelion, in search of inner peace or a skull-crushing pile of wisdom, because she's fresh out.

Helena needs help. Right now, she's a bag filled with shattered pieces. But Kiki won't be the one to hang her insanity on the line for the neighbors to see. Maybe Helena doesn't care now, while her mind lives in its cozy fog, but she will—in time.

In a place like Agria, where the minds lean toward small, one drop of insanity is the same as a bucketful. So Kiki needs to step carefully, lest she drip blood in the water.

Beautiful day, but it barely registers. She's too busy dodging sheep and buses fat with tourists, creeping up and down the mountain. There's no room for speed here; the road threads itself around one sharp, steep corner, then another. Occasionally, a sapling breaks off the main ribbon of faded blacktop and jags left. Houses and shops bud off that one thin vein and form villages.

People live in small pockets all over Mount Pelion, every one its own miniature paradise.

(Pick up any postcard and you'll see.)

She's relieved when it's her turn to cut away from the road, bump down the path that leads to the Holy Mother. Her cousin Max's Jeep is parked outside, so she will have two counselors. Her timing is perfect. Max is a physician—a pediatrician, yes, but he will know somebody who can help Helena. And he knows Agria well enough to fly beneath its omnipresent Cylon-like radar.

Peace washes over her as she tugs opens the wooden door that sits in the rock's face. The cool air rushes out, pulls her into its arms. This unusual church dwells in a natural cavern. Hundreds of years ago, the Greek Orthodox church made itself at home here, and there's been no reason to leave.

It takes a few moments for her eyes to adjust, for the light to come. Pinpricks, at first, then the pale glow of candles left by those who care. Unlike St George's, and most Greek Orthodox churches, the Holy Mother's interior doesn't look like King Midas sneezed on the walls and icons. The real gold here is not a metal.

She lights her own candles, presses their stems into the sand-filled dish. For *Thea* Helena and *Theo* Kristos, for Stavros, for her family. And a fourth for Detective Lemonis, may he find his man—or woman.

Where most Greek Orthodox churches separate the sexes during services, the Holy Mother seats everyone equally. Kiki slides into a pew, bows her head until it's touching the cool wood of the seat in next row.

What now?

Marriage to Stavros has been a fixed point for so many years, an inevitable evening star. His death has left her untethered, free.

It's been so long since she was a loose end. Which way will the breeze blow her next?

It's an illusion. She is anything but free. Not now, when almost every finger in town wants to pin her to a dartboard. Kiki is the flavor of the month, if the flavor is ass. Already she's hearing the whispers. They don't know why she killed Stavros, only that she killed him. Who else would want him dead? Nobody. Stavros was a one-man party. And they love a good party.

Therefore Kiki is the crowned queen of the party poopers.

A warm body slides into the seat next to her. Max.

"Hey," she says.

"Hey. You okay?"

A small shiver as her body adjusts to the cooler clime. "More or less."

"When you're ready, there's *frappe* upstairs with your name on it." He squeezes her hand, then he's gone.

"Tell me what to do next," she whispers. But the man at the head of the class is silent, crying on his wooden cross.

21

KIKI

True fact: There is *frappe* and it is perfection in a glass. Kostas makes it the way she likes it: coffee, cold water, ice, too much sugar, and a splash of milk when the shaking is over and the glass is wall-to-wall foam. He shoves the straw in and sets it in front of her.

"I love you," she tells her cousin.

"I know. I'm a lovable guy."

Max laughs. "He wishes."

There's a sparkle in Kostas's eyes that never fully goes away. "I wish for many things, brother. But that is a fact."

Max laughs harder.

Good-looking men her cousins. Tall, dark, handsome. The kind of faces the camera—and women—love. Kostas's nose leans a little to the side. He was the family's bad boy, and like all bad boys, eventually his nose met an angry husband with a *retsina* bottle in his hand. But that was years ago. Kostas is a changed man, a holy man. He settled down with the Father, the Son, the Holy Ghost, and now all four of them are happy—cozy in this village, in this small apartment above his church. And who wouldn't be happy here? The view alone lifts the weight from her shoulders and sets it aside. If she squints, she can see where the Earth curves away from Greece, toward Turkey.

"Bless me, Father, for I have sinned," she murmurs.

Now both men laugh. "You and everyone else in our family," Kostas says.

She smiles, but the laughter won't come. "What would you do if someone you knew went mad?"

Max takes a short drink of his *frappe*. "Are you talking about your grandmother? She's always been just this side of crazy."

Head shake. "*Thea* Helena. Stavros's mother."

"She lost a child," Kostas says gently. "Let her have her madness. It will fade, in time."

"Not always," Max says. "It's not natural, outliving your children, and the mind knows it. I'd go crazy, too."

Kiki stirs the foam, licks it off the straw. "This is more than grief. She needs help. She really believes Stavros is still alive."

It's not easy, but she tells these two men she trusts about the visit.

Please don't let them laugh.

They don't laugh.

Max is the first to speak. "Do you think she's a danger to herself or to anyone else?"

"Maybe," she says. "I don't know. The doll sounded menacing, like it hates me."

Kostas looks at his older brother. "This one is in your hands. It is too big for the church."

"Are you saying God can't handle it?" Max says.

"I'm saying that for some things, God put the more suitable tools in your hands."

Kiki says, "Max?"

Max nods. "I know some excellent psychologists. But I can't compel *Kyria* Bouto to meet with them, unless she's dangerous or in danger."

"Triantafillou?" Kostas asks.

Max nods. "She'd be my first choice."

That's the rub, isn't it? A benign madness is never a call to arms. "She believes he's alive, Max. *Truly* believes it. She's giddy with joy."

Max nods. "Kostas, maybe we can talk with *Kyrios* Boutos together.

His generation, he won't listen to Kiki. And odds are he won't listen to a doctor, either."

"So the church needs to stage an intervention. I'm not his priest, but I can still speak on behalf of God, for some things."

Kiki slumps on the table. "Thank you."

"What about you, little cousin?" the priest asks. "How are you coping?"

"I'm great," she says, glancing up at him. "This is what I wanted—right? Not for Stavros to be dead, of course. But I wanted my freedom, and now I have it."

Max says, "Until your mother lines up another husband."

She looks at Max in horror. He holds up both hands. "Joking," he says. "Joking."

"He has no sense of humor, that one," Kostas says. "He can joke about arranged marriages, now that he is happy."

It wasn't too long ago, Max was staring down the barrel of an arranged marriage, contrived between her aunt and an old family friend. Max escaped. Barely. She never met Anastasia, but she's heard the horror stories.

Max shrugs. "It's sad about Stavros. He was an okay guy. But that doesn't mean you shouldn't be glad you're free."

"They think I did it."

Two shocked men. Kostas is the first to recover. "Who is 'they'?"

"The police. Stavros's mother. And now everyone."

Max looks confused. "I thought it was a suicide."

"The detective says it's impossible."

"Lemonis?" Max asks. "Not the first time he's been wrong."

"That's what I said."

He winces. "How did he take that?"

"Like a cop," she says. "His mouth told me I could leave, but his face said we'll be talking again."

MAX LEAVES FIRST. IT'S A VIVI THING, NOT A KIKI THING. THE MAN is in love and he wants to hurry over to see her so he can—

Kostas holds up one hand. "Yes, yes. We know why you're going over there. Give her our love, eh?"

Now it's just Kiki and her cousin in black. She looks at the ground-length cassock. "Doesn't that thing get hot?"

"Only if I wear underwear." He grins. "More *frappe*?"

"Sure."

"Good. You can make one for me, too."

Very funny, her cousin. But he chases her out of the kitchen. "It was a joke," he says. "Here you are my guest."

A couple of minutes later he's handing her a refill.

"What will you do now, little Kiki?"

"I don't know."

"You know. People always do. 'I don't know' is what we say when the truth is too difficult to speak, for whatever reason."

"I really don't know. Since I was twelve, all I wanted was to be free."

"And now you are. Max was right, it is a tragedy for the Boutos family, but for you it is a gift."

"Which is why the police thing I killed him."

"They have to start somewhere, cousin. And you are the logical first step. Give them time and they will find another stone on which to stand. Until then, think about what a newly free woman might like to do."

"I guess I can do anything," she says.

Kostas smiles. "You always could. For some of us it takes time to come to terms with our power. Look at Max. He made his stand, and now he's a happy man. Like most happy couples, sometimes he and Vivi fight. But they are fights he chose. Choose your fights, Kiki. Don't let them choose you."

WHICH FIGHT WILL SHE CHOOSE, THE SACRIFICIAL LAMB?

It's a scene out of any old afternoon of Kiki's life: Mama and *Yiayia* sitting in their wood and wicker chairs, under the shade of the overhead grapevines. Mama has her needlepoint and *Yiayia* has dark, beady eyes that watch everything.

A *tableau vivant* she could call it, if only the players would shut up.

"I will find you another husband," Mama says, with only Kiki, *Yiayia*, and a hundred vine leaves to witness her brilliant idea.

"If I want a husband, I'll find my own."

Yiayia pats Kiki on the hand. "Do not listen to your mother. She is a fool if she thinks anyone here will marry you now. Some people think you are bad luck, everyone else thinks you are a murderer."

Great. Best news she's had all day. Where's a rock when she needs one to crawl under?

"Mama!" Margarita cries, "why are you not dead yet? Why are you still here, torturing me? I try and I try to get rid of you, but here you are."

"Good," *Yiayia* tells her daughter. "I enjoy seeing you miserable. You were a horrible child, and now you are a worse woman."

Before the whole conversation devolves into a bickering match, Kiki jumps in "What do you think, *Yiayia*?"

"I think if you killed him, then he deserved it."

"I didn't kill him," she murmurs.

"Then I think you are bad luck, so sit over there." She points to the chair at the far end of the patio.

"Stay right there, Kiki," Mama says. "Do not move a centimeter."

"Turk!" *Yiayia* says. "My daughter is a Turkish cuckoo!"

THAT EVENING, THREE MEN AND A WOMAN WALK INTO A TAVERNA. The woman says, "*Theo* Kristos, *Thea Helena* needs help. These men can help her."

And he says, "I know. But I am one man, what can I do? I see her talking with ... with our son, and a piece of me is envious that to her Stavros is alive. Maybe that makes me as *trelos* as my wife."

Kiki says nothing. It's not her place. She brought these three men together so they could plan a rescue.

"You know where the line between sanity and insanity sits, *Kyrios* Boutos." Max orders a round of *frappe* for everyone. "I know someone who can help your wife."

22

HELENA

"No. No, no, no." Helena slams the lentil soup-filled bowl on the table in front of her husband. "Tell him, Stavros. Tell him we will not go to any doctors."

He will not even look at their son. What kind of man is he who cannot look at his own son when he orders his execution?

A squirt of brown vinegar into the soup, then Kristos stirs. "Perhaps you and Stavros could go together."

"Together?"

"Yes, together." He dips the spoon in the bowl, slurps, proclaims it her best dish yet. "It could bring you closer together."

She watches the careful way he breaks the bread, dips it into the soup, around the rough edges of the feta chunk drowning there. "How?"

"A mother always wants to know her children's secrets, yes? If you go together, maybe this doctor can convince him to share some of his secrets."

It is a trick. A ruse.

"He is lying, Mama," Stavros whispers from the far side of the table. He's not eating. Why isn't he eating? Is it her cooking? He loves lentils.

"*Shh*," she says, but to whom? "Let me think."

"Think," her husband says. "Sleep on it. You do not have to make a decision today, okay?"

❧ 23 ❧

KIKI

Wedding gifts jostle for breathing room on her dining room table. They need to go back to the hands that delivered them, with an apologetic note.

But Kiki's been stalling. How do you pen thank-you-but-no-thank-you notes to people who call you a murderer? Maybe she should leave a little winky face at the end, let them think maybe they'll be next if they keep it up.

Other than the gifts, the only sign of Stavros is a picture on the bookcase. The two of them side by side, his arm curled around her waist, while hers dangles awkwardly in perpetuity. The day was September fourteenth, Stavros's name day, and their parents insisted. They would be glad, the mothers told them. All children should see what their parents were before they become one.

There's a knock on the door—a soft one in Morse code, by a hand that's used to keeping secret visits secret.

A hand she hasn't heard in some time. These days, Soula busts her way in. She enters a room and immediately looks for a way to command it. But tonight, she slips through the door quietly.

"Are you okay?"

Kiki nods. "I'm okay."

Soula smiles. Her sister is a knockout, her features bold. They're similar, two women who clearly belong to the same set. Two equally vibrant paintings, in their own ways.

"Anything you need, you let me know, okay?"

"You know I love you," Kiki says.

"I love you, too."

Soula turns away. Kiki is this close to shutting the door when a small bell tinkles inside her head. A sister's intuition.

"Hey. Are *you* okay?"

Soula nods, but she doesn't look back. "I'm always okay."

No, Kiki thinks, you're not. Lately, Soula is not always Soula.

❧ 24 ❧

HELENA

I t is a quiet waiting room, tasteful with its vanilla walls and its Dutch art.

"Boring," Stavros declares.

The receptionist glances up at them. "Excuse me?"

Helena shakes her head. "It was nothing."

Stavros is smiling, but his voice is rough, angry. "I don't want to be here."

"I do not want to be here either, but we have to be."

"Why?"

"Because your father said so."

"Him! What does he know?"

"Quiet," she says. "He is your father. Show him respect."

The door leading to the inner sanctum opens. A woman steps through, a lovely woman who looks too fashionable to be helpful. Her red shift and impossibly high heels make Helena feel dowdy in her black dress. What can a woman that beautiful possibly know about life and all its troubles?

"Helena Bouto?"

Helena stands, but her feet won't let her move. She doesn't want to pass through the doorway. That woman wants to rip her away from her child. She knows Kristos fed her bullshit. All that nonsense about coming here to be closer to Stavros ...

But she came anyway, did she not?

Why, Helena? Ask yourself why.

Then the psychologist smiles. She is warm, caring, and for a moment Helena feels the sun reaching for her. "Your son can come with you, if you like."

Now it is Helena who beams, and suddenly her feet are okay with moving. Everything will be fine. This doctor understands what it is to be a mother.

DR TRIANTAFILLOU IS HER NAME. TRIANTAFILLOU, LIKE THE FLOWER of love and romance. Helena tries not to think about Kiki and the waterfall of roses she held in her hands on her wedding day.

There is a couch, but the psychologist does not steer her toward it. Instead, she lets Helena choose where they will sit. Helena sits her son on the cream-colored couch, then she takes the chair nearest the window for herself. They are tall things, floor to ceiling, an open invitation to the sun. And it accepts. In it comes and paints them gold. Three people, all of them blessed, all of them angels.

"I am here because my husband asked it of me, not because I am sick."

Dr Triantafillou smiles. "Most of the people who come here are not sick. But they find it useful to have someone to speak with. Like a friend who listens and never judges."

"I have enough friends."

"You're a very lucky woman. Friends—true friends—are wealth."

Helena shakes her head. "You are wrong. Children are wealth." In her lap her hands are curled up the way kittens sleep. For a moment she does not believe the hands are hers. How can they be? They are an old woman's hands, her mother's hands. "Do you have children?"

"One," the psychologist says. "A girl."

"One. A girl." Helena hears her mouth say it in a vague, repetitive way, as though she is the other woman's mirror. "Do you want more?"

"In time. For now I am enjoying this one."

"And your husband?"

"No husband. It is just the two of us."

"How—" Helena cuts herself off. It is not her business, this woman's situation. They are not friends but strangers. Opponents, of a kind. "We also have one—a son. My Stavros."

"Would you like to talk about your son?"

Her hands untangle, fold themselves a new way. "What is there to tell? He is a boy—a man, now."

Stavros's gaze is heavy on her shoulders. He's behind her, listening to every word. The psychologist's attention flicks to Stavros then back to Helena again. This Dr Triantafillou is not what Helena expected. What she anticipated is what the TV shows: heavy furniture, darkness, a large notepad upon which the head doctor would record Helena's every word, furtively analyzing her every movement. But this doctor sits casually, legs crossed, hands resting in her lap as if they are just two women having a conversation about everyday things, instead of the contents of Helena's mind.

"He is an accountant," Helena continues.

"With a big firm or his own company?"

"His own. But he had very big clients. Very prestigious."

Had? What is wrong with her? Has. Stavros has very big clients.

"You must be very proud."

"I will be even more proud when he marries and gives me grand-children."

A red lipstick smile. "My mother always says the same thing. My brothers and sisters and I could have fifty children between us, and still she would want more."

"It is as I said: children are wealth. And people who have many grandchildren are very rich." Her gaze fixes on those shoes with their long, red stems. The doctor reminds her of a geranium, or maybe a poppy. "I am poor. And now I will always be poor."

"Would you like to talk about it, Helena?" Soft. Gentle. It is easy to see this woman as a mother.

"There is nothing to talk about. We are Greek—we do not talk. We yell and we are silent. Nothing lives in the space between."

"It doesn't have to be that way. People come to me all the time just to talk."

Talk! Who goes to a stranger just to talk? She cannot believe people anywhere but on the TV do this—and even then it is for Americans. Greeks do not go to therapy. They go to church or to family. And even then they do not spill all the words and thoughts they've collected. Who wants to see all the monsters that live inside another's head?

"What do they talk about?" Helena asks.

"Many things. What makes them happy, what makes them sad. Sometimes they talk about something interesting that happened this week."

"Nothing happened this week. Or last week. Not for many weeks."

"What was the last interesting thing that happened?"

"A wedding."

"Was this your son's wedding?"

"No." The lie bolts out of her throat. "Yes," she corrects herself. "Yes, it was my son's wedding to that girl." The last word shoots out as if it is an olive pit in an angry mouth.

"You do not like his intended?"

"These days, I do not even like myself."

25

LEO

That damn rooster wakes Leo at dawn. Moments later, he's joined by a few of his buddies from around the neighborhood. All of them competing. Worse than that bratty drill sergeant. He'd strangle the bird, but he likes the way it struts about the yard, chest puffed out like he's somebody, no clue that he's a foot or so tall.

His grandfather's in the kitchen making Greek coffee, toupee on backwards. Leo has never tried the stuff. When they lived here he was just a kid. Back home, his mother makes it the American way. Tall mug. Lots of sugar. Milk. Goes down like candy.

"You want coffee?"

Leo peers at the dense, brown sludge in the tiny long-handled saucepan. A *briki*, they call it.

"Coffee, yeah. But not whatever that is."

"This is the one true coffee! That coffee *xenoi* drink is for people who are not lucky enough to be Greek."

"Looks like mud." He's trying not to laugh. It's leaking out, anyway.

Socrates slaps the air, but he's smiling. "Bah! You are *Americanos*, not Greek. Where did my grandson go? That boy was Greek!"

He pats his grandfather on the shoulder. "For you, I'll try it."

"Try!" The old man mutters something about how trying is for

Turks and Albanians. People who *do*, now they are Greek. King Leonidas and his Spartans did not try defeating the Persians.

"Newsflash, *Papou*—"

"Socrates."

"—the Persians won."

"Only until they lost. Then that girl Xerxes ran home to his mama." He pours the coffee into two demitasse cups, shoves one cup on its saucer into Leo's hands. Then he shuffles out of the kitchen. "Come, we go outside. It is not healthy to be inside all the time."

The early summer sun has sting, but the morning air still has a cool edge. Movement everywhere. Women carrying dishes to the bakery across the way. For cheap, the baker slides the dishes into the wood-burning ovens alongside his bread. At noon, the women will return for their bubbling dishes. Many of the houses here have their own wood-burning ovens. Great in winter, not so much in summer. So they outsource.

"Where's Laki?" Lucky Laki, the statue.

"Asleep. Always he sleeps late. Will you call your embassy again today?"

"They won't help. So I'm going to try something else."

"There you go trying again. Why not go there and camp on their front doorstep until they give you what they want?"

"Good way to get arrested, Socrates."

"A man should get arrested at least once. It builds character. In a cage you learn who you are."

Leo laughs. "When were you arrested?"

"During the *Diktatoria*. Like all the smart people."

ONCE UPON A TIME, GREECE HAD ITSELF A KING, A QUEEN, AND A nest filled with tiny royals. The country stood to the left, politically. Until 1967, when a group of colonels decided the country needed to take a big step to the right. They stuffed the constitution into a drawer, then, within minutes, arrested every notable person standing on the far side of the line, including Greece's acting Prime Minister.

King Constantine shrugged, figuring the coup was for Greece's own good.

Good for Greece, maybe. But not good for many Greeks or their king. Anything tilting left was quickly banned. *Your favorite musician is left wing? Okay, no music for you—you will not play, you will not listen.* Mikis Theodorakis, Greece's most famous composer, was one of the loudest voices against the junta, and for that they tossed him into jail, then into a concentration camp, then, finally, out of Greece entirely.

The king asked for do-overs of the bloodless kind, and tried shooing the colonels out of his yard, but they snatched the broom out of his hand and swept him out of Greece. Then they magicked a kingdom into a republic.

It's only recently, forty-something years later, King Constantine has finally moved back home to his mama: Greece.

"How bad was it?"

Socrates shrugs. "It was the same as being married to your grandmother. But the food and the company were better."

Leo hides his smile. His grandmother, like many Greek grandmothers, was a mostly-benevolent dictator.

"Yeah, I don't want to go to jail. I have plenty of character. I know who I am."

"Oh really?" The old man's wiry brows lurch north. "Who are you, Leonidas?"

Leo laughs. "I'm the guy who's not going to jail."

"Where are you going? You are running from something, or you would not be here."

"Relax, Socrates, I'm not running from anything or anyone. I needed a change of scenery, that's all. Only I got caught up in some of that Greek fly tape."

But Socrates has moved on. He's staring down the street. "*Gamo ti Panayia mou*, here comes a big problem."

Leo looks at the problem. It's woman-shaped. A lot of woman

leverage into one black dress and a pair of unhappy flat shoes. Gray, kinky hair that won't stay in its bun.

"*Kyria* Dora," his grandfather calls out. "Where is your broomstick?"

"I put it in your bottom. Clean it before you give it back, eh?"

The old man cackles. "This is Leonidas, my grandson. Do you remember him?"

"I do not remember where I put my crochet, but I do remember Leonidas."

She moves in on him the way a hurricane makes its moves on Florida. In seconds, his face is wet with kisses and he feels like someone dumped a load of sand in his middle.

He doesn't remember *Kyria* Dora, but there's almost—

(See: Helena Bouto.)

—no going wrong with asking Greek women of a certain age about their kids.

"How are your children?" he asks her.

Kyria Dora pulls away, shakes her hands at the sky. But there's a sparkle in her eyes that says it's thrilled he asked. "My children! The boys, I never see. They only come when they want to eat my cooking. Their wives do not cook—they order takeout. And Effie ... Effie is busy being famous on the TV. When she is not on the TV, she is busy being a lesbian. It is very hard work being a lesbian, I think. She is always protesting something."

Leo hides his smile behind a flat, serious line. "It sounds like hard work."

"You want coffee, *Kyria* Dora?" his grandfather asks.

Leo jumps out of his seat, offers it to the woman. Both chair and woman groan as she settles her backside on its lap. "No coffee. I do not want to wake up yet. Maybe later."

"Leonidas." His grandfather nods at the front door. "Go get Laki."

Again with the hand waving at the sky. "My God, why must you carry that thing around?"

"I feel a vision coming, but it will not come unless I am holding Laki."

"Visions," she scoffs. But she leans closer. "A vision of what?"

"How do I know, woman? I have not had the vision yet."

Leo finds Laki in his grandfather's room. The statue's sitting next to a photograph of King Constantine on the dresser. It's not what he expected, this room. It's still feminine. The walls are covered with photographs of his grandmother. As a girl, as a beautiful young woman, as a wife, a mother, a grandmother. Here is Leo in her arms. She's looking down upon him as if he is her world. Pictures from her very end, his grandparents together. Old but still in love. Socrates holds her hand to his heart.

It's a shrine.

This is what he wants, here in this wall. Someone to do life with.

But not everybody gets that.

Maybe someday. Maybe not.

For now, he's got bigger problems.

He carries the statue outside, sets it on the table, sits on the patio's concrete lip and listens to the grownups jaw.

"Your crochet is in your bathroom," Socrates says.

"Of course! Now I remember. What else does your statue say?"

"It will be hot today."

"It is uncanny how accurate your visions are, old man."

"Eh, sometimes I suspect Laki watches too much news, that is all."

The chair creaks as Kyria Dora settles back on her haunches. "Anything else?"

"Not yet."

"Where is that boy?" She glances around, searching for Leo. "There you are. Is this your coffee? Of course it is. Who else's would it be? Finish it. Turn the cup over. Turn it three times on the saucer, then I will read it for you."

Leo thinks the only thing the cup will say is that he needs a refill. But *Kyria* Dora is obviously friends with his grandfather, so why not do as she tells him?

He chugs the mud and follows her directions.

After a few minutes, she picks up the cup and holds it in her big hands. Then she looks at him, mildly horrified. "Leonidas, did you drink the coffee grounds?"

"You're not supposed to drink the grounds?"

"No! Just the coffee." She sets the cup back on its saucer, pushes it away. "*Po-po*! This one is stupid. If Effie was not a lesbian, I would make them get married. And they could make stupid children, even more stupid than the boys Effie already has."

Socrates cackles. Leo grabs the hairpiece, sets it straight on his grandfather's head. "It was my first time. I didn't know."

"No matter," *Kyria* Dora says. "There is a little in here, but not much."

"What does it say?" Socrates asks.

"I see a door. A door means change. Somebody is coming or something is leaving. That is all. The boy drank the rest of his future. You should meet my niece, Vivi," she tells Leo. "She is American, too!"

"Apparently I'm not American enough for America. They keep telling me I'm Greek," he says.

"That does not matter." She pats his hand. "To us you will always be a foreigner."

❦ 26 ❦

KIKI

Forty days since they laid Stavros to rest. Time for another memorial service.

Is he at rest? Who knows. Kiki can't think of a single person except Lazarus who recovered from death, and his account is sketchy, at best. If popular fiction is any indication, when someone claws their way out of the grave three days later, it's safer to hammer a stake through their heart than to assume divine intervention played a role.

She's at the cemetery, again, standing to the left of Stavros's headstone. Not everyone from the funeral is here for the memorial service —only the major players. And after today, most of them can shuck black for colors.

Not Kiki, though. For her, it's going to be a long, hot summer.

Yiayia is sitting next to her in her wheel chair, wearing big, black sunglasses that make her look like a blowfly. "I hope Stavros does not mind this heat. It is going to be very hot where he is going."

Mama, on *Yiayia*'s other side, jabs her mother's neck with an elbow.

"What?" the old woman says, faking innocence. "You do not think he is riding the elevator up to shake hands with God, do you?"

"Enough! We're Greek Orthodox, we do not believe in purgatory."

"Then Stavros is already very hot." *Yiayia* looks up at Kiki. "I am the mother, but look how she treats me, as if I am a child."

"It is because you say childish things!" Mama says.

Everyone is looking at them.

"Shhh," Kiki says.

Detective Lemonis is there, too. Eyes on Kiki. Eyes on her misbehaving family. Drinking deep from this shallow pool of Stavros's loved ones.

Thea Helena is here, but she doesn't look present. She could be a store mannequin, the way she stands stiffly at *Theo* Kristos's side, head turned toward the road. Whatever she's doing today, attending her son's memorial service isn't scratched on her social calendar.

She does nothing until the very end. Then her statue comes alive, beckons to Kiki.

"It is a trap," *Yiayia* says.

Margarita scoffs. "It is not a trap, it is Helena. She loves Kiki."

"It is a trap, mark my words."

Trap or not, if there's a way to mend what's broken, Kiki's happy to give it a shot, isn't she? Not just for herself, but for Mama. Mama's mood swings these days are seismic.

Her heels peck at the grass. She stops in front of *Thea* Helena. What comes next? There's no protocol she's aware of, so she's winging it. Everyone is watching. Kiki's reputation hinges on how the older woman reacts.

"*Thea* Helena, I'm—"

The flying gob of spit slices off the end of her sentence. *Smack*. Wet drops splatter across her face.

Definitely not a peace offering.

Kiki turns, but her mother is there, stopping her with an iron hand. Holding onto her arm, Margarita gets up in her old friend's face with a clenched fist.

"If you were any other woman I would beat you. It is because we were friends that you are not crying and bleeding on the ground right now. Nobody spits on my daughters! Nobody!"

The memorial service worked. Now no one will forget.

Ever.

SCHOOL IS OUT UNTIL SEPTEMBER. WHICH MEANS ALL OF KIKI'S time is free. Nothing to do. Nowhere to go.

Except the beach. Yes she's in black for almost two more years, but socially forty mourning days are up, and Kiki wants to breathe air she hasn't shared with family.

"Where are you going?"

Yiayia is sitting under the vine-covered trellis, working her way through a bag of sunflower seeds.

"The beach. I could use the sun."

"The sun will kill you."

"I can't stay inside."

"Staying inside will kill you. The best chance of survival is in a doorway. That way when the earthquake comes you will probably live."

Kiki flings her beach bag over one shoulder. "I'll take my chances with the sun."

"Wait!" Her grandmother tosses aside the seeds. "I will come with you. We can look at the men together, yes? Maybe pick out a nice new one for you."

"I don't—"

"Stay there while I find my swimsuit."

Yiayia rolls herself inside. A moment later, Kiki hears the crashing of cutlery forgetting how to fly.

"Why won't you just die?" Margarita yells.

"Kiki," *Yiayia* says, when she comes back, "your mother just tried to kill me with a spoon."

"That's new."

"I am only sorry that my daughter is so stupid she does not know how to kill an old woman. She should take lessons from whoever killed Stavros. Now that is someone who knew how to do murder."

KIKI WALKS. *YIAYIA* RIDES.

Guess who's pushing the wheelchair?

"Are we there, yet?"

"No, *Yiayia*."

"Before we get there, I need a magazine to put over my eyes. Unless ..." She looks up at Kiki's sunglasses.

"I'll get you a magazine."

"You are a good girl, Kiki. Even if you did kill Stavros."

"I didn't kill Stavros."

"So you say. But I will still love you if you did."

"I didn't kill him."

"Okay."

———

DAYS DON'T COME MORE PERFECT THAN THIS. IT'S EARLY BUT THE beach is already full. Every spare inch of the pebbled shore is covered in towels or rattan mats. That's how you separate the locals from the tourists. Vacationers bring towels, expecting the white sands they've seen in postcards. The water is beautiful, yeah, but the beach is a long stretch of pebbles.

The gulf is gentle with the shore and its swimmers. It bobs, sways, but never crashes. The seaweed waves at the sun, as though its wrists are tired, heavy. And the water, it's happy to gently jiggle the small, brightly colored boats that sit on its surface. The boats belong to fishermen—of course—but it is the young who use them to dive. Teenagers and children hoist themselves onto the slippery vessels and dive-bomb the water.

Yiayia is being all kinds of helpful, pointing out potential suitors. "What about that one? He has a big pipe."

Behind her dark lenses, Kiki shuts her eyes, prays for a single-minded tidal wave to wash her away.

"I don't think so, *Yiayia*."

Someone has shoehorned the man in question into a thong. A swimsuit that small would make okra look huge.

"Bah! You should be like Soula. She tries all the men and keeps the ones she likes."

Not all the men, but a lot of men, sure. Which is great for Soula, but not so much for Kiki. Right now she doesn't want any kind of man, especially one who might have to make conjugal visits.

Her grandmother is wearing a bathing suit straight out of the war —one of the early ones. It's black from neck to ankle, with a band of white where her breasts used to sit. She's sweating, fanning herself with *KATERINA*, a popular teen magazine.

"You should have worn something cooler," she tells her grandmother.

"It is not the sun, it is the men! Can you believe what they wear today? How can they fit everything into something that small? It is magic, or maybe witchcraft, I think."

Kiki flops back on her beach mat, closes her eyes and waits for the sun to bake her. It's better this way, with her eyes shut. That way she can't see what *Yiayia* hasn't noticed. Yes, they're surrounded by people, but not a one of them local. Everyone Kiki knows by name or sight is staying back, away from Agria's newest exhibit: Kyriaki Andreou, twenty-eight, alleged murderer.

Good news gains weight fast around here, with so much gossip to swallow.

With her eyes open, she can't help seeing bunches of heads clumped together, swapping stories. *Kiki this, Kiki that. We thought she was a good girl, but no!*

Won't be long before they're pinning every crime in town to her chest.

My chickens are dead.

Kiki.

The store was out of olive oil.

Kiki.

Somebody had relations with my donkey.

Kiki, of course.

She stuffs her head into the metaphorical sand, ostrich style, goes on a mental vacation to someplace where she's not an outcast.

"Kiki!"

One eye open, she sees her cousin Max's fiancée rocketing her way.

Kiki sits up in surprise. "Vivi?"

Vivi's a tiny thing, a V8 engine shoved into a Mini Cooper. American ... well, Greek-American. Which makes her Greek or a foreigner, depending on the crowd's temperature.

Vivi drops down next to her, crouches on the pebbles.

"*Yiasou, yiasou.* I saw you both from the road."

"Are you here to swim?"

"No, I came down for ice cream. Melissa's working her butt off for me this summer, so I figured ice cream would be a nice treat."

"How is she?"

Vivi grins. "Busy!" The smile fades. "How are you?"

Kiki shrugs. "Oh, you know how it is around here when everyone thinks you're a murderer."

Vivi definitely knows. Last summer she and her mother both spent the night in jail for the murder of Sofia Lambeti. Turned out the poor woman killed herself, but half the town buys Vivi's olives because who murders a paying customer?

"They haven't lynched you yet, so that's something," Vivi says.

"Because she comes from a good family," *Yiayia* says. "Although this will not be a good family any longer if she did murder him."

"I didn't murder Stavros."

"Guilty people always say the same thing," she tells the centerfold in her magazine.

Kiki stares. It's those kids from the UK, the ones who influence half the hairdos in her classes. She looks at the American woman. "See what I have to live with?"

Yiayia nudges her with the magazine. "What about that one? Now that man could pull a plow."

'That one' is a big red tank. Could be British with that lobster-colored skin, but the sandals say Germany.

"We don't have a farm or fields."

"Then maybe he can plow something else, eh?"

Jesus Christ. "I'm not looking for a man, *Yiayia.*"

"Of course you are," she crows. "You do not know it yet, that is all."

Vivi laughs. "And I thought my mother was bad."

"Are you hiring?" Kiki asks.

"Thinking of quitting teaching?"

Kiki shakes her head. "I need something to do this summer. If I stay at home, I'll wind up drowning Mama and *Yiayia* in a bucket of rice pudding."

"Your mother's *rizogalo* is terrible," *Yiayia* says. "The worst I ever ate!"

"You won't be eating it, you'll be drowning in it."

"If you have to drown me, make it *retsina*."

Vivi pats her on the shoulder. "Come over later—even during siesta, if you like. I never sleep during the day."

"Still?"

"My blood might be Greek, but my head is American, and it tells me sleeping during the day is lazy."

"I'll be there. And Vivi ... thanks."

Vivi hugs her. "If there's one thing I know it's that things will be okay—okay?"

"Okay."

THEY DON'T FEEL TOO OKAY AS SHE PUSHES HER GRANDMOTHER OVER the pebbles, up to the road.

"That Vivi mentioned ice cream, so now I want ice cream," the old woman says.

Long line at the kiosk that sits on the beach's concrete edge. Everyone wants ice cream, EPSA (a local lemonade that is heaven in a bottle), *frappe*, magazines. The tourists want to try new things and the locals ask for old favorites.

Kiki gets in line with her grandmother.

Casual conversations all grind to a halt—everyone except the tourists. And their chatter dies when they realize the rest of the world has stopped.

Everyone is looking at Kiki.

Hooray. This she needs. "I didn't kill him, okay? Jesus Christ."

The line shuffles forward, and they move with it. Nobody speaks.

"Why would I kill him? It's not like I even wanted to marry the guy."

Everybody looks at her. The locals because her motive is solid, the tourists because—what the hell is she talking about?

Yiayia pokes her. "Say something that makes it sound like you did not kill him."

"I didn't kill him."

"Anything but that."

Jesus. "There's nothing else I can say. I didn't do it."

"Okay. Let me try. You are all Turks!" *Yiayia* shakes her fist. "Or maybe Albanian. They are the same shit!" She looks up at Kiki. "How did I do?"

"Great." So great she's dying.

"Yes, that is what I think, too. Take me to the supermarket and I will tell everyone there what I think of them. After that, the church."

"That's not a great idea."

"Of course it is, Kiki, my doll. All my ideas are good."

"... AND THEN, I CALLED THEM TURKS AND ALBANIANS!"

Kiki's mother closes her eyes. "*Panayia Mou.*"

"The Virgin Mary." *Yiayia* stabs the air. "Now there is a woman who understood false accusations. She would understand. Those Romans were probably secretly Turkish."

Mama opens one of the kitchen drawers, pulls out a pair of gleaming scissors. "Here, Mama. Go play with these, pointy end up. Run."

There's a noise outside, the squeaking of a gate opening.

"*Tsiganes!*" *Yiayia* says.

Kiki looks outside. *Yiayia* is right, but it's only one Romani woman. More girl than woman, sitting on the doorstep between childhood and adulthood. Usually they come in pairs, weathered women with sad-eyed children. The woman always ushers the child forward to be her mouth. But this one is alone.

"Go away." Mama shoots out of the house, shaking a broom. "We don't have money."

The woman doesn't move. The hem of her multicolored, cake-layered skirt sways. Like most Romani women, she wears a mismatched rainbow. "I do not want your money."

"We do not have any work for you, either!"

"I have work," the woman says. "Honest work."

"Then what do you want?"

"Nothing," she says.

"Drina! Come away from there," a voice barks. It belongs to an older woman, her face beaten by the hot sun and its accomplice, time. Her companion shoves her way through the gate, takes the younger woman by the arm. "I am sorry," she says. "She is a girl with big problems." One finger taps her own head.

"*Tsiganes* are all crazy," *Yiayia* mutters.

"We are not all crazy." Her eyes are dark and tired. "We just do what we can with what little we have."

"A curse on you," Drina says. "May an earthquake swallow your whole family."

"Drina! What did I tell you? Small curses only. The big ones come back and bite your ass. Forgive her, forgive her." She looks up at the sky. "You, too, God. Forgive her. She did not mean it."

"A small curse is okay?" Drina asks.

The older woman holds up two fingers, pinches the air. "Very small."

Drina turns back to Kiki and co. "Then I curse you with something very small. Ants."

"That is better."

The walking rainbows leave the yard, gate flapping behind them.

"Ants." Mama shrugs. "It could be worse. I will go and see *Kyria* Dora this afternoon to remove the curse."

LEO

Same circular shit, different day. No help from the US Embassy, no help from the Department of State back home. Three more days and he's going to be AWOL.

Leo's never been a fugitive before. His mother is worth it.

Travel. See new places. Try new things. That was the plan.

Jail will be new—won't it? He can barely contain his excitement.

He dials the embassy again, makes himself a pain in their ass. But they give him the same old no-can-do-story.

They can-do he thinks. They just don't want it hard enough.

But he does.

Options—he needs more.

Idiot. He's wasting his time on the wrong target. So he calls the Hellenic Ministry of National Defense. Tells them who he is, what he wants, and why. Gives them Socrates' address because they want to send paperwork. Paperwork is the key, they tell him. Fill out the papers and then maybe they can do something.

Leo knows Greek paperwork: it'll be choking with red tape. And like Italian mobsters and Pennsylvania Dutch Teamsters, Greek paperwork has a funny way of vanishing.

Papou steps outside in sandals with white socks. He tosses the moped's keys to Leo.

"Where are we going?"

"To see my friend, Takis. I had a vision."

Takis (apparently) lives in the middle of nowhere. A meaningless term. Greek distance and time are negotiable. A kilometer is sometimes ten. Five minutes is sometimes a week.

Turns out the middle of nowhere is about five minutes away by terminal moped, up a small hill and behind a thick wall of slanted olive trees.

Where other trees have a tendency to reach for the sky, olive trees tilt toward their neighbors. They sprawl and grasp and shove, each determined to win a bigger patch of sun. A tree so competitive they're not afraid to fight dirty.

The moped bumps along the dirt road, its tires kicking stones and flinging dust.

"Here," Socrates says, when a chain-link fence appears between the trees. "Takis is a very rich man, but he lives like the pig."

This from a guy with an outhouse.

Nice digs. Swanky house. Old rotting planks held together with luck and determination. Built in the days before building codes made Greece earthquake proof. Maybe built before there were building codes at all. Lots of goats milling around the fenced yard. Leo likes goats; Leo likes animals, period—but goats are cool and easygoing.

Sitting in an ancient chair, puffing tobacco-scented clouds into the air, is an elderly man who is more mustache than face. Younger than Socrates, but not by much.

"Here comes trouble," the man says.

"Takis, you old *malakas*."

Takis cackles. "Too old for that."

"When you are too old for that, you are dead," Socrates says. They slap backs, shake hands. Then Socrates nods at Leo. "This is my grandson. He is divorced and does not have a woman, so he is definitely a *malakas*."

Takis offers his hand. "What do you do, eh?"

"Veterinarian," Leo says, after they shake hands. Takis vanishes inside his shack, comes back with two more chairs.

"You want to eat?" he asks them.

Socrates says, with great authority, "He has the brains of my Greek underwears, but Takis makes the best feta in Greece."

(Old-fashioned Greek underwear is the unfortunate offspring of long johns and that magic underwear they wear in Utah.)

"In the world," Takis corrects him. "A veterinarian, eh? Go, look at my donkey." He nods to a donkey snoozing under the sprawl of an olive tree. The beast is gray with a black cross on his back. What they sometimes incorrectly call a Jerusalem donkey. The cross is a dominant trait in all kinds of donkeys, that's all.

Leo says, "What's wrong with him?"

"Why you ask me? You are the veterinarian! What kind of veterinarian is this you bring me, Socrates?"

Valid point. "I mean what are his symptoms. What makes you think he's sick?"

The mustache jumps. "He is not eating. Always that donkey eats and eats and eats, but now he is not eating properly. And he is getting skinny. There is nothing good about a skinny donkey or a skinny woman. Always it is a sign of poor health."

Leo looks at the donkey. It's lean, but it's not bones.

"Anything else?"

"No, just his appetite."

"How long has this been going on?"

Takis shrugs. "A week, a month."

With that kind of accuracy, Leo doesn't bother asking the donkey's age.

"What's his name?"

"*Gaidaros*."

Nothing to do about that but shake his head all the way over to the tree. "Original guy, your buddy over there," He tells the donkey. "Now you know how cats feel when their owners call them Kitty."

The donkey's not a big talker, but he's okay with Leo taking a look at his gums.

Leo tosses a question over his shoulder. "When's the last time you floated his teeth?"

"Eh?" Takis looks at Socrates. "What language does he speak?"

"Floating," Leo explains. "It's when you file a horse or donkey's teeth."

"Never!" Takis shrugs, palms upturned. "Who would do such a thing?"

Leo gives the donkey's neck a quick rub, then it's back to the chair. "He can't chew properly, so he's not eating. His teeth need to be filed."

"You are sure?"

"Pretty sure."

"Can you do it?"

"I can do it."

"How much?"

Socrates has a look on his face like the man better work for free. So Leo says, "Free. Call it a gift."

"Free is a terrible price. You get what you pay for, and if you do it for nothing, then my donkey will still have trouble eating."

"I have excellent references."

"References!" He slaps at the air. "Bah!"

"My grandson is a professional," Socrates says. "The best veterinarian in America. Free is a very good price for the best."

"Ah, but is he the best veterinarian in Greece?"

"Probably not," Leo says.

Those watery eyes take him in. Thick, yellowing fingers reach for a pocket, pull out a packet of tobacco and roll papers. Takis watches Leo while he makes a new cigarette. He licks the end, balances it on his lip and says, "You might be a terrible veterinarian, but at least you are an honest man. I will let you do it. But be careful, he kicked the last American who touched him. And she was only trying to brush him."

"Is that *Kyria* Dora's niece?"

"The *xena*? Yes. She was stupid at first, but the more time she spends in Greece the smarter she gets. You will get smarter too if you stay here."

"I'm not staying," Leo says. "First chance I can get, I'm going home."

"If you say so," Takis says, grinning. "If you say so."

❧ 28 ❧

KIKI

Ding dong, the town is dead. Kiki is the only one in its streets. Down by the beach there will be people moving, but only tourists taking advantage of every vacation moment. They paid for this sun, this heat, and they mean to get their euro's worth. After lunch, the main meal of the day, everyone Greek sleeps.

Not Kiki. Not today.

She doesn't mind the ghost town. It's a relief. She can walk freely, without accusatory heads and mouths turning her way.

The sun is hot, yes, but it's honest. It doesn't hide its intensity behind puffs of white. Even behind sunglasses, her eyes sting from its assault. Her black dress creates a small breeze around her legs as she walks, but the sun slaps it away fast.

And still it's better than sitting at home.

The houses that aren't white look parched. Once the paved road runs out, the dirt looks just as thirsty as the houses and the cantankerous olive trees.

To her left, just off the dirt road, sits a tiny church on a patch of green. There is grass but it's carefully tended, and trees that aren't olives twist up toward the sky. Fruit trees. *Janera*—a small, sweet, green plum.

When she and Soula were kids, it was tended by a stooped woman with an angry broom that liked to chase children. Even now she can feel the pull of the trees with their ripening fruit. Summer is *janera* time. She wants to climb the trees, sink her teeth into the sweet-tart skin, forget about Stavros rotting in the ground and the people who want to pin his death to her back.

Forget she is Kiki.

A buzzing cuts the silence in two. A vehicle is headed her way. Something small and unhealthy. A moped bounces in her direction from a thin capillary that bleeds up into the nearby olive grove. It leaves a minor dust storm in its wake.

She remembers the moped and the old man perched on back. And she remembers his bragging statue.

Should she wave?

If she doesn't, chances are good rudeness will be tacked onto the bottom of her current rap sheet. In time, people might forget a murder, but they will never forget that one time she didn't wave hello to one of Agria's own.

But if she does, he might stop.

The moped bumps closer, dragging its brown cloud like a half-deflated parachute. Kiki moves off the road, into the scratchy scrub. Seated up front, steering the two-legged vehicle, is a guy she doesn't know. Tall, with the kind of chest that's good to sleep on, dark hair on his head shaved close to the bone. Hard jaw. Big hands. Strong arms.

Vaguely familiar, now that they're closer.

Must be one of the Karas grandsons. Not Leonidas. He (and his ass —and almost her finger) left years ago, thank God. She doesn't see the Karas family around much. Time has scattered them around the area.

Then the moped lurches past. The old man, *Kyrios* Karas, turns around, waving his statue.

"I will see you soon, eh?" he calls out. "I had another vision!"

When the dust lands, they're gone.

Magic.

Kiki picks up her feet and starts moving again.

VIVI TYLER'S COTTAGE ISN'T IN AGRIA, IT'S IN HEAVEN. THE SMALL white-washed house stands away from the road behind a picket fence, an army of trees at its back. Fruit trees, mostly, including a gigantic fig tree sprawling over the yard. The figs are reaching their peak—Kiki can smell their sugar as she trots up the path.

A dog bowls out of the house, catapults her way with a grin on his face.

"Biff!" she says as he knocks her to the ground for a hug.

Vivi is on his heels, mouth loaded with apologies. "My dog is an oaf," she says, pulling the brown behemoth off Kiki.

"It's okay." She cups Biff's face between her hands. "Who's a good boy?"

Biff's a good boy and he knows it. He hangs at her side as the women step into the house.

The cooler air pulls Kiki into its arms. She sags into the sofa, drapes the back of her hand over her eyes.

"Summer is the worst season to be in mourning," she says. "All this black."

"I'm sure I've already said it, but I'll say it again for good luck: I'm sorry for your loss."

"Thank you."

"If you want you can borrow a totally-not-black dress to wear, at least until you leave. No one will ever know."

Kiki smiles. "Thanks, but I'm okay."

"*Frappe?*"

"Yes! I'll be your best friend and love you forever."

Vivi makes *frappe*, and while it's cold and loaded with caffeine, its slap is on the lame side. It's not the coffee, it's her. She's supposed to be sleeping and her body knows it.

"So what have you got for me?"

The American woman groans. "Paperwork. Everything in Greece requires paperwork when you run a business—and lots of it. And I don't understand one end of it from the other."

"I'll do it."

"Yay! I'm saved! It's a miracle. You've saved my life and my ass."

What she means to do is laugh at Vivi's exaggeration, but what happens? Tears. Big, wet, ugly tears. The kind that make noses red and onlookers hunt for an exit strategy.

"Yikes." Vivi leaps across the room for a box of tissues. She pulls a couple out, stuffs them into Kiki's hand. "I know Greek bureaucracy is bad, but it's not that bad."

"It's not that. Everyone thinks I killed Stavros."

"They'll get over it."

Kiki looks at her. Vivi is a woman who knows how violently and quickly the tide changes here. "What if they don't?"

"They will," Vivi says gently. "When Detective Lemonis gets his man or woman, they'll have someone brand new to talk about—someone who's actually guilty."

"There you go, being sensible."

Vivi laughs. "I try, but it's not always easy with my mother's genes."

"I know the feeling." She runs her finger around the rim of the damp glass. Not crystal, but it still sings. "What would you do if you were me?"

"Easy," Vivi tells her. "The same thing I did once I let John go and discovered I was free. Live."

FREE.

Ha-ha-ha. No.

Kiki's nothing like free.

Freedom is for other women, for the Soulas and the Vivis. Not for Kiki. She hasn't known freedom since twelve.

Stavros trapped her in life, and died with his hand manacled around her ankle. He will not let her go. Yes, he's dead, but in some ways so is she. Between this mandatory mourning for a man she didn't love, and the murder accusations, she's already in a kind of prison. And the person holding the iron key is Detective Lemonis. She's not even sure he's looking in any direction but hers.

29

LEO

Where does a guy buy tools in Agria?

"At the supermarket," Socrates tells him.

"Really?"

"Where would you buy tools, clever man?"

"For this? I'd get them from some places that sells veterinary tools or medical supplies. Failing that, a hardware store."

The old man slaps his shoulder. "We have a medical supply store. It is called the supermarket. There you will find your file, vinegar, and rubbing alcohol. With those you can fix anything."

That's not all he's got on his mind, is it?

"Who was she?"

"Who was who?"

"The woman you called out to. The one walking." The cute one with the long legs.

Papou rubs his chin. "The Andreou girl? She is the English teacher at the high school."

"Andreou? Sounds familiar."

"It is a good family, but not for long, I think."

"Why not?"

"That girl is the one I told you about—the one who allegedly killed the Boutos boy."

"I thought you said she didn't do it."

"She did not kill him, but everyone thinks she did, which is just as bad. You have been away so long that you forget how people are here. It does not matter what you do, only what people think you do. And people here are very imaginative. Particularly the women, from watching all those soaps on the television."

"You told her you'd had a vision."

"I did have a vision, thanks to Laki."

"What was it?"

Socrates shakes a finger in his face. "My vision is for her, not for you."

Leo shrugs. Fair enough. "I have to get that file. You coming with me?"

"No," his grandfather says. "Now it is time for sleep. And I am very tired from entertaining you all morning."

Sure enough, the not-so-super market has a suitable file. It's on the shelf between a dusty hammer and dusty tub of *Brylcreem*. The shop is dim, the windows haven't seen a rag in years, and there's an overabundance of chickens pecking around the concrete floor. He wonders if it's like the lobster tank: choose your own chicken.

The proprietor is a woman built like a planet. Her smile starts out big and expands when she sees Leo's money.

"Are you breaking someone out of jail?" she asks, eyes lit up. They're the only thing not dusty in the whole store.

"It's for a donkey."

She doesn't look confused, which he finds mildly disturbing. "The donkey is in jail?"

No, but chances are he will be soon. He might need that file.

But first, time to see a man about his donkey.

"You want to put that in Gaidaros's mouth?"

Leo looks at the file. What he really needs is something to sedate the donkey, but good luck getting that around here. "You bet."

Takis' mustache shakes. His eyes water. He slaps his knee, until the goats wander over to check things out.

"Then I will wish you good luck," Takis says, "because you are going to need it."

———

Less than an hour later, Leo's pocketing the file.

"All that luck worked." He grins at the older man. Behind him, the donkey is facedown in the hay, making up for lost time.

"*Gamo ti putana*," Takis mutters, fingers dancing over his *komboloi*, shifting beads back and forth. (*Komboloi*, AKA worry beads, aren't a religious thing in Greece. They're something to do to keep your joints lubricated for that next political argument.) "The boy is a genius. You cannot be related to Socrates, you are much too clever."

After that, Leo's thinking he could use some fun.

Now he's thinking about those long legs on the road earlier, and how good they'd look around his waist.

Too bad that woman's got all the problems she can handle. Not to mention, she just lost the man she loves. Otherwise he'd look her up and ask her out.

Andreou. Still familiar. Only Andreou he remembers is a kid named Kostas. He laughs. Yeah, Kostas Andreou was a trip. He wonders what Kostas is doing these days.

Time, probably.

30

KIKI

Has Kiki returned the wedding gifts?

No.

They're loitering on her dining room table, fully dressed in their shiny, glittery party clothes. She hasn't unwrapped a one. Why bother? They aren't for her—they're for her and Stavros. For *them*. She's been looking at them every night since his death, learning the patterns on the swarths of wrapping paper, imagining what each box holds in its cardboard arms.

Tonight there's a new box. Kiki doesn't recognize the tiny yellow hearts on the white and silver swirl. It's small, flat, the shape of boxed chocolates—the kind with varied centers.

Someone helped themselves to Kiki's home.

Out the door, down the stairs, through her parents' door with only a brief knock to warn them. They're on the couch watching *Greece's Top Hoplite*. One of the judges is a local woman, Vivi's cousin. She's slashing the contestants to shreds with her tongue.

"My God, the woman is monster," Mama says, but she's rocking with laughter.

"It was the penis," *Yiayia* says, from her wheelchair. "When that man flashed her years ago, something broke inside her head, and now look, she is Medusa."

Kiki butts in. "Did anyone go up to my place today?"

"Why, my love?" Mama's gaze is stuck to a shrieking Effie.

"There's another wedding gift up there. It wasn't there before."

"Probably you miscounted."

"No, it's definitely new."

Mama breaks away from the TV, but it's a reluctant separation. "I do not know what to tell you, Kiki. Nobody has been up there, except me. And I did not leave anything—I took away your cobwebs. Why you not clean that mess?"

"Leave her alone," Baba says. He looks up at Kiki. "Did they steal anything?"

Kiki shakes her head. "I don't think so."

He shrugs. "How bad can they be if they gave you something but did not take anything?"

Yiayia slaps her knobby knees. "You should open it."

Margarita is horrified. "Mama, she has to give the presents back!"

"Why? It is not a wedding present. If it was a wedding present they would have brought it before the wedding, not after the wedding that did not happen."

"Is there a card?" Mama asks.

Kiki lifts her chin. "No."

(A chin lift is the Greek accompaniment to a negative reply. Tilt it down to pair it perfectly with your "Yes.")

"Strange. You should definitely open it. For once, your grandmother is right. And because of that I will not try killing her tonight." She looks at her mother. "Enjoy the sleep while you can, eh? Tomorrow is a new day."

"Then I will go to bed now so I can get good sleep." *Yiayia* dumps a kiss on Kiki's cheek as she passes. "Open the box, but not here. If it is a bomb I do not want to die."

A small alarm goes off in Kiki's head. "You think it's a bomb?"

Yiayia shrugs. "Somebody killed Stavros, yes? Maybe they want to kill you, too."

"A bomb! I have changed my mind," Kiki's mother says. "Step carefully, old woman, because tonight might be your last."

❦ 31 ❦

LEO

You want fun in Agria? Start at the promenade after dark. Barriers seal off the road's ends after dark, leaving a long stretch for walking, for seeing and being seen. Everyone walks when they're not cozied up to the sea, eating, drinking at the *tavernas*. At sunset, the umbrellas disappear and the colored lights come on. Say goodbye to the coffee, to the *frappe*; say hello to *retsina* and ouzo. Greeks tend to be wise drinkers, though. They pair their drinks with *mezedes*—finger food of the Greek kind. Bits of dead octopus, flaming cheese, dolmades (rice wrapped in grape leaves), meatballs, pie made with feta and spinach. They pick at the food, drink, and talk as though an embargo on words has just been lifted.

The promenade at night is where Leo had some of his best times. First as a kid, zipping to the playground snugged up to St. George's side, then as a prowling girl-crazy teenager. The playground is swimming with children tonight, a lot of them teenagers watching over younger siblings. He never came here to watch over siblings. He came here to hit on girls and sweet-talk them into the dark grounds behind the playground. There's a winding path back there that leads to the road, but there are also a lot of trees, and the church itself casts a wide shadow.

Good times.

Those girls still live here, he's sure. But he doesn't recognize many of the faces. And they don't recognize him. Why would they? He's been gone about as long as he was ever here. And somewhere along the way, time smashed them all with a mallet, beat the kid out of them and left the adult to fend for themselves.

Anyway, they've moved on and so has he. They're married (small-town Greek girls don't stay unmarried for long) with kids. And Leo won't touch married women. A married woman isn't necessarily trouble, but her husband sure is.

He likes them beautiful and single. And there are a lot of beautiful women here.

"Leonidas Karas?"

He goes cold for a moment. His animal brain thinks the cops, the army, have found him. Then it kicks in: he's not AWOL yet—just planning to be. He swings around, sees perfection saying his name.

Oh yeah, he thinks.

She's a river of dark hair, dark eyes, smooth tanned skin, poured into a thigh-skimming dress.

"You know me, but ..." *I don't know you, but I want to.*

"Soula," the goddess says. "Soula Andreou. We were in school together."

"Andreou? I've been hearing that name a lot since I got back."

Soula shrugs one slim shoulder. "It is a name that is being said a lot lately. And let me tell you right now, my sister did not kill anyone. Least of all that *vlakas* Stavros Boutos."

Loyal sister. The other woman is lucky to have her on the defense team.

"So he was stupid, huh?"

"He was a man," she says. "You are all stupid."

Leo laughs. "We're stupid because women make us stupid."

When she laughs the angels sing. "Maybe."

"So what do you do now that we're not in school, Soula?"

"I avoid stupid men."

"Too bad," he says.

Her smile is packed with promises of the sexy kind. "There was a time when I was not so picky. We could have had fun then."

A familiar bell is starting to chime. He's remembering her face younger, with less makeup, less polish.

Then it comes back. The high school. *Spin the Bottle.* The disappearing finger trick.

"Oh God," he groans. "You're Kiki's sister."

"Maybe not so stupid." Soula slips her arm through his. "Are you hungry? I am starving. Come, we will get *souvlaki*."

THEY GET *SOUVLAKI*. SOULA BUYS. "NEXT TIME WE GO OUT, YOU can buy."

"Is this a date?"

She bites the end off the meat-stuffed pita, shrugs. "Maybe."

They're standing in a short side street, where there's nothing much except the *souvlaki* place. No chairs inside, no tables, so they eat outside and watch people squeezing into the postage stamp-sized takeout joint.

"This is amazing," he says.

Soula nods, mouth full.

"You want to have sex?" she says, when they're done.

Yes. Yes, he does.

SOULA HAS A CAR BUT IT'S AT HOME, SHE TELLS HIM.

Leo can't say he blames her. Back in the states everyone complains about gas prices, but they've never known the eighty-percent tax Greeks pay at the pump.

Anyway, the walk is good. Gives them time to talk and the tension to build.

She doesn't live alone, she warns him. The family lives Greek-style, one on top of the other. But she's got the top floor, which means there's at least two doors and a sister between her bedroom and her parents' house.

He can live with that. It's not the first time he's sneaked into a woman's bedroom. Or a Greek girl's bedroom. His virginity got lost less than twenty feet away from a good Greek girl's sleeping parents.

Lost. Ha. He was fourteen, and she was sixteen and unstoppable.

What's a guy to do?

Hurl his virginity out the window, that's what.

There's one small square metal table and a short row of chairs in the Andreou family's front yard, but only one seat is taken. In the chair with wheels sits a prune wearing a black nightgown. Short, scrawny legs. Feet lost in backless slippers. She cups a hand over her eyes to kill the glare from the outside light.

"Soula, is that you?"

"Yes, *Yiayia*."

"I thought so. Kiki does not sneak men into her house. Is he good-looking?"

Soula glances at Leo. "Yes, *Yiayia*."

The air smells like perfume. Some kind of flower, but Leo isn't a guy who knows flowers.

"Come closer." Lots of hand waving. "Does he have a big penis?"

"I don't know yet."

The old woman squints up at him. "Do you have a big penis?"

He looks from her to Soula, from Soula to the old woman.

"Well?" Big grin on Soula's face, like she's used to her grandmother's antics and maybe even enjoys them.

"She won't be disappointed," he tells the old woman.

The old woman claps once. "You are lucky," she says to her granddaughter. "Try not to scream too loud, eh? But before you do the sex, go see your sister. Someone sent her a bomb."

🌀 32 🌀

KIKI

"Kiki?"

Somebody is saying her name. Which is weird, because up until now, everyone in the dream has been calling her Batman.

"I'm Batman," she murmurs.

"Okay, Batman. Wake up!" The hand that called her Kiki shakes her.

Kiki leaps out of bed, naked. And ...

Leaps back into bed when it hits her that Soula's not alone.

"My Virgin Mary, Soula! What are you doing?" she says from under the blue cotton sheet.

"*Yiayia* said someone sent you a bomb."

She pulls the sheet off her face, sees Soula standing over her, hand on hips. "A bomb?"

"That's what she said."

"Oh my God. This town—this family—is driving me crazy."

Soula's tail laughs. Who invited him into her bedroom, anyway?

"Who are you?" Kiki says. "Never mind. I don't care. Just go—both of you."

Soula says, "What about the bomb?"

"There is no bomb." She tells them about the new gift, the one she still hasn't opened.

"How do you know it's not a bomb?"

"I don't. But who would give me a bomb?" Everyone. The answer is: everyone. She's on the fast track to pariahdom. The more productive question is: who wouldn't try blowing her up. "Forget I asked. But wouldn't it be heavier if it was a bomb?"

"When was the last time you held a bomb?" Soula asks.

Never—that's when.

He won't quit looking at her, Soula's date. There's something familiar about him, the distinct feeling that they've known each other before. He's tall, dark-haired, holy-shit handsome in an I-like-to-rob-banks-so-hard kind of way. If she hadn't just seen him laugh for herself, she'd think his face never learned how to smile.

"Don't open it, okay?" Soula says. "Promise me."

"I promise."

"Good."

Then Soula and her date are gone.

SLEEP REFUSES TO COME FOR HER. EVERY TIME SHE REACHES THE tipping point, her brain tosses an old memory in her path. Never the good ones. It's a parade of embarrassing moments. Comebacks that arrived too late for a snappy delivery. Stupid things she said in their steed. Opportunities to break her engagement that she missed. Rumors of this woman or that. Any of them she could have taken to both sets of parents and won her freedom.

But she didn't, did she?

Why not?

Because she was all tied up with string. A good little Kiki-puppet dancing on the end of her mother's strings.

And there was never anyone worth cutting them for.

Enough, she thinks. She's free. Vivi was right, after all.

Free.

To do anything. Love anyone. Go wherever she pleases.

Freedom.

A wonderful, terrible word. When you are free you have all the choices, and there are just so damn many.

Kiki picks one.

She pulls on her black dress. Goes into the living room where the presents wait. Sorts them into piles that make some kind of sense to her. Then she loads the first stack into one of those black garbage bags.

It takes until morning, but by breakfast there's nothing on her dining room table besides rings of dust and that one nameless gift.

That she delivers to the police station.

Freedom. It seemed real during the dark hours, but now that it's light she sees she's still on the wrong side of the bars.

33

LEO

Leo's as horny as hell.

Last night came to nothing. A mutual decision. In the end, when the clothes starting coming off, there wasn't any chemistry.

He and Soula laughed, put their clothes back on, then they talked.

It was fun, but it wasn't magic.

That's how life goes. Two beautiful people don't always make fire. But he made a friend, and that's worth plenty.

Soula caught him up on what's what. Everyone else he knew has moved on. Guys he was buddies with followed their wives back to their home towns. Those two goons from Athens come home occasionally, but mostly for funerals and weddings.

Greece marched on without him.

Memory's a funny thing. It assumes time is fixed. People stay young, places never change. The memory doesn't know that the tree you used to climb was chopped down to build a restaurant. Which became a laundromat. Which became a souvenir shop.

The memory only knows about the tree. And when it finds the tree gone, it kind of flips out.

Yeah, Leo's horny.

And it's got everything to do with the other Andreou woman. Soula is gorgeous, yeah, but now it's Kiki he can't kick out of his head.

He remembers her now, remembers *Spin the Bottle*. She was cute back then, pretty, and he couldn't wait to get her alone in the bushes behind the high school. When he won the second spin and they hid from the others, she told him to turn around. What else was he going to do—he turned around. Single-minded teenage asshole that he was, he assumed she wanted to stand behind him and play with his cock. When that finger slid up his ass, he bolted. Left her standing there wondering what the hell just happened.

Not long after, the Karas family shipped out and he never got a shot at apologizing.

Leo still doesn't like a finger up his ass, but now at least he tells a woman no instead of running.

"What do you know about Kiki Andreou?"

His grandfather looks up from the newspaper. It's morning and they're outside again, and Leo's starting to like this coffee. The trick is to let it sit and wait for the mud to sink.

"The Andreou girl? Eh, nothing. She is a good girl. Very pretty. Her mother was very pretty, too. And her grandmother. Her grandmother ... I took her grandmother out a few times. We had a chaperone, yes, but she had one bad eye. So it was easy to sneak a feel of her—" His finger and thumb make a circle in the air.

Leo laughs. Way to go, Socrates. "So if she didn't kill her fiancé, who did?"

His grandfather slurps the coffee before answering. "Maybe Laki knows, maybe not. At first the Lemonis boy thought it was a suicide, but then he decided it was murder."

"Why?"

"Who knows? I just tell you what I hear. What I do know is that it was not the Andreou girl." He looks at Leo through narrowed eyes. "Why do you ask?"

Leo shrugs. "No reason."

"No reason." He shakes his head. "A man does not ask after a girl unless he has a reason. And that reason is always something to do with his *poutso*."

"I don't have time for women, *Papou*. I have to get back to the states."

"How long before the police come for you, now?"

"Three days."

"All a man needs is fifteen minutes with a woman. Many times, less."

"Not the way I do it," Leo tells him.

34

HELENA

Helena cannot say why she goes back, only that she does. Stavros, of course, comes too. He is such a good son, always wanting to be with his mama, but this is the only place she'll allow them to be seen together. Anywhere else ... People will talk if they do everything together. Call him a mama's boy. Whisper about how Helena cannot let him go.

Go where?

Stepping into Dr Triantafillou's office is like stepping onto the sun. The room is so bright secrets have no place to hide—that's what Helena thinks. Today the head doctor is in a pink dress made of scarves. She looks young, carefree. Yet she is a mother, so how carefree can she be? Mothers worry constantly. Look at how she fusses over Stavros. Always there is a pain in her heart waiting to happen. Even when he is in the room with her, she frets he will leave.

"How are you today, Helena?"

"Wonderful," she says. "Who can be sad in summer?"

"Not me," Dr Triantafillous says. "But sometimes people experience sadness all year round. If they experience heartbreak, if they have lost someone, if things aren't good at home." She moves smoothly to her next question. "How are things at home?"

"Wonderful. They are always wonderful."

"Your marriage is happy?"

"Of course. My husband is a good man. A good father. He works hard for our family."

"How did you two meet?"

"How does any Greek couple our age meet? Through our families. Our parents were in business and friendship together."

"Was it an arranged marriage?"

"Yes. But we already liked each other." Helena smiles. "He was so handsome. A lot of girls wanted to marry him, but he saw only me."

"That sounds very romantic."

Helena shrugs. "It would not have mattered if we liked each other or not, the marriage was destined to be."

"Would your parents have forced it upon you?"

"It was expected. And in those days we did not defy our parents. Not like children today."

"How about your relationship with your son? I understand he was to be married." Her words have the lightness of air, yet behind them, Helena believes, is a hammer. And that hammer will strike if Helena is not careful with her words.

"Yes," she says slowly. "He was to marry my friend's daughter, Kiki. We decided when they were young."

"Was he okay with that?"

"Of course. If he was not, he never said so. Stavros trusted me to find him a suitable wife."

He never told her so, but that makes it no less true. It was an unspoken agreement between them.

"What made ... Kiki, was it?" Helena nods. "What made Kiki a good choice for your son?"

"She comes from a good family. We have the same values."

"What does Kiki do?"

"She is a teacher at the high school in Agria. She is the English teacher."

A moment ticks by.

Helena glances out the window into the sun. She can't look it in the eye for long. Her gaze drops to the ground, to the cars bouncing in and out of the parking lot below.

"When were they to be married?"

Helena swallows. For some reason her throat is filled with powder. She makes spit in her mouth to wash it down, but she's too dry. "What was the question? Sorry."

The doctor looks worried. There's a V forming between her brows. "Would you like some water or coffee, Helena?"

"No. No, I'm fine. What was the question?"

"I asked when their wedding was to be."

"April. There were to be married in April. But the honeymoon was not until June when school was out."

"What happened on the wedding day?"

What happened?

"Kiki would not marry him."

Wouldn't she? Helena can't fill in the details. She remembers the church, the waiting, her phone that never rang. She recalls a bride stomping into the church, demanding they leave because there was to be no wedding that day.

Somebody died, then there was a funeral, and Helena vaguely recalls sitting in the bathtub with a towel over her head, hiding from ... from something. Or maybe someone.

There were too many questions in her living room, too many voices asking her how she was doing. Why did they care so much about how she was feeling? Why not ask the mother of the dead boy? She needed their condolences, not Helena.

"Kiki never wanted to marry him," she says. Her words have the thick, slow, stickiness of the honey syrup that drowns *baklava*.

"Do you think she wanted to choose for herself?"

"Perhaps. But what do young people know? They choose poorly all the time. And now we have divorce, even in Greece."

"How do you feel about Stavros and Kiki not being married?"

Winter's finger slides down her spine. "He will find somebody else."

"Will you choose for him again, or let him find his own wife?"

"He wants me to choose. He told me so."

"When was this?"

"This morning. Every morning since he—"

She won't turn her head, meet her son's eyes. His judgment awaits; he has weighed her heart and found it too heavy to be good.

"Do you believe in the old gods, Doctor?"

"Yes, when it suits me."

"That is very honest. And maybe also foolish."

"Truth is what we do here," the psychologist tells her. "Do *you* believe in the gods of Olympus?"

"I do. I believe in our gods more than *the* God. They were as we were—not some nebulous creature poking us with a pointed finger when it suits Him. Our gods walked among us. We drank together. Loved each other. Sometimes we made children and war. They were gods and men in the very best and worst ways.

"I am not Prometheus, but his punishment has become mine, and I do not understand why. What crime have I done? Every day I am happy. I spend time with my son, and we laugh. But at night, when I am supposed to be sleeping, the crows come for me and peck out my liver. All night long, *peck, peck, peck*. I never scream because I do not want to wake my husband. A good mother would worry that a scream would wake her child, but when the crows come for me, the voices tell me I have no son, that he is dead. And I believe them. Until morning comes and I see his smile."

Helena buries herself in her hands, but it's such a shallow grave.

❧ 35 ❧

LEO

The phone takes its sweet time making the connection. When it does, the ring sounds gritty, like it's boring its way through the Earth to reach the other side. But when his father says, "Hello?" his rich voice fills Leo's ear.

"Dad, it's me."

"Leo! Are you still in Greece?"

"Yeah. I'm waiting on paperwork." He looks out the door. Socrates is trotting to the outhouse with today's newspaper. "How's Mom?"

"Better, I think. She looks better."

Lie. But he gets it. Dad's killing two birds with that single stone: if he convinces Leo his mother is better, then maybe he will believe it himself.

"What do the doctors say?"

"Nothing that I can understand. I wish they'd just speak English. They cannot write it, they do not speak it."

His old man can't see him, but Leo hides the smile anyway. All those years in the states and Dad's accent is still as thickly Greek as egg and lemon soup.

"Veterinarians are just as bad," Leo says. "They teach us big words in college so we have fancy ways of saying your cat's got a bellyache."

His father mutters something about how the Virgin Mary is a prostitute. "Put your grandfather on."

"He's in the outhouse. He took the paper, so he's going to be a while."

"The poor chickens," his father says.

They hang up not long after. Not wordy men, the Karas men. They love each other, but they don't say what doesn't need saying.

❧ 36 ❧

KIKI

"You took a bomb to the police station? *Ay-yi-yi!*" Mama shakes her hands at the sheet of blue sky draped over the yard. "Why you do that, Kiki? The doctor, he did not drop you on your head when you were born. Soula—yes—her they dropped. But not you. You are smarter than that. Did you leave a note?"

"Of course," Kiki says. Who does Mama think she is? Only an idiot would leave an anonymous package on the police station's doorstep. Great way to throw the town into panic.

Mama goes from shaking her hands at the sky to shaking her freshly dyed head. Now that her forty days of mourning are up, Margarita has thrown herself overboard with the self-pampering. Today she's not just wearing makeup, she's wearing *all* the makeup. "My Virgin Mary! They will see the bomb, and then they will come for you because you left a note. What do you think they will do to you, eh? A little murder is nothing compared to a bomb. They will send you to Korydallos!"

Korydallos is Greece's high-security prison. It's in the port city of Piraeus, one of Greece's steepest, sharpest edges.

Yiayia pats Kiki's hand. "Do not worry. If they send you to Korydallos, I will sell all your things and rent a helicopter to help you escape.

TRUTH IS STRANGER AND FUNNIER THAN FICTION. ONE PRISONER has escaped Korydallos twice. And twice he made his escape thanks to a helicopter.

Twice.

Once? Eh, that is not so bad. Like shit, it happens.

But twice ...

Very Greek.

"OR," *YIAYIA* CONTINUES. "YOU COULD CAUSE A RIOT AND TAKE control of the prison! Kiki Andreou, my granddaughter the warlord."

THAT HAPPENED, TOO.

In 1995, inmates battled security and the police for days, before all fifteen hundred or so of them were beaten back into cages designed for four hundred. They wanted better food and a less cramped living situation, but Greece said, "You are very funny. No."

"MY VIRGIN MARY," MAMA SWEARS. "MY DAUGHTER WILL BE IN Korydallos with the lesbians and the communists. What will people think? What will they say?"

"What won't they say?" *Yiayia* tells her. "Our family will be infamous."

It's dramatic, the way Mama rubs her forehead. Could be if she presses hard enough, a genie will pop out and make the family's troubles disappear. "I am going to lie down. Kiki, write to me from prison, okay?"

Jesus Christ, the drama. Where's an amphitheater when you need one?

"We don't even know if it is a bomb," Kiki says in her own defense.

"What else would it be?" Mama asks.

"I don't know. It could be anything."

Her mother doesn't look convinced. It's a bomb—she's already decided. Anything less than a bomb and prison sentence will be a disappointment now. Kiki needs to change the subject. Twist it away from her toward something less dramatic.

"Where's Soula?"

"Asleep," Mama says. "That girl always sleeps late. People do not buy houses early in the morning."

Yiayia cackles. "She is probably still playing with the big penis."

It's eerie the way Margarita Andreou turns slowly to face her mother. "What did you say?"

"She came home with a man last night. A man with a big penis."

"A man!"

Kiki shuts her eyes, wishes she were somewhere else. Anywhere else. Maybe a nice one-person solitary cell in Korydallos. It would be quiet there. No shrieking. No gossip. "Soula dates." Someone has to stand up for Soula. "It's not like it's a secret."

Now Mama is multitasking. Like patting your head and rubbing your belly at the same time, simultaneously shaking both hands and head at the sky takes talent.

"For this we build her a house, so she can take men up for sex. Not a husband, but a parade of men. Always a different one. That girl has a revolving door on her *mouni*."

Kiki gawks at her mother. Margarita Andreou never uses *that* word. The world must be ending.

"We didn't have sex," Soula calls out from her balcony two floors up. She vanishes, then saunters down the stairs, slides into the chair next to Kiki. She's dressed and fully made up for work. "Not that it's anyone's business."

"Why not?" *Yiayia* jumps her chair closer, leans in as though they're sharing a secret. But her voice never got the memo. "Did he lie about his penis?"

It's Greece's best actress who rises from the chair and storms into the kitchen. Mama makes her displeasure known with the crashing of pots and pans.

Soula shrugs. "I never saw it."

Yiayia looks horrified. "Why not?"

In the kitchen, Mama rattles the pots and pans harder, mutters a colorful string of swear words.

"No chemistry."

"Really?" Kiki asks, astonished. "No chemistry with *him?*"

"You met him, Kiki?" Mama calls out through the open window.

Yiayia's hand shoots up. "I met him first. A very good-looking boy. He looks like he knows how to show a woman a very bad time." She winks at Soula.

"Is he someone we know?" Mama asks it casually, but it's obvious she's suppressing an explosion.

"He's *Kyrios* Karas's grandson," Soula says. "The one who went to America."

"Socrates's grandson? Then he was not lying about the big penis!"

Mama looks out the window, up at the heavens. "Please, God, do not let my mother speak again. Strike her mute."

"Socrates took me out a few times, before I married your father, Margarita. My chaperone only had one good eye, so he would feel my—"

"Leonidas Karas?" Kiki says. Did she squeak? She squeaked, didn't she? "Leonidas Karas from school?"

There's a wicked grin on Soula's face. "So you remember him, eh?"

Shrug. "Vaguely."

Total lie, and Soula knows it. That's why she's watching Kiki with a very interested look on her face. *We will talk about this later*, her face is saying, *when these hens are not around.*

And Kiki's face is saying, *Not later, not ever. Nothing to talk about.*

"Time to go." Kiki jumps up from the table.

"Where are you going?" Mama calls out.

"Work. Vivi gave me a summer job doing some translating work."

"What about the bomb?"

She shrugs. "If it's a bomb we'll hear about it. I figure Detective Lemonis will have something to say, either way."

First she shoved her finger up Leonidas Karas's ass, and now he has seen her naked.

Fantastic. She's really winning at life, isn't she?

It's a kid's move, but she kicks the road, dislodges a rock, sends it flying a couple of meters.

Leonidas Karas. Wow. It's been a long time.

He was so hot when they were kids. But even as teenagers he was more man than boy. Intimidating. And now ...

Not her problem. But a man like that, he looks like he's some woman's problem. Probably a lot of women's problem. Kiki doesn't need a problem, and neither does Soula. Good thing they didn't have sex.

Different day, but it's the same walk, only cooler. People are scurrying around, getting things done before the sun shoves them into their houses and slams the shutters in their faces.

Kiki tosses out a lot of greetings, waves to everyone she sees, but the waves come back at her limp, the greetings soggy. Agria's people are in a difficult position. They want to ignore a murderer, but what if she's not? They can't not be polite, otherwise, if Kiki is proven innocent, they will be the branded ones.

Reputation matters.

"Hooray, I'm a pariah," she tells Vivi.

"Been there, done that, have the T-shirt. They're going to look stupid when this is over, and they know it. Then you can gloat."

"I don't want to gloat. I just want things as they were."

Vivi pats her on the shoulder, slides a cold frappe onto the table in front of Kiki. "Things are never as they were. Even when they seem the same, they're not."

"You sound like Kostas."

"That's because I stole his words. You don't think I'm that smart on my own, do you?" Vivi grins. "Not even close."

Kiki smiles. "What am I doing today?"

"Paperwork. So much paperwork. We live in the computer age, but Greece's government is too busy dancing to read the memo. Its response is to make more paper, more forms, in protest. This isn't really a paycheck I'm giving you, it's guilt money. I hate dumping this on someone I like."

Kiki takes a long sip of the cold coffee. "It could be worse. I could be in jail."

The other woman sighs. "Been there, done that, too. Twice."

"Was it terrible?"

"The second time I was in a cell with my mother."

Kiki considers that scenario. "My God, so it was hell."

"Hell, but one of the outer circles. The one filled with Greek mothers."

37

HELENA

It is not easy living under a microscope. Everywhere she goes, eyes follow. Home, town, the doctor's office. Eyes delivering messages to analytical minds. Everyone of them measuring her sanity against some invisible scale.

What is the range? she wonders. Who is sane enough to be the beginning point on the measuring stick? And who sits on the farthest edge?

Zeus, of course. There is nobody crazier in Greek history or mythology than the king of the gods. At the other end sits nobody; men and gods all have a little madness in them. Without madness, a person is not fully alive.

She feels those checking her mental pulse while she cooks in her hot kitchen. This summer it is more cramped than ever. The walls seem to inch closer each day.

"How are you?" Kristos asks.

"Fine."

Not ten minutes later: "How are you?"

"Fine."

His mouth opens one more time.

"I'm going to bed," she says.

ALEX A. KING

"Fine," he tells her.

THE NEXT DAY, STAVROS IS ON STRIKE. HE WILL NOT EAT, WILL NOT speak.

"Eat a little something, eh?" Helena begs him. "Or you will get skinny. Women want a strong man, not a feather."

He ignores her. Sits there staring at nothing.

She knows why. It is because of the psychologist. Stavros does not approve. He thinks Helena tells her too much.

"I will not see her again if it upsets you so much. Just talk to me—talk to your mama, okay?"

He smiles but it's the smile of a doll, fixed and flimsy. Wherever she goes, he watches her with his flat, paper gaze, but does not say a word.

"I have to go out. Do you want me to fix you a little snack before I leave?"

Silence.

He will come around, she thinks, *in time*.

Helena has nothing but time. So much that it pours from her hands.

THROUGH THE BUS'S WINDOW THE GULF APPEARS SCRATCHED, DUSTY, ruined. Helena sees only its flaws.

It is a seven kilometer ride from Agria to Volos, all of it waterfront road. The bus rolls toward the *Panayia Tripa of Goritsa* temple—

SOMETIMES TRANSLATIONS ARE ... UNFORTUNATE. THIS ONE IS BOTH unfortunate and funny to people whose senses of humor tilt towards unclean.

Goritsa is a place. Nothing funny about that.

148

Panayia is the Virgin Mary.

A *tripa* is a hole.

—RESTING ON THE ROCKS BELOW. A ROMANI MAN STANDS AT THE side of the road not far from the bleached steeple, peddling bananas.

Bananas.

The sign says he wants ten euros per kilo. A small fortune. But there are people who will pay it because bananas are not an everyday fruit in Greece.

Stavros loves bananas. Maybe these he will eat.

Helena jerks the string that tells the driver to stop.

"I want bananas," she explains. "Stop here."

"It is not a stop," the driver complains into his convex mirror.

"If the bus stops and you let me off, then it is a stop, yes?"

He stops, but only because her logic is flawless.

She gets off the bus, steps into an unforgiving sun. It sees her faults, points out every one. What kind of mother is she? A good mother does not become the accomplice of a doctor who wishes to banish her child.

The sun speaks only truth. It knows nothing of night and its shadows.

When she turns, there is no man, there are no bananas. Only dust from the land and salt from the sea.

Hades, she thinks, is toying with her. She will not be a god's plaything.

Arms outstretched, she screams at the god of the underworld and all his siblings. "What else do you want from me? You have taken everything. Everything!"

❧ 38 ❧

LEO

O uthouses suck.

Not easy trying to figure out which is worse: proper toilet stuck in a closet at the back of the yard, or one of those holes-in-the-ground inside a lot of Greek bathrooms.

The high school used to have a row of holes. He wonders what it's got now.

When he was a kid, every time he came out of the outhouse—this outhouse—sure enough, there'd be a hot girl walking by.

It's hard to be cool when a girl suspects you just took a dump.

He flushes. Opens the door.

"Leonidas!"

Just like old times. Except it's not a hot girl, it's *Kyria* Dora.

"*Kalimera, Kyria* Dora. If you're looking for my grandfather, he's not home."

"For what would I want to talk to that old fool?" The woman jiggles closer, cutting a path through the chickens. "I came to talk with you!"

"Coffee?"

"Maybe a small *frappe*. And a *koulouraki*, if you have one."

They're out of cookies, but Leo finds some personal-sized chocolate cakes in the cupboard. He shakes the coffee, pours, drops the cake on a small plate, all the time wondering what the older woman wants with him.

It doesn't take long for her to get to the point.

"I hear you fixed a donkey."

"True story," he tells her.

"Good." She beams at him. "I have a problem. An animal problem. And they say you are a veterinarian."

"Also true. What kind of animal are we talking about?"

"I do not know, but it is an animal. Every night it comes and bellows outside my window. Sometimes it is on the roof, making that terrible noise. And always, it smells like pee when it leaves."

Leo thinks about Greece and its wildlife. His memory is sketchy. He can't remember what's native, what's not.

"You've never seen it?"

"Never! It is very clever and hides in the dark."

"How long has this been going on?"

"A week. Maybe two."

"And you want me to do what?"

"Catch it and take it away—what else?"

"Have you thought about an exterminator?"

"An exterminator is for ants. This is not an ant, unless it is a very big ant."

"They catch animals, too."

She sighs like it's killing her. "Maybe they were lying about the donkey you fixed, eh? If you cannot help me, you cannot help me." The older woman staggers to her feet. She pockets the tiny cake. "Say hello to your grandfather for me, eh?"

This is what she wants: the chase. She wants him to volunteer and she wants him to do it for nothing. Which is fine, he was going to do it for nothing anyway. He's not here to make a buck—he just wants to get home.

"Wait. I can at least take a look."

"Good!" All smiles. "Come tonight, after dark."

SOCRATES HAS GRAND PLANS—PLANS THAT INVOLVE LEO. HE CAN tell by the twinkle in the old man's eye. What's he up to?

"Come," Socrates says. "We are having chicken for dinner. Can you cook?"

Wary: "Yeah, I can cook."

"Good, then you can make chicken."

Leo knows what's in the fridge and freezer, which means he knows there's no chicken. "Want me to run to the store?"

"For what? Everything you need is here."

"Chicken?"

Papou's eyebrows make a hasty retreat north. "What do you think that is outside, eh? Pick one and kill it."

Leo goes outside.

Walks back inside.

"Axe?"

"Are you a man or are you a girl? Use your hands. Like this." He mimes a snapping neck before following Leo back out.

Leo's euthanized his share of animals before, but only as a last resort. He's not big on killing for fun or food. Doesn't sit right with him when guys hide in the bushes so they can say they bagged Bambi. But he can kill one chicken for dinner—right?

Chickens are silly creatures, but they're okay. And his grandfather's chickens seem to like him. How the hell is he supposed to pick one? They're milling around his feet, looking for food, no idea that one of them is about to be lunch.

Socrates cackles from his chair on the patio.

"Not a word," Leo says.

"What? I do not say anything."

"Don't think so loud, then." He watches them peck. Can't pick one when they're all healthy and happy. "How do you choose?"

"I ask them questions, and whichever chicken gives the wrong answer, that is the chicken." Great joke. Huge. Funny man, that *Papou*. He's slapping his own leg, cackling. "I grab the closest chicken, Leonidas. Whichever one cannot run as fast as the others."

Leo glances from chicken to chicken. He can't do it.

It's the karma thing. Take a life and the universe might take one right back.

What if it's his mother?

He stomps into the house, snatches up the moped's keys. "You want chicken, I'll get chicken."

39

KIKI

July doesn't see full dark until 10 PM, but night is making early threats in preparation. Outside, the cicadas are whining about their itchy skins. Soon they'll shed them, then they'll whine about how the new skins feel too tight. Very Greek, cicadas.

Soula is not on her knees, but she's begging Kiki to come to the promenade. It's been more than forty days, so Kiki's off the mourning hook, socially.

Kiki doesn't want to go. She enjoys socializing, having a good time, but if she goes to the waterfront, everyone will stop and look. Then they'll move on, but their whispers will be deafening.

That's the best case scenario.

There she goes, they'll say. *Walking around as if she never killed a man.*

Then they'll wonder who's next. Maybe it will be them.

Please. As if they're worth killing. The remedy for malicious gossip isn't murder, it's self-inflicted exile.

"Who cares what they say?" Soula cries. "They are nobody. Since when do you care what nobody thinks? The only way to win is to walk down there with your head high. Be polite. Kill them with kindness. Then when this is over and the police have Stavros's murderer, they will be ashamed."

"They won't apologize."

"No, but they will move on to someone else. That is as close as they get to *sorry*."

"Who do you think killed him?"

Soula shrugs. "Who knows? I heard stories. But they are the same stories you heard."

"I can't go," Kiki says. "I just want to hide until this is over."

"Only a guilty woman hides, sister. An honest woman? She enjoys life, because her heart is light."

"Then why does mine feel like a rock?"

"Because you are a good person. A much better person than me. And a piece of you cared about Stavros, even if you did not love him. Me? You know I think he was a piece of shit."

KIKI THINKS HER SISTER IS FULL OF GREAT IDEAS.

Wonderful ideas.

Best ideas ever.

Like going to the promenade. What could possibly go wrong?

So many tourists, you'll blend right in, Soula told her.

Ignore the people staring, Soula told her.

Stay, Soula told her. *Don't let them chase you away. Ignore that old woman spitting in your direction. Maybe she just has rabies. Whatever you do, do not let her bite you, because look at those teeth. Has she never heard of a dentist?*

Kiki bolted, shot straight up the main street leading away from the promenade. Soula followed, her mouth full of curses. Not for Kiki, but for *those* people.

They used to be Kiki's people, but now they won't have her.

Their loss, Soula told her. But Kiki couldn't help feeling she lost something, too.

Now they're standing by the water fountain on Drakia Road, watching Romani bleed out of the dark. There's a woman filling her huge water bottles from the fountain's faucet, but she's faking night-blindness.

(Ask her later and she'll have a good story to tell. But it will be Kiki who's the menace, not the oncoming Romani.)

Soula grabs her arm, tugs her toward home. "We should go."

"Go where?"

They're in an 80s movie, a foreign one that's been dubbed, where the mouths don't match the words. And the good guys are standing back to back, watching the bad guys close in on them.

Kiki doesn't know kung-fu, and she's pretty sure Soula doesn't know kung-fu, either.

"We need a diversion," Soula says over her shoulder.

"Any ideas?"

Soula says, "Only bad ones."

"Like?"

"Offering to sell them a house with a reduced commission."

Jesus Christ

The ring is shrinking by the second. Should she scream? That one woman is scurrying up the street with her bottles. There's an apartment building a few feet away, but if anyone hears her, they'll probably assume she's discussing politics. A political discussion in Greece means yelling. The loudest person—not the most correct—wins.

"Can I help you?" she says.

"Why are you talking to them?" Soula cries out.

"Because they're people who obviously want something?"

"We don't have any money," Soula tells them.

Tsiganes. Yiftes. Gypsies.

Greece has a Romani problem. The government wants to pour oil and water into a jar and shake them until they're a *frappe*. But the Romani aren't big joiners. They prefer to pitch their tents where they please, and move on when the authorities squint in their direction. When they build, it's settlements, not neighborhoods, although minds are slowly changing. But for now, most of them still choose to live on city fringes.

They marry off their children young, rarely send them to school, which sounds like—

Well, Greece. Or rather, Greece as it used to be.

It's not the first time Greece has been a hypocrite. They even invented the word.

Anyway, Greece's Romani are tightly wedged between the proverbial rock and hard place.

The rock? The old Romani traditions fighting for their lives.

Greece, of course, is the hard place.

"GREEKS. THEY ALWAYS THINK WE WANT THEIR MONEY," ONE OF the Romani says. He's either colorblind or a fashion risk-taker. Who else would pair a red *NIKE* shirt with those green pants?

"That's because you usually want our money." Soula sounds brave. Which is good, because Kiki doesn't feel brave.

The man shrugs. "Okay, so we want your money, but not tonight. Although I would not say no to your money, if you want to give it to me." He looks at them expectantly.

Kiki looks at her sister. "I don't want to give him my money. You?"

"No," Soula says. "What do you want?"

Somebody behind them spits. Second time tonight.

GREEKS SPIT A LOT. SOME OF THE TIME IT'S FOR YOUR OWN GOOD.

It's the Swiss Army Knife of gestures.

Spitting wards away the evil eye by canceling out a compliment. *You're so beautiful, so smart, and you have so many shoes! Spit-spit!* Nothing in Greece is more spat-upon than a baby. It's one of a non-Greek's minor parenting nightmares.

They spit to get the gunk out. It's nothing to see a Greek man shooting snot out of his mouth or nose, onto the ground. Sun-warmed gum is a lesser problem. That thing on the ground that glistens like an oyster?

Not an oyster.

And they spit to show contempt. It's an insult for the lowest of the low.

YEAH, KIKI'S SURE THEY'RE NOT SPITTING BECAUSE THEY LIKE HER black dress. She's not keen on the dress either. Or the black. She likes colors.

Soula pivots on the heel of her wedge sandal, points one-fingered. "You did not just spit on me."

"Not on you," the woman says. "Her. You were just in the way."

The spitter is a young woman, destined to look forty before she's thirty. Roma life is tough on its people. She's chicken-shaped: thick around the middle with skinny brown legs.

Before Kiki can say anything, the woman spits again. The wet flecks nail the exposed V of her chest.

Kiki is a good woman from a good family, but there is a limit to her goodness. All this spitting makes her want to reach out and slap someone. "What's your problem?"

The woman moves closer. "You Greeks think you are so superior to us. You would beat us out of the country if you could." She spits again, this time it lands on Kiki's cheek.

One foot at a time, Kiki slides out of her sandals. Her reputation is dirt anyway, so who cares if people see her without shoes and think she's poor? She's past caring. All she wants right now is to throw herself onto her bed and let sleep swallow her for a few hours. Then maybe she'll wake up on a new day, in a new life.

But no. She's stuck here, now, wiping spit off her face.

She picks up the right sandal. It's pretty, strappy, completely unsuitable for walking any great distance. But it's aerodynamic and knows how to find a target.

Bam. Right in the Romani woman's forehead.

Every breath catches. Then the woman hisses, "*Skeela!*"

(It's not the first time one of the Andreou women has been called a bitch, but usually it's Soula. More commonly, they've called her *tsoula*

Soula. *Tsoula* being a charming word that describes a woman who bestows her affections upon many men, far and wide and free.)

Kiki starts to laugh, because isn't this just great? She was supposed to be married to Stavros, honeymooning in Paris, contemplating starting a family, but instead she's here, hurling shoes in a Romani woman's face.

It's laugh or cry.

Kiki doesn't choose laughter—it chooses her. Then—tag—Soula's laughing, too. Both Andreou women doubled over, laughing, even though chances are good they're about to get their asses kicked.

The Romani woman doesn't disappoint. She lunges, knees Kiki in the face.

"Drina, no!"

Kiki lifts her head. Her toes are red with blood, hot. "Drina? Is that your name?"

"Yes. And it is a better name than yours."

Kiki rushes her, slams her to the ground. The woman's not so tough now with all the wind knocked out of her.

Kiki is a teacher, which means she's watched kids fights. A lot of kids, over the years—boys and girls. Her database has been carefully stashing away tips and tricks, not for a rainy day, but—apparently—a warm summer night. She doesn't swing again, doesn't make a chair out of the girl's chest, doesn't pull, bite, slap.

But she does grab the girl's middle finger. And that she bends until Drina screeches, "*Putana!*"

"That's not the magic word." She looks up at the ring of Romani surrounding the three of them. "I know the magic word, and I'm sure that's not it. Anyone want to help her out?"

"That's my sister," Soula declares proudly. But the Romani aren't impressed. They're not intervening, either. They're waiting and watching to see what happens next.

That's strange, isn't it? Kiki figured they'd be tearing the two of them apart. That's how it goes in the school yard.

What happens next is that Kiki tugs on that bent finger.

"I will never say it," the Romani woman bellows. "I would rather die!"

That hits Kiki's OFF switch. Anyone who'd choose death over an apology has bigger problems than she does.

She grabs the woman's arm, pulls her to her feet. "Whatever your problem with me is," she says, "it's not worth your life. Just go home. That's where I'm going."

The girl stands there, swaying in the non-existent breeze. "I would not buy watermelon for a while if I were you."

Kiki scoops up her sandals, dangles the straps over one finger. "Soula," she says, "tonight I feel like going barefoot.

NOT HER BEST IDEA EVER.

Or her worst, so that's something.

She regrets the bare feet the minute they hit the side road leading to home. Road, loosely defined. It's not so much a road as it is a dirt path scattered with rock and other things that like to bite feet.

"Ouch," she says. Two seconds later: "Ouch."

Soula shakes her head. "That's what you get for going barefoot."

"Did I say ouch? I meant, wow, this feels great!" But Soula's not laughing. "Are you okay?" Kiki asks her sister.

"Of course. When have I ever not been okay?"

Kiki stops. "Soula ..."

"What do you think they wanted?"

"The Romani? I don't know. What do they ever want with us? Money or trouble."

"I do not think so," Soula says.

"Then what?"

"I don't know."

Don't you, Kiki thinks. *I think maybe you do.*

But she's a woman who lets the world come to her in its own sweet time, even when the world is her strangely silent sister.

❧ 40 ☙

LEO

Leo makes good on his promise. After dark, he beelines for *Kyria* Dora's house to sort out her wild animal problem. She lives off the main road heading up to Drakia (one of Mount Pelion's larger villages), on a skinny road with a killer incline. Great place to ride a bike no-handed, if you're a kid. The only problems are the potholes and complete absence of fucks given by the person who poured the original road.

Kyria Dora is waiting on her patio in the dark. Her house is a single white-washed story, shaped like an English L.

"Is that you, Leonidas?"

"Good evening, *Kyria* Dora."

Her silhouette clutches its heart with one hand. "My Virgin Mary, that is good! I thought maybe you were the animal."

Not the first time a Greek woman has mistaken him for an animal. Used to be, he and his buddies would sneak around, throwing rocks on roofs in the middle of the night, whizzing on their front doors, making noises like the undead were coming.

Sometimes a woman peeled out of the targeted house, waving a broom at the *animals*, and sometimes it was a man with a hammer.

Boys do things that make sense to them and no one else. Stuff like that is fun when you're ten. It's still fun when you're thirty, but by then you've got to get a good night's sleep so you can work the next day.

"Always it happens around an hour from now." *Kyria* Dora's silhouette nods at the roof. "You should climb up there and hide. That way you can jump on the animal if you see it below. And if comes on the roof, then you will be close, eh?"

Leo nods to the dark cluster of bushes. "Or I could hide there in the bushes."

She laughs, pats his arm. "Those are not bushes, those are my thistles. You will be a very sorry man if you hide there."

He's already a sorry man, and the idea of being more sorry doesn't suit him. So he makes a ladder out of the wood trellis that frames the patio. It's sturdy, built to last. Built to handle a load of climbing man. Which is good, because *Kyria* Dora doesn't own a ladder. He knows because she announces it proudly, as though not owning a ladder is an achievement.

"Would you like a broom?" she asks.

"No, I'm good."

"Okay, but do not blame me when you need a weapon and you do not have one!"

A half hour later, Leo's sitting on the roof, arms loose around his knees, wondering what kind of Greek animal only shows up at a particular time.

Yeah, not an animal at all.

Kids, mostly likely. Kids like he used to be. Either making trouble or making fun—probably both.

He leans back on the flat roof, arms behind his head. Takes his best shot at memorizing how stars look when cities aren't blinding them with their own blazing lights. He's not a sentimental guy, but here he is hoping for a falling star. He's got wishes to make, places to go.

First thing is getting home. Second is finding a place to live. He's thinking about selling off his practice, starting fresh closer to home. Whatever happens with Mom, Leo wants to be close. That's how life goes. When you're a kid you can't wait to run away from home. When you're an adult, you can't wait to run back the first time someone needs you.

Maybe in time he'll meet a great woman, but it's going to be a while before he can set anything in gold again. Maybe never.

Anyway, pointless worrying. Getting home is the only priority right now.

And there it is: *Kyria* Dora's noise.

The gate doesn't squeak because whatever it isn't entering the civilized way. It's clambering over the fence.

And it's got company.

Leo grins. This should be good.

He flattens himself on the roof and watches the new arrivals unpack their pockets. They've come loaded with slingshots and ... not rocks, some kind of fruit. *Janera* or figs, maybe. They load up their slingshots and take aim at the roof.

Leo rolls until he's on the far side of the house, then he drops into the bushes—not Kyria Dora's thistles, but something with a softer landing.

They boys are so consumed with their mischief that they're blind to Leo until he's on them.

"So, either of these look familiar to you?"

One neck in each hand, he gives them a shake.

"Yes," *Kyria* Dora says in one of those voices that heralds trouble's arrival. "Yes, those little animals are *very* familiar to me."

"Don't be angry, *Yiayia*," the smaller boy says.

"Who is angry? It is your mother's job to be angry, not mine." She stomps out of the room, a lot of tectonic movement happening under her nightgown. "Leonidas," she calls out, "do not let them run away."

"Not going anywhere," Leo mutters. He looks at the kids. They're wide eyed and pale under their tans. "Bad night?"

The little one looks up at him, grins. "It was a good night, until you caught us."

Cute kids, *Kyria* Dora's grandsons. Play-dirty clothes. Hair that won't do what the comb says. They look like trouble. Leo knows—he used to see the same thing in his mirror when he was a boy.

He laughs. "Why were you scaring your grandmother?"

They glance at each other, shrug. "Why not?" the older one says. "It's fun."

Little monsters. Yeah, they remind him of him, which is why he can't quit smiling. "You want to make mischief without getting caught, you better learn a thing or two."

"Like what?"

He lets them go, leans against the wall, arms folded. "Don't strike at the same time every night. It's easier to track someone when they have a pattern."

In the other room, *Kyria* Dora is puffing angry words into the phone.

The boys are nodding, eyes big. Not out of fear now, but interest. He's speaking their lingo, this stranger who doesn't think trouble is a bad thing.

"Wear dark clothes. You'll be able to hide better."

The little guy looks down at his shirt. "But I like Spiderman."

"I like Spiderman, too. But all that red? No good. Go black or dark blue."

"What else, *Kyrios*?"

"Be aware of your surroundings. Listen. You should have heard me jumping off that roof, but you were too focused on shooting fruit. If you can't listen while you're working the slingshot, take turns keeping an eye out for trouble."

"Anything else?"

"If, like tonight, you get caught, don't lie. Accept whatever comes your way. Punishment's always worse if you lie."

Nod, nod. "Did you ever get caught?"

"All the time. Until me and my buddies got good at it. Then we almost never got caught. People knew it was us, but there's not much they can do if they don't catch you."

Kyria Dora rushes back into the room, gushing words. "Your mother is coming, and then you will be her problem!"

The kids don't howl this time. Leo just dumped a pile of gold in their hands, so they're in their own timeout, waiting until they're alone so they can plot their next strike.

"I need to get moving," he says.

"Stay! Effie will want to thank you."

Effie rolls in five minutes later, and *thanks* is the last word she's got for anyone.

Yeah, he remembers Effie now that he's looking at her. There was some kind of scandal when they were kids. He can't recall what. But anyway, he definitely remembers her, though she was skinny back then, not muscular like she is now. Less makeup in those days, too. Tonight she's all spackled pores.

Effie doesn't waste time—she launches right into the shrieking. Within seconds, she's dialed all the way up to eleven. But her words bounce right off the kids like they're rubber. Effie sounds like she's had a lot of practice yelling, and the boys look like they've had a lot of practice listening to her yell. They've mastered the art of tuning out while they nod.

Eventually she runs out of steam. Hands on hips, she glares at Leo.

"Who are you?"

"I'm the guy who caught your kids."

"Are you?"

He can almost hear the whirring of a fisherman rewinding his line, getting ready to cast again. Then her mother steps on her foot —literally.

"Mama!"

"Where are your manners? Effie, this is Leonidas Karas, Socrates Karas's grandson."

"I thought you went to America."

"I did. And now I'm back."

"Why?"

If he was a guy with fur or feathers, she'd be rubbing them the wrong way. But he's a pretty chill guy, so he says, "What can I say? I love Greek women."

"Have you met Vivi?" She shifts her focus to her mother. "Mama, has he met Vivi?"

"Is that your American cousin?" Leo asks.

One sour word: "Yes."

The older woman rolls her eyes at the ceiling, mutters the Virgin

Mary's name. "There is a small rivalry between Effie and Vivi, but blood is blood, and they secretly love each other."

Must be a story there, but Leo doesn't care. Agria is filled with stories, many of them petty and founded on nothing.

"I remember your mother," Effie says.

"Really?"

Effie frowns, as if mildly confused by his reply. "Yes. Nobody thought she had the power to make your father leave."

Kyria Dora waves her hands. "Effie, always you talk too much." But nothing is stopping the Effie train.

"How is your mother?"

What does he say? Not the truth. Say something out loud that way and it has a way of becoming real. It's a desperate man who tells the lie and says: "She's great. Much happier back home."

"In America." It's a question without a hook.

"In America," he confirms.

She looks away. Leo knows when he's been dismissed. The next words fizzing out of her mouth aren't for him. They're all about Kiki Andreou and some fight she got into with a bunch of Romani.

He barely knows Kiki, but when Effie gets to the part where Kiki walked away, barefoot, a piece of him is proud of her.

❦ 41 ❧

KIKI

"Now you know what it is like to be poor," Mama crows. "It is a good thing nobody saw you."

"The *tsiganes* saw her," *Yiayia* points out. Very helpful for a woman who isn't in the conversation—or in the room.

"Like I said," Margarita hollers, "it is a good thing nobody saw her!"

The prejudice goes way back. Times are changing for Greece's two people, but it's moving on Greek time. And Greek time moves how it pleases—sometimes fast, sometimes slow. An hour can be a week or a minute, depending on its mood.

"You have very bad luck with the *tsiganes* lately, eh, Kiki?" *Yiayia* calls out. The old woman is down the hall in her room, but her hearing is keener than a dog's. "What did you do to them?"

"Nothing." Kiki's mulling it over, but the way life has been lately, her mind is slow at making connections. Now it makes one—hallelujah? "The Romani woman, I think she's the one who came here."

"When?" Mama wants to know. "*Tsiganes* come all the time to our door, begging for money."

"The other day. The weird one who cursed me."

"Always they give us curses, because always we kick them out and do not give them money. You must be more specific."

"The one with the ants."

"Her! She is a terrible *tsigana*. Why they let her make curses, I will never know." Mama waves her wooden spoon at the floor. "I forgot to see *Kyria* Dora, but do you see any ants? I do not see any ants. We have no ants. Not a one. Not so much as a fly without wings that we can mistake for an ant."

Yiayia rolls into the room in her wheelchair. "In my day, they made good curses. They cursed me with a terrible daughter, and look, I have your mother."

Mama drops the spoon back into the béchamel sauce. Tomorrow morning, early, the *moussaka* is taking a short trip to the bakery. "I thought you were in a coma today?"

"I was." The old woman shrugs. "But I do not want to miss out on something interesting."

It's like watching a game of tennis, and Kiki doesn't like tennis. "I'm going to bed," she says, dropping kisses on every cheek in the room.

"Not me," Soula says. "I am going back out. The night is still young."

"Live the way you do, and soon you will not be so young," Mama says.

"You are full of good advice, Mama," Soula says. "You should write a book."

"It will be the world's shortest book," *Yiayia* says.

Kiki leaves Mama and *Yiayia* to their bickering, Soula to her vanishing act. Bed is waiting, and it's impatient. But by the time she's traipsed up the stairs, washed the evening off her feet, and wrapped herself in a robe, sleep doesn't want anything to do with her.

She doesn't spend much time with her computer when school's out, but tonight she flips open the lid and goes straight to the browser.

It's asinine, childish, and something she secretly scoffs at when she overhears her kids talking about it, but she goes to *Facebook* and pulls up Stavros's page. They're not "friends," but Stavros wasn't a careful guy, and his life's highlight reel is open to all audiences. Funny, you'd think an accountant would be cautious. But no, there he is in color, women hanging off him like streamers. Not just his pictures, but women who've tagged him in theirs.

Popular guy, which she already knew.

Lots of women, which she also knew.

I love yous and kisses and promises to do it again.

Did Detective Lemonis see all this? Did he invite all these faces to that airless room for a conversation about murder?

Scroll, scroll, scroll. Down and then up again.

Woman of every flavor but Romani.

42

LEO

Two more days—after today—until he's a wanted man.

Good thing the postman's got his paperwork. He waves the thick yellow envelope at Leo, then putt-putts away on his red motorcycle.

Fast. Extremely fast for Greece.

Leo empties the packet on the kitchen table. Big stack. Thicker than a couple of *IHOP* pancakes. When he looks them over, he understands the bits where his name's supposed to go, and his address, but that's about it. They're Greek forms made for native Greeks—ones who've run the educational gamut, beginning to end. Not part-time Greeks like Leo who've forgotten more Greek words than they remember. They may as well be Hebrew, for all the sense they make.

No way does he have time for this. Even with a Greek-to-English Lexicon he'll be here forever. And time has a funny way of vanishing quicker when you need more of it. It likes the thrill of the chase, the being in-demand.

"*Papou?*" he hollers in the direction of the open door.

His grandfather shuffles out, hair in hand. He's raking through it with a wide-toothed comb. "Take the dirt road toward Taki's place.

But keep going until you see a white cottage with a big dog out front. That is where the American woman lives."

"How—"

Socrates dumps the hair on his head. "If you have to ask, you are very stupid. And maybe your mother had a man on the side, because my blood would not be so stupid, eh?" He's grinning as he says it, gold tooth twinkling. "Go. Take my motorcycle."

Leo goes.

IT'S HARD TO FEEL BADASS ON A MOPED, BUT LEO MAKES IT WORK. The dark sunglasses help. There's no trail of broken hearts behind him, but there's one hell of a dust cloud.

He finds the cottage where his grandfather said he would. The dog, too. He finds the American woman when she wanders outside to see who her dog is rolling over for this time.

"That dog," she mutters in English, but she's smiling, isn't she? Cute woman. Petite. Lots of dark hair held up high in a ponytail. Doesn't look much older than a college kid, but word is she runs her own company.

"I'm Leo Karas," he says. "And I really need some help."

"You're American!" The smile grows. She's one of those people who smiles like life is always sweet. "Whereabouts?"

"My family lives in Florida, but I grew up here. You?"

"Oregon. You get all our sunshine, we get all your rain."

He laughs because she sounds like home. "It's good to meet you, Vivi."

"You know my name?"

"Your aunt mentioned it the other day."

"It's a miracle." She shakes her hands at the sky—Greek-style. "Usually everyone calls me the foreigner." Then she nods at the cottage, ponytail swinging. "Come on in, Leo. I'll make you a real cup of coffee. Then we can talk about what kind of help you need."

"I think I love you, Vivi," he says. "Vivi what?"

"Tyler," she tells him. "Soon to be Vivi Andreou."

The same Andreou family? What are the odds?

HIGH. VERY HIGH. BECAUSE KIKI ANDREOU IS SITTING AT VIVI'S kitchen table, not even close to naked this time. She's in a black dress, hair scraped into one of those no-nonsense buns that's begging to have its pins pulled out.

Pretty woman. Bright eyes. Full lips made for kissing—and lots of it.

"We meet again," he says.

Vivi looks from one face to the other. "You two know each other?"

"From school," he says, just as Kiki says, "From my bedroom."

"Not like that," Kiki is quick to add.

Vivi is a woman who looks hungry for a good story. "Okay, I know I've been in Greece for way too long, because there's a story here and I'm dying to hear it."

"There's no story," Leo tells her. "Kiki was a year or two behind me in school."

"There is a story." Kiki ignores him. "He was in my bedroom the other night with Soula."

Vivi holds up her hand. "Forget I asked. The good news is that I'm not completely Greek yet, otherwise I'd be begging for more."

Leo grabs a chair. Sits. Grins at Kiki. She's doing a great job of pretending to be busy with the pile of papers in front of her. The dog leans against him. Leo rubs his head; you don't say no to a dog.

"So how's it going?" he asks her.

"Wonderful," Kiki says, not looking up. "A Romani woman attacked me last night. We fought."

"So I heard."

"I'm sure you did. Just out of curiosity, where?"

"*Kyria* Dora's daughter, Effie."

"Effie." Over at the counter, Vivi laughs. "Of course. My cousin is real sweetheart. I thought about selling her on eBay, but you can't sell family."

Leo looks back at Kiki. "Did you win?"

"You know, I'm not sure. I ended it."

"Then you won."

"It's good to win something," she says, glancing up for a moment.

"What was it about?"

"The fight? Who knows?" Kiki says it absently, like she's already moved on.

Leo leans back in the chair, crosses his arms. "Men get into fights over nothing. Over a look. Over a word. But women? You don't get into fights about nothing. There's always a reason."

"Sexist," Vivi says, but she's smiling.

He laughs. "*Almost* always a reason."

"Better," she tells him.

Kiki's shaking her head. "If there was a reason, she never said."

"Doesn't mean there wasn't one."

Vivi gets busy with the coffee maker. It's the real deal, not a *briki*. "So how can I help you?"

That. For a moment he almost forgot. "Long story short, I have to get home. The Greek army wants me to complete my national service, so they took my passport. The US Embassy won't replace it. The Hellenic Ministry of National Defense *might* help, but only if I submit all this." He dumps the packet on the table. It lands with a thud. "The problem is, I don't understand a word of it."

Vivi says, "Why not finish your service? Why the hurry to go home?"

Both women are looking at him with interest, waiting to see if he's going to toss some shallow excuse out there. And why would they think any different? They don't know him.

"Ugh, sorry," Vivi says. "Greece is making me nosier every day. Forget I asked."

"It's okay. It's a family thing," he tells them. "A now or never thing."

Not a blip in the man code. He could elaborate, but why? He's here for the paperwork, not the sympathy. Sympathy won't get him home.

Vivi nods like she knows. "How do you take your coffee?"

"White. Two sugars."

"Greek paperwork is a pain in the ass," she continues. "And it sounds like we're in the same babelboat: spoken Greek is fine. Written, not so much." She gestures toward Kiki. "Kiki's saving my bacon. If you ask nicely, she might save yours."

Leo shakes his head. The Andreou woman has enough problems, including a broken heart. Last thing she needs is a plateful of his.

"I appreciate the recommendation," he says. "But she looks busy."

The coffee comes, and it's incredible. Best coffee he's had in weeks. Then Vivi sits a cookie jar in front of him.

"Chocolate chip and oatmeal raisin. No powdered sugar or syrup in sight."

"You're engaged? Lucky man."

She laughs, pats him on the shoulder. "My daughter made them, and she's only sixteen. What do you think, Kiki?"

"I'm not busy enough," Kiki murmurs. She looks up at him from the nest of papers stacked on the table. "I can do it."

He eats a cookie. Perfect ratio of chips to dough.

There's something in her eyes. A thread of desperation.

He gets it. Yeah, he really gets it.

"Let's do it," he says.

❦ 43 ❧

HELENA

That policeman comes. The one who—

"Detective Lemonis?"

The detective stands at her gate, watches her sweep leaves from one side of the concrete yard to the other. She finds it relaxing to sweep, while the gardenias pour perfume into the air. She should invite him in, serve him coffee in a tiny cup, sweets on a tiny plate, but she can't seem to stop sweeping.

No matter. Doesn't look like he expects hospitality.

"*Kyria* Bouto, good morning."

Swish, swish. "Is there a problem?"

He shakes his head. "No problem. I have questions for you."

"Questions? Then ask. I hope I can be useful."

"Your son—Stavros—he was engaged to Kyriaki Andreou. Was there anyone else? Another woman?"

What a question. Her Stavros is a good boy. A faithful boy.

"No, of course not," she tells him. "When he was younger, yes. Boys will be boys and men will be men, eh?"

"Another man, perhaps?"

She laughs. "My Stavros is not a *pusti*."

The detective nods. "Okay. Do you know the name of his last girl-friend before Kyriaki?"

"Who tells their mother such things? There was a time when he told me everything, but not since he was a little boy. So sad, but that is life and sons." A hiccup in her sweeping. "Why not ask Stavros himself? He can tell you."

His expression does not change. "Ask him?"

"He is inside, reading the newspaper."

"Inside?"

The poor man, he looks confused. It must be the heat. It is morning, but summer is in a merciless mood. And there he is, out in the full sun.

"In the kitchen. I will stay out here, that way he can keep his secrets, eh? Boys do not like to talk about sensitive things in front of their mothers."

She whistles as she sweeps, an old Jenny Vanou song about love and how it finds its way to lost

---

"How are you, *Kyria* Bouto?"

Helena jumps. She didn't expect the detective to be done with Stavros so quickly. Of course, maybe the sweeping made it seem faster.

"Did you get your answers, Detective Lemonis?"

He rubs a hand over his head. His face is that same blank he always wears. A uniform, of sorts.

"I think so," he says. "When do you expect *Kyrios* Boutos home? I have questions."

Now his face speaks: so many questions.

"Who knows? He comes and goes as he pleases. The way the wind does."

"What did he say?"

"The detective?"

"No. Him"

"You mean Hades?"

Not a word out of Stavros.

"You do mean Hades." Her bones creak as she settles them on the bed beside her only son. When did they start this—this complaining? Yesterday she was a young woman, today she is her own grandmother. Soon she'll be complaining non-stop about her feet and how they hurt. "He refused to speak to me. He wants more than I have to give."

"What does he want?"

"My boy ..."

"Mama."

She sighs, because Hades' demands are too great. "A life for a life."

"People die every day, Mama. Look at me. What am I if not dead?"

"What are you saying?"

"Lives, people, are disposable. If you take one, the world will deliver another to replace it in seconds."

"You cannot ask that of me, Stavros."

"Why not? Who else do I have?"

Helena is a sponge, soaking up her son's poison. He is the doll, yet here she is dancing to a tune only she hears.

Take a life, Mama. Do it for me. It's the only way to bring me back and we both know it. For the right price, Hades is merciful. But you must walk carefully. Take your time—I can wait until you have the right ... sacrifice. It's not easy, I know, but nothing worth having comes easy.

No. She can't kill someone.

No? Whose mother are you?

He stands, leaves her sitting on the bed's cold edge alone. He's done with her, repulsed by her cowardice. Whose mother is she?

A life for a life.

She has only one life to give: her own.

❧ 44 ❧
LEO

L eo makes a date. Not for love, but for paperwork. Kiki's house after lunch.

"You know where I live—right?"

Is she mocking him? God, he hopes she's mocking him; he likes a woman who can give him hell.

"I don't know. So many women ... You know how it is. I'm a busy man."

She laughs. It's a beautiful sight, a beautiful sound. "After lunch. And I'm not responsible for anything my mother or grandmother say."

He remembers the old woman—and her questions. "Is your mother anything like your grandmother?"

"No." It's a wicked smile she gives him. "Mama is a very different kind of worse."

45

KIKI

"I'm not saying anything," Vivi says, contradicting herself.

"When I was a teenager, I shoved my finger up Leo's ass."

Blink, blink. "Oh wow. Okay, consider yourself a prisoner in this house until you tell me everything."

Kiki tells Vivi the *Spin the Bottle* story. By the time she finishes, Vivi is facedown on the table, crying.

"That's the funniest thing I've ever heard," she wails. Which triggers a fresh torrent of laughter and tears.

Kiki can't help joining in. Laughter—the good kind—has a transmission rate any self-respecting virus would envy. It leaps from person to person, until it hits a sour puss.

"I thought it was his vagina," she says in her own defense.

Vivi's panting and crying on the floor when her daughter walks in.

"Guess what?" Melissa's bright, excited as she looks from woman to woman. "The police station's on fire."

THEY TAKE VIVI'S CAR. HER IDEA.

"I've never been to a fire before. For the record," Vivi says, "I've never felt more Greek than I do right now."

Half the town is watching. Great show. All that fire, licking the building, licking the air. That counter? Mine. That filing cabinet? Mine. Flames and water chase each other up the hall, into the offices. All that hissing, sounds like a hundred cats stuck in a room with a couple of two-year-olds.

Kiki says, "My Virgin Mary!"

Translation: *Oh my God, this is my fault! It was that gift. It had to be. It was some kind of incendiary device, and now the police station's on fire. They're going to throw me in jail. If not for murder, then for arson. Argh!*

Firefighters are trying to keep everyone in the safe zone, but how can people see if they stand too far back? A handful of old men have worked their way to the front of the crowd. They're barking orders at the firefighters, telling them exactly how they'd put that fire out—if their feet didn't hurt and their children were respectful.

Detective Lemonis is standing off to one side, looking pissed off at the world.

Kiki acts invisible. Which is easy when there's a fire. Unless you're the one burning, no one cares.

"I'm going home, okay?"

"You want a ride?" Vivi asks.

Kiki shakes her head. "Stay, watch. If anything super-exciting happens, call me."

"Hey, Kiki?"

"Yeah?"

Big grin. Huge. "Keep your fingers to yourself."

"I hate you," Kiki says, but she's laughing as she says it.

❧ 46 ☙
LEO

On time. Leo's good at showing up exactly when he means to.

He lets himself into the jungle, looks side to side for grandmother-shaped trouble. Fifteen years ago he would have stood at the gate and hollered Kiki's name until she showed, but living in the US taught him all about walking up to the door and knocking.

"Who are you?"

Kiki and Soula's mother. Easy to see where the women got their looks. She's put together, too dressed up to be sweeping the yard.

Yeah, he should have taken the time to check for mother-shaped trouble, too.

"Hello, *Kyria* Andreou." He tells her his name, tells her why he's there.

She looks him up, down, up. "Leonidas Karas, eh? First you have sex with one of my daughters, and now you are back for the other one? Who is next? My mother?"

"At last!" Kiki's grandmother appears through the screen door. "It only took you fifty-five years, but you finally had one good idea."

Kyria Andreou shakes the broom. "Shut up, old woman."

"Leo!

He looks up to see salvation waving at him from her second-floor balcony.

But Kiki's grandmother isn't done with him yet. "Did Kiki tell you she burned down the police station?"

"Enough, Mama," Margarita Andreou says, expression on her face like this is just another day in the madhouse.

"No. I say when it is enough."

Leo butts in. "The police station burned down?"

"Not all the way down," the grandmother says. "Just part way. It is a good thing Greece builds things strong."

"And Kiki burned it down ... how?"

"With the bomb, of course. It is a good thing she gave it to them and it was not us who burned."

❧ 47 ❧
KIKI

I f Leo's wearing anything other than a smile, it's hard to tell. That's how big it is.

The smile, not ...

(Whatever her grandmother's got, it's catching.)

"Oh God." Kiki closes her eyes. "They told you I burned down the police station, didn't they?"

"They might have."

"I'm going to jail," she says, "so we better get this done fast."

She brings out all the usual suspects: *frappe*, tiny cakes wrapped in plastic. Onto the dining room table they go. It's good to put something on this table. It looked naked without the wedding gifts. Now it could be any table in any house, one where the people who live there are normal, their lives murder and fire-free.

Leo looks good in her house. He moves easily. He's tall, broadshouldered, but he's not one of those guys who sucks up all the air. He gives her room to breathe.

"Did you burn it down?"

"Not on purpose, if I did."

"Look on the bright side: they can't toss you in jail if there's no jail."

Leo Karas is an optimist. What she thinks is that if they believe she's to blame for the fire, they'll just find another jail to put her in.

That's how the world works.

"Sit. Eat," she tells him.

"Why do Greeks feed everyone?"

Good question. "You're Greek—don't you know?" Headshake. He's wandering around her living room, touching everything with his eyes. They linger when he gets to the photo of her and Stavros, then bounce away to inspect her books.

"Half-Greek. Tell me," he says lightly.

"It's a cunning trick. If we feed you, give you coffee, then you're more receptive to answering questions."

"So it's like a truth serum?"

She laughs. "How many people answer questions honestly? It's more like a social lubricant."

Back to the photograph of Stavros, with her trapped in his arms. Forever. "What is it like when someone you love dies?"

On the outside, his question is casual, soft. But the comfortable cotton is wrapped around something sharper.

"It's everything you fear—and more."

His back is to her, and she's glad. This way he can't see the lie. Kiki is sorry—so sorry—Stavros is dead, but it was not the worst moment of her life. That will come when, one day, she loses the man she loves. But Stavros never was that man, and never will be.

"I'm sorry for your loss."

"Thanks." She slides into the dining room chair, nods to the papers. "May I?"

"That's why I'm here." He takes the other chair, the one to her left. Good choice. With the blinds open you can see the horizon stitched to the gulf. It's a snippet of the view from the Holy Mother, but it's a beautiful one. But she doesn't have time to enjoy the water, and from the looks of him, neither does Leo.

"Most of this," she says, leafing through the pages, "is repetition. The same questions, the same information, over and over. I think they do it so they don't have to spend money on photocopies and computers." She looks up into his smile. "Very sensible, the Greek government."

That smile breaks down into laughter. "Thrifty."

Now she's laughing, too, because if there's one thing the Greek government is, it's bad with money. And now the whole world knows it.

"Okay. They're asking for proof to go with your reason for wanting to bail out of your national service. Do you have proof?"

"I can get it. I'll call home later. Do you know where there's a fax machine around here?"

"Fax machine? Can't someone email it to you?"

"If we were talking modern people, yeah, they could. But these are my parents. They've barely got a grip on how their DVD player works. My mother can't even figure out how to schedule a show on DVR. And my brother ... he's just a kid. Last thing I want to do is put more on his shoulders."

"It could be worse. We don't even have cable here. And my mother thinks the Internet is a shop that sells porn. Lucky for you, I know where there's a fax machine. When you're ready, I'll take you there."

He rubs his head. His jaw stays hard, but his eyes are warm.

"How do I thank you?"

"Help someone who needs it, when the time comes."

"I can do that," he says.

She doesn't look up at him; she doesn't want to get lost.

"Good."

BY MID AFTERNOON, SHE KNOWS TOO MUCH ABOUT LEO KARAS. And she knows nothing.

❧ 48 ❧
LEO

Leo feels like an asshole for letting Kiki do all the work. But what choice does he have? All those years in the US meant he never had a chance to learn the big Greek words adults use.

He's normally a giver of help, not a taker. So this doesn't sit all the right with him. Whether this all works out or not, he owes her—owes her big.

But what do you give a woman who's giving you a shot at saying goodbye before it's too late? What do you give a woman who lost love herself?

No idea.

"What are you doing tonight?" he asks.

49

KIKI

"Why?"

The next words out of his mouth are about how he wants to take her out to dinner. As far as ideas go, it's a sweet one. But she can't accept.

"Why not? You've got to eat, and so do I."

"You've been away too long, and you've forgotten the way things are here. If we go out—it doesn't matter that it's a platonic thing—people will think it's a date. The same people who think I killed Stavros. It won't just be bad for me, but you also. And your family. A bad reputation smears everything, and everyone, it touches."

"Is that how it is for you?"

"That fight I got into last night with the Romani woman? Soula and I went to the promenade, but I had to leave because somebody spat on me. And before that, they were looking and talking. And they weren't doing it quietly. The smallest minds in town are attached to the biggest mouths."

Leo gets up. Vanishes into her kitchen. She hears the refrigerator creak open.

A moment later he's back.

"Are you hungry?" she asks.

"No. I just wanted to see if you're vegetarian or not."

"Why?"

"Because I'm taking you our tonight, Kiki Andreou—gossip or no gossip. But I'm not a madman or an asshole. I don't care about my reputation, but I want to protect yours. So we'll go somewhere that isn't here. And I'm cooking."

50

HELENA

Stavros stays home. His choice.

"I won't be too long," Helena says. "I promise."

He doesn't care about her promises.

When did he become so cold? Her son was always a warm boy, a happy boy. Even as a baby he was sweet-tempered. Now he is as sullen as his father. The two of them watch her from the corners of their eyes, measuring her moods and sanity.

Both men are waiting for her to act out a play of their choosing.

She doesn't want to leave the house, but she must. Outside her gate, everyone looks. And like her husband and son, they pretend not to. They wave and smile as if she is not a strange thing moving amongst them.

In the meat shop, carcasses dangle from arm-sized hooks. Whole sheep and pigs swing in the breeze. Behind the counter, the *kreopolis* slams his cleaver between the bones of a lamb. Between whacks, he shoves hair out of his eyes with the back of his hand. He's a small man who seems too delicate to swing a cleaver. Yet, every fall of the blade is heavy and true.

For a moment, she imagines kneeling at the wooden block, resting her head on the smooth maple. After the blade's fall, how long would it be before her head registered the loss of its body?

How long will it take if she fulfills her promise to her son.

Those bloodless bodies sway ...

Gelid thread binds her mouth. When the *kreopolis* greets her, all she can do is shake her head and bolt out into the hot glare of the sun.

"*Kyria* Bouto? Are you okay?" someone asks. She doesn't know who; they are just a voice to her.

She's standing in the middle of the street, mesh bag dangling from one hand.

"Of course I am all right."

SHE PULLS THE TELEPHONE INTO THE BATHROOM WITH HER. DIALS the number on the card that lives in a secret corner of her handbag. She keeps it there where her son will not find it.

"Help me," she says. "Please."

51

LEO

The cupboard is bare, so Leo goes shopping. None of this supermarket business—two different shops.

Tomatoes. Lettuce. Bacon.

BLTs. Not very Greek, but very American.

All he's missing is the bread. Thing is, the bakery (well, three of them now) are locked up tight. He's starting to get the feeling bread is a morning-only thing. Makes sense when the main meal of the day is lunch.

"I need bread," he says to no one in particular. Two women scurry past the madman talking to himself. He goes into the dust shop—uh, market—where he bought the file, pokes his head in the door.

"Do you sell bread?"

A different person at the lone checkout this time. The old man looks like someone crumpled him in their filthy hand.

"Does this look like a bakery?"

Leo glances around. "No."

"Then why would we sell bread?"

Crazy, Leo thinks. He must be crazy. What on earth would make him think a market sells bread. "Where can I get bread at this time of the day?"

"Volos. They are not so civilized there."

HE COULD BE A BOWLING PIN, THE WAY THE WOMAN KNOCKS HIM down. She's a tiny thing, but the way she moves, she's designed for football.

American football, not the kind with the black and white ball.

Leo hasn't played soccer in years. Not since the last time he and Greece danced. For a while, after his family moved, he clicked from sports channel to sports channel, looking for soccer matches, but friends and sports bars made an American football fan out of him.

The middle-aged woman's fight was for nothing—the bus is three-quarters empty. But she found herself a good seat up front, near the exit door. Now she's glaring at him, face sullen and creased and begging for whatever it is women slap on their faces these days to keep their skin soft. He smiles, flips her a wave, drops his coins into the conductor's hand.

Then he sits at the back of the bus. Leo Karas: rebel.

Never really a bad boy, but he knows he looks like one.

A bad boy wouldn't be riding the bus into the city. And he wouldn't be riding that bus to buy bread for a woman's sandwiches. Especially not a woman who isn't his.

Truth is, he'd like to take Kiki on a real date, but she lost the man she loved, and there's no time for him to wait. Couple of days from now, he's either going home or going to jail. The dating options are dismal behind bars, and Leo's not a man who switches teams. And he's not about to do the long-distance thing.

So he's doing this. Making sandwiches. Taking her to a gossip-free zone.

Best case scenario, he'll convey his gratitude, and have fun looking at a beautiful woman while he's doing it.

Who knows, maybe they'll wind up friends, lobbing emails at each other across the globe. *Facebook* friends, scrolling past updates.

There are worse things than making friends.

The bus bumps in to Volos. He gets off and the rock-faced woman stays.

VOLOS IS A SMALL BIG CITY. FEWER THAN TWO-HUNDRED-THOUSAND people. It's the newest of the port cities and number three when it comes to commercial traffic.

There's some debate over how the city scored its name.

It's been called Golos by some historian in the 14th century.

(In the Michael Bay world, winners go home and fuck the prom queen, but in reality they go home and write historical non-fiction.)

And Folos after some rich local guy.

And Gkolos—

Never mind. Who can pronounce that last one, anyway?

The V was something the city picked up along the way. Nobody really knows how. None of us are that old, except maybe Larry King, and he's much too busy collecting ex-wives to divulge what he knows about history.

Volos sits at the foot of Mount Pelion, clutching its three rivers. And it's home to one of the biggest cement companies in the world.

For a good time, ask anyone.

SURE ENOUGH, VOLOS SELLS BREAD IN THE AFTERNOON. SOME uncivilized heathen sells him a loaf. She draws the line at slicing the thing, though. You want sliced bread? Go home, American.

GREEKS CUT THEIR BREAD AT THE TABLE IN ROUGH CHUNKS. THEN they pull each piece apart and use it to push food onto the fork.

In English-speaking countries, this is a called a knife. Except a knife is sharp and doesn't crumble.

If you go to Greece and ask for a knife with your meal, it's entirely possible they'll deport you. On the off chance they give you one, they'll lay it on the table. Not because you're the idiot asking for a knife instead of bread, but because handing someone a knife is bad luck.

Best thing to do is just sit up, shut up, and pretend your bread is a knife.

———

ON THE WAY HOME, HE STOPS AT THE OTHER KIND OF BAKERY, THE one that sells cakes and cookies. Sugar and salt are the matter and anti-matter of Greece. Sell them under one roof and the whole country might explode.

The sugar rush hits as soon as he walks in. They're having a sale on diabetes today. Leo wants to buy one of everything, but that's more boxes than he can carry.

He leans against the counter. The woman jumps to attention. Leo isn't just a customer, he's an attractive customer. And she's around about the age when marriage gets important.

For a moment, he considers asking if she knows Kiki, and if so, does she know what Kiki likes? But he's not going to make trouble for her. She's got enough of that.

The door opens and two women are swept inside by the heat. They remind him of chickens, the way they're chatting.

"All these cakes, I don't know where to start," he tells the woman behind the counter.

"What do you like?"

"Everything."

"Everything?"

His gaze dances from her eyes to her waist and up again. Nice. Pretty with her dark curls trapped in a barrette. If he was shopping for fun he might bite.

He smiles at her. Friendly, but not inviting. He's about to tell her he likes chocolate when the other two women slice into the conversation gap.

"... And she teaches children. A murderer! What next?"

"They will have to find a new English teacher before school starts."

Leo turns slowly. He looks them up and down, but there's no appreciation in the move, only disdain.

They're too busy yapping to notice.

"Give me two of everything on the top row." He nods to the middle cabinet with its tiny cakes and pastries. The other cabinets are filled with messier Greek desserts: the syrupy *baklava* and its cousin *kataifi; Loukomades*, fried sweet balls drowning in syrup (there's a trend here); *finikia* (semolina cookies, also swimming in syrup); *kourabiethes* (a shortbread cookie smothered in confectioner's sugar); *koulouraki*, one of the few Greek sweets that isn't overly sweet; and short mountains of *loukoumi*, in a half dozen flavors, including the omnipresent rose and pistachio. Greeks, he thinks, would have a collective heart attack if they knew Americans call *loukoumi* Turkish Delight. It's the kind of thing that starts minor wars. Greece and Turkey are always looking for an excuse to arm wrestle across the Aegean Sea.

The woman's hands move quickly as she builds a cardboard box, but her gaze keeps flicking up to the other women. It's obvious she wants to jump in, but who wants to lose a customer?

On and on they gossip, mouths outrunning their brains. Kiki's sins are confetti, and the women are flinging handfuls all around the shop.

What's a guy to do when a good woman isn't here to defend herself? They're pissing him off, talking about Kiki like she's not a person.

So yeah, he jumps in. Both feet.

"Word on the street is that Stavros Boutos was screwing a lot of women on the side. Maybe one of them killed him—not his fiancée."

The conversation doesn't lie down and die—it runs off a cliff. There's no death rattle, no gasping, no begging God for a window seat in heaven. Only silence. Because those two gossipmongers haven't thought up a Plan B. They're too busy renovating Plan A, building new sins on top of Kiki's old ones.

Finally, one of the gaping fish says, in a voice straight out of a freezing January morning in Alaska, "Who are you?"

"Leonidas," he tells them. "Leonidas Karas. And if you want to gossip about me, go ahead. I'll give you a list of all the bad things I've done. And I'll throw in a list of the bad things people think I've done. And man, it's a long, long list."

"It's true," the saleswoman says. "Stavros had many women on the side." The women look at her. She holds up her hands. "Not me! But I can think of at least three names."

"Who?"

She wags her finger. "No. I will not tell you anything. But the police will not be looking at Kiki for long if they are smart."

Leo nods his thanks. Then he and his cakes are out of there.

52

HELENA

"Stavros is not with you today?" Dr Triantafillou asks.

Helena shakes her head at the window. The woman trapped in glass mirrors the move. Who is the lesser woman—the reflection or the Helena made of blood and bone? Their fingers touch, and still she cannot say which of them is real.

"No. He does not know I came." To her ears, she sounds distant, absentminded. Barely here—or anywhere. "I had to sneak out."

"He won't let you go out alone?" The doctor's reflection speaks. Like its original, it's in yellow jeans and shirt tailored to be their perfect accompaniment. Her shoes are flat, but still she seems tall, endless. It's not the psychologist's body, it's her spirit that seems all-encompassing.

"No. I mean yes, he does not mind if I go out. But he does not like me coming here."

"Why do you think that is?"

"He thinks you want me to kill him."

"And you, Helena, what do you think?"

She and the mirrored woman both shake their heads. "I think he is already dead." Now she turns away from her other self. "But if that's true, why do I still see him? Why does he still speak to me?"

"Helena, what you and *Kyrios* Boutos are dealing with is a parent's very worst nightmare. There is nothing natural about outliving your children, and your mind knows it. So be gentle with yourself. It is okay to feel ..."

"Crazy?"

The doctor's smile is warm. "Not the best word, but yes. In time, sanity can come from what feels like insanity."

"How do you know?"

"Are you asking if I have experienced loss?"

Helena nods. "Yes. What are your qualifications?"

"I have lost, Helena. Not a child, but I have lost. And I know what it is to go temporarily mad."

"How did you make it through?"

"Who says I did?" Now Helena sees it, the sting in her eyes. "But every day I come here and I help people. Between my daughter and work, I find hope."

"You help people. That is good. Useful. I do not know how to help anyone."

"Start small. Try one little thing. You may find you like it. And if you help enough people, perhaps you will find some measure of peace. Not today or tomorrow, but in time."

53

KIKI

Black is the new black. Lucky, because black is all she's allowed to wear.

Kiki shimmies into a black dress. A different one. No heels for her tonight. She's aiming for comfort in flat sandals.

Also black.

Her underwear isn't black. It's the color of fire. It's not for Leo (this isn't a date—remember?), it's for her, in case she forgets she's alive. The dress is to remind everyone that Stavros is dead, so they can judge her behavior accordingly.

She goes downstairs to wait for Leo. From their yard they can see a good chunk of the street. People wander past, on their way to the promenade, to parties, to the places people go when they're not at home. In the evening, those whose plans involve staying home sit in their front yards, greeting this small piece of the world as it passes by. Being social without being sociable. Each new passerby throws a new spin on the conversation, once they're out of sight. Some nights her mother does crochet, other nights it's needlepoint. Most of the time *Yiayia* is in one of her comas, but lately she's been part of the sedate festivities. Tonight she's defacing magazines, drawing faces on top of faces. One of Greece's most popular actors has balls swinging from his forehead. Anna Vissi, mega pop star, is riding a broom.

Kiki doesn't do needlepoint or crochet, and she can't draw. So when she's out front she reads. Tonight, it's something post-apocalyptic, written in English.

The front yard is filled with questions.

"Where are you going?" Mama asks. "Who are you seeing?"

"Do you need money?" her father wants to know.

"I don't know. Leo. And no thank you, *Baba*. I have a job —remember?"

He's a good man, her father. Sturdy. Reliable. And he always asks if she needs money. Kiki hasn't needed her parents' money for years, but it's sweet that he still asks.

"Leo Karas with the big penis," *Yiayia* explains, in case anyone forgot.

"Jesus Christ," Kiki's father mutters into his newspaper.

"It's not a date. He's just thanking me for helping him today."

"Did you see his penis?" *Yiayia* wiggles her eyebrows, smacks her gums.

"No! I helped him with paperwork."

Yiayia elbows her son-in-law. "Paperwork."

Mama drops her needlepoint. Stamped onto the fabric is a picture of the goddess Athena clutching a shield and spear. "Enough! Every time you open your mouth, Mama, I feel like Hera. You are my Hephastus, so ugly that I want to throw you off Mount Olympus!"

Yiayia scoffs. "You are not Hera, you are the goat who raised Zeus. Every time you open your mouth, all I hear is 'maa-maa!' *Katsika*! You are the goat woman!"

Either her mother is too disgusted, or she hasn't conjured up a good comeback, because her attention swings back to Kiki. "Where are you going with this man?" she demands.

"I don't know."

Kiki shuts her eyes, shoots for that invisibility thing, but Mama's got her own magic. Doesn't matter what her daughters are doing and where, Mama has a way of knowing.

Not every mother is a god. Just the Greek ones. What they don't know, they think they know.

"She does not know!" her mother declares. "You agreed to go out with him and you do not know?"

"It's not a date."

"If you go out with a man, it is a date, unless he is your brother or cousin—"

"If it is a cousin it can still be a date," *Yiayia* chimes. "I went out with a cousin once. And your mother—"

"Ignore her," Mama continues. "If people see you, they will talk."

Is Mama high? Doesn't she listen? "They're already talking!"

"They will talk *more*." She punctuates with her needle. "And the things they will say will be worse—much worse. Already they think you killed Stavros, but if you go out with this Leo they will call you an adulterer, too. They will not see *thank-you*. All they will see is you with a man who is not your dead fiancé. Then what will you do, Kiki? When it gets back to Helena, what will you do, break her heart some more? Stavros's death and her belief that you killed her son have ruined my friendship. Helena and I have been friends since we were children. And now that is gone!"

"For once, your mother tells the truth," *Yiayia* says. "Listen carefully because it will not happen again."

"*Skasmos!*" Mama barks.

"So what, am I supposed to crawl into the grave alongside Stavros to prove devotion I never felt for him?"

"That would be a good start," Mama says, but it is too late now."

"Then tell me, what do I do now?"

"You go back upstairs and stay home." Stab, stab with the needle. "No men. No going out. You stay there until people forget or the police decide someone else killed Stavros. That is what you do."

Kiki deflates. A night out sounded like fun, but Mama pricked the balloon. Now she wants to go upstairs, climb into bed in her black dress, and sleep.

Baba lowers the newspaper. "Go," he says, "and have a good time. You have not had a good time in too long. Stavros is dead. Staying home will not bring him back and it will not make you happy. Just because he is dead, does not mean you have to live like you are dead, too."

"It is about respect!" Mama glares at her husband.

"Respect," he scoffs. "What respect do they show our daughter, eh? Everybody in town knows Stavros was a philanderer. How was that respectful to our daughter? And when people talked about his bad behavior, how were they respecting our daughter? That marriage was your idea, not mine."

Holy fatherly intervention, Batman! Kiki wants to cheer, but only a stupid person would jump into that volcano.

"But you loved Stavros!" Mama cries.

Baba scoffs at that. "I did not love him. And I did not love him for my Kiki. She deserves a much better kind of man."

A cobra rears back before it strikes, and so does Mama. When she lurches forward, it's with a single steel fang. She drives the needle into the thatched fabric.

When it comes to her husband, her protests are small. Why waste drama on the man, when she can save it for somebody who can be more easily crushed

"*Kalispera!*"

Leo.

Salvation and damnation in one. The man looks like the devil, but his eyes are soft, kind. Her eyes want to stare, but her common sense kicks their ass. Greece is filled with hot men, so Leo's nothing special, is he?

No.

If she had her way, she'd be dragging him down the street, away from the snake pit, but her father is already out of his chair, slapping Leo's back, shaking his hand.

"I know your father," he says. "Lefteris and I were in school together. We did terrible things when we were young."

"Of course you did," Mama mutters.

"How is your father, your family?"

"They're great," Leo says.

"Are they well?"

Anyone else notice the pause in his delivery, or just her?

"They're well."

"Tell your father I said hello, eh?"

Eyes focused on her needlepoint, Mama's voice gets ready to drill. "Where are you taking my daughter?"

"I'm taking Kiki on a picnic."

"At night? Who goes on a picnic at night?"

"Mama, enough," Kiki says. To Leo she says, "A picnic sounds great."

A picnic. The two of them alone.

Leo's brave going anywhere with her fingers.

❧ 54 ❧
LEO

Houses everywhere. Hulking, squatting behemoths where the church and its grounds used to sit.

Leo laughs, because what else can he do?

"Greece moved on without me."

"Did you think it would stay in stasis, and all of us along with it?"

"Have you ever seen Brigadoon?"

Kiki shakes her head. "No."

"A couple of American tourists in Scotland discover a village called Brigadoon. It's only there for one day every hundred years. In between, the village vanishes and its people sleep. Agria was my Brigadoon, until I got back."

"We haven't been sleeping. We've been living and loving and dying without you."

"I know." He flashes a smile at her. "So. I don't have a Plan B."

"Lucky for you all my plans are Bs. I know a place we can go."

55

KIKI

Good thing she's a resourceful woman—a resourceful woman with a key.

Arms loaded with two white boxes, a plastic bag looped around one wrist, Leo laughs. "The high school?"

"The high school."

"Is there going to be homework?"

Her turn to laugh. "Just get inside before someone sees us."

"Who's going to see us?"

Nobody, that's who. But Kiki is all kinds of paranoid. Which is why they're standing at the high school's back door. The double doors out front sit in plain sight of two residential streets. But the school's backside butts up to nothing but trees, bushes, and a small dirt road that winds past an abandoned half-built house before spilling into an asphalt artery.

"Around here, you never know."

"Sounds like the NSA," he says.

"I don't know what that is, but it sounds Greek."

Inside there's nothing but silence. When she closes the door behind them, it's as if they're sealed off from the world and all its noise. She only knows this place filled with the constant tapping of soles on marble, the chatter of students as teachers flit from class to class, toting lesson plans and textbooks.

Empty, she and this building do not know each other.

Leo's reading her mind, because he says, "In American schools it's students who move from class to class, not the teachers."

"What was it like, leaving here, moving to America?"

He shrugs. "It was a long time ago."

Oh yeah, there's a story there. But what's it to her? Leo owes her nothing. She doesn't have a right to hear his stories, just because she helped him with some paperwork.

"That's the good thing about life," she says. "Even the bad stuff gets left behind, sooner or later. Do you want a tour? I know someone who can give you one."

"I can guarantee the only thing that's changed about this place is me."

"Come on, then."

She lifts one of the boxes out of his arms, heads for the marble stairs. When they reach the second floor, she leads the way down the hall to a smaller staircase hidden behind a metal door. Up the stairs, until they burst out into the dying light.

They're on the school's flat roof, along with the solar panels that keep its motor running.

The view from up here is really something. Laundry pinned to clotheslines on other, lower, roofs. An old man peeing against a wall. Two women, three children, rubbing corn off cobs in their front yard. After a few ears, Kiki knows your thumbs turn red and numb. Then your mind quits dishing out mercy, and the fire comes.

At one of the houses a party is full tilt. A man holding a handkerchief dances on his own, until he is joined by another. Soon the family has formed a dancing chain. They move with a fluid synchronicity— mostly. There's a wild beauty to the dance, and even the dancers with no rhythm don't detract from its charm.

(It's not often you meet a Greek with no rhythm, but once in a while, they happen. What they lack in skill they make up for with enthusiasm and comments about how the gods wish they were this talented.)

"Looks like fun," Leo says.

Does he mean it? She can't tell. "Nobody has more fun than Greeks. Just ask us." She smiles. "This is Greece—the real Greece. The view you see from Pelion's villages, that's the catalog copy. It's how we sell our country to tourists. But if you want to know Greece, here is where you come." She nods at the formerly pissing man who has turned his attention to shooting snot. "It's as ugly as it is beautiful."

Side by side, they lean against the school's top lip. Between them stands an invisible wall, a respectable wall. Kiki is glad it's there. Leo radiates something Kiki wants—needs—but he's temporary.

Oh look, there's a conclusion, and Kiki jumped right to it. Well done, she tells herself. For all she knows, the quiet hum of potential she feels is one-sided.

"I remember," Leo says. He turns his head just a fraction, enough for her to see his smile is meant for her. "Leaving here sucked at first. Greece was all I knew. Unless you count a few vacations to the states to see my mom's family. Everything got left behind. Most of our stuff. All my friends. But it didn't suck long. As soon as we got on the plane I decided it was an adventure. Not a tree-climbing, dirt-digging adventure. A real adventure, into an almost unknown place. Man, it was great!"

"Why did you come back?"

He laughs. "I wanted to join the army."

One eyebrow raised, she asks, "Really?"

"No. After my divorce, I figured I'd see Europe. And last time I checked, Greece is still in Europe."

"I'm sorry ..."

"I'm not. Tracy is a good woman, but we weren't a good match. I'm out of here tomorrow," Leo says. He looks down at her with those dark eyes. They're warning her that there are rough seas ahead. "Have to go to Athens and deliver those papers in person."

"I hope they approve your request."

"Thanks. I want to swing by and see you before I go."

"For that fax?"

"For that. And to say goodbye."

She moves on without him, but he follows as if they're tethered.

He leans over the lip, laughs at a pair of teenagers making out in the alcove below.

"Remember—" he starts.

"No."

"I didn't finish."

"You don't need to."

"So you do remember!"

"I was a kid."

"So was I."

"You looked like a man, even then."

"Man on the outside, kid on the inside. I was pretty though, wasn't I?"

"You were pretty," she admits. "Why are you in such a hurry to get home?" Way to change the subject, Kiki.

"Family stuff."

"You said that already."

The feverish teenagers below break their seal, glance up. Leo grabs Kiki, pulls her down with him so they're both crouching. For a moment, he's as silent as marble.

When he speaks, it's in a low voice riddled with hairline fractures. She's reminded of an ancient vase, trapped in a museum. "My mother's sick. The kind of sick that doesn't magically get better. I don't want to say my goodbyes over the phone."

Now is the perfect time for a woman to take a man's hand and swear a caring allegiance. But Leo is one small step up from a stranger. She has little to give him.

Except the truth as she knows it.

"Earlier you asked me what it's like when someone you love dies —remember?"

"Yeah, I remember."

"I lied," she continues. "The truth is I don't know."

He blows his breath out in one long stream. "You didn't love your fiancé?"

"No. And time wouldn't have changed that, I don't think. We knew each other since birth. That's plenty of time to fall in love, but it never happened. And after our childhood, we weren't even friends anymore. So I don't know what it's like. But I'm sorry that you *will* know."

She doesn't take his hand. But there's something about Leo, something that tells her a hand isn't everything to this man.

"LIKE IT?"

Full mouth, so she nods. When the food scoots down her throat she says, "What is it?" Because—Virgin Mary!—it's delicious. The bacon's crisp, the tomatoes sweet.

"BLT. Bacon, lettuce, tomato. It's an American thing."

She inspects the half-eaten sandwich. "It's so good I'm surprised we didn't invent it."

The sun's leaving, but Leo keeps her warm with his laugh. It feels good to be with him. It feels free.

A dangerous, tantalizing thought.

Leo says, "Greece: the birthplace of civilization and everything else."

"We do have kind of a complex."

"The expats are worse. We put Greece on a pedestal when we leave. No place is better, more wonderful. All the people are friendly, it's more beautiful than anywhere. The food is the best.

"What's wrong with that?" she says, deadpan. "It's all true."

"Shut up and eat the sandwich. I slaved in the kitchen for hours making that thing."

Now she's a puddle of laughter and tears. Her mascara runs for the border, but she catches it with the back of her hand, smears black across her cheek.

It doesn't matter. This isn't a date.

It's just two people sharing what she hopes will be a secret.

❧ 56 ❧

HELENA

H elena saw that ... *putana* Andreou woman with that man. Seducing another one the way she seduced her Stavros.

"She was cheating on him—I know it," she mutters.

Kristos lifts his head from the pillow. "Who?"

"Kiki! Who else?"

"Kiki was not unfaithful. She is a good girl."

"Then why was she with a man?"

"Maybe he was a friend. Why are you following the poor girl?"

"I know Kiki's friends. I know Kiki."

"Then you know she was not unfaithful to our son."

Betrayal wears many faces. Tonight, it wears her husband's.

"Maybe you are right," she says.

We will see.

57

A SMALL ASIDE

Helena's eyes are not the only ones watching Kiki Andreou live.

58
LEO

Morning moves sluggishly into Agria, dragging its peach and gold train. Leo and his grandfather are already out on the patio when the roosters start hollering at the sky.

"What does Laki have to say this morning?"

The old man taps the statue's head—the big one. "He says that *tsiganes* burned the police station."

"Did you tell them?"

"I called them. But did they listen? No. If that Detective Lemonis's father was still alive, he would believe me. But his son is a *kolos*."

Leo has never met the guy, so he can't judge if he's an ass or not.

"Kiki thinks they'll pin that on her, too."

Papou makes a small *tsst* sound. It's Greek shorthand for 'No.' "For that, no. But other things, yes. Good thing she is a strong girl. Being unhappy in love has tempered her. Everybody should be unhappy with love at least once in their lives."

"Were you unhappy?"

"No! I was too happy." He nods at the happy, happy statue. "Like Laki here."

"It's good *Yiayia* made you happy."

"Your grandmother, Kiki's grandmother, a lot of grandmothers—

even a few great-grandmothers. A lot of women contributed to my happiness. Your grandmother was the last and the longest."

Leo laughs. *You go, old man*, he thinks.

"When will you come back?" *Papou* asks. "It is good to have you here. The rest of the family, they drive me crazy. But not you."

"Doesn't Laki know?"

"No. He prefers to tell me about women."

"I don't know," Leo says. "I don't know how long—"

How long it will be before Mom dies.

How long it will be before it's okay to leave Dad and Soc.

"I still have a business to run," he continues.

"You could run it here. Agria needs a good veterinarian. We have one, but he is also a doctor. Always he wants to put the thermometer ..." He mimes shoving something up his butt.

"I have a life back there." Yeah, he says it, but even he can hear his words are pliable tin, not steel.

"Work is not a life."

"It is when you've got nothing else."

Silence.

Time drags its legs around the clock.

"Let's go, eh?" The old man slaps the table, two-handed. "You do not want to miss your bus."

"I have to see Kiki first. She's got a fax for me."

Papou's gold teeth flash in the sun. "Is that what you call it?"

❧ 59 ❧

KIKI

K iki can't help reading the fax. Not because she's Greek, and therefore terminally curious, but because she's human. It's not as though she had to steam open an envelope. The school's machine burped the whole thing out in flat, readable pages.

Leo's mother has cancer, and she's going fast.

Now she feels like an unclean thing that has tainted something sacred. She shouldn't have looked. This is Leo's business, not hers.

She slides the papers into a yellow envelope, unfolds the metal butterfly wings to seal it (temporarily) shut.

This morning, the school feels even more empty than last night. Turning in a slow circle in the atrium, she wonders if she'll be here when this great white lung draws its first September breath. What's she going to do if that call from the principal comes, and he tells her that Kyriaki Andreou is no longer the school's English teacher? Teaching is all she has ever wanted to do. Where do teachers go when they're no longer teaching?

Who knows? Maybe they'll put her in a temporary pasture, where she'll stay, bored and useless, until the detective wipes a damp sponge over her name. But even then, when life returns to a new sort of normal, she'll be a *remember-when?* until it's her turn to take a permanent, underground leave of absence.

Okay, so she'll be a *remember-when?* after she's dead, too. But death has a way of keeping a person too busy to care.

The sun greets her on the other side of the door with a slap. It's the school bully, striking out at her because she's in black—and who wears black in summer? Freak.

Not much she can do except live through it. It's not like she can shoot Helios out of the sky. He's had his own problems in the past, what with his son stealing his chariot and crashing it into the earth and setting the whole place on fire. So if he's harsh ... Eh, who wouldn't be?

The putt-putt of a moped follows her up the street. Already, she knows it by heart. Sure enough, it's Leo with his grandfather perched on back.

They stop beside her.

"Oh my God," she says. "You brought your grandfather."

"Why does she say it like that?" Socrates Karas looks at his grandson. "What is wrong with me, eh?"

Leo's grinning. He pats his grandfather on the shoulder. "It's the statue, old man."

"It's the statue," Kiki agrees. Because he'd be at least fifty-percent less strange without the thing. The remainder of the strangeness is self-made.

"Poor Laki. And after all he does for you." The old man winks at her.

She gives Leo the envelope. "I looked. Sorry."

"Don't be."

He traps her gaze. She can't look away, though her heart is demanding she turn and run. It's not so bad defying her internal organs; her eyes like him, and her head likes him, too. He's a good man. Too bad he's leaving. They might have been something.

"Goodbye, Kiki Andreou. Good luck."

She offers her hand. He takes that hand, and with it, a piece of her heart.

"Goodbye, Leo Karas. Good luck and Godspeed."

✤ 60 ✤
LEO

H e has to reach, but *Papou* slaps him around the ear.
      "A woman looks at you like that, you kiss her."
"Maybe I didn't want to kiss her."

"Why not? Are you a *pousti* or just a *vlakas*? She is beautiful and also allegedly dangerous. What is more attractive than beauty and danger? Nothing!"

"I've kissed a lot of women," Leo says. "And they liked it. And most of the time, after they liked it, I forgot them. But something tells me Kiki Andreou isn't a woman you kiss and forget."

"That is wonderful! Every man needs one woman he can't forget."

"Not when she's thousands of miles away."

"Especially then," his grandfather says, waving Laki for emphasis. "That way she cannot cause trouble."

KIKI WON'T GET OUT OF HIS HEAD.

It's starting to feel like he's spent half his life saying goodbye to Greece in a rearview mirror. First time he didn't care so much.

Nothing but adventures ahead. And Agria was a small place that looked even smaller in retrospect.

But this time when he turns in his seat at the back of the bus to look, his world is filled with the place.

And Kiki as he remembers her.

In that black sundress.

In those short shorts and that top with the barely-there straps.

Naked, leaping out of bed that night with Soula.

He wants to throw her down on the floor and fuck her until his name is the only word she remembers.

Jesus, Karas. Take a chill pill. She's one woman in a world filled with women.

But he's been around a lot, and he's never met a Kiki until now.

He almost wishes he could stay and find out what she looks like on her knees.

But fate has other plans for Leo Karas. It's the bus for him, or a lifetime of regret. Maybe he can say hello again to Kiki someday, but when it comes to his mom, he's only got one shot at saying goodbye.

KIKI

There's a sudden void in her world, and Kiki means to shovel something into it.

'Something' being Vivi's paperwork.

"Where are you going now?"

Margarita is a spider and this yard is her web. And Kiki, in this cruel documentary, is the fly.

"To see Vivi—remember?"

Her mother makes a dissatisfied noise as she sweeps. "Better if you stay at home."

And do what—rot? "*Yia sou*, Mama." She trots toward the gate, but suddenly Mama is in front of her with her broom.

Like God, Mama is everywhere.

"Stop right there. If you have to go out, fetch water first."

Big, fake groan. She doesn't really mind staggering home with two giant water bottles, each of them shifting and sloshing their load. But it's fun to gripe the way she did when she was a girl.

Mama has the uncanny knack of poking her inner twelve-year-old.

It's nearing midday, and the sun is ramping up for the big shine. The walk to the water fountain is a light one. The maroon bottles bump against her legs, but it's no hardship.

Not too many nights ago, she and Soula sparred with the Romani near this very water fountain. It's little more than a faucet trapped in marble—not really a fountain at all—on the edge of a tiny triangle of trees. The shade they provide is negligible, but it's better than a punch in the teeth. Kiki waits her turn; ahead of her are a pair of boys, somewhere between six and nine.

When they see her, their eyes go wide and wild. Their elbows smash together, each of them frantically pointing her out to the other. Then the little one steps forward with a question.

"Hey lady, is it true you killed someone?"

Laugh or cry? Cry or laugh?

Laugh. They're kids and they're cute. "Not even a little bit true."

Their small shoulders slump.

"That's too bad," the bigger boy says. "We were going to ask you what it's like."

"To kill someone?"

It's a wonder their heads don't fall off, the way they nod.

Kids. She can't even be mad; curiosity goes with the territory.

"Well, I don't know what it's like. But I bet it's awful."

"Why?"

"Because it's forever," she says. "When somebody dies, they never come back. There's no magic REWIND button. So by the time you realize you did something very wrong, it's too late."

"Zombies come back."

The older boy pokes the little one. "Zombies aren't real."

"Hey lady, are zombies real?"

"I hope not. Because they're kind of ugly. I bet they smell horrible, too."

"Like rotten meat? The kind with maggots?"

"Exactly like that."

They drift away from the faucet, so she shoves the first bottle into place, turns the water on.

"Hey lady?"

"Yes?"

"We're friends now, which means you can't kill us, okay?"

"I promise," she swears.

Then they're gone.
When the bottles are full, she hurries home, head up.
Facing the world.

✺ 62 ✺

LEO

A man can do a lot of thinking in five hours. His mind can travel a lot of roads.

His cock's been hard a dozen times between Agria and Athens. The trigger is always Kiki.

But she's not the only thing on his mind.

Leo's been making plans. First, the Ministry of National Defense. Then he's going to hole up in a hotel for the night, or however long it takes for the Ministry to stamp his papers and hand over his passport.

Then the airport.

Maybe he'll go out after he checks in, find a decent bar where the drinks are cold and the women are sociable. Rinse the memory of Kiki away.

Thing is, Leo knows he can come back. Back to Agria and Kiki. Coming back isn't the problem.

It's the why of the whole thing stopping him.

If he comes back it's because Mom's dead.

His head won't go there. If he makes plans to come back he's making plans for her death.

Leo is a man who plans for life.

✥ 63 ✥

HELENA

In the bed beside her, the enemy sleeps.

How can he?

Maybe it is because he does not know the things she knows.

That must be it. The alternative is unthinkable.

Helena eases out of the bed. This summer, she has mastered the art of stealth. She moves through life without touching anything—including people. She finds if she feigns normality, then nobody will see her. Strangeness is what draws attention. If you want to be invisible, be a sheep, moving from pasture to pasture, along with all the other sheep.

Quietly, quietly, down the hall, into the kitchen.

"Where are you going?"

Stavros has caught her once again. Every night, the same thing.

Always clever, her son.

"Nowhere."

In the dark kitchen his outline is still. "Somewhere, I think."

"It's not important."

"Then why go?"

Helena wraps the black robe around herself. Never a big woman to begin with, she is diminishing. The tie on the robe and the looseness of the cotton tell her so.

"One day you will have children, then you will know."

"Dead men don't make children, Mama."

She crosses the kitchen in two steps, slaps his face so hard he falls on the floor.

"Don't you say that," she says, her voice a husky whisper. "Don't you ever say that again."

"Why not? It's true."

"Just because something is true, does not mean we should believe it!"

Then she's alone in the kitchen, heart beating her throat with its fists, skin frozen yet covered in a light sheen of sweat.

Stavros is gone, back to bed with the red tattoo of her hand on his face.

Helena opens the front door. The night grabs her; they have plans.

THE STREETLIGHT KEEPS HER SECRET; IT'S TOO DIM TO SPEAK UP. And wrapped in black, who would see her anyway? She is a shadow.

The three-layered Andreou house sits in darkness. The doors are unlocked, she knows. The windows, too. Cool night air gently blows the heat away.

Air conditioning is not for the Greek people, only the largest of their city shops and office buildings. Everyone else is used to the heat. What else have they known? All their lives they and the heat have lived side by side. Spend your days and nights in refrigerated air and you will wilt in the outside world. That false spring makes a person weak.

Helena eases though the gate soundlessly. A million times she's pushed and pulled the metal frame, so she knows how to hold its tongue.

Through the yard, clinging closely to its sides, then up the concrete steps to the second floor. There is a small, open stairwell here, and Kiki has made it beautiful with flowers.

Yes, the door with its decorative glass arch is unlocked. With splayed fingers she presses her hand to the wood. But it is only a touch, not a suggestion. The door stays shut.

Kiki is behind this door, in her room, sleeping.

And somewhere out there is the one who killed Stavros.

Helena remembers that now. The knowledge comes and goes as it pleases. From one minute to the next, she does not know which is truth and which is a lie. But in this moment she is certain he is dead, and that Kiki would never have killed him. That will change again, soon.

But for now she sits in the stairwell, wrapped in her black, cotton robe. There she waits, a faithful hound, watching over her dead son's fiancée. They did not love each other, but she loves them both.

For this moment.

What a disaster she is.

"WHY DO YOU GO?"

Helena says, "I don't know."

"I think to help her. To protect her, maybe?"

"From what? Who is she that she needs protection?"

"It's just a thought."

A ridiculous thought.

Dr Triantafillou uncrosses her legs, swings them the other way. Normally the woman is perfection, but today there's a tightness around her eyes.

"How is your daughter?"

The psychologist smiles. "Beautiful. She is a beautiful monster."

"Are you eating properly?"

Now the younger woman laughs. "Yes, I'm eating fine. When I have time. There is not always time.

"Mothers. We take such terrible care of ourselves."

"How is your appetite, Helena?"

"What appetite?"

"You've lost weight."

"I have lost more than weight, yes?"

"Would you like to talk about what you've lost?"

Helena shakes her head. Her hands stay knotted in her lap. "It is unhealthy to dwell on what is lost."

"It's unhealthy to live in that place, yes. But sometimes you must speak about it to put it in its correct place, so that you can move on."

"When you lose a child, you never move on. You stay there forever with them, so they are never alone."

"So they're not alone, or so that you are not alone?"

Her nails bite into the thick skins of her palms. "What is the difference?"

✿ 64 ✿
LEO

A thens. Now there's a city that's seen a lot of churn. Athenians have been to war a lot—with themselves and others.

The glorious city sits in a bowl and brews its city-made smog. Above it all, the Parthenon hunkers on the Acropolis.

Acropolis is just the Greek way of saying "edge of the city." Which it was—once. Today, Athens is a mishmash of architectural styles, classical and modern, Greek and foreign.

The building Leo needs is concrete, cut in a severe rectangle. Very sixties. The Public Enquiries office is filled with statues—behind the counters and in orange plastic rows in the waiting area. Leo isn't a man who does interior decorating, but if ennui was a color, this dull green on the walls would be it. This is where hope falls on its own sword. He takes a number, sits and becomes one of them, until the red number on the screen matches the number the machine spat into his hand.

Bag slung over his shoulder, packet of papers in hand, he goes to the designated counter. It's standing room only on his side.

On the side of the counter with the chair, there's a coat hanger wearing a horseshoe mustache. He doesn't look like a man who knows happy. He barks his greeting, holds out his hand. The plaque sitting askew on the counter says his name is Yiannis Papadopoulos.

Leo hands Yiannis Papadopoulos the stack. Mustache guy flips through them, facial expression never breaking bored.

"You are on leave?"

"Until tomorrow."

"Okay. Leave these with me and we will contact you."

"When?"

"Eh ..." He looks up at the wall. Nothing there but a portrait of the current Prime Minister and his buddy, the Greek President. "Six weeks. Maybe four. Maybe eight."

"Maybe today?"

"Ha-ha-ha!" Yiannis Papadopoulos rolls his chair backward. "Hey," he says to his cohorts, "this man thinks we can process his paperwork today." Lots of laughter. Best joke they've ever heard. He rolls back into place. "No." Deadpan.

"I have to get back to the states immediately."

"Immediately, in your case, is nine weeks."

"You said maybe four."

"That was before I realized you are a comedian. For comedians it is at least nine weeks."

Leo leans forward, both palms flat on the counter. For the other guy this is business, but for him it's as personal as personal gets. "My mother is dying. I have to be there."

"Do you have proof?"

He's losing patience—fast. "There." He singles out the faxed pages from Mom's doctors. Yiannis plucks it off the pile.

"This?"

"Yes, that."

The man dangles them between his fingertips. "I don't know what this is. What I know is that it is not Greek. It could say anything. For all I know, it is your grandmother's shopping list. You are not the first foreigner to deny your obligations."

Leo wants to hurt the man—with fists and fire.

"I had no problem with staying until I found out my mother is dying!"

"Do not shout. We are having a nice conversation, yes? So why shout?"

The tectonic plates in Leo's jaw shift and grind. "Just tell me: What do I have to get home tomorrow?"

"Can you swim?"

"Yes, of course."

"Then that is what you must do. You cannot leave Greece legally until we have processed this. In the meantime, report for duty tomorrow, or they will be coming for you."

❧ 65 ❧

KIKI

W hat was it? One day? Two? Not long, but now there is a gap in her world.

Kiki wonders if Leo made it to Athens safely, if he took his papers to the Ministry of National Defense, if they rained stamps of forgiveness on those papers.

With luck he is on his way home, where his family needs him to be.

To miss him is to be selfish.

Isn't it?

"YOU LIKE HIM."

Two sisters in the dark, side by side on Soula's couch, feet on the coffee table. In the background, Anna Vissi is singing that 80s song about midnight.

"Of course I like him. He's a good guy."

"That is not what I meant."

"I know. Just let me pretend it was, okay?"

"Okay." Soula nudges her sister's leg with her shoe. "It doesn't have to be like this. You don't have to stay in mourning. Why don't you take that honeymoon, maybe meet a Frenchman and fall temporarily in love?"

"I don't want temporary."

"Relationships are all temporary. Even relationships with family. Someone dies, and—*kaput*! What is that if it is not temporary?"

Kiki looks at her sister. Soula is a shadow of a woman in the darkness.

"It's not like you to be so pessimistic. Are you okay?"

"I am a realist, that is all. Name one great love in history that survived."

Kiki thinks. It takes a while. Every candidate is quickly knocked down by divorce or death.

"You can't think of one, can you?" Time stretches. Soula stares into the darkness. "Me either."

"Are you in love with someone, Soula?"

Soula laughs. "When have I ever fallen in love?"

Never … and every other week. Soula has only ever done love-lite, the commitment-free, limerence version of love, that withers as it ages, until she kicks it out of her bed.

"What's stopping you?"

"I am," Soula says.

Two floors down, somebody screams. *Yiayia*.

"Snakes," Kiki explains. "Mama put snakes in *Yiayia*'s bed."

"Again?"

"Mama is not a woman of great imagination."

"I am not like Mama," Soula says. "And I do not want you to be, either."

✸ 66 ✸
LEO

Leo phones home from a tired, old payphone, but nobody's answering. There's a cold rock sitting in his stomach as he dials his father's cell phone.

Nothing.

Smells like stale beer and *souvlaki* in this plexiglass stall. Nothing to eat in hours, and the stink only exacerbates his vague nausea. On the bright side, if he pukes, he won't be the first guy who puked in a phone booth.

Next, he calls his brother. Socrates is sixteen, which means he and his phone are conjoined. Sometimes they're attached at the ear, sometimes at the hand. You almost never see a phone in a teenager's pocket.

"Yeah?"

"Hey, Socrates." He pronounces it the Bill and Ted way: *so-crates.* "It's me."

"Leo?"

"Yeah. What's going on?"

"When are you coming back?"

"Soon."

"How soon?" A hint of panic in his recently deepened voice.

"Why? What's going on?"

That rock in his gut is turning to ice, and it's spreading. No more nausea. No more anything except that frozen water.

"Mom has pneumonia. They moved her to the ICU. Dad's with her."

That explains Dad not answering his phone. ICU means no cell phone.

"Where are you?"

"At home. We had a gig tonight, but I bailed."

His brother is in a band. Guitar. It's a high school thing, but the kids are good. They play a lot of parties.

"Are you okay?"

"What do you think?"

Leo thinks his brother is anything but okay, but boys are men waiting to happen. After a certain age, tears aren't something they make unless the wall breaks down. Leo knows about the wall—he has a strong, tall one of his own. Even Tracy couldn't put her fist through that sucker.

"Leo, you have to come home."

"I know. I'm trying. I have to go—okay? I'll call again later, I promise."

Soc doesn't say anything, but Leo hears the nod anyway.

"I love you," Leo says. "Tell Mom and Dad I love them, too."

"Yeah." His brother's voice crackles. "Okay."

HE WANTS TO PUNCH A WALL. NOT JUST ONE WALL—ALL THE WALLS.

Starting with the Parthenon. Maybe if he punches a few ancient statues in the face, the gods will come down from Mount Olympus. Then he can swap his liver or his soul for a ride home.

He doesn't punch a wall.

He doesn't punch anything.

Because the man part of his brain knows what the animal part doesn't: punching leads to cops. Leo doesn't want to be a signal on their radar. He needs to go invisible.

He checks into a hotel, but only for the one night. Cash. Today he's on leave, but tomorrow he'll be a wanted man. Doesn't seem smart to wave his credit card and say, "Here I am!"

Once he's back on base they'll have him so hogtied there won't be time to chase his paperwork. And chances are good they won't let him know there's a phone call with his name on it, if it comes at all.

Six weeks. Too late.

Nine weeks. Unacceptable.

Leo isn't one to shuck responsibility, but family trumps all.

He stays up late. Can't sleep. Doesn't have it in him to go out into the night. The city is buzzing in the false day it makes with millions of lights. Usually he likes the night—it's shown him a lot of good times.

But tonight he doesn't want a good time—he just wants time, and more of it. More sand—twenty years worth, at least—in the top half of his mother's hourglass.

NEXT MORNING, FIRST THING, HE PLANTS HIMSELF ON THE MINISTRY of National Defense's doorstep again—the Public Enquiries office. When they come with keys, he follows them upstairs and takes a number. Today he's number one.

And number two.

All the way up to twenty.

If one person won't help him, maybe someone else will.

He goes from counter to counter. Hears a lot of bullshit about how paperwork takes time to work its way through the ministry's piping. Which is their way of saying, "That's not my job. I have no power."

"Who's your boss?" he asks the last one. Yiannis and his super-cool mustache again.

"Greece is my boss. I work for her."

Enough of the existential bullshit. "Where's Greece's office? I want to talk to her."

"*Kyrios* Karas, the only thing you can do is report for duty and wait."

No can do. "Wait" is not an answer he can live with.

❦ 67 ❦

KIKI

K iki buries herself in Vivi's paperwork. At night, she buries herself in sleep.

What she wants to do is walk in the sun, head held high.

So she does ... behind dark sunglasses, under a hat.

Very brave.

She's walking to Vivi's cottage when she hears the hum of an approaching vehicle. It's a police car, spitting dust. It pulls up alongside her.

"*Despinida* Andreou?"

She lifts her glasses. "Detective Lemonis."

"I'm sorry, but you're under arrest."

Blink-blink. Then his words sink in. "On come on. We both know I didn't kill Stavros."

"Assault," he says

She stops. Gawks at him. Is he *kidding?* Assault? Really? Hands on hips, she asks, "Who?"

People wander out into their yards to watch the show. Kiki Andreou is good entertainment value.

"A Romani woman."

Kiki slaps her own forehead. Her sunglasses dive-bomb the ground. She stoops to pick them up, then goes back to staring at the detective in disbelief, because—clearly—he has lost his mind. "Are you insane?"

"Did you or did you not have an altercation with a Romani woman the other night?"

My Virgin Mary ... "She started it!"

"Started it how?"

"She spat on me! Ask my sister. They spat on her, too!"

Her feet are on the ground, but her voice is rising. If this continues she'll be well into shrieking territory. Kiki doesn't like shrieking; it reminds her of her mother.

But the people? They're loving it. No pretending to sweep, to water the flowers, to call for their absent children who are playing God knows where. They're unabashedly enjoying *The Kyriaki Andreou Show*.

Their enthusiasm lights a small fire inside her. So they want a show, eh? Why not give the people what they want?

There's a bit of Soula in Kiki, a bit of their grandmother. That piece of her shoves common sense out of the way and grabs her wheel. Kiki leaps onto the cop car's hood, bounds up onto the roof.

"Take a good look," she yells. Then palms facing each other, she points at her crotch.

(A very generous Greek gesture, an invitation to partake in sucking one's male appendage.)

Kiki doesn't have a penis, but she makes it abundantly clear she wants them to suck it anyway.

Shocked faces. Kyriaki Andreou, formerly good woman, once-beloved English teacher, telling the town to blow her. Who saw that coming?

Nobody.

But soon—very soon—they will say they always knew. Because nobody here wants to admit they're lacking insight into human nature or their neighbors' lives. At least now when they talk about her they can reference something she actually did, instead of making up stories based on nothing.

Soula will be so proud.

Done with telling them to suck it, she shows them the *moutsa*—flat palm facing out.

(As previously mentioned, it means the recipient has a chronic, brain-mashing masturbation habit. But it also has a second meaning: to rub fecal matter in the recipient's face.)

So many two-faced people, not nearly enough shit to rub in them.

✻ 68 ✻

KIKI

Mama says, "I saw you on the *You Tube*."
"I know, Mama."
"You told them to suck your *poutso*."
"I know, Mama."
"Then you rubbed *skata* in their faces."
"I know, Mama. I was there."
Margarita Andreou's finger pokes accusatory holes in the air. "I know you were there, *Kiki*, because I saw you on the *You Tube*!"
"I know, Mama."
"I thought I raised you better than that! What do you think they are saying about our family now, eh?"
"I can only imagine."
"And now you want me to bail you out?"
Kiki takes a good look at her new digs. Boy, she's really going to miss this fancy place. "No."
Mama's eyes widen. When she blinks, one of her false eyelashes is left clinging to her eyebrow. It's threatening to jump. "No?"
Arm reaching between the bars, Kiki says, "Did you bring my purse?"

Margarita holds it up, just out of range. "Yes, Kiki, I brought your purse."

"Get my credit card out and give it to the nice policeman at the front desk. Well, what used to be the front desk."

"Oh, you want me to give your money to the police, is that what you want?"

"Yes, please."

"Now you have manners, eh? Where were your manners when you were insulting the town?"

"Where were their manners?"

Hands raised to the sky, pleading for divine intervention: "What daughter is this You have given me?"

"The same daughter the gods gave *Yiayia*?"

Mama shoves Kiki's purse into her skirt pocket. "You want me to give them your card, eh? Want to pay your own bail?"

"Yes?"

"No! You stay there until you learn some manners!"

BEING BEHIND BARS DOESN'T MAKE KIKI FEEL TOUGH.

It's because of the distinct lack of prison tattoos. If she had those, she'd be strutting, instead of sitting knees-to-chin on what she suspects is meant to be a bed.

It's hard to hide in the corner when you've got a scowling Jesus Christ inked on your chest, and blue-green tears streaming from one eye. She hums that old song about working on a chain gang, but the guys in *Cadence* did it better.

For a while, she lies down, stares at the ceiling.

Time in here is running on Greek time, which means it could be any day, any time. Too bad she doesn't have something to scratch markers into the paint.

Eventually, one of the cops wanders in. He's fresh out of police school. One of the kids she used to teach. "How long have I been here?" she asks, running to the bars.

"Two hours."

"Two hours?" she wails. "That's it?"

He shrugs. "Two hours. Can I get you anything, *Despinida* Andreou?"

"No." She sweeps a hand at the cell. "I have everything I need. All that's missing is a roommate with crazy eyes. Preferably a drunk who hasn't bathed in a week."

"My mother used to bath us once a week when we were kids. In the same water, too. Saturday. That was bath day."

"How many kids?"

"Five," he tells her.

"Did you sleep together, too?"

He nods. "All piled into the same bed in the kitchen."

"No bedrooms?"

"Two. My parents used one. The other they turned into a guest room."

Kiki and Soula don't have guest rooms, but Mama does. It's set up with a big table, fancy chairs, embroidered cushions, and a hundred photos of the family. In that room she keeps her good china and other nice things children aren't supposed to touch

Kiki and Soula used to touch them while Mama was out. They'd lick each decorative thing, then put it back in its place.

That room has seen a lot of saliva over the years. It's crawling with bacteria.

"Can I get you anything?" the boy cop repeats.

"Out of here. You can get me out of here."

"Sorry," he says. "Your mother said we had to keep you for your own good."

Then he's gone.

But she's still here, isn't she?

This place smells like the end of a fire. No flames in sight, but smoke has burrowed its way into the walls. Even the rock-stuffed pillowcase reeks of stale smoke. Kiki sniffs her hair. Smoke

Kiki doesn't want to think, so she sings.

❧ 69 ❧

LEO

Does Leo take the bus back to Kalamata so he can report for duty?

Hell no, he doesn't.

When it's time to rejoin the herd, he's riding the bus north-east instead. There's no going back to the Ministry's office until they've stamped his papers. He shows his mug there, he's going to wind up in a military prison.

Leo has no intention of going to prison—military or civilian.

He's going home.

With a passport or without one.

Do-overs.

The bus rattles into Volos, dumps him onto the hot sidewalk. *Papou* is there holding Laki.

"Vision?" Leo asks his grandfather.

"Vision. Laki tells me you are on the run."

Leo slaps the old man's back. "It's true, Socrates. I'm a fugitive."

"Eh, it could be worse. You could be a Turk or Albanian."

THE FOLLOWING IS AN OVER-SIMPLIFICATION OF AN OVER-simplification of an over-simplification.

Albania is to Greece what Mexico is to the USA—minus the drug cartels and their passion for violence. The eastern European people flocked to Greece after Albania ditched its communist regime and the economy tanked, most of them tiptoeing across the border sans papers.

Greece was—and still is—a country without jobs to give, yet there they were, close to a half-million Albanians looking for work.

They're hard workers, but that's never the point, is it? Not when you've got people already looking for work.

Time traveling further into the past, Albanians buddied up to the Ottomans and adopted Islam as their primary religion. Turkey's BFF and Islamic? Two strikes against them—if you're Greek and have an old-school leaning towards prejudice.

LEO ISN'T A TURK OR AN ALBANIAN, BUT BEING A FUGITIVE IS BAD enough. None of this sits right with him. He'd be okay with doing his service if not for Mom. He'd even be okay with coming back to complete it when—

He doesn't want to think about that.

He's not in denial, but why fixate on something he can't change?

Leo chooses to focus on the problem he can solve.

"How do I get out of Greece?"

Socrates hands Laki to him, lifts his hair, scratches his balding pate. Then he drops his hair back into place and takes Laki from Leo.

"Thirty years ago, I would have told you to sneak across the border. But now all the borders in Europe have more eyes than before. And the countries have agreements. Agreements! Seventy years ago we agreed on nothing, but we were honest. Now we pretend we are all friends."

Next thing he does is call his dad's cell phone.

"Leo?"

"It's me."

"How are you?"

"Okay. How's Mom?"

"Eh," he says. "Better, I think."

"Where are you?"

"At the hospital. Your mother ordered me to go home and get some sleep, but I cannot—" The end of his sentence cracks, breaks away. "I cannot leave," he eventually says. "I will not leave her."

Leo's staring at the blue wall, through hot, sand-filled eyes. This is the part where he's supposed to promise his dad that she'll make it, that he will be there soon to ... to do whatever it is Dad and Soc needs him to do.

But he can't, can he?

Because Mom's not going to make it. And he won't be home in time to do anything except give her flowers she'll never see.

❧ 70 ❧

KIKI

No office this time. Detective Lemonis takes her to an interrogation room.

It's the room they save for company they don't like.

Everything in the square box is metal. In this case, *everything* means two chairs and a rectangular table. On the smoke-stained wall there's a two-way mirror. She waves, because why not?

"There's nobody on the other side," he tells her.

The speaker above the mirror crackles. "*Yia sou, Despinida* Andreou."

"*Yia sou*, Nobody!" Then she turns her attention to the detective. "Why am I here when that Romani woman isn't?"

"She says you attacked her."

"And of course she has eyewitnesses." Of cooooourse.

"Quite a few."

"And all I have is Soula. My own sister." Nothing from the man with the badge. "Did they tell you they surrounded Soula and me?"

No comment. Not even a twitch. "Why don't you tell me how it happened."

So she tells him, and he scratches words in his notebook that she can't see from the guilty side of the table.

"They came out of nowhere?"

"Yes."

"You did not see them bothering anyone else?"

"No. We didn't see them at all until they were there." She laughs, because who wouldn't? It's the summer of insanity. "I thought you were arresting me because of the fire."

"Why would you think that?"

"The wedding gift."

"You mean the one you dumped on our doorstep?"

"Hey, I left a note."

"What did you think was in it?" The man looks genuinely puzzled.

"A bomb?"

"So you brought it here?"

"I wasn't going to keep a bomb."

He rubs a hand across his mouth. "It was not a bomb."

Wow. Not a bomb after all. She can almost feel her mother's oncoming disappointment.

"What was it?"

"Despinida Andreou, something is wrong here. This room is where I ask questions—not you."

"Can I ask one more?"

"Fine. Ask. But it is the last one."

She leans across the table has far as she can—which isn't far. "How did you know it was me?"

"What do you mean?"

"Why did you come straight to me? How did you know I was the one who bent her finger?"

"The Roma woman told me your name."

"Don't you find that interesting?"

Because Kiki does. Kiki really, really does.

❦ 71 ❦

LEO

Leo looks at the old woman. "Nice snake."
The roll of scales is curled around her shoulders, stole-style.
Kiki's grandmother beams. "My daughter put him in my bed to kill me,
but she is so stupid she does not know a venomous snake from a non-
venomous snake."

Her stupid daughter sighs like it's killing her. Stab, stab, stab at the
needlepoint. He wonders what she'd stab if she didn't have a creative
outlet. "It wasn't supposed to bite you, Mama. You were supposed to
get a fright and have a heart attack."

"If you want to kill someone," Kiki's grandmother says, wagging
her finger at him, "do not ask Margarita. She is a terrible killer. With
her skills, she should be a heart surgeon. That is how bad she is at
killing."

Kyria Andreou saves her glare for him. "Which of my daughters are
you here for this time?"

"Kiki."

"What, my Soula is not good enough for you?"

He can't tell if she's the rock or the hard place; he suspects she
might be both. "Soula's a great woman. But I'm here to see Kiki. I
wanted to thank her for her help."

"You already thanked her."

"I want to thank her again. That's how grateful I am."

"Listen to this one," Kiki's mother says. "He could be a politician, the way he argues. What do you do?"

"Veterinarian."

"Animals, eh?" The old woman elbows her daughter. "Margarita, look, I have found you a new doctor."

It's all he can do not to laugh. Yeah, he wants to see Kiki, but her family gives one hell of a comedy routine.

"Is she here?"

"No, she is not here," Kiki's mother says. She doesn't volunteer further information.

But the grandmother is happy to squeal. "Kiki is in jail!" The older woman is almost bouncing in her seat. "It is very exciting. Nobody in this family has been to the jail before."

"You were in jail, Mama," her daughter says absently, not looking up from her needlepoint.

"That does not count."

"It counts." She looks up at Leo. "My mother smacked an English tourist with her handbag. This town relies on tourists, and what does she do? Beat them."

"He pushed me."

To Leo: "She smacked him with her handbag so hard he fell off the bus. And it was moving."

"Very slowly. You always forget that part where the bus was moving slowly."

"Why is Kiki in jail?" Leo wants to run to the police station and break her out, but he's already showering with a hairdryer, as far as the legal system goes.

Shrug. "The police say she attacked a *tsigana*. Then she jumped on top of a police car and told everyone to suck her *poutso*."

"That is my girl!" The older woman looks proud. Leo gets it. He's proud of Kiki, too. This town has been heaping shit on her for weeks. About time she gave some back.

Kiki's mother sets aside her needlework, stands. "Sit, Leonidas. I will bring you coffee and something sweet, eh?"

It's a test and he's going to fail. "I'm sorry, *Kyria* Andreou, but I can't stay."

Social suicide, more or less. Family and friends can get away with saying no, but if Leo is aiming to impress, he just threw himself off a cliff.

"Where are you going in such a hurry, eh?"

"To get Kiki."

The rest of the conversation follows him down the street.

"To get Kiki," the old woman says. "This one she should marry!"

"Mama! *Skasmos!* No one will marry Kiki now."

"This one will. He is very brave and very stupid."

LEO THE VERY BRAVE AND VERY STUPID GOES TO WHAT'S LEFT OF THE police station.

Which is most of it.

Greek buildings say no to earthquakes, and—apparently—fires.

He's not sure Greece even needs firefighters. All they need is one average Greek mother to command the fire to stop. Fire would tuck its tail between its legs and run back to the stone ages, where it was wanted.

If his mother was Greek, he's sure she could command the cancer to stop spinning its webs throughout her body. Too bad she's American all the way to her red, white, and blue blood.

Inside, a couple of policemen are sitting in office chairs, papers balanced on their laps. No desks. No front desk for him to lean on while he asks the cost of getting Kiki out.

Greek buildings say no to fire, but Greek furniture is happy to burn.

They look up at him when he walks in. He nods, says, "I'm looking for Kiki Andreou."

"She's busy."

"Doing what?"

"Singing."

The second cop looks at the first one. "Can we really call it singing?" He gets up, waves for Leo to follow him. Leo follows him down a hallway with half-assed doors. Looks like they used to be white, but now they're sooty and smudged.

The jail is at the back of the building. Leo remembers seeing the tiny barred windows from the street that runs parallel to the one out front. Standing between the jail and the rest of the building is a steel door.

"Listen," the policeman says, sliding open the rectangular peephole. "If you can stand it."

Behind the door, someone is choking. It's like listening to a Vogon recite poetry.

"Is she hurt?" Because if she is, he's going to wind up in the adjoining cell.

"No! She is singing Madonna songs."

Leo is seriously confused. "That's a Madonna song?"

The cop's head bobs. "*Laik Is Fur Gin.*"

He doesn't recall a Madonna song about fur or gin, but he's not about to tell the cop that. He's too busy trying not to laugh, because Kiki's singing could strip paint off the walls.

Throw her into a battlefield, watch armies fall.

Greece has no idea it's harboring a bio-weapon. Alexander the Great wishes he had just one Kiki Andreou.

And suddenly, so does he.

"What's it going to take to get her out of here?"

"Why? You going to post her bail?"

"Yeah, I'm going to post her bail."

"Praise the Virgin Mary."

"No," he says. "Praise Leonidas Karas."

❧ 72 ❧

KIKI

I t's a one-woman concert, audience of zero.Kiki sings every song she knows.

She's a woman who knows a lot of songs.

The mattress had to go bye-bye. It's leaning against the wall, sleeping off its misspent youth, while she dances on the flat-topped frame.

Madonna's catalog is over. Now it's onto Mariah Carey.

Kiki puts her heart and soul into *I Can't Live*. She's on her knees, howling at the ceiling when the door flies open. Filling the doorway is Leo, wearing jeans and a T-shirt that shows what he's made of.

"Ha-ha," she says weakly. "Ha-ha."

Leo shakes his head. "Man, it's a crime to put that kind of talent behind bars." He swaggers into the room (what else can she call it? That's a definite swagger, and it's all Greek), leans against the bars like it's, well, a bar. "I leave for two days and you wind up in jail. What am I going to do with you, Kiki Andreou?"

Kill her—kill her now.

She looks up at him. "I take requests."

73

LEO

F uck her, he thinks. He wants to fuck her.

But he can't. Obviously.

"Come on. I'm taking you home."

She stands there in her black sundress, sunglasses balanced on her head, nothing but disbelief on her face and one question in her mouth. "You posted my bail?"

He shrugs. "It's nothing. Don't sweat it."

"Leo ..."

"You helped me out. Now I'm helping you out. Paying it forward."

"Wow. Thank you."

"Did you really tell everyone to suck your dick?"

"They were asking for it."

He laughs, because he believes it. This woman is something else. The world falls on her, shoves her to her knees, and she sings. Who wouldn't want her on their team? Who wouldn't want to be on *her* team?

"We'll have to walk," he tells her. "You okay with that?"

"I've been walking for twenty-seven years. I'm pretty good at it."

"I mean are you okay with us being seen together?"

"You posted bail when even my own mother wouldn't. I'm proud to be seen with you, Leo Karas. If they don't like it, they can—you know."

Oh, he knows.

✣ 74 ✣
KIKI

They walk. Late afternoon, so they're not the only ones in the streets. Everyone else is slowly venturing out to see if the sun has quit blasting its furnace.

Kiki kills them with kindness. They choke on their hellos, but they can't ignore her, can they? She waves to *Kyria* Maria, one of the worst offenders, and her aunt's closest friend (that would be Kostas and Max's mother). "How are you?" she calls out.

"I am well, Kyriaki. How are you?" She's a squat woman with a frog's mouth and a forked tongue.

"Wonderful! Never better." She nods at Leo. "This is my friend Leo Karas. He's wonderful, too. Aren't you, Leo?"

"Leo Karas—Socrates Karas?"

(That's a Greek thing: adding and elder's name to the younger. When you've got a family stuffed with people with the same first name, it helps to identify them by an extra characteristic. You're never just you—there's almost always a plus one. There is no escaping bad family in this small town; everyone knows to whom you belong, to whom you will always belong.)

Leo, bless him, knows how to play Kiki's game. Of course he

would, he's part of this place, whether he recognizes the belonging in himself or not.

"I'm wonderful. It's a beautiful day, and here I am with a beautiful woman." He winks at the older woman. "Two beautiful women."

Kyria Maria, that old hypocrite, smiles, and for a moment it touches her eyes. An attractive man is an attractive man, no matter his age. But when he is also charming, he is ageless.

"Give my regards to your family, eh?"

"I will," Kiki sings over her shoulder. Then she and Leo turn right, toward home.

❧ 75 ❧

LEO

L eo tells her his sad tale, only he paints it several shades of less tragic. No mention of the calls back home, the cracking of his father's voice and his unwavering devotion to his wife of thirty-five years. Not a hint about the fear in his brother's voice.

Why fill her head with his bullshit? She's got enough of her own worries.

Yeah, she's got her own worries, yet here she is worrying about him, asking, "So, what now?"

Leo rubs his head. His hair is making a fast comeback. "The way I see it, I've got two choices. The legal way or the illegal way."

"You can't wait."

"Right."

"And you can't sneak across all those borders. How would you get into America?"

"I don't have to. All I need to do is get to a country that isn't best buddies with Greece—one that has a US embassy."

He has said too much already, so he stops right there. Plausible deniability. The less Kiki knows, the less Kiki can say if the authorities squeeze her.

They're at the gate, the one that leads to Kiki's safe home and her safe, crazy family.

"Good luck, Leo Karas," she says. "If there's anything I can do, you know where to find me." She points at her castle.

She's a good woman. That face, that body, they're just syrup on an already-delicious cake.

"Good luck, Kiki Andreou."

76

KIKI

Mama glowers.

"So they let you out, eh?"

"Leo posted my bail."

"Leo posted your bail?"

Kiki nods.

It's one of those rare times when it's the two of them alone in the kitchen. Kiki's busy stringing beans, and Mama's busy showing her how to do it properly for the millionth time since Kiki's childhood.

Someone has micromanagement issues.

"What do you think he wants?" Her voice is low, dangerous. There's a storm coming.

"What do *you* think he wants?"

"I know what he wants. What all men want."

Kiki snaps the end off a bean, tugs on its strings. "Some men want other men. And if you look on the Internet, some men want farm animals and baked goods."

"The Internet! What does the Internet know about normal people? Everyone on the Internet is crazy. Only pornography and the YouTube."

"Leo doesn't want anything." *Snap. Pull.* "When I helped him out with his papers, I told him to pay it forward. So he did. And here I am."

"That man does not want farm animals or men, he wants my daughter."

"So what if he does? It's not like I'm married."

Mama snatches up the beans, strings and all, dumps them in the huge pot. "You are right, Kiki, you are not married. Whose fault is that?"

"Let me guess: mine?"

"Who else, Kiki? Who else?"

"You think I killed Stavros?"

"No! But I do not think you mind too much that he is dead, otherwise you would not encourage that man."

"Mama, you taught me to be kind. I helped Leo out of kindness, and now we are friends. You are seeing something that isn't there." Kiki stands, touches a hand to her mother's shoulder. "I do mind that Stavros is dead. I mind a lot. There's a wide open territory between love and apathy. I liked Stavros. I didn't want to be his wife, that's all."

Nothing. Her mother is a cold, turned back.

"Will you tell Helena that?" Mama says in a small, choked voice.

"Tell *Thea* Helena? Why?"

When her mother turns around, Kiki sees she's bleeding tears. "I want my friend back. You helped Leo. Okay. Now help me." She reaches for the big, wooden spoon, dips its scoop into the beans. "Bring my friend back. I cannot do life without her."

GARDENIAS. THERE IS NO OTHER FLOWER IN THE WORLD LIKE THEM. Give them enough acid and they will change your world with their perfume.

Thea Helena has almost as many gardenias as Mama, and like Mama's, hers live in captivity. The women used to paint empty cans and containers together, then sip *frappe* while the paint dried. Now both women sweep in their separate yards, their friendship gone, the way of the contents that once filled those containers.

"*Thea* Helena?" she asks the sweeping woman.

Nothing.

"Will you talk with me?"

When she speaks, it's slow, exhausted, as though it has climbed up to the monasteries of Meteora, one bloodied hand at a time. "What do you want, Kiki?"

Kiki leans against the gate, her chin resting on the top of the warm metal frame.

"I'm not here for myself. I came for my mother."

"Margarita and I have nothing to say to one another."

"Maybe not. But she thinks I should tell you something anyway."

"I cannot care, Kiki. Whatever it is."

"Okay." She looks around at the quiet street with its invisible eaves-droppers. She can't see them, but she feels the collective breath-holding taking place behind the shutters. "Okay. Maybe I will say it and then you can decide if you want to hear it or not."

The broom continues to scratch at the ground like a chicken, but *Thea* Helena doesn't speak.

"I'm sorry about Stavros. I didn't want to marry him—and he didn't want to marry me—but that doesn't mean I'm glad he's dead. I cared about him very much. He was a good man. And my whole family —including me—wants to see whoever killed him pay. I didn't kill him —I would never. All I wanted was to not marry him. But that's not worth murder."

Silence. Even the broom has stopped its back and forth.

"My mother misses you. She's making us all miserable, and she's hardly tried to kill *Yiayia* at all lately. Which should tell you everything."

Nothing from the other woman in black, nothing to indicate a single one of Kiki's words have drip-filtered into her head.

It's no use. Kiki came here to fight a battle in a war that has already been lost.

"Go home, Kiki. Let us never speak again."

LEO

Ambush.

If he was playing *Jeopardy*, his answer would be: What do you call your entire Greek family shoehorned into your grandfather's front yard?

"Leo!" they shout.

Leo is a trooper. He gets down to the happy business of shaking hands, slapping backs, kissing and being kissed.

Even with his problems, he's glad to see them.

The names, the faces, they come back, as soon as he rips fifteen years off their faces. Lots of new faces with old names, too. Socrates, Socrates, and Socrates. Very original with names, the Greeks. Everyone is named after somebody else.

Greek naming conventions dictate that he should be a Socrates, but Mom wanted him to have his own name. So instead of his grandfather, he's named after the warrior king of Sparta.

Yeah, that one. The ate-Persian-steel one

This is not Sparta, it's Agria. Which means his mother spent a lot of her days in social purgatory after that episode.

Somebody shoves a cold beer into his hand. When that one's gone, there's another. There's food to go with that drink. Mountains of it.

Dishes crammed onto a long table on the patio. No way does he remember what every dish is called, but he remembers them by sight, and he definitely remembers how good they taste.

Another somebody thrusts a plate at him, piled with snippets of everything, looks like. But there's no time to eat; they're bouncing him from conversation to conversation.

How is your father? How is your mother? And your brother? We have never met him! Po-po, why your father does not bring him to meet his family?

Leo doesn't say Dad's got his hands full with Mom's cancer. He just shrugs and tells them he doesn't know. They're not looking for answers anyway; questions are just something they throw into the air to keep silence distracted.

He works his way through the crowd. Says the right things. Makes the appropriate noises. Fake-spits on the family's newest members.

The idea is to work his way to his grandfather, but *Papou* isn't around.

One of his aunts shoves money at him. Cash. Monopoly money, this whole euro thing. Drachmas at least looked like money.

He tries "No thank you" on for size, but she waves away his objection.

"Take it for your brother."

Soon more money is flying at him—a lot of money—all of it for his brother, after word gets out Leo won't take it for himself.

"Has anyone seen *Papou?*"

His question zips around the room, but everyone is too busy auditioning for *Greece's Loudest Voice*. Nobody has brought their inside voice to this shindig.

Want something done right, do it yourself. He sets the beer on a window sill, grabs a fork, jams a chunk of rotisserie lamb into his mouth. It's good—it's better than good. Herbs and lemon explode in his mouth, leaving him weak and dying for more.

Room to room, he stuffs his mouth with food.

He finds *Papou* in his bedroom, sitting in the edge of the bed in the dark. Who can blame him? It's a zoo out there.

"Not having fun, Socrates?"

"Eh. Even dead, your grandmother is better company than those goats."

Leo sits beside his grandfather. "I'm not in a party mood myself."

"I tried to stop them, but they came anyway. Your aunts are like the ocean. Hold up your hand and say, '*Oxi!*' still they keep on coming. Even the Turks eventually took 'No' for an answer—but not your aunts. I would lock them out, but I cannot find the key."

"Look on the bright side," Leo tells him. "All these people. One outhouse. I can't see how that could go wrong—can you?"

"Wait until they discover there is no paper!"

They share a laugh, which is more therapeutic than any drink.

"You are a good boy, Leo. I wish you could stay. But I understand that you have to go."

"I don't suppose you've had any visions?"

"Nothing that will help you. But soon—very soon—we will hear screaming."

"Who?"

The outline of his shoulder rises and falls. "I do not know. Laki was not specific."

Right on cue, the screaming starts.

Leo runs.

YEARS AGO THERE WAS A MODERATELY FUNNY MOVIE WHERE BEN Stiller, pretending to be a teenager, got the ol' frank-and-beans trapped in his zipper.

Son-less women and girls everywhere wondered how that could possibly happen. Who gets their dick caught in a zipper?

Guys, that's who.

THE KID COULD BE A CHAMPAGNE BOTTLE, THE WAY HE'S SPRAYING curse words all over the yard. To him everyone is a *putana*, and he tells his mother to do something anatomically impossible, unless she's a snake with a penchant for incest and necrophilia.

Leo shakes his head. "Wow. Where does a five-year-old learn those words?"

"Life," his grandfather says.

They're standing there looking at the boy's mother—Leo's cousin Toula—tugging the zipper in all the wrong directions. It doesn't help that the kid is leaping around, slapping her hands away.

"Stop it, you little bastard!" she yells in his face.

"Like I said," Socrates tells Leo, "he learned those words from life."

Leo can't watch this. He shoves the plate into his grandfather's hands and snatches the boy up by his armpits.

"Fuck the *putana!*" the boy hollers. "Suck Zeus's *poutso!*"

What is it with these people? Everyone wants somebody to suck someone's dick. If there's dick sucking going on, it better be his dick and Kiki's mouth.

He carries the kid inside where there's light. Cousin Toula follows, spitting out questions. Stupid ones, mostly. But when someone you love is hurt, the stupid ones come more easily.

"Relax," he tells her, dumping the boy into a chair. "You'll still have grandchildren."

"Are you a doctor?" she demands.

He remembers when his cousin was a kid herself. Cute little thing with messy hair. She was bossy then, she's bossy now.

"Veterinarian."

"What do you know about fixing ... this?"

He grabs her by the shoulders, pushes her into a second chair. "Sit. Stay. Shut up."

"What—"

"You think your kid's the only one who got his dick caught in a zipper? Been there, done that. What's your name?" he asks the boy.

Toula looks at him like he's lost his mind. "His name is Socrates!"

Socrates. What else?

"Okay, Socrates," he tells the spitting, hissing boy. "Take a deep breath."

Socrates doesn't listen, he just keeps on kicking and screaming like he's part cat, part donkey. That's okay, Leo's dealt with worse. Try a kicking, squealing pig. He grabs the kid's shorts, either side of the zipper, jerks the metal teeth apart. The cotton makes one hell of a ripping sound, but better the shorts than the boy.

"You ruined his shorts!" Toula cries.

"Think of me when your first grandchild is born." He stuffs twenty euro into her hands. "Get him a new pair."

THREE MAIN GROUPS FORM AS THE EVENING WEARS ON: MEN, women, and children. Those first two groups are talking about one thing: Kiki and Stavros.

And why wouldn't they? Murder is the third most exciting thing that can happen around here—football and basketball take first and second, depending on the season.

("How can America call themselves world champions of basketball when they do not play against the world, only themselves, eh?" one of his cousins asked earlier.)

"They say you are seeing Kiki Andreou," someone asks.

"She helped me with some paperwork. We're friends."

Are they friends? Leo's not sure. Maybe they are, but it sure feels like they could be something else under the right circumstances.

"Friends." His cousin nudges one of the uncles. "Friends."

"Friends," Leo confirms.

"Careful with that one. If she thinks there is another woman she will kill you."

He takes a long pull of cold beer. "Come on, Kiki didn't kill anyone. Do you really believe she did?"

His cousin shrugs, palms up. "Who knows? She is a woman, and women are capable of anything."

"Except common sense," one of the uncles says.

Lots of laughs, but not from Leo. He doesn't mind a sexist joke when the women are giving back as good as they get, but this isn't a fair fight. All over town right now there are people talking about her, and she doesn't get to defend herself to a one of them.

It's a rerun of the bakery—the one with all the cakes.

"I'm capable of pissing in your beer." He nods at the bottle in his cousin's hand. "Doesn't mean I would—or did. That you know of."

His cousin looks uneasily at the beer. "You didn't—"

"No. And Kiki didn't kill Stavros."

Someone else says, "Who could blame her if she did?"

"What do you mean?"

"There were a lot of women. Stavros was just a life-support system for his *poutso*."

A round of laughter.

"Kiki never dated anyone else?" They're not telling him anything he didn't already know about Stavros, but about Kiki, yeah, he's curious. Too curious.

Another shrug. "Some. But not for years."

"Let me ask you this," Leo says, after another swallow. He points to the men with the bottle. "Let's say Kiki didn't kill Stavros. Who would you say did?"

Glances move from person to person, followed by the shrugs.

Greeks shrug a lot, he thinks. Their body language is almost as loud as their voices.

"Maybe someone who did not want him to get married to Kiki," Leo says. To his ears he sounds almost like one of those old Greek philosophers, trying to push these clowns to think.

"Why do you care, eh?" one of the cousins asks.

Laughter streaks around the group. "Because he wants to sleep her, of course. Why else does a man care?"

Leo ditches his beer, heads out into the night.

It's not children that are better seen and not heard—it's family.

LEO DOESN'T FIND KIKI IN THE DARK, BUT HE DOES FIND SOULA.

The other Andreou woman is sitting in her own patch of night at the foot of her street, the long skirt of her dress wrapped around her legs. This little light, her toenails appear as if they've been dipped in black paint.

"Soula?"

"Leo?"

"Come here often?"

Her laugh is low, husky. The kind of laugh men hurl themselves against rocks to hear. Not Leo, though. Not when he knows Kiki's clear bell.

"Only when I'm waiting for someone."

"Anyone special?"

Shrug. "If he wasn't special, I wouldn't be waiting. I'd be living."

"Is he going to show?"

"Sometimes he does, sometimes he doesn't. If he doesn't, you want to have a drink?

"Yeah," he says. "But not with you."

A low laugh. "Another woman would be offended, but not me."

"That's why I said it. Better to be honest."

"Is it Kiki?"

"It's Kiki."

Soula shakes her head. "Leo, Leo."

"Yeah, I know."

"My sister is too good for you."

"I know."

"No, you don't. My sister is too good for anyone. She is the best person I know. There is no one like her." She nods to the patch of ground beside her. "Sit and I will tell you something."

Leo sits. He wants to hear whatever it is she wants to tell, especially if it's about Kiki.

"I am glad Stavros Boutos is dead. It is the best thing that could have happened to her."

Boy does she deliver. "Okay. Why?"

"If they were married, he would have been a faithless husband. There is no way he could have made her happy. And if he had broken their engagement, Kiki would have been left wondering what was wrong with her that he didn't want to marry her. It is better this way. Not for anyone else, but for Kiki—yes. Once her mourning time is over, she will be free to find love. Not purchased love, but real love of her own choosing."

"You think we get to choose who we love?"

Soula laughs quietly. "No. I am proof that we have no choice at all. Love comes for us in its own way, and sometimes it makes fools of us all."

"You sound like you know."

"Don't you?"

In the distance, some kind of vehicle is rolling their way. It's growling along the streets.

"Yeah, I know."

Soula stands, reaches out for Leo's hand. She pulls him to his feet. "I like you, Leo Karas. And if things were different, I would be proud to have you join our family. But your life is elsewhere. You are temporary. My sister deserves more."

"Why don't we let her decide what she wants. It's about time someone gave her the chance."

She laughs. "As I said, I like you."

Then Soula's gone, nothing left of her but the memory of a beautiful woman in a flowing dress.

❦ 78 ❦

HELENA

"Did you go out last night?"

"No. Why?"

Kristos unfolds the newspaper. "I woke up and you were not in bed."

"Maybe I was in the bathroom."

"That long?"

"I must have eaten something bad."

"Like the Chernobyl fruit?" There's the ghost of a smile on his face.

Everyone in Greece over a certain age remembers the Chernobyl disaster. Helena recalls the panic, the warnings not to eat fruit and vegetables without a thorough washing, the food inspections, the closing of the borders to foreign foods.

Helena's aunt, *Thea* Kalliope, ate food by the bucketful. (*Thea* Kalliope was a woman known for breaking more than one toilet seat in the family.) When the Chernobyl disaster happened, her eating didn't slow one bit. She worked her way through a box of plums, and when it gave her the runs she blamed Russia.

For years afterward, whenever her aunt caught a stomach flu or ate something bad, she claimed Chernobyl and its radiation were the culprits.

It's almost normal the way he says it. How can he make jokes?

She tries but she cannot join in. She cannot pretend this house keeps a room made up for humor and good times.

"Like the Chernobyl fruit," she manages, by some miracle. But the smile that used to go along with it never comes.

His gaze stays on her face too long, as if he's trying to discern whether his wife is still tucked away inside her somewhere.

"Where do you go, Helena?"

"I am still here," she says.

"Are you? I wonder. I have not seen you for so long."

❧ 79 ❧

KIKI

Stupid refrigerator. She's been standing in front of it for fifteen minutes, gazing sightlessly at its contents, and still it refuses to give her what she wants: a solution to the Leo problem.

Or rather, a solution to Leo's problem.

On the walk home from the police station, he dialed down the drama and kept things light. But she can't help knowing what she knows, thanks to that fax.

She's not much of a do-nothing person when it comes to helping people she likes—and she really likes Leo.

"Come on, refrigerator, think."

But the only thing it's telling her is that it's too late for Leo and his mother. All she gets are flashes of a future where Leo goes home—months from now—to a cold grave where the turf has already stitched itself to the surrounding grass.

"Who do you know, Kiki? Who can help him?"

Theo Kristos works for the government, but she can't go to the Boutos family now. No way can she ask for their help when she couldn't help them.

"Who else?"

The feta says nothing.

It's on the way to bed that she has an epiphany of the semi-religious kind.

She makes a call—just the one. That's all it takes. After that, there's no time for sleep.

Leo doesn't have the luxury of time.

SOULA'S NOT HOME.

Kiki scribbles a note, pledges undying, sisterly devotion, snatches Soula's car keys out of the wooden bowl where she keeps odds and ends.

Then she jogs down the stairs, sprints through the yard.

A wall stops her, of the flesh and blood kind.

"Kiki?"

"Leo? Leo! I was coming to find you."

He laughs. "Great minds. I was coming to find you."

"No time to ask why. Let's go."

"Where are we going?"

"Church."

80

HELENA

Helena is a small patch of shade in the night.

A mosquito latches itself to her arm. The slap leaves a dark smear. Red, but without light it appears black.

Inside Kiki's house there is movement. Kiki is awake. Is she like Helena, where she cannot sleep?

Footsteps, moving her way.

Helena dissolves into the deeper shadows.

She hears the slap of Kiki's shoes as she runs upstairs, then down and out, through the yard.

A small smattering of talk, half of it Kiki's. The other half of the conversation belongs to a man.

All these nights she has been watching over Kiki, but she did not deserve it.

Worthless. Faithless. Good for nothing except—

Helena smiles in the dark. Life is tasting sweeter. Stavros is gone, yes, but with Kiki's help she can bring him back.

A life for a life.

LEO

Well, everyone is right: Kiki is a killer. Just not the kind of killer they're talking about.

Her driving is—

"Why are you swerving?"

"Snake," she tells him.

Jesus.

She zags right—to the correct side of the road, at least.

"And now?"

She shrugs at the wheel. "Another snake."

"Snakes," he mutters.

A quick glance in his direction. "Have you been to Mount Pelion before?"

"Years ago. Not since I got back."

"Where did you go?"

"My mother loves Makrinitsa, so we went there a lot." His voice stays strong, steady. Good. This is no time to crack.

She smiles at the winding road illuminated in the headlights. "I love Makrinitsa, too. But not as much as where I'm taking you."

"Where's that?"

Headlights coming their way. They're weaving left, right, left, right. Got a serious case of the Kikis.

"Relax, Leo," Kiki says. "You're so tense."

The super-cool dude isn't tense. No way. He's just forgotten how Greeks drive: like they're the only ones careening through a rubber-padded world.

"You know this isn't a bumper car, right?"

She laughs. "Sometimes I forget. I don't drive much."

No kidding.

The lights pass. Pushing them is a convertible packed with loud, waving people. Kiki honks, waves.

"Do you know them?"

"No, but they're having fun. It's good to see people enjoying life."

She means it. He can tell. "What do you do to enjoy life, Kiki Andreou?"

She doesn't look at him. "I watch other people enjoying theirs."

That doesn't sound to him like it's enough.

LEO DOESN'T DO CHURCH. IT'S NOT THE GOD THING, IT'S THE people thing. Leo is okay with God, but he's not okay with the frenzied devotion some religious groups put on display. As far as he's concerned, if you're protesting at funerals, your heart is more than two sizes too small. And he's not big on people bashing on his door, peddling their favorite flavor. So if he talks to God, it's on the quiet.

"This is a church?"

Can't be a church. Not a Greek one. Greek Orthodox churches scream, "Come get me! And don't forget to leave your money." Like anyone else trying to lay for pay, they dress up fancy. Yellow gold is their jewelry of choice.

This place, yeah, it does its decorating in wood and stone. Its open hand is a simple box with a narrow mouth, sitting near a basket of new candles.

Kiki smiles, but it's not for him. It's for this place; he can tell by the way her finger caresses the back pew's shoulder. "It's a church. My favorite one."

A door opens, clicks shut. As his eyes adjust, he sees a man in head-to-toe black hurrying down a small set of stairs cut into the church's left side.

Things in Greece have definitely changed. The *pappas* isn't clean shaven, but he's not far from it. Used to be Greek Orthodox priests never left home without a beard. No long hair for this guy either. Looks like it's almost as short as Leo's own, under the soft *skufia* on his head.

The priest takes one look at him, starts laughing. It's a big, full sound that fills the church. "Leonidas Karas, is that you?"

Leo remembers that laugh. "Kostas Andreou?" He looks at Kiki whose gaze is swinging from man to man. "I didn't realize you were one of *those* Andreous." Then it's back to the man in black. "What are you doing in a church? Hiding out?" Because the Kostas Andreou he used to know was trouble's drinking buddy. No way would you find him in a church, unless he was panning for gold.

"God beat me over the head with a stick, and then put me to good use." He hugs Kiki, kisses her forehead, hugs Leo. "Where did you find this clown?" he asks Kiki.

"He followed me home."

"Technically I'm a fugitive," Leo adds. Not that he's proud of it, but it doesn't seem right to lie to a priest in his own digs.

"What—"

Kiki interrupts. "I'm going to make coffee to take with us, okay?"

Kostas nods. "Okay."

"Take with us?" Leo says.

Kostas steers him toward the pews. Nothing else to do but sit, so Leo sits.

"My cousin tells me you're a man who needs help getting out of Greece."

On the wall, Christ is sleeping or dying, Leo can't tell which. "Yeah, I do. My mother has cancer. She doesn't have long. Greece won't let me go, and America won't twist their arm."

"This country ..." Kostas shakes his head. "It is no wonder we have problems. I love Greece, but I do not always love her behavior."

"No offense, but I'm not sure how a priest—even you—can help."

The reformed man smiles. "I help a lot of people, my old friend. Most of the time it is people who want to come into Greece because their own countries are inhospitable. But sometimes I help people like you, who need to get out quickly and quietly."

"You're a Coyote?"

"A Coyote?"

Leo fills the gap in his education, tells him about the booming smuggling business between the US and Mexico; it's a sad, desperate story.

Kostas shakes his head. "Yeah, then I guess I am a Coyote of sorts, but I don't take money from anyone. Helping people is not a business opportunity. What I do, I do because I can when they cannot."

There's something in his eye. Feels like hot sand. It's been happening a lot lately. There's a *thank you* coming, but he can't say it now, or that desert in his eyes is going to manifest an ocean.

His voice is thick when he asks, "So what happens now?"

"My cousin is making coffee, then we will drive north to the border."

"Which one?"

Bulgaria, Macedonia, Albania, Turkey. Those are his options.

Kostas grins. There's the boy he used to know. "Hold on tight, Leo Karas. You are going to Turkey."

MACEDONIA. NOW THERE'S ANOTHER PAIN IN GREECE'S BUTT. Nowadays everyone knows Macedonia as one of the former Yugoslavia's shards. But—like everything in Europe—it goes way back, wearing a bunch of different outfits of varying sizes. It's been part of this empire, part of that, with much of it slopping into modern day Greece. Macedonia is still a region in Greece—which, in this instance, means it's a state. It's the largest region—basically Greece's Texas. And it butts right up against the other, newer Macedonia.

After Yugoslavia became just another broken home, Macedonia—the new country—argued with Greece over its newly-adopted name. Macedonia's coming-out conversation went something like this:

Macedonia: *Rawr*, we're Macedonia!

Greece: No, we're Macedonia!

Macedonia: No, we are!

Greece: No, Macedonia is Greek!

Macedonia: Nuh-uh.

Greece: How about you call yourselves Northern Macedonia, eh?

Macedonia: Nope. Macedonia.

Greece: Here is a much better name for you: Macedonia the Country That is too Stupid to Think of an Original Name, So it Must Steal One From Greece.

Macedonia: Hahahaha—No. Macedonia.

NATO and the UN mediator weep openly.

Greece: Grrrrr!

Macedonia: (To Everyone) Hey, did you know Alexander the Great was Macedonian?

Greece: We hate you.

The custody battle over the name *Macedonia* is ongoing.

BEFORE THEY LEAVE, LEO PULLS OUT THE CLUMP OF EUROS HIS family spent the evening shoving into his hands. About five-hundred US dollars, he figures. He stuffs them into the collection box, picks up a candle. Lights it in his mother's name.

The second he lights for Kiki.

❧ 82 ❧

HELENA

All of Agria knows Kyriaki Andreou is a *putana*.
They know because Helena tells them so.

"I saw her with my own eyes!" Two fingers pointing at her face. "She went off with that Leonidas Karas to cheat on my son!" she tells the sun-scorched man.

"You what? " He glances at his mate. "I don't think she knows we're British."

"I don't think she knows she's crazy, either."

The first guy leans in close to her, thumb pointed at his chest, and says, "I no speak Greek. English!"

TRAVEL TIP: WHEN ENCOUNTERING FOREIGNERS, SPEAK LOUDLY, clearly, and in broken English. The more stupid you treat them, the more easily they'll be able to understand you. Stupidity is universal.

"*MALAKAS*," HELENA MUTTERS BEFORE MOVING ON TO THE NEXT person.

By the time she's done, all of Greece will know what Kiki Andreou is made of, even the *touristas*. Soon Kiki will come to her and speak her mind. That is Helena's plan.

"Worst plan ever, Mama. Kiki won't come."

Silence.

It's a first, Helena ignoring her son's voice.

But children, what do they know about the terrible prices parents pay, the bargains they strike with any of the universe's open ears?

Nothing.

Not until they are parents themselves can they know.

A SEETHING, BUBBLING WOMAN WALKS INTO DR TRIANTAFILLOU'S office. Today she does not sit. When she's not pacing, she's staring out the window at the helpless world, milling in and out of the hospital's doors. She has a plan, yes, but she needs this anger to steer her ship.

"You seem upset today," the psychologist says.

"Why would I be upset? Do I look upset? I am not upset."

What does this woman know about being upset? All she has to worry about is fashion, about what clothes she will wear that day.

When Dr Triantafillou says, "Is that how you see me? As a woman who only cares about clothes?" Helena realizes the words have escaped from her head through her mouth.

"I—"

The psychologist holds up her hand. "It's okay. In this room we must be honest with each other, otherwise we have nothing."

Her words touch a pin to Helena's fury. Her shoulders slump. "I misspoke."

"It is true, I do like clothes. A different color can change your whole mood. Red for confidence, yellow for happiness. At home, I wear white or blue, because they are cool and calm. And when I am cool and calm, my daughter is cool and calm also."

Today she's in a bright orange shift that would make anyone else look like a piece of fruit. Her heels are the same bronze as her tan; they make her legs go forever.

Helena remembers orange, but it's a color from a lifetime ago. "Many years ago, I, too, loved fashion. Today I am an old woman in black. My time for fashion is gone."

"You can still look good in black."

"Bah! You cannot fix grief with a new dress."

Dr Triantafillou shakes her head. "I'm not trying to fix your grief. But it is easier to do life when you wear clothes instead of them wearing you."

Helena sags into the chair. It is comfortable, as though it is glad she has chosen to sit.

"That girl is cheating on my son," she tells her hands.

Smooth, easy, barely a pause: "How do you know?"

"I saw her last night, sneaking down the street with a man. He was tall and handsome." *Alive.*

"Perhaps he was family."

Helena shakes her head. "No. I know the family as well as I know my own. We were inseparable, Margarita and I. Since we were children."

"Were?"

"I do not want her pity."

Silence, then she glides to the next question. "What about your other friends?"

"Other friends?" Helena laughs. "Nobody wants to be friends with the dead man's mother. What if it is contagious?"

HELENA WILL NOT BE BACK. SHE HAS ALREADY DECIDED.

✣ 83 ✣

KIKI

I t isn't long before they turn their backs on the sea. Here Greece is thirsty, her lands covered in stretch marks, nature-made. Lots of invaders have tried to leave their own set of scars on Greece, but where are they now?

Not here, that's where.

"Music?" she asks her traveling companions. Leo's riding shotgun, while her cousin sprawls in the backseat, as much as a Mini Cooper will let a grown man sprawl.

"Only if you don't sing," Kostas says.

"I hate you," she tells him. Leo tries the whole not laughing thing, but it's not easy, she can tell. "I hate you, too," Kiki tells him.

"No you don't. I'm charming and handsome."

Yes, yes he is. Too charming. Too handsome. "All Greek men think they're charming and handsome."

Kostas laughs. "That's because we are."

Leo turns in his seat. "Did Kiki tell you she went to jail?"

"Kiki!" False outrage. The priest is grinning. "All this time I thought you were the good cousin, like Max. What did you do?"

Kiki shrugs. "It was nothing. A very small fight with a Romani woman."

Kostas looks at the Mini's ceiling. "Forgive her, Father, for she is truly an Andreou. What did you fight about?"

She gives him the barely dramatic highlights.

The priest frowns. "It is not like the Romani to go to the police. They make a habit of avoiding the authorities."

Kiki bobs her head. "I know."

"You're a smart woman, what do you think?"

Her cousin's eyes are dark in the rearview mirror. Kostas has an uncanny way of seeing into a person. Always has, long before God chose him for service.

"I think bending a woman's finger backwards until she squeals like a pig is not a good reason to file an assault charge. But perhaps I offended her some other way."

"So close," Kostas says. "You're almost there."

Does she dare say it? "I've seen her before. She came to the house begging for money." But she didn't ask for a single euro—did she? "And I think I saw her across the street at Stavros's funeral."

"You think he was—" Leo starts.

"Fucking a Romani woman? Why not? He fucked everyone else." Kiki speaks plainly. And why not? Stavros had no shame—why should she?

"You knew?" Leo says. Thanks to her stellar peripheral vision she witnesses his shock. Very fish-like.

"Everyone knew, except maybe his mother." Kostas tells him. "Stavros did not know the meaning of discretion."

Leo won't quit staring. "And you were going to marry him? Why didn't you say no?"

"I might have, if there was someone worth the fight."

"What—you're not worth the fight?"

Kiki's gaze meets her cousin's in the mirror again. "I'm not an angel, Leo. I haven't been waiting for marriage all this time, not to a man I didn't love. There were men. Stavros's affairs outnumbered mine by a lot, but there were still men."

"Wow."

She glances over just as he turns back to the road. Is he horrified?

Disgusted? She can't read him, not when all she's got to work with is his profile, one stolen glance at a time.

"Are you shocked?"

"Sex doesn't shock me. Sex is amazing," he says. "You surprise me, that's all."

"I surprise you?"

"You're unexpected," he says. "Surprising at every turn."

"Everyone is surprising, Leo. That's one of the most interesting things about being alive."

With one finger, she flicks on the radio. Music pours from the speakers, fills her world. Kiki sings. Sometimes it's fun to watch grown men beg for mercy.

❧ 84 ❧

LEO

The Vale of Tempe has seen its share of war. During World War II, the Germans (playing the part of Xerxes and the Persians) threw ammunition at a combination of Greek, Australian and New Zealand forces (playing King Leonidas and his Spartans), because they had the audacity to stand between the Germans and the city of Larissa, a geographical bottleneck, through which allied troops flooded north.

Spoiler alert: The Germans won that battle, but lost the war. So both sides went home with a plush toy.

The pass still sees a lot of death. Greece builds its statues and houses to last, more or less, but its roads ... not so much. If it's not the pitted roads and rolling trucks, it's the falling rocks.

"TEMPE IS A COPYCAT," KOSTAS SAYS OF THE VILLAGE SQUATTING ON the far side of the river. "They put a church in the mountain, too. But my church is better." There's a twinkle in his eye as he says it.

A suspension bridge hangs between the road and the village. Pedestrians only.

Kiki says, "Not the whole church."

"Not the whole church," he agrees. "Some of it sits outside."

Ten degrees cooler in this green corridor. The river chatters as it crosses under the bridge, on its hunt for the Aegean Sea.

"Are we stopping?" Leo asks. His legs want to walk, but his brain and heart want to charge the border.

"No. I just enjoy complaining about their church."

But it's obvious the man is kidding. The Kostas Andreou he knew was the same guy, he didn't have a mean bone in his body.

A handful of miles down the road, the gorge spits them out near the coast. The land flattens as Kiki pushes the Mini Cooper north-east.

"Want me to drive?" he asks.

She shakes her head. "I'm good. Just enjoy the ride."

Hard to enjoy the ride when Kiki drives like she's one of the Four Horsemen of the Apocalypse. But Kostas is relaxed, so maybe he should just chill the hell out, too.

He leans back, closes his eyes. Replays the plan over and over. He doesn't skip forward to the end point, to the getting home. There will be time for that later—if the plan works.

It's not that he doubts Kostas, it's that he knows people. People have a way of screwing up a great plan. Throw in high stakes and a slow rotating finger at the law, and the chance of disaster increases exponentially.

But he's got to get home, and this is the only plan that ends without him saying his goodbyes to a marble slab.

His mind wanders a few inches left, to the woman with the lead foot. What are the odds he can come back and make things right with her?

Time. Leo never has enough of it. Hasn't since childhood. Those early years were tortoises, then somewhere along the way, they turned into race horses. Probably around the time he took out a mortgage. Banks hurry you from month to month so they can empty your pockets sooner.

By the time he makes things right with family, Greece and Kiki will be out of reach. Won't be long before the men come calling, with more to offer than Leo.

Ha! He barely knows Kiki, yet he already misses her.

He thinks about how he almost took a wrong turn at Soula. Good thing they both recognized zero chemistry when they saw it.

Eyes open. "Where are we?"

Kiki glances over. Dark smudges under her eyes. Messy hair. Creased dress. His cock thinks she looks amazing—and so does he.

"Katerini," she says.

Fields on both sides of the highway, growing crops he doesn't recognize. There's a faint perfume in the air he knows on some primal level, but his base self isn't speaking to the rest of his brain.

"Tobacco," she says.

"You reading my mind?"

"No. Just the question mark on your face. Greece is one of Europe's largest tobacco producers."

"I didn't know."

"Who thinks of tobacco when they think of Greece? Most people think of Santorini and other white islands, olives, beaches, and—now—our economic problems."

"Mention the word Greek back home and people think college."

She shoots him a confused look.

"Fraternities," he says in English. He gives her the abbreviated version of how Americans do college. Doesn't explain to her the other meaning of Greek in America. That's a show thing, not a tell thing.

Kiki shakes her head when he's done. "We go, we learn, we socialize. But it's not party, party, party until we're sick."

"Why teaching?"

"I like kids. Why veterinary medicine?"

"I like animals." His gaze coasts from the curve of her ankle all the way up to her dark hair. "And I like you."

A chuckle erupts from behind him. "Do not mind the man in the back seat. I am sleeping."

Leo laughs. "How long until we reach the border?"

"Not long," Kostas says. "About an hour."

Not a big country, Greece. From end to end it's about a twelve-hour drive—if you drive the American way. If you drive the Greek way, file off a couple of hours and set aside a few euro for speeding tickets, unless you know a guy who can pull the old my-uncle-is-the-law trick.

An hour.

And then it's goodbye.

85

KIKI

An hour until goodbye.

Her foot launches a protest on behalf of her heart by easing off the gas just a little. Good thing her head cuts in, shoves that rubber square back where it belongs. She likes Leo, which means the best thing she can do for him is drive as fast and safely as she can.

The second best thing she can do is say goodbye and never look back.

Not even to wonder: *what if?*

"TURN HERE."

Kostas is awake now, alert, watching everything. He touches Kiki's shoulder and follows his gentle instruction with a nod in the right direction.

The border is about a couple of kilometers ahead (about a mile, if you're American), but now she's jumping off the main road, onto a smaller stream that trickles to the right.

The road turns to dirt. She eases off the gas to shrink the dust cloud on their tail.

"A little further," Kostas says.

Leo looks cool, but his hands are balled into fists on his thighs.

"It's going to be okay," she tells him.

"Listen to Kiki," the priest says. "She is one of my smarter cousins."

Kiki reaches back, gives him a half-hearted slap on the head.

Leo swivels to look at them both. Small car; it's a short trip. "I can't tell you how much I appreciate your help—both of you. Whatever happens ..." He hands a piece of paper to each of them. Printed on both is his family's address, phone number, email address. "If you need anything—ever—name it and it's yours."

Kostas claps him on the shoulder, nods. "We're here."

❧ 86 ❧

LEO

He can see the border from here. No road, but there's something about the trees that suggest their allegiance has shifted. Those straddling the border look confused. Are they Greek? Are they Turkish? They don't know.

Leo doesn't know, either. Not about the trees, but about himself.

Kiki kills the gas near a guard shack. A couple of guys outside—soldiers, or guys doing a Hollywood imitation—slouched in chairs, weapons resting within reach.

One of them gets up, swaggers their way. He and Kostas slap hands, then the soldier nods at Leo."Is this him?"

"He's the one," Kostas says.

"Greek?"

"Greek-American," Leo says.

Stone Face looks him up and down. No movement, just his traveling eyes. Then he shrugs, spits on the ground. "No problem. You have your uniform? Put it on."

Kostas and Stone Face stand in their own huddle, swapping whatever it is they have to swap. Promises, prayers—who knows?

Leo has questions, but he doesn't stop to ask them. He does what needs to be done, and he does it fast.

Kiki watches him strip. He watches Kiki watching him strip.

Turnabout is fair play. He's seen her naked, hasn't he?

He'd like to see her naked again. But he'd settle for fully dressed, like she is right now. The woman is just plain good company.

Pants up and buttoned. "I like you," he says.

"I like you, too."

"I'd stay if I could, maybe see what this could be."

She shakes her head, waves at her dress. "Leo, this is my life for the next two years."

"Could be you're worth waiting for."

She laughs. Again with the head shaking. "Leo, look at you. You're not a man who needs to wait. Men like you do very well out there."

Ouch. "You think I'm a player?"

"No. I think you're very handsome and very single. And whether a man like you wants them or not, a lot of opportunities will come your way. I'm just one Greek woman in a tiny nothing of a village, with nothing to offer you but wasted time."

"Is that how you see yourself, as a waste of time?"

She bends down, picks up his clothes. Folds. "No. I'm telling you I'm a waste of *your* time. There's a difference."

He shrugs into the shirt, leaves it hanging open while he rolls the sleeves, until they're sitting neatly above his elbows.

She's eating him with her eyes—no shame. It's turning him on, her lack of shame. He figured that was a Soula thing, but it's also a Kiki thing.

And he likes it.

She drops his folded clothes on top of his bag. Then she's in front of him, up close, fingers dancing over his buttons. Her breath is a small puff of hot air on his neck.

"I can do buttons," he says.

"Yes, but do you want to?" Husky, warm, no ambiguity.

Perfectly still. "No."

"Karas, you ready?"

Leo looks over his shoulder, sees his immediate future waiting.

"Ready," he says.

❧ 87 ❧

KIKI

Kiki falls away. One second changes everything. Present to past in a heartbeat.

"Email. Write. Call. Anytime," Leo says.

"I will."

His fingers curl around her wrist, reel her in. "Promise."

"I promise."

Then the man who is never coming back kisses her. He keeps her close, one hand behind her neck as he goes deeper.

First kiss, last kiss in one.

Normally when she kisses a guy, they're on their way to naked, but Leo is on his way to dressed and gone. She wants to go up in flames with him, but there's no time for their bodies to burn.

"Karas!"

"Let them have this one moment, eh?" she hears her cousin say.

Then it's Leo who falls away. "It's time."

And she's not sure if he means it's time for him to go, or if it's time who is the other woman standing between them.

"Go," she tells him. "And be careful. Turkey is not Greece."

He joins the other soldiers, jumps into the back of a Jeep.

She watches them bounce away, destination: Turkey. Leo's gaze stays on her until trees swallow the slow-moving vehicle.

"Good guy," Kostas says.

Kiki says, "I know."

"So?"

"I'm in mourning and he's gone."

"You will not always be in mourning, and he can always come back."

She shakes her head. "Once he crosses that border, Greece and I, we will be forgotten."

He puts one black-clad arm around her shoulders. "Kiki ... You and Greece, you are both unforgettable. Have a little faith."

❧ 88 ❦
KIKI

Kiki crawls toward home, metaphorically speaking. Figuratively, the Mini is moving at a good ten kilometers below the speed limit. A car zips out from behind them, cuts in front of her just in time to miss an oncoming tour bus.

Kostas says, "He will be back."

Yeah, vacationing with a wife and kids.

MAMA'S NOT SO MUCH COOKING AS SHE IS PLAYING PERCUSSION IN the hot kitchen.

"Where were you, Kiki? I was worried sick. Your father was worried sick."

"I was worried sick," *Yiayia* says.

A wooden spoon points its scoop the old woman's way. "You will impress me more if you are worried dead."

Yiayia doesn't flinch. "Is my snack ready, yet?"

"A snack before lunch! In a minute, Mama. I am trying to yell at Kiki."

"If you are trying, very good, you are successful. Everybody in Agria can hear you."

Mama slits the candy wrapper, dumps the entire wafter in the blender, hits the red button. Brown and tan dust fills the jug.

"You cannot just leave without telling anyone," she shrieks over the mechanical whirring. "I thought you were in a gutter, dead. Or maybe alive and in a Turkish harem."

"Do they still have harems?" *Yiayia* asks. "I would not mind being in a harem."

"With all those women?" Kiki asks.

"I did not think about that. A harem would be awful. Dozens of women like your mother ..."

The idea of her mother in a harem is preposterous. Kiki closes her eyes, wards away the image by crossing herself, forehead to chest, shoulder to shoulder. She crosses herself a second time to banish the image of *Yiayia* shimmying up to a Turkish prince.

"I was with Kostas."

"Kostas Andreou? Your cousin Kostas?"

"That's the one."

Mama dumps the powder in a bowl, throws in a spoon. It lands with a crash in front of *Yiayia*. "Here is your chocolate, Mama." To Kiki: "What were you doing with Kostas? What took you so long?"

"We were talking."

"Talking!"

"I was helping him tend to the poor."

"Tending to the poor? If only that was true!"

"I can't tell you."

"Why not?" She slams a lid on the pot. "I am your mother. You should tell me everything."

"Do not tell me everything," *Yiayia* tells her daughter. "I do not care."

"No one is asking you, old woman." She gives Kiki a sharp look. She could cut steel with that intensity.

What can she say? Not the truth, that's what. Because she will never—ever—hear the end of it. "We were helping someone, Mama. Leave it alone."

"Helping. And while you were helping someone, I was looking for you everywhere. And not only could I not find you, but I could not find your sister."

"Soula's missing?"

"I'm not missing." Soula bounces into the kitchen in white linen pants and a turquoise top, bracelets dancing up her arms.

Mama points a fork at her. "And where were you?"

"Out."

"Out where?"

Soula leans over. "How old are we again?" she says in a stage whisper.

Margarita slaps her across the back of the head. "Not too old that I cannot smack you. And not so old that I cannot worry about my daughters. If you were sons I would not worry, but anything can happen to a daughter."

"Anything can happen to a son, too, Mama," Soula says lightly. "Look at Stavros. Being a guy didn't help him."

The kitchen doesn't go still, it goes empty. Every bit of sound and air sucked away, through Margarita's teeth.

It's like waiting on a volcano to blow. Mount Margarita. Her explosions are legendary, and they flatten whole families and turn enemies to salt. God and Zeus could call her for advice on that whole eye-for-an-eye thing. She doesn't just take one eye—she snatches out both and crushes them beneath her slippers.

When Margarita speaks, it's with a strange calm. Trouble is coming. Big trouble. "Are you hungry?" She doesn't wait for an answer. She heaves the pot off the stove, leaves the blue ring of flames flickering. "Wherever you girls went I hope you worked up an appetite, because I worked very hard to make this." Then she upends the pot on the kitchen table.

Hot lentil soup hits the Formica. What doesn't splatter, splashes, leaving the three seated women covered in brown-green soup.

Baba pokes his head through the door, takes a long look at the scene of his wife's crime. "I cannot stay for lunch. I will grab a *souvlaki*, okay?"

"Okay," Mama says brightly. "I hope you choke on it."

"I will try." Then he's gone.

Kiki gets up. Grabs three spoons. Gives one to Soula, to *Yiayia*, and keeps the last for herself. She dabs the table with a chunk of bread, shovels it into her mouth.

"Thank you, Mama," she says with a full mouth. "It's delicious. Best you ever made."

✖ 89 ✖

LEO

I t's not a piece of cake, but close.
     Leo could die from the shock. The American Embassy spits out a temporary passport overnight.

He's tough on the outside, Jell-O on the inside while he waits for the plane. The airport is crowded. Everything sounds harsh, jangled. At the same time, it's muted. Doesn't make sense, but sometimes the world is that way.

He drops his bag on the ground, scoots it between his feet. Zips his credit card through the payphone's vertical mouth. Punches his Dad's cell number.

"I'm on my way home," he says.

"Thank God," his father says. "Thank God."

He wants to call Kiki, but he doesn't have her number. Somehow the information swap got messed up before it was complete, and now he's slouched in an airport seat, staring sightlessly at foot traffic, wondering if she got back okay, if she's happy.

THE PLANE LEAVES THE TERMINAL, THEN IT LEAVES THE GROUND, and soon Turkey is patch of brown and green somewhere behind him.

Closer to Mom, closer to home.

Farther from Kiki. Or is it further?

Doesn't matter, he left her behind.

❧ 90 ❧

KIKI

She watches her world for signs. Not street signs—the other ones. Every day occurrences, meaningless to everyone but a mildly desperate person.

Kiki's not desperate, she's ...

Yes, she is. May as well admit it, because it's true.

Which is why she's careful that her shoes don't flip over when she slides them off. (If one ends up in the upside down position, she'll have to mutter "garlic" to ward away the bad luck.) And why when that crow flits past, she wishes it well.

A good sign. She needs one. Just one that lets her know Leo made it home okay.

It's not long before Vivi's paperwork is a solved and signed mystery, flitting away in its paper envelopes. Which means she's back to whiling away her afternoons with books and daydreams.

Daydreams are dangerous things. They are where longing is born.

KIKI'S NOT IN A BENEVOLENT MOOD, WHICH IS WHY SHE LEAVES

Detective Lemonis to fend for himself when he comes calling at the front gate. Let him suffer. Only the strong survive Mama and *Yiayia*.

"What do you want, eh?"

"Is *Despinida* Andreou home?"

"Which one? I have two daughters."

Mama knows perfectly well which one. Only one of her daughters is a murder suspect, but she enjoys being difficult. Kiki's okay with it when someone more deserving is on the receiving end.

"Kyriaki."

"Maybe. Last time I looked I was not her keeper. She comes and goes as she pleases without my permission. What do you want with her, eh?"

"I am looking for answers."

"What are the questions? Ask us, and we will tell you if we know the answers." She looks at *Yiayia* for confirmation.

Yiayia shakes her head. "Why you want to ask young people questions? They know nothing. If you want answers, ask an old person. But not my daughter, because she is very stupid for an old woman."

"I'm not that old, Mama."

"Your face is not old, but inside you are a *strigla*."

"Yes, yes, I am a hag. I get that from your side."

The detective clears his throat. Looks like his patience is wearing thin. Good. Maybe he'll go away. "I want to know if Kyriaki had any lovers."

Mama crosses herself. "Kiki!" she hollers up at Kiki's balcony. "This one is your problem."

Kiki jogs down the stairs to join them.

"I am going," Mama says, crossing herself again.

"Not me," *Yiayia* says. "You two talk and I will listen."

"Mama!"

"What? You will hide behind the curtain like a thief and listen. I am more honest, that is all." But it's an empty protest because Margarita grabs the wheel chair, rolls her inside.

"I apologize," Kiki says. "My family ..."

"I have two sisters and a mother. And I'm the youngest child."

"My condolences."

It's a dry laugh, but better than nothing.

She says, "To answer your question, yes. But not for a couple of years. Maybe a bit longer."

"Leonidas Karas." *Yiayia*'s voice trickles out the window.

"Don't listen to her," Kiki says. "Leo and I are just friends. And he wasn't in the country when Stavros was killed."

"Who else?"

She laughs, because it's better than crying. "Detective, you're wasting your time with me. Unlike Stavros, I was discreet. Any men in my past are long gone. Not one was local, and I made my lack of intentions very clear at the time."

In the kitchen, Mama gasps.

"She thinks I'm a virgin," Kiki tells him. She turns around. "I'm not a virgin, Mama!"

"That is okay," *Yiayia* calls out. "Your mother was not a virgin when she got married, either."

A moment later, there's a symphony of screaming silverware.

"Welcome to my life, Detective. If you want to find a murderer, you won't find one by picking at the bones of my life."

Whatever she expects next, it's not his reaction. He drops down into one of the shaded chairs, rubs his head, eyes cast on a patch of sun that's made a heroic journey through the densely layered vine leaves overhead.

"I'm chasing a ghost. You're the only lead I've got."

She sits next to him, pats him on the back. It's unprofessional, but the guy looks like he could use some kindness.

"I'm not a lead. I'm just a bystander who got caught in the crossfire."

❧ 91 ❧

LEO

" Welcome home."
        Stamp.

Just like that, he's on American soil again. The air is alive with Americans speaking English words the American way.

It's jarring.

Nothing to declare. The Customs officers and their dogs look through him as he rolls on by with his luggage.

Then it's out the doors into the space filled with people wearing (mostly) happy faces. None of them are waiting on him. That comes later, after another flight, another airport.

No payphone this time. He got online back in Turkey, paid the phone bill, charged his cell on the plane, and now it's three bars and counting. Four. Five. His phone shakes with unacknowledged alerts. From Dad, from Soc, from spammers peddling spam.

He checks. Nothing he doesn't already know, except he'll win a cruise if he comes to some timeshare thing.

He inches toward the domestic terminal on a slow-moving shuttle. Sunny day, but it's missing Greece's blinding edge. Smells different. People look different. His people, but they seem foreign. Nobody on the shuttle is carrying a sack of live chickens or wearing black knee-high stockings. It's a mixture of faces, from dark to pale, with every variation in between. Not a lot of golden tans, though, or skins browned and lined from years of honest work under the sun's wicked glare.

So this is it: culture shock.

"What are you looking at?" the guy across from him barks.

"I don't know," Leo admits

What is he looking at?

Nothing, that's what. His eyes are pointing in the other guy's direction, but there's no looking going on. Leo's seeing Kiki all over again, beautiful in that rumpled black dress as she stood at the border waving.

Too bad he couldn't pack her in his luggage.

He wonders if she has a passport, if he can fly her here when his mother is—

When things return to the kind of normal his family has to face here on out.

He open his email, considers shooting her a note, but he never got her email address, did he? That damn one-way swap. He's at her mercy, unless he bugs *Papou* for her digits or email.

Off the shuttle, into the terminal. The flashing board tells him his flight is on-time. He checks his bag, knocks back a latte at Starbucks, glances at the *New York Times*'s front page.

Nothing but bad news.

Leo is a man with a lot bad news headed his way, so he doesn't bother buying the newspaper. He wants to hear something positive, something good.

He texts Dad, his brother, gives them his flight info again, in case they forgot. Only his brother replies. He'll be waiting, Soc says, because Dad's at the hospital. He uses a kind of teen shorthand that makes Leo's eyes want to bleed.

Then it's boarding time ...

Departure time ...

Wasted time in the air, where he's got nothing to do but percolate

...

Landing time, but the pilot is goofing around, waiting on permission to land from the FAA gods.

On the ground—finally.

Everyone surges in the same moment, causing gridlock in the aisle. Luggage falls from the overhead compartment, onto heads, into arms. No grace, only chaos.

Leo's tall enough that his bag pops out with minimal persuasion. Then he gets busy helping the women next to him. They're grateful in a polite, detached way. They're less polite as they near the front and it's every woman and man for themselves.

Leo remembers the days when a person waiting on you could walk right up to the gate. Not anymore. He does a lot of walking before he sees Socrates the younger slouching against a wall, thumbs dancing over his phone.

"Hey," he says.

His brother glances up. Tears explode out of him.

Leo thinks: *I'm too late.*

❧ 92 ❧

KIKI

Summer drags Kiki along behind it. The passing of time is in no way awesome, as far as she's concerned. The missing of Leo never wanes. Soon August is coming, then September, and with it, school.

What's going to happen, then?

The principal has assured her that she still has a solid place amongst his faculty, but he's not from Agria. He lives in Volos, where Agria can't squeeze him.

"Are you coming to the festival?" Soula asks.

"No."

"You're coming to the festival," she says decisively.

The Fishermen's Festival. Or the Fishermen's Night. Whatever you want to call it, the festival happens in late July, early August. This year it falls in July.

And Kiki is not going.

"I can hear you thinking," Soula says. "And we're going together, okay? If anyone attacks you, I will punch them in the throat."

Kiki believes her. But she's still not going.

"Yes, you are."

"Stop doing that."

Her sister shrugs. "Don't think so loud, then."

"YOU CANNOT GO TO THE FESTIVAL," MAMA SAYS. "WHAT WILL people say? You are in mourning, which means no festivals for you."

"It's been more forty days."

"It is still disrespectful! Two years!"

Kiki hadn't considered that angle. Mostly she was worried about the taking-a-beating-and-being-spat-on-for-murder thing.

"Soula told me I have to."

"Soula, Soula, Soula. Who listens to Soula? Would you ask a man with no legs how to walk? No! Then why would you listen to anything Soula says?"

"Soula is like a man with no legs?"

"It is a metaphor," Mama says. "Your sister has no etiquette and a very big mouth."

"Just like her mother." Her father drops a kiss on his wife's head on the way out the door. She swats at him.

"Careful, or I will spit in your food."

He winks at Kiki from behind Mama's back. "Again?"

"Relax, Mama," Kiki says. "I'm not going to the festival."

IF SHE'S NOT GOING TO THE FESTIVAL, WHY IS SHE AT THE FESTIVAL?

Soula. Of course.

The bulldozer in high heels pushed her all the way down here, despite their mother's shrieks.

"It's not so bad—see?" Soula says cheerfully.

Kiki is temporarily dazed. The promenade is lit up from end to end with multicolored lights, and people stroll beneath them, from St. George's to the bumper cars. In between, the tavernas hum with conversation and the sounds of glasses clinking. Everyone is toasting to good health, good fortune, good life.

Before they left, Kiki made her own toast with a bottle of EPSA lemonade—a toast to invisibility.

So far, it's working. Everyone is dazzled by the lights, the noise, the corn toasting over hot coals. Bowls of fish soup and other freshly-caught seafood dance across the promenade from taverna to table.

"Kiki, Soula!"

Kiki's blood plunges to freezing, then warms back up when Vivi, Max and Melissa push out of the crowd.

Hugs, hug. Kiss, kiss.

"Look at you," Kiki says to the pretty blonde girl, "every time I see you you are more beautiful."

Melissa closes one eye and winces. "You're not going to spit on me, are you?"

Kiki laughs. "I'm not going to spit on you."

Fist pump. "Hooray! Greece is finally coming around to my way of thinking."

"Melissa, Vivi!"

More bodies out of the crowd. This time it's Vivi's aunt *Kyria* Dora.

"Look at you, Melissa," she crows. "Prettier every day." Then she dry spits in Melissa's direction.

"Great," Melissa mouths. Kiki tries not to laugh, and succeeds —mostly.

"Hello, Soula, Kiki." The bigger, older woman nods at them both. "Kiki, where is your friend?" A very innocent-sounding question, that —underneath—is the equivalent of a backhoe.

"Which friend is that?"

"*Kyrios* Socrates's boy. Leonidas."

Vivi wags a finger in her aunt's face. "No! We've had this conversation."

Palms up, *Kyria* Dora says, "I was just asking. Leonidas is a good boy. I read his cup the other week. But there was not much inside because he drank the coffee and the grounds. Then he caught some wild animals for me."

"How is Effie?" Kiki asks.

"Still a lesbian. All she needs a good man and she will change her mind."

Kiki thinks that's not how it works, but what does she know? Effie had a husband for a long time, and before that—rumor has it—she and

Detective Lemonis had a fling. But she knows how gossip is here. It's like popcorn, mostly filled with hot air. Mostly.

"My family loves her show," Kiki tells her.

The big woman beams. "In Germany, they worship her. This is because they do not know how stupid she is. But these are people who voted for Hitler and love David Hasselhoff, so they have no taste." Despite her words, it's obvious she's proud.

"Have you heard from Leo?" Vivi asks.

No, she hasn't heard from Leo. And Leo hasn't heard from her. The paper he gave her sits in her desk between the pages of a diary she never uses. She keeps meaning to fire an email across the ocean, but when she sits at her computer, her fingers find the backspace faster than SEND.

What is she waiting for?

A miracle.

"Leo? He is well. He is back home," Kostas says, pushing into the circle, black robes swirling around his calves. "He sends his gratitude and good wishes. And I sent him ours. He has a new address." He gives Kiki a meaningful look.

Kyria Dora double-takes. "*Skordia, skordia,*" she mutters. She's old school, which means catching sight of a priest going walkabout in the street is potentially bad luck. But the mere mention of garlic chases the bad luck away.

Like vampires, bad luck doesn't like garlic.

"Is his mother—?" Kiki starts.

"Holding on," Kostas assures her. "I think *Kyria* Kara must be a very strong woman. She had to be to survive here."

"His mother was very strange woman," *Kyria* Dora says.

"You mean she was American," Vivi says.

"Eh, it is the same thing. Even your mother is strange—" She points to her head. "—after all those years in America. It must be the radiation."

Vivi blinks at her. "Radiation from what?"

"The satellites."

The older woman doesn't see her niece shake her head slightly, or the tiny smile flitting across her lips.

"I'm starving," Soula says. "Anyone else?"

"Good luck finding a table," *Kyria* Dora says, glancing back. "Every chair is full of bottoms."

Soula's large hooped earrings rattle in time with her head shake. "No table necessary. Every time I come to the *paralia*, I eat the same thing."

"*Souvlaki*," Kiki says.

"*Souvlaki*," Soula confirms. "And not just any *souvlaki*."

Vivi slings her arm around her daughter's shoulder. "You want *souvlaki*?"

Melissa jerks her head up, makes a *tst* sound.

"Oh my God," Vivi groans. "Can you not do that?"

"They all do it." Kiki shakes her head at Melissa. "Try listening to a whole classroom full of them making that sound."

"No," Vivi tells her daughter. "The word is no. Learn it. Use it. Or you're grounded."

Kyria Dora is the first to snap off the group. She staggers over to the stage set up at the promenade's concrete lip and finds a chair. The music is on, the dancers are dancing to a traditional Greek folk song. Kiki danced there once, when she was a girl. The clothes were hot, heavy, not made for summer nights.

"Kiki?" Soula says.

"I'm fine. Go get your *souvlaki*."

"Will you be okay?"

Maybe.

"Wait right there," Soula says. "Do not go anywhere."

———

KIKI DOESN'T GO ANYWHERE—ANYWHERE COMES TO HER.

"Kiki, what are you doing here?" Stavros's best friend, Akili, appears at her elbow. *Retsina* fumes roll off him. "It's disrespectful."

"Then it's a good thing I care about your opinion."

He glances side to side, then back at her. He tilts his head toward the meandering crowd. "Walk with me, Kiki."

Kiki doesn't want to walk, she wants to scream. "I'm not going anywhere with you."

"It's just a little walk. Come on."

His fingers are an iron manacle around her wrist. She's going nowhere, except with him. Unless she screams. And all this noise, who can separate a cry for help from a cry for more?

"You like to ride, Kiki?" He nods to the Ferris wheel, making its slow tour of the night sky.

"I don't like heights."

Not true. Kiki has never minded heights. It's the falling that worries her, and the crash at the bottom.

"I'll protect you," he says.

She thinks about flinging herself on the ground, throwing an epic toddler tantrum, but who would notice? People here act out their own personal melodramas all the time—hers would be minor. And anyone watching would shake their heads and say, 'We knew Kiki Andreou was crazy, just like Candy Box.'

So she goes, hoping for an intervention between here and there.

No such luck. Akili buys two tickets from the guy working the wheel. Kiki doesn't know the man—they're a package deal with the equipment, moving from town to celebrating town. Akili shoves her into a swaying red bucket, then they jerk up and away so the next couple can take their seat.

"How are you, Kiki? Are you well?"

They're staring into the same darkness ahead, his arm casually curved around the bucket's back. Possessive, but not touching her.

If he touches, she'll break his finger off, throw it to the fish. No mercy like she showed the Romani woman.

In a bored voice: "Fine."

"Are you going to ask how I am?"

"No."

"Come on, Kiki, why not? I thought we were friends."

"You were Stavros's friend—not mine."

"And now I do not have my best friend. So you owe me."

Now she looks at him, nothing but disdain on her face. "I owe you nothing."

"Yes, you do. You killed Stavros, now you owe me a friend."

The wheel jerks again. Higher. On the promenade, people are shrinking like they've been hit with a ray gun. A cold needle makes frozen stitches up and down her spine. Her fight and flight is malfunctioning: she wants to punch him in the face first, then do the running.

Anger. Fear. Kiki's feeling both. "God, I'm so tired of defending myself."

"Good," he says, glancing her way. "Confess, then you will feel much better. Did you get the present?"

"What present?"

"I left it for you on your table."

"You left the bomb?"

He looks confused. "Bomb? Hey, I don't know anything about a bomb. All I did was deliver something Stavros told me to give you. He said to give it to you at the church, but then—"

A lightbulb flicks on in her head, brighter than all the lights on the promenade combined. That little bastard. "You knew, didn't you? Stavros meant to stand me up, and you knew."

"He wasn't supposed to get mur—"

"I don't have time for this *skata*." She stands. The bucket sways, but it's more stable than the guy still sitting.

"Where are you going?"

"Away from you."

The wheel moves another bucket higher.

"You'll fall!"

"Oh, please," Kiki scoffs. She was one of those kids who used to scale trees—sometimes to steal fruit, sometimes to throw it at Soula and the other kids. This metal giant is nothing—nothing.

It's a short drop to the next bucket.

"Hi," she says to the bewildered people sitting inside. "I'm Kiki Andreou. Nice to meet you. Hey," she calls out to the wheel operator. "Can you stop this thing? I need to get down. I'm trying to get away from a crazy person."

He gives her a look that says the other crazy person must be certifiable, because Kiki's not looking too sane herself. But he stops the wheel, because who needs that on their record?

Kiki clambers over the two people in their bucket, straddles the wheel's arm, shuffles forward a meter or so, then drops to the next bucket. From there it's just a short fall to the ground.

She lands with a gymnast's flourish.

"Thanks," she tells the operator. Then she dusts herself off and curtseys to the people waiting on their turn to ride. She looks up. "Hey, Akili?"

He's leaning over the bucket's edge. Even under the colored lights he looks pale. "What?

She thinks about all the things she could say—should say. But she can't do it. Akili is an ass, yes, but he's an ass in pain. He lost his best friend in this whole world, so she can't twist a knife in him.

"Take care of yourself, okay?"

❧ 93 ❧

KIKI

Mama's performing a post-mortem on Kiki's evening. Because everything Kiki did, everything Kiki said, showed up at home before she did.

There's no way to beat gossip home, unless you're one of those flying superheroes.

Kiki isn't a superhero. That should be obvious by now.

"...And then she jumped from the Ferris wheel onto the ground!"

She should be in the theater, Margarita Andreou. None of that modern day performance, where subtlety lives, but theater circa Ancient Greece. They'd eat her performance and beg for more in one of those stone amphitheaters.

Deep breath. Kiki waits for the perfumed air to work its magic, but the gardenias are sleeping, thick petals pulled tightly around their shoulders.

Thanks for nothing, flowers.

She doesn't tell her mother about Akili's unintentional revelation, not when she's unsure how she feels. Too bad Stavros wasn't man enough to deliver the news himself. Too bad he didn't feel like he could. Overjoyed is how she would have felt if he'd come to her with his breakup plans.

It's all just too, too bad.

"I jumped," Kiki says, "but not onto the ground. Not at first."

"Not at first," Mama repeats, like she's dying.

"You act like I had a choice."

"You did have a choice! To jump or not jump! What will people say?"

"Margarita, leave the girl alone, eh?"

Reasonable man, her father. He has to be to balance out his wife. Can't have two crazy people in a marriage, unless the family is the kind of wealthy that can buy an island or two.

"What will they say? There's nothing else to say, because they've already said it!"

"Your logic has no place here, Kiki." *Baba* shakes his head. "You should know that by now."

"*Ai sto dialo*!"

(Which is the cheap and dirty Greek way of saying, "Go to the devil.")

Soula pushes through the gate, carrying two paper-wrapped *souvlakia*. When she sees Kiki, her pretty mouth droops. "Where did you go? I told you to stay right there."

"A problem ran into me."

"Good thing you're my favorite sister. Here." She hands one of the parcels to Kiki on the way past. Then she vanishes up the stairs, sandals slapping the steps as she runs.

Squinting up at the stairs, Mama hollers, "What are you doing, Soula?"

"Going out!"

"Going out," Mama says flatly. "Always out."

"It is called being young and single," *Baba* tells her.

"I was young and single once, and I was never like that."

"No, you were worse," her husband says.

Footsteps on the street. One voice. "Margarita, Kiki, come quick!"

Yiayia. For an old woman, she's spry. The wheelchair is just part of the act. When she wants to—like tonight—she can run, skirt's hem bunched in her hands.

"Mama, what?"

"It is Kiki!"

"Kiki's right here."

"Yes, I see that. I am not blind, just old. Kiki," she says, out of breath. "Everybody is talking about you and the Karas boy. Helena has told everyone you are a *putana*, doing the sex with him while you are still in mourning."

"I didn't touch him!"

Not completely true, but Agria doesn't have eyes on the Turkish border, does it?

Does it?

Anything is possible.

Mama wags a finger. "It does not matter what you did or did not do, only what they say you do."

"Was it good?" *Yiayia* looks much too happy about all this.

"No! We didn't do anything," Kiki says.

"That is too bad. If my granddaughters will not have sex, then I suppose I will have to find some men for myself."

Margarita glares at her. "What are you talking about, Mama?"

"Life is interesting lately, yes? Before, it was boring. Being in a coma was the only fun I had. The things people will say when they think you cannot hear them ..."

"Life is interesting," Mama mocks, but her eyes are cold, hard. "So Helena is the one saying this, eh?"

"Yes, it was Helena. What a mouth she has. I always knew she was a problem."

"Do not worry about Helena," Mama tells Kiki. "I will fix her."

Uh oh. The wrath of Margarita is coming, and Kiki's just glad it's not coming for her. But Helena? She better start enjoying her final moments.

"Oh my Virgin Mary," *Yiayia* says suddenly. "I think I left my wheelchair behind."

"Yes," Mama says dryly. "It is a miracle."

✤ 94 ✤

HELENA

Late afternoon and the sun is still visiting, but its conversation is dying out. The village is shaking off its sleep, stretching, and in the street there are signs of movement. The air smells dry, scorched, thirsty. Before long, she'll go outside armed with the hose and show she is merciful.

"Helena, come out!"

Margarita. Helena knows her friend's call by heart.

"Helena! I know you are in there, coward!"

Helena considers sliding down the wall, curling into a ball until the other woman leaves. But she knows Margarita like she knows her own self. Margarita will not go until she has cut and weighed her kilo of Helena's flesh.

What else can she do but face her accuser?

Nothing.

Her plan is unraveling. She expected the daughter not the mother. A mistake. A sloppy calculation. The Margarita Andreous of this world do not sit by while somebody shovels *skata* onto their daughters.

Now she needs a new lure to bring Kiki to her.

In the meantime ...

She opens the door but does not step through it. The cacti that frame the opening (it's a good luck thing), the geraniums, the gardenias, they are silent, beautiful witnesses. They know it is coming, the *coup de grâce* of what was once the strongest friendship.

"What do you want, Margarita? I am a busy woman."

Margarita is Artemis, goddess of the hunt, with a broom for a bow. "What are you telling people about my daughter?"

"The truth."

"You called my Kiki a whore! And you told this to everybody!"

"Like I said, the truth."

Margarita shakes her broom in the air. "If you were another woman, I would kill you where you stand. I only let you live because you have bigger troubles than any woman should have."

"You speak as if you are doing me a favor, when it is your daughter who is a cheating *putana*. I feel sorry for you. Two daughters and both of them—"

"Cheating? Oh you want to talk about infidelity, eh? I do not think you will like where this conversation goes if you want to talk about who was faithful and who was not!"

"I saw her with that man," Helena says, measuring and cutting her words. "Walking around with him in the middle of the night, whispering like they had secrets."

"Okay, Helena. If this is what you want ..." Her old friend looks both ways for open ears. And her neighbors ... Helena knows they will be listening. "Your son was fucking a *tsigana*! Now you tell me who is the *putana*, eh? Your precious Stavros was a man-whore! Put your *poutso* in a *tsigana* and you will put it in *anything*, even a goat! Maybe even a chicken."

What a liar Margarita is. It is a pity she didn't see it years ago. "He would never!"

"If you say so. But people are saying it is true."

"I will ask him!" She turns around. "Stavros!" But her son is silent. He's staying out of this argument between women. "Stavros, come out here now!"

"My God," Margarita whispers, her face stretched in horror. "What are you doing?"

"Stavros will tell you himself! He will tell you—then you will believe me!"

❧ 95 ❧
KIKI

A T-shirt. A very small one.

A gift from Soula.

On the front, in English, it reads: *I Did Not Fack Leo Karas.*

"I can't wear this." Kiki lobs the shirt at her sister, who catches it one-handed and tosses it back. The shirt lands on Kiki's head.

"Why not?"

(Fack. It's the Greekest typo ever. See a kid spray painting a wall and chances are he'll be misspelling the word the same way. Overpasses and walls all over Greece are facked.)

"Did you miss the part where I'm a school teacher, and this is wildly inappropriate?"

Soula shrugs. "So don't wear it to school."

Down below, the gate creaks. Mama rushes into the yard, carrying her broom. Moments later, sandals slap their way up the concrete steps and land on Kiki's front doormat.

"Kiki? Kiki? Are you here?"

"We're here, Mama. What's wrong?"

"Thank the Virgin Mary!" She stomps into the living room, whisk broom still tucked under her arm, eyes wild. "It is Helena, she has gone mad!"

"Gone mad how?"

Mama uses the broom to punctuate. "She thinks Stavros is still alive—can you believe it? I went over there to tell her you are not a *putana*, that it was Stavros who was doing the sex with a *tsigana*, and she said he would tell me himself that it is a lie!"

Kiki blinks. "Stavros was sleeping with a Romani?"

Carefully-spoken words, lest Mama ignite. And no way does she want Margarita exploding before she's siphoned off everything she knows about the Romani situation. Sometimes the grapevine yields gold. This could be one of those times.

Mama shrugs. "So they say."

"Who, Mama? Who says?"

"People."

Kiki gives her a verbal prod. "Which people?"

"Eh, just people. You know how people here are."

Like Mama. People here are just like Mama. If they don't hear a good story, they take a bad one and spin it into a better story.

"What else do you know?"

"About the *tsigana*?" Mama shrugs. The broom moves with her. "Eh, nothing. A *tsigana* is nobody."

Rattle, rattle. Shaking the gift. "Was her name Drina?"

Another shrug. It's almost becoming a tic. "Maybe. If they told me a name I forget. Who remembers such things? It is much more important we do something about Helena. She is crazy, the poor woman."

"I know," Kiki says. "And she's already getting help."

"Help from who?"

"A psychologist."

"A psychologist? *Po-po*." She shakes the broom. "That is not help, that is madness pretending to help madness. What Helena needs is a priest to do an *exorkismos*!"

Margarita has been watching too much TV again, of the pulpy horror kind. "She's not possessed, Mama. She's grieving. Kostas has already been to speak with her. It's because of him and Max that she's seeing a doctor."

"You knew?" Suddenly, her mother deflates. "And Kostas and Max knew about Helena, too?"

"I told you and you brushed it off!"

"Still, you should have told me!"

Margarita Andreou, philosopher. Her logic is circular and nonsensical.

Soula jumps into the fray. "Mama you know what people here are like. Gossip, gossip, gossip. Tell one person and it spreads like a disease. What Kiki did was a kindness, otherwise everyone would be talking about how *Thea* Helena is crazy."

"If people do not talk, how will anyone learn anything, eh? My own daughters, keeping secrets from me."

"I didn't know about *Thea* Helena," Soula tells her. "At least not until just now. And see, my world didn't end because I didn't know. Yours will not end, either."

Margarita drops onto Kiki's couch, broom and all. Underneath her, the cushions sigh. "You are children," she says. "Children who have never lost a friend. All our lives Helena and I were best friends. We knew everything about each other. I told her when I lost my virginity to a French actor, and she told me about how she stole from the church."

Soula pounces on the catnip. "You lost your virginity to a French actor? Which one?"

Their mother waves a hand in the air. "Eh, one of them. I do not remember his name. He smelled like cheese."

Kiki swaps glances with Soula. Mama must be losing it if she's admitting there was anyone before their father. The way she usually talks, she was a virgin until her children were in school.

"What is that in your hand?" Mama nods to the T-shirt Kiki's still holding.

Uh oh. "Nothing."

"It looks like something. If it was nothing I would not be able to see it."

Kiki can't argue with that, can she? "It's just a T-shirt."

But Margarita knows her daughters. She missed one secret, and now she's not about to miss another one—not when it belongs to this family.

Arm outstretched, palm up: "Show me."

"It's mine, Mama," Soula says.

"I do not care who it belongs to, I want to see it. Unless there is a problem. Is there a problem?"

"No problem," Soula says.

Except there is a problem. A big *I Did Not Fack Leo Karas* problem. And it's stained on the front of the shirt in big white letters, typo and all. Mama's English isn't good, but it's good enough.

Kiki hands her the T-shirt. Margarita sets aside the broom, unfolds the shirt, takes a long look. Then she folds the T-shirt neatly, sits it on the coffee table, gets up, and leaves with her broom.

Not a word.

Until Soula says, "That went well."

"Soula." Kiki throws her arm around her sister's shoulder. "It's like you don't even know our mother. That went anything but well."

LONG NIGHT. A HOT ONE, TOO. THERE'S NO SEA BREEZE TO SWEEP the heat out of the room. It's as if the weather knows she wants to brew.

She and the night sit side by side on the narrow balcony and watch the stars unfold their drama. All that shining, it's obvious they want the attention.

What to do?

Mama—with the whole town standing behind her—confirmed Kiki's suspicions, that Stavros was—to use one of her favorite English language words—*boning* Drina, the Romani woman.

The problem is this exact same mob's other battle cry is that she killed Stavros.

Which isn't the truth or anything like it.

They've been wrong a lot.

But ...

But they've also been right.

Even in death, Stavros's best friend stands by his side, keeping his secrets. There are no answers to be found by poking Akili with sticks.

But he's not the only snake in this pit, is he?

❦ 96 ❦

HELENA

Mouth closed, ears open. She has been talking so much that she missed the other stories creeping around the village.

Now she's hearing them. Terrible stories. About Stavros, about the women he collected like *komboloi* beads.

About a *tsigana* they say was her son's favorite new toy.

Who sleeps with tsiganas? they whisper. *The Boutos family must not be such a good one. No wonder Kiki killed him. She is better off.*

They care nothing for Helena's shattered heart.

Akili comes on his way to the promenade. He swaggers into the yard, surrounded by a cologne-scented cloud.

"Is it true?"

He stops. "What have you heard?"

"Akili, do not play games with me. I hear the stories and now I want to know if they are true. You are the only one who can tell me."

"Not the only one," he says. "Sorry. Sorry. I didn't mean that."

"Oh, I think you did." She nods at the chair she keeps at her side for him. "Sit."

Her son's best friend hesitates. Coward. Yet she cannot be angry with anyone who loved Stavros. He lifts the chair, moves it slightly left —away from her—and sits. "What do you know?"

"It does not matter what I know. Tell me the stories."

Nod, nod. But he will not look at her. He prefers to stare at the road.

The road cannot save him.

"Stavros was popular. Girls liked him, and later, women. And he liked them."

"What about Kiki?"

"What about Kiki? They had an arrangement where they would see who they pleased, until after the wedding."

"Stavros agreed to this?"

Still fixated on the road: "It was his idea."

"He would never!"

"What did you expect? He didn't want to marry Kiki."

"He never said."

"Stavros was a good Greek son, and he didn't want to lose your blessing. But he had no intention of going to the church that day. You pushed him too far."

"Tell me about the *tsigana*."

"What is there to tell? He was ... he was sleeping with her. But he was sleeping with a lot of women."

"She was not special?"

He shrugs. "Who knows? He saw her more than some of the others, but that's all I know."

"Does she have a name?"

"Drina," he says. "Drina is her name."

✾ 97 ✾

KIKI

K iki wears the T-shirt—wears it all the way to the outer edge of Volos where the Romani live.

It's not hell, but it's one neighborhood to hell's left. No paved roads. Nothing but dirt, with the occasional burst of dehydrated grass spidering between lean-tos, shacks, and the rare house built with cinderblocks and desperation. The Romani vehicle of choice is the dilapidated pick-up truck. From the back they sell produce or collect the kind of garbage that yields euros if you take it to the right place.

Kiki locks Soula's car, while she figures out where to start.

She's not paranoid, but the Roma have ... a reputation.

But—if she's being fair—so does she now.

The encampment seems impossibly huge, but it's still much smaller than Agria. And if everyone in Agria knows everyone else, then logic dictates that everyone knows everyone in a much smaller place—and knows them too well.

People stare at her, but they don't make eye contact. As soon as her gaze collides with theirs, they dart away.

Kiki is the *xena* here—the foreigner. This is the Romani's world, and they have their own rules. Maybe it's not rule Number 1, but one of the top rules definitely involves kicking Greek asses if they intrude —Kiki is sure of it.

Where to start?

At the beginning, of course. She unpicks the loosest thread, the slowest-moving target. By slow-moving she means he's not moving at all, except to slap the occasional fly out of his personal space. That shack behind him doesn't look like much, but it's casting a decent swath of shade. She trots towards the man and his shade. He's maybe forty, maybe fifty, maybe—

Does it matter? He's lived hard and it shows. But now he's relaxing in the shade, the bow-legged man in the yellow shorts. It's a battle of the colors between those shorts and the orange T-shirt that covers a basketball belly.

Not a word out of him, even when she plants herself in his shade and says, "*Yia sou*."

Silence.

"It's a beautiful day, isn't it?" She tugs at her shirt, makes a pitiful excuse for a breeze. "Hot."

Maybe there's a secret Romani code. Mama would say the only thing Romani respond to is cash, but she's going to try this the cheap way, with politeness.

If that fails … Money.

"I'm looking for a woman named Drina. Can you help me, please?"

He takes his sweet time answering. But he speaks when she's *this* close to pulling out her purse.

"Are you looking for Drina, are you? Why? Are you the police?"

"Do I look like the police?" Would the police wear short black shorts with an *I Didn't Fack Leo Karas* T-shirt?

"Eh, who can tell? Police always try to not look like the police. Then—" He smacks his hands together. "—they catch you like that. And you go to jail."

"Oh, I know all about jail," she says cheerfully. "I've been there."

"Really? You?" Jaundiced eyes wide and disbelieving. "For what?"

"For assaulting Drina. But she started it."

He spits on the ground. "There is no Drina here."

"Not even one?"

Shrug. "Do I look like a telephone book?"

"No. You look like somebody who knows everything and everyone worth knowing around here."

He stares at her, eyes locked onto hers. Still she gets the feeling that the eye contact is a distraction so he can rifle through her pockets, looking for money and secrets.

Then he laughs. It's a big laugh, but then he's a big man.

"I maybe know a Drina. But could be she does not want to know you. Why you want to make trouble for her?"

"Who says I want to make trouble?"

"What else could you want? It is a rare Greek who wants anything but trouble with a *tsignana*." He spits out the epithet. Coming from his mouth it's even more uncomfortable than usual.

"I just want answers, not trouble."

A long silence follows—the kind that leaves a person wondering if the other party in the conversation died. Even a donkey twitches its ears when it's ignoring you, but not this guy.

"Come back tomorrow," he says finally. "I will ask if there is a Drina here. And if there is, I will ask if she will speak with you. But I make no promises."

Friendly guy. Helpful.

She's not even being sarcastic. She has a feeling that he's as friendly and helpful as friendly and helpful get around here.

"Tomorrow."

He says, "Tomorrow."

"What time?"

Shrug. "When you are finished with your sunbathing and painting your toenails and whatever else pampered women do."

Soula would bite, but not Kiki. What's the point? Romani-Greek prejudice runs both ways. She saves the sharp edge of her tongue for a battle worth winning, and thanks him for his time.

The Mini is still there. Kiki hates that she's surprised.

But it's not alone.

Leaning against the shiny red paint is a guy who looks like trouble. The kind of guy who looks like he's punched a lot of faces, and maybe has had his punched a few times, too. But he's a big man, stocky and solid, and she'd bet he ends more fights than he starts. Attractive, in a wild kind of way.

A lot like Leo. But then Leo has a killer smile to neutralize his gruffness.

"Nice car," he says. No smile.

"Thanks."

"Yours?"

"No."

"Whose?"

"I'm leaving now. Goodbye."

She unlocks the car, slides inside.

He points at her, doesn't look away. "I know you," he says. "And one day maybe you will know me, eh?"

———

MAMA AND *YIAYIA* ARE A PAIR OF BIRDS. PARROTS. CONSTANTLY they chatter, chatter, bicker. Always pecking at each other, unless they have a softer, tastier target.

"Kiki!" Mama calls out from her perch in the yard. "Where did you go?"

"Nowhere. Out."

"Which is it? Nowhere or out?"

"Out nowhere."

Yiayia slaps her black-clad leg. "Clever that one. She takes after me."

"Virgin Mary help us if that is true."

May as well use their bickering to her advantage, dart upstairs, shut the door.

Too bad Mama is hip to the ways in which her daughters evade questions. The tornado spins, blocking the stairs. "Where is my answer, eh?"

"When I lose my sunglasses, the first place I check is the top of my head. Have you looked there?"

"Yes, I have looked there," she says dryly. "And your answer is not there. It is still in your mouth. Talk."

Kiki sighs. "Mama, I'm twenty-eight."

"I know how old you are. I was there when you were born, remember?"

"Not really."

"Not really. You sound more like Soula every day. Soon I will have two Soulas, and one is enough trouble."

"As I was saying, I'm twenty-eight. And a grown woman shouldn't have to tell her mother everything."

"Somebody killed your fiancé, Kiki, and I am worried maybe they will kill you, too. So when you disappear without saying a word—first with Kostas, and now with who knows—then I worry you are dead somewhere."

For once, Mama's reasoning is reasonable. Too bad she didn't capture the moment on camera and upload that to YouTube.

"One of these days, you will have children," Mama continues, "and then you will understand the fear mothers feel every moment of every day. Every time you walk out of the room I feel afraid that I will never see you again. That is what it is to be a mother."

"Not me," *Yiayia* says. "I am happy when your mother leaves the room."

Kiki kisses Mama's cheek. "I went to find answers."

"Answers. Did you get them?"

"Not today."

THE ANTS HAVE ARRIVED.

Three of them.

And about nine thousand of their closest relatives.

"Ants." Mama assassinates a few with the bottom of her slip-on shoe, but, like the Persians, the ants keep marching. "Kiki," she says, a cold steel edge to her words. "This morning, did you go to see the *tsiganes*?"

Uh oh. "Maybe."

The hand waving is epic. "What have you done? Get out before you bring disaster into the house. Go. Go and see *Kyria* Dora."

It's not far to *Kyria* Dora's house. About a two-minute walk from the high school's back door to her front yard. Along the dirt road, then up a concrete street that looks like it's seen a lot of skirmishes. At the top of the hill sits a yellow BMW that's cultivating rust bubbles.

Rust is everywhere here. The sea air keeps it well-fed.

She treks up to the blue peeling gate and white-washed house standing behind it.

"*Kyria* Dora?"

A short spell passes, then a graying head of hair pops through the side door. "Who is calling me?"

"It's Kiki. Kiki Andreou."

"Kiki! Come in, my love." She wobbles into the yard, packed loosely into her black dress. "I was doing crochet in my new bathroom. Vivi fixed it for me, you know. Very beautiful. That woman can work better than any man!"

Kiki hopes this visit won't take place in the bathroom.But she's worrying for nothing, because the older woman ushers her inside, past the *iconastio*—

ICONASTIO. OR: ICON STAND. IT'S A SMALL TABLE COVERED IN religious icons of the gaudiest kind. If beautiful, harmonious decorating is your thing, look away when you encounter one of these often-present shrines. The most common subjects of these pieces of art are the Virgin Mary and her Son, and maybe a saint the family holds dear.

—IN THE HALLWAY, INTO THE GUEST ROOM, AND ASKS IF SHE WANTS *frappe* and maybe a little something sweet to eat. And Kiki is a good Greek girl, so she says yes to both, although it's the idea of a *frappe* that's making her drool.

When it comes, balanced on a black lacquer tray, she almost hurls herself into the tall glass. Next, *Kyria* Dora pushes a tiny crystal plate into her hand. On top is what looks like a small, barrel-shaped haystack lying on its side. *Kataifi*. Almonds, walnuts, shredded pastry, honey syrup, and a splash of heaven.

"Tell me, my love, why have you come to visit this old woman?"

"Mama says I'm *matiasmeni*."

"Yes, probably you have the evil eye. You have had very bad luck this year, and many people in town say terrible things about you. Not me, of course, but others. Bah!" She reaches for her own damp glass. "All they do here is gossip. You would think it is air the way they scramble for even the smallest news."

Says one of the largest mouths in town. But *Kyria* Dora isn't a bad woman, just a loud one.

"You eat and drink, Kiki. And I will get everything ready, okay?"

EVERYTHING MEANS: A BOWL OF WATER, OLIVE OIL, AND *KYRIA* Dora herself. The cursed person—that would be Kiki—is already present and accounted for.

Kyria Dora is one of the chosen ones, a person who believes they can banish curses and the evil eye.

A big piece of Kiki believes in the evil eye, too, otherwise she wouldn't be here. What if everything *can* be fixed with a simple ancient ritual? She has witnessed fortunes changing at the hands of a *Kyria* Dora.

THE OLDER WOMAN PERFORMS HER MAGIC. SHE COMBINES A BARELY audible prayer with a frantic crossing over the bowl of water.

Kiki yawns. She could be an anaconda the way her jaw almost unhinges.

"Your mother is right, you have the evil eye! It is a good thing you came to me before you died in a terrible accident."

One drop at a time, oil drips into the bowl.

Kyria Dora gasps, grabs the table's edge. "Never before have I seen this!"

When it comes to vanquishing the evil eye, the oil can do one of two things: it stays neat and tight, zero sprawl, or the drops separate.

The first one means you're a-okay—for now. The second one means you're getting the super-duper evil eye treatment.

But Kiki's oil isn't doing either of those things. All three drops sank. They're sitting on the bottom, defying the laws of physics.

The older woman turns pale. "*Panayia mou*, what have they done to you?"

"Who?"

"Everybody! This cannot be a good sign. Many people wish terrible things for you."

"Can you fix it?"

Kyria Dora gives her a mildly offended glance. "Of course I can fix it, though it may take time. Then we will turn bad fortune around, yes?"

"I just want the bad luck to go away. I don't want anyone else getting it."

"Kiki, my love, bad luck must go somewhere. It cannot just disappear. Think of this as returning a terrible gift you do not want to the person who gave it to you."

"What will happen to them?"

Kyria Dora shrugs. "Eh, who knows? Most likely a small misfortune. Catching a little toe on the furniture, or bending a fingernail all the way back. One time I turned the evil eye around, and the person who made the evil eye began sprouting hair from her chin. Every morning she had a shadow like a man. She has it still. But sometimes it is a bigger misfortune. I heard of one woman—not here, but in Kala Nera—who was pecked to death by her own chickens."

Kiki winces. Almost nobody deserves to be pecked to death by chickens. "Okay."

"Okay!"

Kyria Dora performs the ritual nine times in total—three is a lucky number. Three times three is an even luckier number.

By the ninth time, the oil drops float like miniature lifesavers.

Kiki swishes her finger in the water three times and licks the oil and water off her finger.

ALEX A. KING

"Good girl. Now we must turn it around, eh? Give the evil eye someone else to look at." She vanishes into the kitchen, reappearing with a fresh bay leaf and a square of paper. She folds the paper over and over, until it's a small triangle. "Keep the leaf and this prayer with you at all times. When you sleep, put them under your pillow or mattress, but do not forget to take them with you. Otherwise the evil eye will find you again. Think of this as a disguise!"

When Kiki leaves it is with lighter shoulders. With luck—and *Kyria* Dora's help—things will change.

———

KIKI DOESN'T TRIP, FALL, OR ROLL. WHICH DOESN'T MEAN MUCH. She didn't trip, fall, or roll on the way here, either.

What does happen is that somebody calls her name.

Somebody at the bottom of the hill.

Somebody old.

Socrates Karas. AKA Leo's grandfather.

Kiki's heart doesn't skip beats—it makes more. By the time she's face to face with Socrates, she's a sweating, light-headed mess in a wrinkled T-shirt and shorts.

"*Yia sou, Kyrios* Karas."

He beams at her. "Laki said I would find you here."

Laki. The wooden man of exaggerated proportions.

"You're looking for me?"

"Who else? This street is filled with old crones. Why would I want to see them?"

She hates to say it, but the old man doesn't look well. His leather is on the faded side. "Are you well?"

"Never better. I am like good wine, not that *retsina skata*. Good wine."

She doesn't point out that wine gets better only if it's kept in controlled temperatures and not left in the sun for prolonged periods. But she does say, "Maybe you should sit in the shade awhile."

"Bah! Shade is for the women and children. Sun is what makes men and crops strong." Then his face blanks and his scaffolding collapses.

"Help!" Kiki yells.

Kyria Dora rushes through her gate, coming at them like a bowling ball. "What is it? What is going on? *Kyrios* Socrates?"

"Sunstroke, I think," Kiki says.

"Stupid old man." *Kyria* Dora nods to Kiki. One woman on either side, they lift him and stagger toward the older woman's house. "Put him in the shade," she says.

Kyrios' Socrates's breathing is shallow, fast. He's the color of putty. They place him under the shade of the grapevine that covers most of Kyria Dora's yard.

"Wait there," Kyria Dora says. "If he tries to die, do not let him."

Kiki gets busy popping his buttons, pulling off his sandals and the thick socks he wears with them.

The old man's eyelids flutter. He lifts his head slightly. "I see an angel ..." Kyria Dora stomps out with a plastic bottle of rubbing alcohol and a glass of water. "And now I see a horrifying demon. I thought there would be a tunnel and light and my *Yiayia* carrying a plate of her *baklava*. But no, I get an angel and a monster. Are you going to fight over me? I will not mind dying if I get to see a fight between two women. Loosen your buttons first, eh?"

"Foolish old man," *Kyria* Dora mutters. She squeezes the plastic bottle, shooting rubbing alcohol all over his chest. "I will rub his chest, you rub his feet."

Socrates lowers his head. "Is this what it takes to get a beautiful woman to rub my feet? I should have died sooner."

"*Skasmos!*" *Kyria* Dora tells him. "You are not dying, old man. But if you did it would be your own fault. Who goes for walks in this heat? Fools, that is who."

"And me," Kiki says.

Kyria Dora says confidently, "Fools and Kiki, and sometimes *touristas,* because they have no sense. Where were you going in such a hurry, eh? To a feta sale?"

"What makes you think I was coming to see you? You flatter yourself, old woman. It was Kiki I wanted to see."

"Me? Why? Is Leo okay?"

"He is fine. He called this morning and asked about you, but that is not why I came. I had a vision!"

"Always he has a vision," Kyria Dora mutters.

He sits up, gulps the glass of water. "Do you have anything sweet?"

"Inside."

He looks at her. "Well, are you going to bring it?"

"After you tell Kiki about the vision. How will I hear if I go inside?"

At least she's honest about her thirst for real-life soaps.

"The vision," Kiki prompts him. *Kyria* Dora settles herself into a chair; she's not going anywhere.

"Yes, I had a vision that *Kyria* Bouto would strangle a *tsigana*. The same *tsigana* you are looking for."

Kyria Dora throws her hands in the air. "You are crazy! Why would Kiki have any business with those people? Any why would Helena care enough to strangle one of them?" Then she stops, looks at Kiki. "Oh."

The old man shrugs. "I am just the messenger, and it is not a message for you, old woman, so if I hear anyone gossiping about this I will know who to spank, eh?"

"Okay." *Kyria* Dora heaves herself out of the wood and wicker chair. "I will bring you something sweet, then I will drive you home. Kiki, my love, do you want me to drive you home, too?"

Kiki shakes her head. "Thank you, but I'll walk. It's not far."

She heads toward the gate. Heat rises from the street in shimmering sheets. Through them, everything is distorted, off-kilter.

Something has been forgotten.

She goes back to the vine-shaded yard. "When?" she asks Kyrios Socrates.

"Eh, soon."

❦ 98 ❦

LEO

When he left for Europe, Leo said goodbye to a woman. She was whole, vibrant, and the grey threaded through her hair was a suggestion that her end was coming, but not for a good twenty, thirty years—at least.

Now he's in a hospital room, looking at a husk that wears his mother's name on its wrist. But that's not his mother. It can't be. It's not.

She shatters his lie with the smile he has always known. "Leo."

"Mom."

He wants to hug her, but he's afraid she'll shatter in his arms.

Don't let her see you're freaking out, stupid.

"I leave for a couple of months and what happens? You all fall to pieces."

Grief is already practicing its chokehold; when Dad laughs, it's more pain than mirth.

Mom grimaces. "Only your father and brother. I'm as awesome as ever."

He sits on the edge of her bed. She lists slightly his way, so he stands and takes her hand instead. The vampires have been busy punching their holes and draining their pints of blood. Why don't they leave her alone? She can't spare what little she's got. And they've already divined her future from the vials they took: she has no future.

LEO ISN'T GOOD WITH EMOTIONS. HE FEELS THEM, BUT HE'S GOOD AT packing them in boxes until later. Then later comes and it's too late, he can't remember where he hid the boxes.

Hide your feelings from a woman long enough and she gets tired of never meeting the man behind the wall.

That's what happened with Tracy, more or less. She got tired of being married to a robot after her no-kids tirade. Then they drifted to separate sides of the bed, until they both fell out onto a cold, hard floor.

Yeah, those boxes don't help when it comes to women, but they're great when you're watching someone you love die another inch every day. Cancer isn't swift and merciful. It's a hulking spider that paralyzes its prey and takes one careful bite here, one careful bite there.

Cancer is a fucking asshole.

Leo wants to shove his hands inside her and rip the spider out, crush it beneath his boot. Then set the mess on fire.

But the doctors have tried that, with a bunch of different treatments most of which he can't pronounce. Nothing worked. Nothing came close.

Mom wants to be cremated, so in a way that spider will burn.

He does what he can, which isn't much. He brings coffee for the thirsty, snacks for the hungry. He sleeps in a chair at the foot of Mom's hospital bed, while Dad sleeps at her flank.

"Don't you have to work, honey?" she says in one of her lucid moments.

"It's Sunday."

She smiles. "Liar."

Is he? He thinks it's only going to be Sunday for him for a long, long time. Sunday. Kyriaki. Kiki. He calls *Papou* every other day to ask after her.

"I met someone," he tells his mother. "A woman."

"In Greece?"

"In Greece."

"Then what are you doing here?"

"Slumming it with my family."

"Leo ..."

"I know. You don't need me. But Dad does."

"I wasn't going to say that. I'm glad you're here. It's funny," she says. "In movies, the dying person always has something wise to say. It's like impending death is magic, and even idiots gain insight and wisdom. It's bullshit. I'm dying and I can't give you a lick of advice. Not a single pearl." She looks over at the window, where the sun comes daily to watch her life set. "I loved Greece at first, but it hated me. And in time I came to hate it, too."

"Why?"

"It wanted to dictate how we lived. Not your grandparents—they were good people. But everyone else—the family, the town. Everybody had an opinion. I was a foreigner, so I couldn't possibly know what was best for my own family. It's funny how people so often see foreigners as slightly mentally challenged. It's as if speaking and thinking in a different language is a disability.

"But it's not just Greece, we all do it. That's what I've learned since we left."

Leo says, "They're still the same way. A lot of things have changed there, but not that."

"Nobody likes change, especially in small villages where even the tiniest shift is like an earthquake. It was different for you, Leo. You were born into the place. No matter how long I stayed there I would have been an outsider. But you, no matter how far you travel, you will always be Greek."

"Careful, you might be rebutting your own comment about wisdom."

Her smile is cracked and peeling. "What's she like, this woman you met?"

"Kiki?" He rubs his head absentmindedly, while his mind goes back to Greece. "She's magnificent. She went out of her way for me—about five-hundred miles out of her way—so that I could get home. Who does that for someone they barely know? If I went to war, I'd want her by my side."

"Sounds like you'd be the one at her side." The smile stretches. "You have to go back for her. As soon as I'm gone, you have to go. Don't feel like you have to stay—you'll be staying for nothing."

That nod turns into a shake. "I can't just up and go. Dad and Soc need me. And work needs me, or I'm going to wind up broke." He's still got money, but it won't last forever.

Mom's hand curls around his. "What about you, Leo? What do you need?"

99

KIKI

Evening comes, and with it a strange lack of people to and fro-ing. Kiki doesn't notice, until *Yiayia* says, "It is like aliens came down in the spaceship and took their people back home."

Mama scoffs, but the needle in her hand doesn't stop jabbing at the Athena's cross-stitched face. "Always with the aliens, Mama."

"What? Do you think we came from monkeys?"

"Monkeys. Aliens," Baba mutters into his newspaper.

Yiayia leans forward, shakes a finger at her son-in-law. "Why are you still reading the newspaper? Have you not finished it by now? If you have read one newspaper you have read them all."

He lifts the paper higher, blocking her out.

"God put us here," Mama says.

"Yes, he put us here. But before that we were in His spaceship."

Round and round.

Kiki cuts in. "You're right, there's almost nobody."

"See," *Yiayia* gloats. "Nobody."

Footsteps on the street. High heels clicking out a rock-n-roll beat.

Soula.

"It's the plague!" she says quickly. "There is nobody at the *paralia* except the *touristas*. Everyone else is sick!"

Mama and *Yiayia* cross themselves. "What kind of sickness?"

"A stomach thing. Everything coming out both ends."

"Everybody?"

"Not everybody, but many. Half the town—at least."

More crossing of the feverish, frantic kind.

"This is the work of the Turks or the Albanians," *Yiayia* mutters. She clutches her belly. "I need to go to the bathroom."

Baba stands, moves his chair six feet to the right. Away from *Yiayia*.

"Never mind. I feel better now that you have moved," she says.

Kiki winces. "I don't think it's the Albanians, the Turks, or the plague." Everyone looks at her. "I think it's me."

"You?" Mama says. "What did you do now, Kiki?"

Kiki shakes her hands at her mother. "You were the one who told me to go to *Kyria* Dora to remove the evil eye and whatever curses I've been collecting. So I went. When she was done, she turned everything around."

"*Panayia mou.*" Mama closes her eyes. "We will have to move away from here. All my life I have lived in Agria. Our family was one of the first families. And now I will have to leave because my daughter gave everyone diarrhea."

Soula is laughing. "She did not give them anything they didn't ask for."

Mama chooses not to hear her. "They will come with brooms and they will chase us out of town. And we will have no choice but to flee from our home." She gets up. "I will go and pack."

"Sit down, you silly woman," her husband says. "No one is chasing is anywhere. How could they possibly know this is Kiki's doing?"

"They will know," Mama says darkly. "They know everything."

Kiki can't argue with that. Besides, if *Kyria* Dora knows, everyone knows. "Oh well," she says. "Tough luck."

Everyone gapes at her.

She shrugs, because Soula's right: they brought it on themselves, didn't they? When you're an asshole, sooner or later the world is an asshole right back to you. All *Kyria* Dora did was speed up the process. Now they're eating the shit *souvlaki* they grilled by themselves.

Baba laughs. "That is my girl. If they *kaka* themselves, they deserve what they get. Maybe it will teach them to mind their own business."

Not likely. But it's a nice sentiment.

Kiki grabs her sister's arm. "Come on, Soula, let's go to the *paralia*. I want to enjoy my handiwork. Maybe we can eat a *souvlaki* in peace."

SOUVLAKI AND *RETSINA*. FOOD AND WINE OF THE SIMPLE GODS.

Kiki tosses her second empty bottle in the garbage can and goes in for a third. When she comes back out, Soula is gone.

Which is weird, because even though she's had two bottles of wine, she knows she left her sister right here, on the sidewalk outside the *souvlaki* shop.

Garbage blows away, not sisters.

"Soula?"

Nothing.

IT'S A MISSING PERSON REPORT, BUT THE TWO COPS ARE LAUGHING.

"Ha-ha," she says weakly. "Now go do your job."

"You want us to find your sister?"

"Yes."

"And she's been missing how long?"

Kiki glances up at the clock on the wall. "About thirty minutes."

"Thirty whole minutes?"

"Now it's thirty-one."

They go back to their brand new desks, back to their paperwork. Back to their stack of *koulouraki* cookies.

"Are those homemade?" She nods at the heaped plate.

"My Mama made them." The younger cop looks at her suspiciously. "Why?"

"No reason."

The wine is turning to vinegar fast in her stomach. Where the hell is Soula? Nobody just vanishes unless they're a magician. And Soula is a lot of things, but a magician is not one of them.

Her heart's in panic mode, leaping around her chest, hands flailing. Blood sloshes in her ears, blocking out ambient noise. Last time someone she knew didn't show up when he was supposed to, he wound up dead, so yeah, she's jumpy. And these blue clowns are sitting there stuffing *koulouraki* into their mouths.

She leaps over the new counter, snatches up the plate, runs for the door.

Bang. Right into Detective Lemonis.

Koulouraki everywhere.

As soon as she regains her equilibrium, she starts stomping on them, making crumbs.

"Those are my mama's *koulouraki*," the cop groans.

"Wow," Kiki says, in a very unKiki-like way. "I feel so bad."

"You again?" Detective Lemonis doesn't look thrilled to see her, but he doesn't look surprised, either. Resigned is the word.

"My sister is missing. One minute she was there, then she was gone."

"I'll take you to look, okay?"

"Okay."

Please don't be dead, she prays. *God, if you have to take one of us, take me.*

LEMONIS DRIVES HER BACK TO THE PLACE SHE LOST SOULA.

"Does your sister look like that?" He nods at the sidewalk, at the woman standing there.

No way.

But it's Soula, all right. She's looking around like she lost something.

Something being Kiki.

"I hear you've been visiting the Romani," Lemonis says. "Why?"

"I have questions and could be they have answers."

"What's the question?"

"How do I get my life back?"

"And you think they know?"

"My Virgin Mary," Kiki says, "it's like you're the dumbest cops in history. Stavros was sleeping with one of them. And maybe that same someone killed him."

"Do not mistake slow for stupid, *Despinida* Andreou. The police cannot just arrest people when all they have is thin air and town gossip."

"Why not?" she says. "You arrested me at the word of the person who might have killed Stavros."

"Do you think she killed him?"

"I don't know anything. Which is why I want to speak with her."

"Stay away from the Romani," he says. "That woman didn't kill Stavros. And you're interfering with an investigation if you go there."

"Good," she says, unable to hide her bitterness. "At least interference is action."

KIKI SHINES THEIR MOTHER'S HARSH LIGHT ON HER SISTER. "WHERE did you go?"

"I saw a friend."

"What friend?"

"My God, Kiki, when did you turn into Mama?"

Kiki shakes her hands at the sky. "You vanished. I was worried."

"You worry too much."

"Somebody has to worry about you."

Soula laughs. "My little Kiki. Everything is fine. Half the town is sick, we have good food and wine in our bellies, and—"

A horn cuts her off. Loud, insistent, with a jeering edge. Soula doesn't turn, but Kiki does. A pickup truck. Romani.

"I've seen that truck before," Kiki says.

Now she's panicking, waiting for the truck to run her over.

Soula turns, gives it the once-over. "How can you tell? They're all the same shit."

"I went to the Romani encampment outside Volos earlier. I remember it from there."

Soula gives her an incredulous look. "You did what?"

"When I borrowed your car, I went over there."

"Why?"

"Because Stavros was sleeping that woman who attacked us."

Her sister grinds to a halt. "Are you sure? I thought maybe it was just Mama and her gossip."

"I don't think so. Even Kostas seemed consider it a possibility."

"Then be careful, sister. The Romani are ... difficult. If you expect to get answers, you could be disappointed. And what does it matter who Stavros was sleeping with, eh? You did not love him."

"No, but maybe she did. Which maybe she knows something about his murder."

Soula puts both hands on Kiki's shoulders. "Then be doubly careful. If they know something about his death, then there is no way they'll talk with you. They are not like us. They keep each other's secrets."

❧ 100 ❧

KIKI

Yesterday the camp buzzed with life. Today it limps.

Kyria Dora is magic.

She finds the man from yesterday where she left him, sitting on the same rickety chair outside the same rickety shack, slapping at the same persistent flies.

He spits on the ground. "You are back."

"I'm back."

"I did not think you would be stupid enough to come."

"Ask around. I'm all kinds of stupid."

"Heh." He nods at the camp. "Most people here are sick today. You might want to leave."

"Oh," she says brightly, "somehow I don't think it's contagious."

"No? Are you a doctor?"

She's done answering his questions. She looks past him, searching out the reason for her being here.

"Where's Drina? Is she sick?"

Spit, spit. "She does not want to speak with you."

"Well," she says. "That's just life, isn't it? We all do things we don't want to do, every single day. I don't want to be here. I'd rather be on the beach, relaxing in the sun with a magazine and a cold drink. But I'm here talking to you when I'd rather be talking to Drina."

"About what?"

"It's a woman thing."

"Pretend I am a woman."

"I think she's in danger."

"In danger?" He slaps his knee. Laughs until he wheezes. "Every Roma in the world is in danger every day, because people do not like us. Greece wants to hammer our Roma edges until we are smooth and Greek. We do not want to be Greek, we are Roma."

Kiki shakes her head slowly. "Look, I don't care if you're Roma or Romani or Greek or Martian. I just want to speak with Drina." She shoves her hands into her pockets, pulls the fabric flaps out. "See, no weapons. No hammer to hammer her edges."

The man spits again. Then he fixates on some distant spot to Kiki's left. All the same, she gets the feeling he's staring into her. At this rate she's going to die of old age.

"What do you want?"

"I told you—"

"No. What do you *want*? If Drina speaks to you, then what?"

Kiki's tired of this game. It's circular, childish. She's had enough of circles. A straight line is what she wants, one with an arrow at the end, pointing away from Stavros and his death. She wants to move forward from this place, from this time, to a future where there are no black dresses, and where there's gossip, but never about her.

"Closure."

"Closure." He laughs. "Talking to Drina will only open more boxes. There is no closure to be found here." Then he hollers, "Drina!"

There's a small movement in the shack behind him. The door opens, but it whines about doing its job. Out steps the Romani woman. She seems so young, but her eyes are flint. Looks like someone wrapped an old gift in new paper.

Chin up. Arms folded. "I have nothing to say to you."

"Did you know Stavros Boutos?" Kiki asks.

"Of course I knew him." Drina stabs the air with her finger. "Stavros and I, we loved each other."

It's what she expected, more or less. But she figured the love thing was a single lane.

"Stavros loved you?"

"Yes. He did not love you." She says it proudly, like she should be waving a flag.

"I didn't love him either. And I didn't want to marry him."

"Who would not love Stavros? He was a good man."

"He was a good man, but not a faithful one."

"He was faithful to me!"

Poor kid, swallowing Stavros's bullshit. "There were a lot of women."

"After he met me, there was only me. Every night, he was with me."

Maybe it's true—who knows? Not Kiki. She approaches her next question the way one does a wary dog. No way does she want to get bitten.

"Did you kill him?"

"No!" The fire in her eyes adds a half dozen more exclamation points to her answer.

"Do you know who did?"

"If I knew, I would cut their throat and make them pay. At first I thought it was you, but I hear nothing but stories about good things you do for people."

"I definitely didn't do it." Kiki sits on the dirt. A small dust cloud puffs up, then sinks. She's a minor, cross-legged disturbance. "Do you believe in prediction?"

The fire dies. "I am Roma."

Okay, so she'll take that as a yes. "Have you met Stavros's mother?"

A headshake. "No."

Stavros, Stavros, what did you do? "A man told me she would try to strangle you. A man who knows things."

"I would like to see her try!"

"Drina!" the man barks.

"Sorry, Papa."

He shakes a finger at her. "You speak like that, you invite trouble."

But invitation or not, trouble is already here. And it looks exactly like Helena Bouto. Her mother's former best friend is shoving money into a taxi driver's hand. Then she marches toward them, looking like the old gods elected her to mete out vengeance.

"*Thea* Helena?" Kiki asks. "What are you doing here?"

The woman she's called aunt all her life doesn't look at her. She's too busy glaring at the Romani woman, shooting daggers, knives, and several pairs of non-safety scissors with her eyes.

"I came to see if it was true, if my Stavros was fucking a *tsigana*. I thought we taught him better." The words shoot out of her mouth like bitter olive pits.

Drina's father doesn't so much stand as he unfolds. Sitting, he's a big man. Standing, he's a smallish giant. He moves his mountain until he's separating his daughter from the woman with the crazy eyes. "And Drina's mother and I thought we had taught her better than to keep company with Greek boys."

But Drina's not having any of it. "I can fight my own wars, Papa."

"Okay. But if you must fight, aim for the eyes," he says.

Kiki jumps up, waves. "I'm still here."

Drina's father looks at Kiki. "Do you want to kill my daughter?"

"No."

"Then stand over there and be quiet."

The previously dead encampment is coming to life. Its people don't look well, but they do look curious. They remind Kiki of goats, the way they amble over to see what the fuss is about.

Kiki touches *Thea* Helena's arm. She's much too thin. Her arm feels hollow, like a bird's empty bone. "Come, *Thea*. I will take you home."

There's a fever in older woman's eyes. "Did you kill my Stavros?"

"No," Kiki says gently. "And I don't think Drina did, either."

"Drina?" She turns back to the Roma woman. "Are you Drina?"

Drina, the girl with only one name—apparently—doesn't speak. Got a look on her face like she wants to stab the world.

"I asked you a question," *Thea* Helena barks.

Drina's father glances back at her. "Answer her and maybe they'll go away quicker, eh?"

"Yes, I am Drina. Drina Bouto."

Kiki blinks, because she never saw that sharp stick coming at her eye. Stavros was married?

Stavros. Was. Married?

If Stavros was already married, what was she doing at the church, dressed up like a cake?

"Ha-ha," she says. A laugh with no muscles.

Thea Helena doesn't laugh—she flies. She rains slaps on Drina's head, face, chest. In all that black, she reminds Kiki of an oversized bat, the way she's flapping.

Drina fights back—and the woman fights dirty. It's a battle of hair-pulling and biting and comments about how *Thea* Helena's mother had repeated sexual orgies with farm animals, biblical figures, several politicians, and an exorbitant number of inanimate objects.

This is some daughter-in-law, Kiki thinks. No way could she have competed with that.

Big audience now. Looks like the whole encampment is here, watching the cats fight. Nobody moves to separate the woman—including Drina's father.

"Somebody should stop them," Kiki says.

Stavros's father-in-law says, "Let them fight. You must have a war before you can have peace."

She doesn't think that's true; lots of people have peace without fighting a war first. "Okay," she says. "Time to go."

She reaches into the cloud of dust and fighting women, and pulls out a leg. Eureka! She strikes gold the first time, according to *Thea* Helena's black shoe. Kiki tucks that foot under her arm and draaaags.

Thea Helena howls.

"You want to go?" Drina flops back on the ground, panting. She looks up at Kiki, face flushed and filthy. "Go. But she stays."

Goodbye, leg.

The battle continues, with Drina ripping the hairpins out of the older woman's hair. *Thea* Helena shrieks.

A collective laugh bubbles up through the audience.

Then it dies when Drina takes an elbow to the face and squeals.

A woman cuts a quick path through the crowd. She is Drina with an extra twenty, thirty years taped to her face. "Drina did not kill your son! Your fight is with me, *skeela*!"

If a woman wants to fight with a woman, calling her a bitch is a good way to declare war.

Except that's not what happens.

The two fighting women fall apart, each in their own breathless heap.

"Mama?" Drina says, face painted with blood—hers and Helena's.

"He was trouble, Drina. For you, for her—" She points at Kiki. "For all of us."

"You killed Stavros?"

"I had no choice," the mother wails. "You would do the same if your daughter was married to that animal!"

"My son was not an animal," *Thea* Helena screeches. "He was a good boy!"

Drina's mother spits on the ground. "I piss on your son's body. He was a *putano*. A man-whore. He stuck his *poutso* in everyone! Even after he married my daughter!"

Almost everyone. Kiki is one-hundred-percent sure she never saw Stavros's dick. Kiki remembers every dick she's seen. Not that there's been too many. But still, she remembers them. And contrary to her mother's opinion, if you've seen one you haven't seen them all.

Every ounce of energy in Kiki's body ups and leaves. She is her mother's pasta, boiled long past the point of *al dente*.

"I'm too tired for this. I'm going home. Don't call, don't write—any of you."

❧ 101 ❧

KIKI

K iki doesn't say a word, but the story spreads anyway. Ebola could learn a thing or two from Greece.

PARIAH ONE MOMENT, SWEETHEART THE NEXT.

Poor, poor Kiki Andreou, deceived by that monster Stavros Boutos. He was married—and not just to anyone, but a *tsigana*! And of course, her mother killed him, because Greeks hate *tsiganes* and *tsiganes* hate Greeks right back.

The story spins round and round the town until it's only a distant relation to the truth.

The sympathy sucks as much as the murder accusations.

Kiki never wanted sympathy, she wanted freedom.

Now she has it, what will she do?

GOODBYE, BLACK. HELLO, COLORS.

Not a word from Mama. The slamming pots and pans speak for her.

Yiayia interprets the clangs and bangs. "She thinks you should wear black for a full year."

"It's not my place," Kiki says.

And it's not. Stavros has one grieving widow—more than enough for any man.

Soula is a puzzle piece. Kiki pushes her into place with one question: "You knew, didn't you?"

"About Stavros and Drina? No. But I suspected."

"Why didn't you say something?"

Soula shrugs. Like Kiki, the summer sun is painting her a darker shade of gold. "You are my sister, and I love you more than anything in this world. How could I come to you with nothing but suspicions? I tried to grab something tangible to bring to you, but then Leo came along and you seemed happy."

"He was in my life for maybe three days."

"So? Three happy days, compared to what? A lifetime of mediocrity you would have shared with Stavros? So I stopped asking questions."

"Asking who?"

Then the alarm rings in her head, grabs her by the shoulders and screams, "Wake up, stupid!" Kiki remembers now. The Romani man and his comment about Soula's car. The honking pickup truck the night Soula went missing.

"Oh God, Mama is going to kill you," she groans.

Soula drops onto Kiki's soft couch. "I know. That is why she can never know. At least not until I am ready."

"How did you meet him?"

"He wanted to buy a house. He's been saving since he was a boy to buy his family a home away from the encampment. All the banks turned him down, but he almost has all the money saved for a good house here in Agria."

"Roma living in town. People will flip."

"Times are changing. And with it, the population is turning over. The older people with their prejudices are slowly dying out, and they're being replaced by those of us who care about the actions of the individual, not their family tree. A time is coming when sins are not visited upon the sons."

"Mama is still going to kill you."

Soula grins. "Mama is still going to kill me, but not for a long time. We are just starting out, Marko and I. And the road is filled with rocks and dirt."

The laugh bursts out of Kiki's chest. This is all too ... too ... *something*. It's funny, yes, but that's not all it is. There's no word in Greek or English for a comedy balled up with tragedy—is there? She can't think of much right now.

Loose ends. Everything but work is dangling in the air, waiting on a good breeze. Now that her hands are unshackled, it's time to tie some knots, tether her life to something solid.

"I have to go." The words burst out of Kiki's chest.

"Where are you going?"

Kiki shrugs. "I don't know."

102

KIKI

Yeah, right. She knows.

103

KIKI

Kiki twists the travel agent's arm until he gives her what she wants.

"Thank you, cousin," she says on the way out the door.

At home, she throws a week's worth of her life into a suitcase.

Mama glares at the luggage. "Where are you going?"

"America."

"To see that man?"

"To see that man."

"Why? I will find you another husband. Now, it will be easy. Everybody knows you are innocent."

"If you do, you'll lose a daughter."

Mama looks shaken. "What about school?"

Kiki kisses her mother on both cheeks. "Relax, Mama. I'll be home in time for work."

"You cannot go!"

"Yes, I can," she says. "I can do anything."

Waiting at the front gate is a car. Not the taxicab she called for, but a police car.

Detective Lemonis.

He gets out, holds open the passenger door. "Get in."

"No. I know for a fact that I haven't done anything. And ..." She nods at her suitcase. "I have a plane to catch."

"Get in. I'll drive you."

Is he crazy? "To Athens?"

"To Athens."

Apparently he is crazy. Not exactly confidence-inspiring. "Why?"

"We are having a slow crime day and I am bored."

"But my taxi—"

"Not coming."

Oh.

She who hesitates winds up with a police detective tossing her suitcase into the trunk of his car, one-handed.

"You can take me as far as the bus station. I already paid for the ticket."

He stares at some point past her head. Kiki glances back, sees Soula standing on her balcony, nose in a magazine.

"Okay," he says, finally.

"I can sit in the front, right?"

"Unless you would prefer the back."

Kiki gets in, clicks the seatbelt. "Home, James," she tells him in English.

Detective Lemonis doesn't apologize for getting it wrong. This ride he's giving her, that's his *sorry*. He pulls up to the curb outside the bus station, lets the car idle, contributing his share to the pollution. From the pent up look on his face, it looks like he's a man with something to say.

He reaches past her, pops the glove box. Inside is the wedding gift her family mistook for a bomb. Okay, so she mistook it for a bomb, too. But only because the drama was mildly infectious.

"The case is closed. That belongs to you."

"What's in it?"

"Absolution."

Absolution. The word is heavier than the gift she lifts from the glove box.

"I'm not sure I want to open it."

He nods. "I understand."

"Do you?"

"When someone releases you from obligation or guilt, sometimes their generosity can be a bigger burden than you anticipated."

"Will the contents be a problem at airport security?"

"No. It's not a bomb." There's a tiny twinkle in his eye.

"How—"

He holds up a hand. "Drina's mother. When I went out there asking questions, she started the fire, hoping to ... I don't know. Burn any evidence connecting her daughter to Stavros, I guess."

She slides the box with a carefully slit belly into her handbag. "I'm not ready for absolution."

Lemonis's nod is that of an exhausted man. "Don't be surprised if you discover you are never ready."

❧ 104 ❧

LEO

His mother leaves on a Wednesday, on the hottest day of summer. Her husband begs her to stay, but it's too late, she's already gone.

The hospital is sorry for their loss—so, so sorry—but they need the bed, because the Reaper is one greedy bastard. He touches his finger to everything and calls it his.

I shit on Death, Leo's Greek half thinks. The other half is nodding, telling the hospital staff to do what needs doing.

Three Karas men. His brother is stone, his father is water. And Leo, what is he? He signs the paperwork that okays Mom's cremation, so he must be fire. Cremation is a sin to the Greek Orthodox church, but his mother isn't—wasn't—Greek.

A funeral happens, filled with wordy people. They're all so sorry, Mom was such a good woman, she has left a hole in the world. Nothing he doesn't already know.

Tell me something, he thinks. *Tell me one thing I didn't know about her*. If he learns one new thing, then it means she's still alive out there, somewhere. Not here, but somewhere.

But they tell him nothing new.

Dad speaks. Leo speaks. His brother can't speak with a stone in his mouth.

After the funeral, there's food. So much food. Who can eat with all this death? Leo tries, but everything tastes like *Made In China* plastic.

For two days and nights, he sleeps on Mom and Dad's couch, still wearing the black suit. His old room is there, but it's a home office now. His new apartment is a stranger, and right now Leo doesn't need strangers.

When he's not asleep on the couch, he's thinking about Kiki. How he's glad they're not together, because he couldn't be Dad, couldn't be *Papou*, and set love on fire.

"Go home," Dad tells him on the third day. "I'm glad you're here, son. But you need to move on with your life and let your brother and I find our way."

So he drives away in the Chevy he used to love. Now it's just a vehicle, headed towards an empty apartment. Either he's gone colorblind or the world has turned gray while Mom was dying. Is this how it's always going to be now, everything shades of ashes? He's got to stuff this into its box. Put it on a high shelf in a closet he never opens. Look at it sitting up there once a year, but only when he's holding a bottle of *Jack* in one hand.

His new place has no soul. It's one of those places built to look like it cares, but the residents are transient and temporary. Everyone here looks like an inbetweener; stuck between college and marriage; between divorce and marriage number two. Beige walls with white balconies tacked on. Palm trees. Kidney-shaped pool that goes ignored by everyone but the kind of people you don't want sharing your water.

Leo climbs the stairs to the second floor, tugging at his shirt collar. Every step is a broken bell's hollow toll. Footsteps bounce his way. Sounds like they're happy to get out of here. A moment later, some guy —looks like a college kid—hits the stairs, headed down. Leo moves back into his lane.

"Hey, man."

"Hey," Leo says on autopilot. His fingers are hunting for the new key. It's the one that still feels foreign when he picks up his key ring. No way is this place ever going to be home.

With Mom gone, he's not sure where home is. Where does the boat drift once its anchor is gone?

He'll figure it out. In time. For now, it's this gray world for him.

Life is one funny, cruel bastard. There's no knowing which way it's going to twirl you, when it's going to shove you out of a plane at thirty-thousand feet.

When it's going to make amends and beg for forgiveness.

Today, Leo thinks. *It's making amends today for its major fuck-up.* Because on his doorstep, sitting next to a bright red suitcase, is the sun.

❧ 105 ❧

KIKI

H is mother is already gone. She can tell by the stoop of his wide shoulders, by the dark shadows that say bad news punched him in both eyes before absconding with his heart. And still he looks gorgeous in that dark suit, with the tie hanging loose around the shirt's collar, top buttons undone.

Now she feels awkward. Maybe coming wasn't the best idea. Impulsive, grand gestures are for the Soulas of this world. Kiki does things small and with great care. A phone call, an email painstakingly crafted to offer friendship and comfort without prying or assumptions about the future—not jumping onto a plane without an invitation.

She looks at the dim, cream-colored walls, the white ceiling, the other doors lined up like soldiers. If they're taking a side, it's not hers. She had every opportunity to call, to email, to do take things slow. Instead, she got on a plane. For better or worse.

"You look like you need a friend," she says.

"I need you." Plain. Honest. There's something boyish about the way Leo rubs his head. His dark hair is longer than she remembers, his face harder. "And not just because of my mom. I need you because I need you, because there's no one else like you." He laughs—at himself, she can tell. "And I'm not a man who has ever needed anyone."

Her hand finds its way into his.

"Then it's a good thing I'm here."

"Yeah, it is." He nods to the door at her back. "You want to come in?"

"Yes," she says. "I do."

❧ 106 ❧

KIKI

He starts in the kitchen. "This is the kitchen. I think."

"It looks like a kitchen."

"It does look like a kitchen."

It is a kitchen—one of those tiny spaces built for people whose idea of cooking is zapping food in the microwave.

Bathroom next.

"No hole in the floor," he tells her.

"Very civilized."

"But not very Greek."

"Hey, I have a real toilet."

"Did they kick you out of Greece for it?"

"For that? No. I stopped being a source of gossip, so they voted me right out of town."

"Their loss. What happened?"

She tells him in the tiny guest bedroom. By the time they make it back to the kitchen, he's laughing.

He still laughing when he picks up her by the waist and sits her on the kitchen counter.

"I thought this was the kitchen," she says. As far as precautions goes, her babble isn't a good one. The heat spreads anyway, from his hands to her skin, to that faucet that switches her on.

"Small apartment. Everything doubles as something else."

"Good thing the kitchen doesn't double as the bathroom."

"Very good thing."

His hand moves, but not far. The fire moves with it.

Logic kicks in, tells her this isn't the best time—not for her, but for him. "Are you sure now is a good time?"

He lifts her off the counter, turns her so she's facing away.

"What did I say?" His voice is burnt around the edges, raw.

"You need me."

"I need you," he whispers. "And you need this."

This turns out to be Leo. All of him.

❧ 107 ❧

LEO

He keeps his secret for a couple of days. On the third, he's ready to share Kiki with the rest of his world. But she doesn't look convinced.

"Your family is grieving. The last thing they need is to feel like they have to entertain me."

They're not like that, and he tells her so.

"Okay." She looks at his pathetic excuse for a kitchen. "I'll go with you. But I have to be useful."

"What did you have in mind."

"Your father is Greek, isn't he?"

———

"LEONIDAS! WHAT'S ALL THIS?" DAD IS IN GREEK MODE, HANDS AND shoulders shrugging at the bags Leo's carrying.

"What's it look like?"

"Food. What do I need with food?"

"Who says it for you? Maybe it's for me."

His fathers laughs. Good. Feels like it's been a lifetime since Leo heard his dad laugh. Then he notices Leo brought company.

"Who is this?"

"Kyriaki Andreou, Lefteris Karas. Dad, meet Kiki."

"You are Greek?" He looks at Leo. "Is this the one?"

"She's the one."

He shines his light back on Kiki. "So you're the reason my son made it home when he did."

"It was nothing," Kiki says, offering her hand. "I'm very sorry about your wife."

Funny, because to Leo it was everything.

Dad pulls her into his arms, hugs her like she's one of his.

His old man won't leave Kiki's side after that. He lingers in the kitchen, drinking coffee while she cooks. This is good for him, it's what he needs—something from his first home.

Leo lets the two of them do the talking. She catches him up to fifteen years of scandals and stories, culminating in the adventures of Socrates and Laki. By then, all three of them are howling with laughter.

Feels like a family. Except there's more than just his mother missing.

"Where's Soc? He get tangled up in groupies?"

Dad shakes his head. "On the dock. Always he is there."

❧ 108 ❧

KIKI

This house ...
"It's beautiful." Very American with its large, bright rooms and two-point-five bathrooms. Everywhere she turns the walls are shades of white. Not the furnishings; those are bright, bold, the antithesis of sedate.

Leo hasn't stopped watching her since he saw her on his doorstep. "You're beautiful."

Kiki laughs. "What, are we in a romance novel? It is, as Americans say, cheesy."

"Hey, I like cheese. I love cheese."

"I like cheese, too."

Kyrios Karas wanders into the living room. He nods at Leo.

"Son, a moment?"

"I'll be right back," Leo tells her.

———

LEO'S BROTHER IS SITTING AT THE END OF THE DOCK ALONE.

Kiki sits, too. She doesn't speak. He's heard enough words—he doesn't need more.

369

There is a rumor that Greece and Florida share the same sun, but Kiki isn't sure. This sun is a more forgiving sun. A cooler, yellow sun.

In time, he says, "Where do you think she is?"

Kiki points at the sun. "There." Then at his chest. "And here."

❧ 109 ❧

LEO

F loor length sheers. White shutters thrown open to catch the breeze—the opposite of the way Greece does it. A queen-sized bed with matching furniture in the cherry wood Mom loved. Over the bed, a painting of flowers immortalized at their peak.

Everything identical to how it was, yet it's not the same, is it?

Dad sinks into the bed's edge.

"You do not look stupid, Leo, so why are you acting like a *vlakas?*"

Say what? Dad's looking at him like he—Leo that is—pitched his marbles overboard.

"Huh?" Very eloquent. His education really paid off.

"Why are you here?"

"I came for Mom. And for you and Soc."

His old man nods. Sometime between losing Mom and today, he shrugged on ten extra years. They've settled on him like a thick winter coat. "I know, I know. And that was the right thing to do. But now?"

"The family needs me."

"No. The family needs your mother, but she is gone. Now ... now we go on alone, without her—me, your brother, and you. None of us can do anything but remember her and be the best men we can be *for* her." He sighs. "I want you here, but if you stay, the life you are meant for will move on without you."

"What else am I going to do, Dad?"

"Go back to Greece. A man gets one chance at a good woman. I know. That is why we left Greece." He nods at photograph on Mom's vanity. The camera caught his parents cuddling at the end of their dock last summer. Leo knows, he was the photographer. "Your mother hated Greece. The family … it is not that they mistreated her, but their way was not her way. You know how they are with their questions and their gossip and their interference. Every day they wanted to be in our business and dictate how we lived and raised our family. You were young, and you did not see how hard it was for her or how much we fought. She asked me to choose." He laughs. "What a silly woman, your mother. There *was* no choice. They were family, yes, but she and you— and in time, your brother—were *my* family. So we came here. And I have no regrets, other than not walking away from Greece sooner.

"But you, Leo, I think maybe you belong in Greece with your Kiki. She has heart, strength—" He holds up his fist. "—and courage. And if she is not already in love with you, she will be soon. Go back with her. Finish your time in the army. And do not forget to call and visit us, eh?"

Leo stares at the photograph, at the moment he captured. He can't quit thinking about the woman in the other room and how he wants to frame her on their wall.

"Fine. Cast me out into the street." But he's laughing as he says it.

Dad slaps him around the back of the head. "*Maimou!*"

"If I'm a monkey, I get it from you."

"So my son is a comedian, eh?" He nods at the open door. "Come on, let us go find your woman. I want to know what else she can cook."

TIME. THERE'S NEVER ENOUGH OF THE STUFF.

He's in bed, curled around his woman, both of them fully dressed. So it's summer, so they're sweating—so what? He'll get her naked soon enough.

"What are we going to do?"

She tangles her fingers in his. "I'll go back to Greece. School starts in a week. And I have to be back before that."

"What about me?"

What about him? Jesus. He sounds like a petulant kid. *What about meeeee?*

"We are impossible. I belong in Greece, and you belong here."

"You see a problem. I see a challenge. C'mon, Ariadne, throw me some string and I'll find a way out of the labyrinth."

"You want string?" She glances back at him. "Okay, here's your string. If you come, I'll be waiting."

"Oh, I'm coming." He hooks his fingers under her dress's slender strings, pulls until his mouth is warm against her ear. "I'm coming with you."

❧ 110 ❧

HELENA

Helena is still broken—that will never change. But the cracks are thinning. Time cannot move backwards, but it can move forward. This is not the mercy those who grieve hope time will give, but it is something.

"Have you spoken to the girl?" Dr Triantafillou asks. Today, she is the silver-green of the olive leaf.

"Drina? Yes. I thought she would hate me—she should hate me—but every day she comes. She is a good girl. I can see why Stavros cared for her."

"You have lost a son, and while she has not lost a mother, her mother cannot be there to mother her. I'm not surprised she has turned to you. You need each other."

Drina's mother is in jail. Detective Lemonis had been watching the encampment for some time, trying to hammer and chip his way in. Soon there will be a trial, but not a long one. The woman confessed. She was almost proud of what she had done for her daughter.

In a quiet place deep inside her, Helena thinks that she would have done the same for a daughter—she who almost killed for her dead son.

374

IT IS A PENITENT WOMAN WHO BAKES THE *GALAKTOBOURIKO*. SHE covers the golden top and walks her gift to the Andreou house.

Margarita's mother is in the yard, supervising her daughter's sweeping.

"I know how to sweep!" Margarita snaps. "I have been sweeping for many years now."

"Yes, and always you do it wrong. Sweep away from the house or the bad luck will come in."

"I am sweeping away from the house!"

"Then you do not understand the meaning of away!"

Margarita grabs her mother's wheelchair, rolls it—and its passenger —into the house, slams the screen door behind her and gets back to the business of sweeping.

"You are still doing it wrong," her mother bellyaches.

"Margarita?"

The woman stops. "Helena."

She came unprepared, without words, hoping the right ones would follow her here. But they haven't, and now she is standing on the wrong side of Margarita's gate, alone.

"Take this and give me the broom," she says, finally. "Your mother is right, you're doing it wrong."

"Oh?"

Inside the house, the older woman cackles. "Even the stupid woman knows you're doing it wrong. What does that make you, eh?"

Margarita and her broom come to the gate. There, the women swap. Helena takes the broom and Margarita takes the tray of custard pie.

Not all apologies contain words.

Sometimes food is enough.

❧ III ❧

LEO

The plane is breathing heavy, and Leo expects any moment now the military police will elbow their way aboard and drag him away.

But they don't. Nice guys—they don't pounce until he's pulling their luggage off the conveyor belt.

"Hey, *malakas*," his old buddies say. "Do you know what time it is?"

"You better go," Kiki says.

"They look like they mean it," he tells her.

"They do look like they mean it."

"We mean it," the MPs tell him. "Passport?"

He slaps his new passport into Yianni's outstretched hand. "Add it to the collection." Then he gets down to the serious business of saying goodbye to Kiki—again. This was his idea, coming back now, doing his time in green. After that he's a free man.

"As soon as they give me leave, I'll be back."

Tweedledum nudges Tweedledee. "Very funny man, he thinks he's getting leave."

"Leave or no leave—" Kiki scowls at them. But when she looks up at Leo all he sees is her sunshine. "—I'll be waiting."

❧ 112 ❧

KIKI

I t's an empty house, but her heart is full of Leo.

She closes the door, shutting out the sound of her family and all their craziness. Yeah, they're crazy, but they're her lunatics. And for that, she loves them.

It is time to open that one gift, time for absolution.

She's ready.

The lid comes off easy. With one finger, she parts the lavender tissue paper. Nestled inside is a sheet of paper, a photocopy of wedding certificate. Stavros and Drina Boutos.

Nothing she didn't already know, although now she understands why Lemonis told her to keep clear of the encampment.

The paper's not alone. Underneath is a white stick with one pink line blazing in its small window.

❧ 113 ❧

KIKI

Sometimes the best place for absolution is at the bottom of the garbage, with the other secret things.

❧ 114 ❧

DRINA—THE FINAL WORD

A person can only lose so much before they shatter. Good thing a Roma woman is steel, not glass.

It is a steel woman who staggers into the hospital's emergency room on her father's arm when night is at its thickest. It is a steel woman who understands her love killed her husband, and now her grief has murdered their unborn child.

Thank God she did not tell Helena she was pregnant. The glass woman has lost enough.

NOT READY TO LEAVE GREECE YET? YOU DON'T HAVE TO! STAY in Agria with *Freedom the Impossible*, book 3 in the *Women of Greece* Series.

LONG BEFORE SHE WAS THE JUDGE GREEKS LOVE TO HATE (AND Germans love to love) on *Greece's Top Hoplite*, Effie Makri was hurling rocks at flashers and falling in love with Nikos Lemonis, the local police detective's son. Now she's about to answer

379

the most important question she'll ever be asked. Yes or no, everything will change ...

Turn the page for a sneak preview of *Freedom the Impossible*.

FREEDOM THE IMPOSSIBLE PREVIEW

Dora looks at the lie on the paper. It's a big one. The lie, not the paper. The paper is small, but it's stacked on other small, lying pieces of paper.

That man takes her for an idiot.

Dora Makri is not an idiot.

Uneducated, yes, but not stupid. It is Haralambos Kefalas who is the fool if he thinks she is so simple.

"What is the problem?" he says to her now. "I see nothing."

She stabs the paper with her finger. Which triggers a fresh round of "What?"

The man is starting to sound like a scratched Jenny Vanou record: What, what, whhhhaaaat? It is all she can do not to slap his head. If his mother and father were alive, they would beat him for his stupidity.

But maybe, knowing the Kefalas family, they would applaud his swindling. Before they were olives, the family was ouzo, and before that, disorganized crime.

"You are blind or stupid or a crook," she tells him. "Which is it?"

Two palms up. "I don't see the problem."

Haralambos—Harry—Kefalas is a cheating man—in life and business. A man who lies to his wife, sneaks another woman under his desk, will think nothing of pinching drachmas from his workers' pay envelopes.

And that is what has happened. Harry Kefalas, who owns the biggest olive factory in town, steals from the people who help make him rich.

Look at him in his expensive clothes, with that chunk of gold on his little finger.

How did he pay for it, eh?

With stolen wages, that is how.

"You are stealing," she tells him. "And from people who can not afford to be stolen from. You steal from someone rich ... okay, that is not so bad."

He leans against the desk, arms folded. His face stays serene. "*Yia sou*," he says. Goodbye. Although maybe he is saying hello. That is the problem with *yia sou*. It is ambiguous, unless somebody is coming or going.

When people first meet Harry they think he is a handsome man. He is one of the fortunate ones, modeled after the gods, they say. Fifty-something, but he is tall, fit. His clothes are always expensive, designed by French and Italian *poustis*, but stitched in third-world countries by hungry children.

They don't see the weasel skulking around in the man-skin. She knew he was no good when her George worked for him. But George was a good man, a loyal man. Kefalas gave him a respectable job and George repaid him with hard work. And what did Kefalas do? He did not throw out that batch of olives—that is what he did not do.

He pushes away from the desk, opens the office door.

"Oh no, no." She wags a thick finger in his face. "You cannot say *yia sou* to me! I quit. I will not work for a thief."

He points to the office door. "Go."

"Maybe I will see you in church this Sunday—yes?"

His eye twitches.

"Maybe I will see you in church and I will watch how much you pay for the candles you light, eh?"

Dora storms out, but only because it is noon. Any earlier and she would hide in the factory's shadows. She does not want Effie to know she has lost her job. The girl works too hard, worries too much. Not once has she complained about leaving school to work.

What a brave girl she and George made.

Too bad her mother is a disappointment.

It's the 1990s and Cyndi Lauper still won't shut up about girls and how they want to have fun.

If she's even singing about that. Apostolia told Dina who told Katerina who told Effie. And Effie knows Apostolia is half English, which isn't American.

And Cyndi Lauper is American.

So how does Apostolia know what Cyndi's singing about?

(For the record, Effie isn't the sharpest rock on the beach.)

Apostolia (she of the Greco-English breeding) laughs. "It's like you're an idiot, Effie." That mean little laugh dies when Effie slams her bumper car into Apostolia's and the blonde girl takes a bite of her own sharp tongue.

Cyndi Lauper grabs her song and leaves. Kriss Kross, those kids with the backwards pants, take her place. The bumper cars die with Cyndi. Time to refill the attendant's pockets or make way for paying customers.

Effie is all out of spare change, but she wants to have fun. She's all itchy on the inside and she knows why: it's Apostolia—she's begging for a slap. One of those heartfelt strikes, where Effie pulls her arm back almost to its breaking point before letting it fly.

But it's late July and it's the second night of Agria's Fisherman's Festival, so she's supposed to be happy. And when you're happy you don't hit people.

Effie isn't happy, Effie is employed. Six days a week. Seven hours a day, which usually bleeds into nine. The extras go uncompensated.

Long, long days for a seventeen-year-old girl who should be in school.

That's what happens when your father dies when you're fifteen, and there's only you and Mama to make money. Leave school, find work.

Tell me, she thinks. *Tell me about how girls just want to have fun.*

"I'm going home," she says to her friends. "Work in the morning."

"See you," they say. Not one of them tries to convince her to stay. Some friends.

Her mother always says that friends are fickle; there is loyalty only in blood, and even blood will betray you when there is money or a dead relative's jewelry involved. Still, it would be nice to be wanted. Effie wants one friend who'll beg her to stay.

She threads through the crowd, looking for Mama. So many people. The festival pulls everyone into its celebration. Locals, out-of-towners, tourists. They all flood into Agria for these two nights, out of ... she can't remember how many nights in a year. Only that is sometimes changes. Normally Agria is small. Everyone knows everyone. But tonight she only recognizes one face in twenty.

She finds her mother with her friend (and their neighbor) *Thea* Elektra (who isn't really her aunt), eating a *tiropita* near the wooden stage set up for dancing. It's packed tight. No one can pull out their best dance moves because there's no room to swing a dead chicken.

Mama is on the round side of chubby. Dora's not fat, but she expects to be, someday. Even jokes about it. Effie's grandmother was fat, her mother will be fat, and one day Effie will be fat too, Mama's always telling her.

Effie won't let that happen. She's bony now, in that seventeen-year-old way. A cute girl, but Effie never really sees herself in the mirror. She's too distracted by her father's dark hair and his big mouth. They look funny on a girl, she thinks. And not a good kind of funny.

"Effie!" *Thea* Elektra says. "Are you having fun?"

Effie shrugs. It kind of started out that way, but the return is diminishing the closer she gets to opening time at the Very Super Market.

"Can we go home?" she asks her mother.

"Effie, my love, go home if you want to go home. I will see you later."

Effie goes, the unwanted girl. Back toward home.

The night sky is a sheet of black glass, cracked in places so that the yellow winks through. In one corner, the moon is paddling toward morning. It's not a long walk between the promenade and home. Seven minutes if she walks fast. Longer if any of Agria's people throw questions at her.

How is your mother?

How is your father?

What news of your aunt in America?

No news about *Thea* Eleni in America, or Effie's two cousins, Vivi and Christos. Her aunt almost never calls and Effie's mother almost never calls her.

Yet Mama can never shut up about them.

No one ever says, "*Effie, how are you?*"

Agia Eleni—Saint Eleni—is how Effie thinks of her aunt. Everything her aunt and their children do is brilliant and miraculous. Effie has never met her, or her gifted cousins. Her aunt threatens to come, then never does.

Down at the bottom of her street sits a forgotten house. Two stories, mostly concrete and rebar bones. The owner ran out of money somewhere between the roof and the walls, so now it's an oversized jungle gym or playhouse for Effie and the other neighborhood kids—when she was younger, anyway. Keep walking past it and you'll hit the high school's hidden back gate in about a minute. The road is dirt and stones, but Effie's street is pocked and pitted concrete.

Effie stands at the T where dirt meets concrete. There's a noise coming from inside the abandoned frame. It's small beneath the throb of the festival's music, but definitely present.

It could be trouble, but this is Agria. There's no trouble, unless someone is stealing a chicken.

"Who's there?" she calls out.

A man steps out of the dark into the slightly lesser dark. There's one streetlight here, but the light loses its way before it touches the ground.

Thirty, thirty-five, she thinks. Old. Black hair that might be brown in the light. Built like a chicken: skinny legs, chubby belly. Face that makes her wonder if his mother had relations with a ferret. Effie doesn't know him, and she knows pretty much everyone in town. Agria's that kind of place. Everybody knows everybody, and anyone they don't know, they know *of*.

The guy says, "Hey."

"I don't have any money," she tells him.

He shrugs like her empty pockets don't matter. "What's your name?"

"Effie."

"You want to see something, Effie?"

"Is it money?"

"No."

"Is it chocolate?"

"No."

"I don't want to see it," she tells the weirdo. "I have to go home."

"Come on," he says. "It's something worth seeing."

Effie doubts it. He doesn't look like a guy with anything worth seeing.

"I don't think so."

She turns away. Two steps up her street she hears him say, "Hey, pretty Effie."

That's new. Pretty isn't an adjective anyone ever hitches to her name. For a girl who never hears she's pretty, he has thrown out a shiny silver hook. It's bright and it speaks to her the way no one ever has.

"What?"

"Come look."

He's standing there not doing anything. Not dissolving into the shadows, not moving toward her. Inside her head there's a small alarm ringing, but she slaps it aside. She's pretty, he said so. How bad can he be? Bad men don't shower girls with compliments—the TV says so. Bad men get right down to the being bad.

"Show me from there," she says. "And I'll decide if I want to come closer."

The man shrugs. "Okay."

He turns around for a moment. A zipper whispers. When he turns around something about him is different, but it's not light enough to see what.

"What?" she says. "I don't see anything."

"Really?" Disbelieving.

Now he moves closer, just a few steps. Effie holds her ground.

"See it now?"

"What is it?"

"My best friend. It could be your best friend, too, pretty Effie."

Yeah, no. "It looks like a tiny penis," she says.

"It's not tiny! It's a big, brave soldier!"

Effie picks up a rock. It's no empty threat. Effie can pitch a rock, thanks to her older brothers.

"Put it away," she tells him.

"Do you want to touch it?" Another step closer.

It's not the first penis Effie has seen. Europe is nude-friendly. A few years ago, Italians elected a porn star into their parliament and nobody blinked, even when she was naked on the news. A penis is nothing. They're on the beaches, filling up the late-night TV screens, dangling from Greece's most famous statues. But Effie's starting to feel like this old guy shouldn't be waving his stick at young girls.

So she throws the rock. It sails through the air, makes a soft landing.

He screams.

Effie runs, leaving him bent over the ground, making a thin mud out of dirt and tears.

Read *Freedom the Impossible* today!

ABOUT THE AUTHOR

Alex A. King is an American author (by way of several countries, including Greece), who divides her time between writing, thinking about writing, and reading Seuss's HOP ON POP for the millionth time. She lives in the Pacific Northwest with her family.

23278255R00232

Printed in Great Britain
by Amazon